VOICES
OF THE
ELYSIAN
FIELDS

VOICES
OF THE
ELYSIAN
FIELDS

A JONATHAN GRAY, M.D.
MYSTERY

MICHAEL RIGG

LEVEL
BEST BOOKS

Author Photo Credit: Martha C. Rigg

First edition

ISBN: 978-1-68512-924-8

Cover art by Level Best Designs

This book was professionally typeset on Reedsy.
Find out more at reedsy.com

America has only three cities:
New York, San Francsico, and New Orleans.
Everywhere else is Cleveland.

— Thomas Lanier Williams III

Contents

Praise for Voices of the Elysian Fields

"Michael Rigg takes the reader deep into the world of forensic pathology and the complicated political realm of the coroner's office. His main character's desire to "find the truth" is the driving force which leads him into a complex web of political corruption and hidden motives. In so doing, he must be true to the "ghosts" of his own past and give them a voice so that future victims have a hope of justice. *Voices of the Elysian Fields* is a complex tale of family, greed, corruption, and, in the end, justice."—Rebecca Barrett, author of *The Rat Catcher*

"Robby O'Malley is dead. Jonathan Gray must step into the shoes of his mentor and friend as the Chief Coroner of Orleans Parish on that same chill December night to deal with a murder/suicide of a prominent Garden District couple. But things aren't what they seem. Michael Rigg has woven a complex web of political corruption, family greed, and betrayal. And he has created a hero of quiet conviction and deep moral courage."—Rebecca Barrett, author of *The Rat Catcher*

"Passions run high in the Crescent City. Forensic pathologist Jonathan Gray is fighting his own private battles, but so is everyone else. Can he pull them together when a whirlwind of forensic science must shred an avalanche of politics, corruption and murder? Michael Rigg's *Voices of the Elysian Fields* keeps you riveted on the way to that answer."—Lisa Black, *NYT* bestselling author of the Gardiner & Renner series

"Atmospheric, suspenseful, and propulsive, *Voices of the Elysian Fields* is must-read, especially for readers who love mysteries set in the Big Easy.

New Orleans coroner Jonathan Gray is a complex and deeply sympathetic protagonist haunted by a personal tragedy that instead of undoing him, propels him past doubts and indecision to fight corruption even when it endangers his life. Author Rigg's passion for the Crescent City shines through every page as he balances both the beautiful and dark sides of America's most unique city, creating a truly immersive experience for readers — one I eagerly look forward to revisiting in future novels featuring Coroner Gray and his compelling cast of coworkers."—Ellen Byron, *USA Today* bestselling & Agatha Award-winning author

"*Voices of Elysian Fields* is a multi-layered mystery of rare depth and intrigue. Michael Rigg has fashioned a beautifully crafted tale where each revelation uncovers not just secrets, but the very essence of human nature, weaving together complex characters, multiple plot-lines, and hidden motives to keep readers guessing until the final page. As vibrant and drenched in color as the city of New Orleans in which the book is set, this is a major debut."—Jon Land, *New York Times* and *USA Today* bestselling author

"Rigg captures the mood, the atmosphere, the taste and smell of New Orleans and builds a suspenseful story from one of the few cops in the city who believes police are seriously meant to serve their community. Come visit the Big Easy and be prepared for some serious bumps along the way."—Don Bruns, *USA Today* bestselling author of the New Orleans-based Quentin Archer mysteries and editor and contributor, *Bat Out of Hell*

"Followed by the mysterious death of his mentor and the apparent murder-suicide of an elderly couple, New Orleans' Deputy Coroner Jonathan Gray must navigate the dangers of the city's corruption to solve the seemingly unrelated crimes, and stay alive. *Voices of the Elysian Fields* is what a thriller should be."—DP Lyle, award-winning author of the Jake Longly and Cain/Harper thriller series and co-creator of the Outliers Writing University

"Michael Rigg's medical/legal thriller, *Voices of the Elysian Fields,* is as twisty as the famous streets and seedy back alleys of New Orleans. Thrust into the role of Coroner when his predecessor dies mysteriously, Dr. Jonathan Gray is faced with an onslaught of murders and assaults that Rigg masterfully weaves into a deadly tale of betrayal and greed."—Heather Weidner, author of the Jules Keene Glamping Mysteries

"Michael Rigg's debut medical/legal thriller, *Voices of the Elysian Fields,* is as twisty and seedy as some of the famous streets and back alleys of New Orleans. Thrust into the role of Coroner when his predecessor dies mysteriously, Dr. Jonathan Gray is faced with a rash of murders and assaults that Rigg masterfully untangles to create a deadly tale of betrayal and greed."—Heather Weidner, Author of the Jules Keene Glamping Mysteries

Chapter One: Bayou St. John

Tuesday, December 23, 2014

S hortly after 2:00 a.m., Jonathan Gray drove his aging Chevy Blazer out of his courtyard and turned right onto Bienville Street. After-hours calls usually fell to the on-duty pathologist. But Robby O'Malley—Coroner of Orleans Parish and Jonathan's friend and mentor for almost forty years—had been found dead in his home near Bayou St. John. So, he got dressed and left a note for his still-sleeping wife, Emma. Best not to mention Robby, though, until he knew more.

Sidewalks teemed with pedestrians. Unusual, given the late hour and crappy December weather. Likely, tourists celebrating Christmas early. He focused on his unplanned trip Uptown. What the hell happened? Even at seventy-four, Robby looked healthy as they toasted the end of another workday, about eight hours ago, over shots of small-batch. He had been so full of life. *Had been.* It was difficult to think of Robby in the past tense.

Within minutes, Jonathan guided the Blazer onto Moss Street. Almost there. He lowered his window and shivered at the rush of cool air. A slight, musty breeze tickled his nose. Heavier fog from before had dissipated into a thin, patchy mist. To his left, lights from the surrounding neighborhood reflected off the bayou's ebony surface. All in all, an idyllic portrait of holiday serenity—except for the police cruisers, their flashing blue lights, and a CSI van parked about a hundred feet ahead on the right.

He eased his vehicle to a stop in front of Robby's place, a two-story, white-brick structure with a wide front porch and a gallery above. Christmas lights flickered from a tree in the front room on the left side of the first floor. On the right side, large French windows stood open. Sign of an unannounced entry, perhaps, or a hasty retreat by some as-yet-unidentified visitor.

Jonathan exited his vehicle, pausing to fiddle with duct tape securing his gas-tank cover. That the body shop couldn't locate a replacement part was an irritation. He shook his head, chastising himself for dawdling. Now wasn't the time for distractions. He needed to focus on the task at hand, while accepting Dante's literary missive about abandoning hope as he entered the metaphorical inferno of a death scene. So, he breathed deeply, as if to brace himself for the emotional trauma awaiting him inside, and hastened toward the uniformed police officer guarding Robby's front porch.

"Morning…" Jonathan showed his badge and squinted at the patrolman's name tag. "Officer Michaud."

"Morning, Doc. I've added you to the access list." He handed a clipboard to Jonathan. "If you'd be so kind as to give me your John Hancock."

"Sure thing," Jonathan said, as he signed the access list.

"Body's in the back of the house." Michaud grinned. "Got your booties?"

Jonathan held up a pair of cloth shoe coverings. "I'll put them on before I go inside."

"Thanks." Michaud chuckled. "You know how picky those crime-scene techs can be."

"Sure do." Jonathan cocked his head and smiled. "That's their job."

He passed under the yellow tape draped around the porch and turned back toward Officer Michaud. "Betsy Sprance inside?"

"Yes, sir." Michaud nodded. "Detective Lieutenant Sprance."

"Good." Jonathan entered the already-open front door.

Robby's house smelled of Christmas—evergreen and cinnamon—as if someone had been baking cookies after decorating the tree. Cold air flowed through the open windows. Voices resonated from a hallway leading away from the foyer. Must be where Robby was.

The O'Malley family room. He'd been there on dozens of occasions over the years. Often on his own. Many times with Emma. So, the layout was familiar. A well-stocked bar off to the right. Adjacent, a state-of-the-art entertainment center with a seventy-inch TV screen evoked memories of watching LSU's football team while sitting on Robby's ugly-as-hell purple, green, and gold faux-leather couch. Tonight, the TV remained dark and lifeless.

A pair of CSTs in white Tyvek protective overalls went about their business of documenting the scene. One concentrated on lifting fingerprints from an open briefcase while the other observed. A crime-scene photographer, not wearing any protective gear beyond cloth booties covering her shoes and a pair of purple exam gloves, took pictures of what must be Robby's lifeless body—he couldn't quite see to be certain—and the surrounding area. Frequent bursts of light from the camera's electronic flash added to the surreal, almost noir atmosphere.

Books and papers lay scattered around the room, but there was no blood that Jonathan could see. Nearby, Betsy Sprance spoke with a uniformed officer wearing corporal's chevrons.

Despite the noise and activity, Jonathan might as well have been there alone. He tuned everything out, as if he had tunnel vision. Everything except the tacky Mardi Gras sofa and what was on the other side.

He took a step closer, and his face warmed. Next to a sturdy wooden coffee table was a man in his mid-seventies, lying face up, motionless, his arms crossed neatly on his chest. Robby O'Malley, with his eyes wide open, staring God knows where, looking at God knows what. Jonathan's thoughts returned to the last time he saw his friend alive. Lightheaded, his knees wobbly, he shuffled to his right and sat on one of the bar stools. His temples pounded.

Betsy Sprance approached. "Thanks for coming so soon. I know it has to be a shock."

"Right." Jonathan stood, placing his hand on the bar for support.

"You going to be okay, Doc?"

Jonathan nodded. "Semper Fi, Marine."

Betsy closed her eyes and smiled. "Ooorah." She opened her eyes. "I knew you'd want to be here."

"Yeah. Good instincts." His eyes moistened. "Thanks for having them call me."

"Don't mention it," Betsy said. "You'd do the same for me."

"Aren't you out of your normal beat?" Jonathan asked. "This isn't the Sixth District's area—"

"About that." Betsy nodded, looked toward the floor, and then back at Jonathan. "I recognized the address when Dispatch made the radio call. Figured I'd drop by and see if I could lend a hand."

"Got it. Glad you did." Jonathan sniffled. "Any clue about…" He raised his right hand and gestured toward Robby.

"Corporal." Betsy motioned to the uniformed officer. "Got a minute?"

As the officer walked toward the pair, Betsy spoke. "Doc, this is Corporal Grace Jividen. She and her partner, Officer Michaud, were first on scene."

"Morning, Corporal. I'm Jonathan Gray, Chief Deputy Coroner."

"Yes, sir. I know." Jividen nodded. "Most of NOPD knows who you and Dr. O'Malley are."

"True that," Betsy said. "Corporal, can you bring Dr. Gray up to speed?"

"Sure." Jividen crossed her hands in front of her utility belt. "Not much to tell, really. Officer Michaud and I responded to a call from Dispatch about a noise complaint. Loud music. When we got here, the windows were wide open, and Louis Armstrong was belting out "What a Wonderful World" at about a million decibels. And it kept repeating, over and over. My ears are still ringing."

"I see," Jonathan said. "Occupational hazard, I guess."

"Right," Jividen said. "And when no one answered our knocks, we found the front door unlocked. We entered with sidearms at the ready and followed the music."

"A CD on replay?" Jonathan asked.

"On the money, Doc." Jividen nodded. "And then we found Dr. O'Malley."

"Already dead?" Jonathan winced.

"Yes, sir." Jividen paused. "Still warm."

Jonathan closed his eyes, then exhaled a loud sigh as he reopened them. "Anyone else around?"

Jividen shook her head. "We did a quick sweep and cleared the house."

"No Mrs. O'Malley?" Jonathan asked.

"Negative," Betsy said. "But we think she might be out of town. We're contacting family members."

Jonathan nodded. "She's probably already at their beach house for the holiday. I have Jacki's cell number if you need it."

"Thanks," Betsy said. "That'll save us some time."

"Sure," Jonathan said.

"Say." Betsy paused. "You ready to take a look?"

Jonathan swallowed. "Yeah."

They walked toward Robby and stopped about a foot from his body. Jonathan put on a pair of latex exam gloves, then squatted beside his friend. He had to remain objective and keep his emotions in check. He stood and looked at Betsy.

"Thoughts on cause of death?" she asked.

"Seems pretty straightforward. Like a heart attack or stroke." Jonathan pursed his lips. "But there's something out of place. I can't put my finger on it." He shook his head. "And the timing. If he was going to stroke out because of job pressures, seems like he would have after Katrina. That was almost ten years ago." He paused and breathed a heavy sigh. "Anyway, we'll know more after the postmortem."

"Roger that." Betsy nodded. "We'll deliver him to the morgue as soon as possible after you give us permission to remove the body."

Jonathan nodded, acting as if Robby's autopsy would be just another day at the office. Jesus, he hadn't even taken over officially as Coroner. Although, the mayor's office had already ordered him to be at city hall at 10:00 a.m.—hardly seven hours away. That the swearing-in ceremony couldn't wait until after Christmas was a bitter pill. But with Emma beside him to hold their family Bible as he took the oath of office, he'd be there. Grief would have to take a back seat to duty.

"I'm on the overnight shift tonight at eight." Jonathan gritted his teeth, then exhaled a cleansing breath. "No use canceling now. It'll be a great opportunity for the exam."

Betsy raised an eyebrow and spoke softly. "Don't you think it's too soon? I mean—"

"Emma will probably think I'm nuts, too." He shrugged. "But I prepared the schedule before Robby died. Besides, giving the staff extra time off over the holidays is always a morale boost. No reason to change horses in the middle of the stream."

"All right, Doc, you know best."

"Thanks, Betsy." Jonathan swallowed hard, then took a deep breath. "Guess there's not much we can do but dig deep and find out what the hell happened to one of the finest people ever to grace the Big Easy. Let's check in with the CSTs."

Chapter Two: The Garden District

Tuesday, December 23, 2014

Fifteen-year-old Hunter Dejarnette stumbled, then righted himself without falling, as he raced along Chestnut Street. He was big for his age and athletic. Pap said he could be a championship wrestler or maybe a linebacker. He had walked through this neighborhood dozens, maybe hundreds, of times on his way to his great-grandparents' house. So, he should have remembered the spot, just past Washington Avenue, where tree roots made the sidewalk bulge upward. But it was nearly nine o'clock— his first time after dark. And the first time he'd been in such a hurry. He needed to get to Gram and Pap Haldeman's place on First Street as quickly as possible.

Tomorrow was Christmas Eve. Especially at this time of year, family members should get along—even those relatives you don't see that often or fathers and sons who disagree and fight like, well, fathers and sons. Before the argument, the holiday party had been so much fun. He'd beaten all of his cousins at *Mario Party*, including Timmy and Tammy, the snobby twins from Baton Rouge who thought they were so much smarter than him. And everyone had been singing carols and eating the delicious food. Oh, wow, the food. He had eaten so much of his two favorites: the Haldeman family recipe for boudin balls and Aunt Evie's Polish *potica*. He could probably hibernate for a month, like a bear, he was so full.

But his face fell when he thought about the confrontation. Why did his cousin Joe and Uncle Ben have to yell at each other? Hunter hadn't meant anything by it, not really, when he threw the wine on Joe. He certainly didn't mean for it to start an argument between Joe and Uncle Ben. He'd wished they would go into another room to talk. But they hadn't.

Uncle Ben and Joe must have known it would upset Gram and Pap. Gram was so sick. Hunter's eyes moistened. They had left the party early so Gram could rest. At least, that's what they'd said. But he knew the real reason—they were upset about the argument. Hunter wiped his eyes and moved forward, slower now, but still hastening toward his great-grandparents' house. He would apologize for what had happened and tell them how much he loved them. His breath visible in the chilly December air, Hunter exhaled frosty rings of moisture. Just a few more blocks. Not much longer.

The corner of Chestnut and First Street. He could turn right and go home across Magazine, to Mom and Dad's camelback. Or he could keep going to Gram and Pap's. It wasn't a difficult decision. Left up First Street for just over a block, a couple of houses past Coliseum. He would tell them everything. He had to make it right. *Then* he could go home.

Gram and Pap would understand. They always did. Maybe Pap would give him another lesson on how to repair jewelry while Gram napped. Napping eased her pain. Working with jewelry helped Pap not to worry so much.

He paused at his great-grandparents' driveway. Their Buick was there. But why hadn't they left the front porch light burning or turned on the Christmas tree in the front room? Maybe they didn't want to be bothered by anyone. A flickering, multicolored glow from the back of the house caught his eye. They must be in the family room watching TV. And he wasn't just anyone; he was Gram's Special Angel. He was always welcome at Gram and Pap's.

Hunter rang the doorbell three times, counting to ten-Mississippi after each ring, exactly as his mother had taught him. No answer. By now, someone should have turned on the light in the hallway on their way to answer the door. Despite the cold air, sweat dripped from Hunter's face. His heartbeat seemed to travel from his chest to his throat. Something was wrong.

A few steps carried him from the porch, along the gravel walk, toward the family room in the back of the house. Small stones crunched underneath his shoes.

"Pap, it's me. Hunter," he called, as he stood six feet from the family-room window.

No response, except for the voices coming from the television. He moved closer, his nose almost touching the windowpane. "Pap. Gram. Are you..."

Peering through the hand-blown glass, which distorted the images inside slightly, he stood like a statue—as if he had stepped into the Arctic Circle and become frozen in place. Gram slept peacefully on the couch, but Pap lay on the floor, a yard or two away. He looked unconscious, but then he stirred.

A quick blur. Then there they were—two figures standing off to the right. Why hadn't they come to the door? They must have thought he'd gone away. At least, they didn't act as if they saw him. Hunter smiled to himself. Maybe he'd become the Invisible Man.

One figure wore black clothing, a ski mask, and gloves. A ninja? Why would a ninja be at Gram and Pap's? The other—the larger of the pair—stood at an angle, face hidden. The larger figure wore a hoodie and baggy jeans, just like Hunter's. They spoke, but he couldn't hear the words. The ninja held a shotgun. Pap's favorite, his L.C. Smith double-barrel.

Hunter's jaw quivered. His eyes stung. A corona of rainbow colors surrounded everything. Maybe he was having an episode. Maybe it was a dream. Maybe...

The ninja looked toward the window, so Hunter flattened himself against the outside wall of the house. He held his breath. Then came a muffled bang, followed by a second one. He gasped in the night air, then gagged as bile crawled up his throat. But he didn't vomit.

He ran, then slipped on the gravel and fell. He stood up, brushed the debris off his pants, and sobbed. Tears and mucus made breathing difficult as he dashed helter-skelter down First Street. He had to get across Magazine and head for the camelback. He'd be safe there. He could get a handle on what he'd seen and figure out how to make everything right. It was his fault. If he hadn't thrown wine on Joe and made Gram and Pap leave, none of this would be happening.

Chapter Three: Snow White

Tuesday, December 23, 2014

Betsy Sprance pressed the backlight on her wristwatch, revealing her official time of arrival: 9:52 p.m. Not her best performance, but still pretty damn good. She had made it to the house on First Street, between Coliseum and Prytania, in just over thirty minutes after the radio message dispatched officers to a reported domestic disturbance. She would have been there sooner, but the officers, following proper protocol, had waited to radio for Homicide until they'd confirmed there were fatalities involved. Then, per procedure, they cleared the premises, searching for other victims and the perpetrators.

Being the first investigator on the scene and doing whatever it took to solve the crime had become Betsy's hallmarks. Maybe she owed them to the efficiency and doggedness she had learned in the Marines...or to her grandmère, who had often reminded Betsy she needed to be better than everyone else if she wanted to succeed in a world where people with testicles and lighter skin were often in charge. Whatever the reason, her job as Chief of Detectives in the Sixth District meant she had become the de facto protector of the mansion dwellers living in the picture-perfect haven called the Garden District.

Murders didn't happen there. Mayor Jamerson and Police Superintendent Bondurant wouldn't tolerate it. Let the lesser humans in the outer wards bludgeon one another to death, but keep the Garden District pristine. Yet, here she was, charged with investigating not one, but two gunshot deaths. And the identity of the two victims underscored the tragedy. William and Margaret Haldeman, both in their mid-nineties, were prominent, upstanding citizens. Who would want to kill these two pillars of the community?

Betsy approached the mansion, one of the few Greek Revival homes in the neighborhood. It looked more like a fortress—a blockhouse—with columns and a double gallery. Not exactly her cup of tea for a place to live. The moderately priced Arts and Crafts–style house—some referred to it as a Craftsman—she and her family bought Uptown off South Carrollton suited her just fine. Besides, the Haldeman place wasn't anything she could afford on her police salary, even if she added her husband's Army retirement pay.

A uniformed officer tied a piece of yellow crime-scene tape to the wrought-iron fence separating the front yard from the sidewalk, then turned toward Betsy.

"Evening, Vogel." Betsy's words seemed to hang in the cold air before dissipating.

"Evening, L.T. Great night to be out." Vogel rolled his eyes.

"At least it's not raining," Betsy said.

"True dat. But I hear the Northshore's getting hammered."

"Guess we're lucky. The bodies are inside, out of any bad weather, planning to drop by." She glanced briefly toward the sky, then turned her eyes back to Vogel. "Were you one of the responding officers?"

"Yes, ma'am. Me and Corporal Templeton. She's inside. We called the CSTs—they're on their way. And Sergeant Broussard should be here soon. I just finished marking off the yard with tape."

"Log-in sheet started?" Betsy asked.

Vogel nodded. "Here you go."

"Good." Betsy signed the access list and returned it to Vogel. "First impressions?"

"Looks like a murder-suicide."

"Out-freaking-standing." Betsy sighed. "What's the world coming to? Kill your life-partner, then yourself. It's always a gut punch."

Vogel nodded. "I've only been out of the Academy six months, and already I've seen three."

"You never get used to it," Betsy said. "Each time, I get butterflies when I arrive. By the time I'm done, the butterflies turn into jackhammers." She gritted her teeth, then exhaled a loud sigh. "Reckon there's nothing to do but get started."

"Right," Vogel said. "Bodies are in some sort of family room off the kitchen. We did a quick sweep and established an access corridor along that pathway near the driveway." Vogel pointed. "Best entrance is through that gate."

Inside, Betsy greeted Corporal Templeton, the other officer who had responded to the domestic disturbance call, and surveyed the room.

"You and Vogel did a good job protecting the crime scene."

"Thanks, Lieutenant."

"CSTs will have a lot to work with. Ought to make everyone's job easier. I'm hoping we can put this one to bed before Christmas."

"That'd be great, L.T."

"You know, Templeton, I've lost count of the times I've responded to reports of murder-suicide. Seems like it ought to be a calm, calculated act. But the actual event is always messy. Bodies don't fall neatly. Blood touches everything. A rusty copper scent from the blood drapes the room. Empty liquor bottles or scattered pill containers, sometimes both, are evidence of the extreme sedation either the victim or the killer—maybe both—needed before completing the act."

"But look at this." Betsy gestured with a sweeping movement of her arm. "None of the gore you usually find at a murder-suicide... See the body on the floor near the coffee table?"

"Yes, ma'am." Templeton nodded. "That's the husband—William Haldeman—I think."

"Right," Betsy said, "there's what looks like a blood stain on his shirt and a couple of drops by his head. But there should be a pool of blood, and all sorts of spatter... It's like someone came through with a WetVac."

"Well, *something* happened. Two dead bodies, husband and wife. They wasn't exactly making groceries."

"Yeah." Betsy allowed herself to smile, a slight snicker. "That's why they pay me the big bucks, isn't it? Figure out what in God's name happened, who did it, and why."

"A real puzzle, L.T."

"Right. Search warrant just came through. Don't want to disturb anything before the CSTs get here." She pursed her lips. "Maybe they'll find more blood evidence using the ultraviolet or Blue Star." She nodded and paused, as if trying to identify the best next move. "At least we can look at the pieces, see what we can see."

"I'm all ears," Templeton said. "Maybe I'll get some pointers for the upcoming sergeant's exam."

"That's the spirit. Tell me what hits you first about the crime scene."

"Well," Templeton said, "there's Mrs. Haldeman. I believe her name's Margaret."

"Affirmative."

"There she is, lying on the couch, as if she's taking a nap."

"What else?"

"The small entry wound to the top of her head means she *isn't* taking a nap. But there's no sign of a struggle. No blood spatter, no rusty odor, nothing—just like you said." Templeton paused and looked at Betsy. "Her arms." Templeton pointed at Margaret Haldeman's corpse. "They're folded, undisturbed, across her torso. Jesus, it's as if she's in a coffin waiting for her funeral." Templeton sighed. "Or, hell, like Snow White waiting for her Prince."

"Good observations," Betsy said. "And on the coffee table, there's a pistol lying on top of an old photograph. I'd estimate the weapon to be a twenty-two."

"A twenty-two seems consistent with the small entry wound on her head," Templeton said. "Probably the murder weapon."

"Affirmative," Betsy said. "And the photograph. I can't quite see it from this angle. But I'd bet my paycheck it's a family portrait of some sort, given the circumstances. Best guess? It's the two of them in their younger days."

"Sounds logical. I suppose we'll find out when the CSTs get here."

"Likely so," Betsy said. "On top of everything else, there are no liquor bottles in sight. There are several prescription medication containers, all lined up neatly, on that end table near the couch. But no open bottles or pills scattered all over the place."

"And look at her husband."

"Right." Betsy nodded. "William Haldeman. Seems almost as serene."

"Look at him. Lying on the floor. Just a few feet from his wife, but not right next to her. On his back. Other side of the coffee table. What do you think? Table's about two or three feet from the couch?"

"About." Betsy nodded. "Body's stretched out on the floor neatly, with a shotgun propped up against his chin—thumbs on the trigger."

"Yeah." Templeton crinkled her nose, like a human bloodhound. "Smell that? Gunpowder—acrid with a hint of Sulphur—kind of lingering in the air."

"Sharp sense of smell. Good. And the odor's not surprising, considering the pistol and shotgun must have been fired inside."

"But still. There's hardly any blood."

"Odd, isn't it? Damned odd."

"Yes, ma'am." Templeton smiled. "But, like you said, that's why you get paid the big bucks."

Betsy suppressed a smile. "Call the Coroner's office yet?"

"No, ma'am."

"Okay. Let's get in touch with Dispatch. I think Sonny Rabideau's on duty tonight as lead death investigator."

"Shame about Dr. O'Malley."

"Yeah. Heart attack or stroke. At least that's the scuttlebutt." Betsy sighed. "Anyway, sure looks like Dr. Gray'll be up to his elbows in this Haldeman mess soon enough."

Starting a murder investigation the night before Christmas Eve. Betsy cursed silently. No doubt this was one holiday season she wouldn't get back.

Chapter Four: Plan B

Tuesday, December 23, 2014

Just over two hours into his shift, Jonathan pushed a cadaver tray into place and closed the door on the last of the morgue's two dozen storage lockers. He shuddered at the hollow clang when its metal handle clamped shut. As chief deputy, he hadn't had to work nights very often. When he did, he held his breath. Operating with the shift's typical skeleton crew increased the likelihood he'd be forced to autopsy an infant or child victim—an emotional trigger. And tonight, his luck had run out. With the extra strain of having the Coroner's political and administrative burdens thrust on him without warning, his emotions had been even harder to control.

But it was more than that. How things had changed. Twenty years ago, such cruelty would have been unthinkable. Now, children were caught in the crossfire all too often. Every day, it seemed. What was wrong with people? New Orleans wasn't a war zone. Or was it? And images of his latest autopsy subject—an eighteen-month-old girl—added to the anger. There she was, the innocent young victim, lying on a cadaver tray, lifeless, mutilated by bullet wounds and the incisions and sutures from her autopsy.

Susan Miller, an emergency-room physician at Tulane Medical Center who sometimes worked in the morgue, approached. She carried a clipboard, glancing at it as she walked. Her raven-black hair, tied in a bun, stood out in contrast to her white lab coat.

Jonathan took a deep breath, closed his eyes, and exhaled slowly. He opened his eyes, then shook his head. "All this shiny new equipment doesn't mean squat. We're barely a quarter of the way through the night shift, and the lockers are full. A brand-new building, and we've already outgrown it." He bit his lower lip to keep from cursing.

Susan lowered the clipboard to her side and nodded. "Too bad the politicians cut corners."

"What's our turnover rate? Might be time for Plan B."

Susan studied the clipboard. "We have nine corpses ready for release. And they're all scheduled for pickup tomorrow morning between nine and eleven." She looked up. "For the next ten hours, there's no room at the inn."

"Guess that makes the choice for us. Plan B it is."

"Plan B?" Susan cocked her head to the side. "Something tells me you don't mean the emergency contraceptive."

"Our Plan B is very basic, almost prehistoric. You're lucky we haven't had to use it when you've been here. Until local morticians ease our storage capacity problem, any new cadavers received will have to be kept in the hallway, out in the open. We'll send someone to the convenience store down the street to buy ice, lots of ice. Then we'll crank the air-conditioning down as low as it'll go and pray the combination is enough to delay further decomposition."

Susan grimaced. "Does sound kind of Neanderthal. So, what if your air-conditioning and ice strategy doesn't work?"

Jonathan stroked his cheek and chin. His nostrils flared as if he had just smelled rotted flesh. "Well, it could get rather unpleasant around here."

"Got it."

Jonathan sighed. "But at least it's not summer."

Jimmy Caplan, a former Navy Corpsman who attended premed classes by day and moonlighted in the morgue, mostly on nights and weekends, arrived. He wore a flannel shirt—part of his standard work attire. It seemed he had dozens of them, or at least a different color and tartan for each day of the week. Therapy, he often said, for so much time in camouflaged battle-dress uniforms.

Susan pointed at Jimmy with her thumb. "How about we have His Nibs pick up some air freshener, too, if we have to send him out for ice?"

"Plan B, huh?" Jimmy said. "Let's invite those peckerwoods on City Council to visit their new morgue. Then they could see and smell the problem for themselves. *That* might convince them to give us additional cold-storage units."

Jimmy removed five brown-paper bags from the refrigerator before grabbing the keys to the morgue's van.

"Doc, I'm going to run these specimens over to Pathology. Should be back in an hour or so. You know, I'll sure be glad when the lab gets moved to this new facility. Call my cell if you need me to swing by and pick up some ice. I'll have them add it to your tab."

"Will do. We'll take stock when you get back. Keep your fingers crossed. Maybe we'll get lucky and won't have any more arrivals."

Chapter Five: The Conference Room

Tuesday, December 23, 2014

"With Jimmy off to the lab," Jonathan said, "why don't we discuss tonight's autopsies?"

"Sounds good," Susan replied. "I could use a rest."

As Jonathan sat down near the small desk they often used to review files, he jumped back up. "Man. These chairs are cold as ice. It's like sitting on frozen concrete."

"That may be true." Susan sat down and crossed her ankles. "But it feels good to take a load off."

Jonathan eased himself onto the chair slowly. "Inexpensive metal chairs. Yet another gift from the troglodytes on City Council."

"Right," Susan said. "We should do what Jimmy suggested and invite them for an up-close and personal tour. They *should* see the impact of their inadequate funding. At least we didn't have to use Plan B for Robby."

"Jesus, I'd forgotten about Robby. I've been going a million miles an hour since he died." Jonathan paused, his face warm with embarrassment that he had been so self-absorbed. "Haven't been to see Jacki or their kids yet."

"Was she there when he died?" Susan asked.

"No, she was at their beach house in Destin. Robby was supposed to drive over tomorrow. But he had some kind of meeting he needed to take care of before he left."

"God, married nearly fifty years and not together at the end. I can only imagine how she must feel."

"Yeah, not much I can add." Jonathan paused and cleared his throat. "Listen, I really appreciate you performing Robby's autopsy." He exhaled slowly, his eyes moist. "Not sure I could have gone through with it. It's just too close—"

"Understood. Perfectly natural. I'd still be in shock too."

Jonathan nodded and sighed. "So, how about his autopsy? I'll need to tell Jacki what happened. Maybe provide closure, to a degree."

"Cause of death seems clear," Susan said. "Robby suffered a massive hemorrhagic stroke. No doubt he died quickly and didn't suffer. But we need the test results before we draw final conclusions."

"Anything remarkable? I talked to Robby just a few hours before he died. Nothing. Absolutely no warning signs he might stroke out."

"Nothing major comes to mind, although—"

"Although, what?"

"Some small, barely noticeable contusions on his neck. Police report shows Robby lying on his back next to a big wooden coffee table near the sofa. I mean, it's possible he fell against the sofa or table, maybe both. Although...if that's the case..." Susan looked toward the lockers. "If that's the case, I'm surprised the bruises weren't more extensive..." She looked back at Jonathan. "Or there wasn't bleeding from when he hit the table."

"Hmmm." Jonathan glanced at the cold-storage lockers. "Sounds like you did your typically thorough job. Thank you."

He focused on the lockers for several long seconds before turning back toward Susan, his chest tight. His temples throbbed—likely signaling a headache on the way. "I'm thankful we didn't have to use Plan B with my autopsy subject, either. A female, approximately eighteen months old. Another drive-by shooting in the Upper Ninth."

Jonathan shook his head. His fingers twitched at the image of a dead infant, left in the hallway exposed to passersby, the tiny body surrounded by bags of ice. He prayed the next cadaver wouldn't be a toddler.

"Child autopsies are a major reason I could never work here full time," Susan said. "At least when I see injured kids in the ER, I have a chance to save them. But when they get to the morgue, all we can do is determine cause of death—and hope we can help police put whoever killed the child in jail. Maybe bring closure to the family."

Jonathan nodded. "When I was on active duty, I dealt with a lot of blood and gore at Navy field hospitals in the Middle East. Children, too. Arms and legs blown to smithereens by an IED or smart bomb." He paused and gritted his teeth. "I should be used to it." He paused again, his eyes moistening. "But I'm not."

"Can't blame you."

"What really gets to me are the dumpster children. Or ones found in secret graves in the bayou. Or…" Jonathan dabbed his eyes with the sleeve of his lab coat "…kids murdered in cold blood when all they're trying to do is go to school." He sniffled and cleared his throat. "I mean, any child's death is bad enough. But tiny innocents facing torture and death alone and unprotected is something I just can't fathom."

"We can only do so much," Susan said. "That's kind of hollow, but I don't know what else to say."

His hands shook, so he put them in the pockets of his lab coat. He was so damned tired. "I'll tell you what. It's been a long day. I'm exhausted. They haven't delivered our conference table yet, so I'm going to grab some Zs in the conference room. Bang on the door if you need me."

"Sure thing, boss. Thought I might get some caffeine, anyway. See you in a few."

Jonathan yawned, picked up some spare scrubs off a nearby rack, and hastened toward the mostly empty conference room. Hopefully, a little rest would cure his looming headache and the tremors. He entered and closed the door.

Sparse, perhaps, but here was refuge, privacy, and plenty of space to sleep without distraction until they needed him. Move the chairs out of the way. Use the shirts as a sheet and pillow. His lab coat would make an excellent blanket. He stretched out on the carpeted floor—affording some warmth. Not exactly the lap of luxury. But given his long, emotional, frustrating day, sleep came instantly when he closed his eyes.

Almost immediately, the nightmare started. Just like most of the other times he'd autopsied an infant or child. An innocent young victim—tonight, the eighteen-month-old girl from the Ninth Ward—lying lifeless on a cadaver tray, disfigured by bullet wounds and the incisions and sutures from her autopsy. Jonathan slid the tray into a locker and closed the door. Each of the twenty-four doors started opening and closing on their own, repeating that damnable, hollow-metallic clang again and again.

He was asleep, but it was as if he were fully awake, thinking aloud. The self-doubts arrived. There was still so damned much to accomplish, and they were always behind the proverbial budgetary eight ball as they dealt with a system that forced the Orleans Parish Coroner's Office to conduct more than twice as many autopsies as St. Tammany and Jefferson Parishes combined, though Orleans had fewer personnel and a much smaller budget. Robby had always been there to talk him out of his funk. But now, without Robby...

What if, at age fifty-four, he'd lost his edge? What if he couldn't measure up to this latest test of his mettle and resilience? He couldn't worry about that yet. Not much he could do except power through, jump in with both feet.

The noise morphed, sounding like someone hitting a nail with a hammer. Or like a fist pounding on the wall. His temples echoed with each loud bang.

"Dr. Gray? Dr. Gray, it's Jimmy. Time to get up. We've got deliveries inbound."

He sat up and sighed as he wiped sleep from his eyes. It had been twelve years since the CSTs delivered the children's bodies—victims of a mass shooting at their school—to the morgue for autopsy. Twelve years since the single most horrific day of his life. For a dozen years, the nightmares had forced him to live through it time after time. Each nightmare seemed worse than the one before. Now, the mantle of leadership had fallen on him. He had to find a way to deal with the nightmares, the self-doubts, and the stresses of his new duties—all without Robby's guiding hand.

Another knock at the door. "Doc?"

22

"Coming." Jonathan inhaled and exhaled slow, deep breaths. Despite the fitful rest, his head no longer ached, and his hands were now steady. Joining Susan for a shot of caffeine might do him some good.

Jonathan opened the conference room door. Jimmy stood just outside.

"Greetings and salutations, Doc. Dr. Miller called me on my way back from Pathology. A police van's pulling up to our loading dock with two new guests, both gunshot wounds. Looks like someone forgot Christmas is a time of peace and goodwill."

Jonathan grimaced but hoped it looked something like a smile to Jimmy. "All right, let's roll." Jonathan threw the scrubs into a hamper as they walked toward the examination room. "Guess we might need to send you out for some ice after all."

Chapter Six: The Old Couple

Tuesday, December 23, 2014

J onathan shook his head at an all too familiar picture. The proverbial
déjà vu all over again. The CSTs—in this case, Smithwick Hebert and
Michelle Tranh—working in tandem, guided two gurneys, each with a
body bag on it. Tonight, at least, brought a little comic relief. Susan walked
alongside the CSTs, a cup of Seattle's Best coffee in hand, laughing. Smitty
told a story in Cajun French, a dialect mostly spoken by the older population
of South Louisiana. The pair tried to one-up each other in a never-ending
contest of archaic phrases and idioms.

Michelle—Shelly for short—coughed and pointed toward Jonathan and
Jimmy.

Smitty looked up and stopped his story midsentence.

Susan smiled. *"Bon jour, mes amis. C'est bon de vous voir."*

"It's good to see you, too, Susan," Jonathan said. "What, no Starbucks?"

"Not enough time," she replied. "Had to settle for what's in the vending
machine. Number Two's not bad, by the way. Got a large café mocha for
a buck twenty-five. I wonder if Starbucks ever looked into developing a
push-button barista."

Jimmy helped Shelly and Smitty transfer each body bag onto gurneys
owned by the morgue.

"Dites-moi, Monsieur Hebert," Jimmy said, "what sort of *cadeaux du cadavre*
have you and Mademoiselle Tranh brought to brighten our holiday season?"

"Tonight's gifts are two gunshot victims, a husband and wife." Smitty looked up from the paperwork. "William and Margaret Haldeman. Both, ninety-plus years old. Suspect murder-suicide. Not much left of the husband's lower jaw or face. Looks like a snapping turtle's beak, if you ask me."

"And the other?" Jonathan asked.

"A single bullet struck Mrs. Haldeman on the top of the head," Shelly said. "Based on the size of the entry point, and lack of an exit wound, we think it was from a small-caliber handgun."

"Did you say *Haldeman?*" Susan's face appeared pale, almost ghostlike.

"That's right," Smitty said. "William and Margaret."

Susan opened the smaller of the two body bags enough to expose the female victim's face. She closed her eyes and pursed her lips as her chin dropped to her chest. Slowly, she raised her left hand to her forehead and massaged her temples. The morgue fell silent, except for the steady sounds of the ventilation system.

"It's Maggie Haldeman," Susan said, her face no longer hidden. "My family is, or was, very close to the Haldemans. They had four kids. Two boys and two girls. My parents went to school with their two oldest children, Ben and Evelyn. You'll probably recognize Ben as Judge Haldeman from the Louisiana Court of Appeals. Evelyn—Evie, as I knew her—used to babysit me. Hank, I mean Henry, and Connie were their other two children. I didn't know them very well."

"I recognize all four," Jonathan said. Hopefully, his interruption would give Susan an opportunity to compose herself. "Each one is a prominent member of the city's social elite, either in their own right or by marriage or association. But Judge Haldeman is probably the most well-known."

A yawn overtook him mid-speech. "Sorry. It's been a long day." Café mocha for a buck twenty-five sounded fantastic. "Ben Haldeman administered my oath of office at ten o'clock this morning." He paused. "Actually, it's almost yesterday morning at this point. And Max Jamerson was there as well. I think Max must have been self-medicating again for his old knee injury."

"The one from the Sugar Bowl?" Jimmy chuckled. "Or was it the Super Bowl?"

"Sugar Bowl." Jonathan snickered. "Or maybe he was just hungover. He reeked. You could smell alcohol through the mouthwash and cologne."

Susan sighed, as if she hadn't heard anything Jonathan had said. "Maggie and Bill Haldeman were two of the nicest people you would ever want to know. They got married when they were both Navy officers during World War Two. I was at their *seventieth* wedding anniversary party a few years ago when they renewed their vows under an arbor in their backyard in the Garden District. There wasn't a dry eye in the crowd."

Jonathan placed his hand on Susan's arm, guiding her away from Maggie's corpse. "How about sitting down in the conference room? Take as much time as you need."

"Thanks," she said. "But I'll be fine. I suppose this one hits closer to home than most. It should sharpen my focus. I owe it to Bill and Maggie to hold it together and press on. Let's figure out what happened."

Impressive—Susan's emotional control. Any lingering softness had already disappeared from her eyes. Her piercing gaze signaled she was ready for business. Jonathan turned back to the group and accepted the chain-of-custody documents Shelly presented to him.

"Okay," Jonathan said. "We'll make certain we conduct an inquest sufficient to determine the exact method and manner of death."

Jonathan signed the forms and handed them to Shelly. "Who's lead detective?"

"Betsy Sprance," Shelly said. "She'll be here once she secures the victims' house and outlines how she wants the crime scene processed. Probably in three hours. But she wanted us to get you the bodies as soon as possible so you could conduct your preliminaries."

"Betsy's good. One of the best," Jonathan said. "Was Sonny Rabideau there?"

"Yeah. He came maybe thirty minutes after we did," Smitty said. "The original call to 9-1-1 was from a neighbor reporting what sounded like a domestic disturbance. No mention of gunshots. Police notified your office once they realized there were deaths involved. Sonny watched us secure the bodies. Told us it was okay to bring them here when we did."

"Great, thanks. With Betsy Sprance and Sonny Rabideau working together, I know this will be a solid investigation. Given the visibility of the victims, we need their experience and attention to detail. Robby taught me two very important rules. First, *all* autopsies must be thorough. Second, autopsies involving rich, influential people must be *perfect.*"

"Anything unusual at the crime scene?" Susan asked.

"The placement of the bodies, maybe," Shelly said.

"How's that?" Jonathan asked.

"Mrs. Haldeman," Shelly said, "was lying on the couch like she was sleeping."

"And Mr. Haldeman?" Jonathan asked.

"On the floor, maybe five feet away," Shelly said. "There was an enormous coffee table between him and Mrs. Haldeman."

"Anything else seem out of place?" Susan asked.

"Well." Smitty paused and scratched his head. "I mean—"

"And...?" Susan tilted her head toward Smitty.

"It all seemed relatively clean and neat, given two dead bodies and all," Smitty said. "There wasn't really much visible blood."

Jonathan exchanged a glance with Susan. There should have been a lot of blood in plain sight.

"And then there's Judge Haldeman," Smitty said.

"What about him?" Susan asked.

"The judge came to the house," he answered. "I overheard him tell Detective Sprance that Mr. and Mrs. Haldeman had been at a family holiday party at his house approximately an hour or two before, and they left because Mrs. Haldeman wasn't feeling well."

"Interesting," Jonathan said. "Any weapons?"

"We recovered a double-barrel shotgun," Shelly said.

"It wasn't just *any* double-barrel shotgun," Smitty said. "It was a classic L. C. Smith twelve-gauge Ideal model with dual triggers in a fore-and-aft configuration. Hunter Arms manufactured the Ideal between 1912 and

1950. And they only made about 18,000 of them. I mean, this shotgun is—"

"All right," Shelly said, rolling her eyes and sighing. "We got it. The shotgun is special. It has two triggers, one in front of the other. We also found a plain old twenty-two caliber handgun. Nothing special about it. And it has only one trigger. We sent both the shotgun and the pistol to the lab for fingerprint and ballistic analysis."

"Tell her where they found the twenty-two," Smitty said.

"Oh, yeah. It was on the coffee table, on top of a framed photograph of Mr. and Mrs. Haldeman together in their Navy dress blue uniforms during the war."

Jonathan shuddered internally. There must have been something significant to bring these two patriots to the point of a possible murder-suicide. "I'm curious. Was there a note?"

"We didn't see one," Smitty said, "but Detective Sprance took a lockbox and a handful of documents into evidence. You got a hunch, Doc?"

"Could be." Now it was Jonathan's turn to be officious and dour. No use letting anyone else outside his team know his thoughts, at least not yet. "We'll know more once we complete the autopsies. I hope to have some insights for Detective Sprance when she arrives."

"Thanks, Doc," the CSTs said in unison.

"And to all a good night," Smitty added, as they turned to leave. "Hope y'all don't get any more presents till after Christmas."

"Two cadavers, two deaths by gunshot," Jonathan said. "An exciting way to greet Christmas Eve."

"Okay, Jonathan, now what?" Susan asked.

"Time to hit the scrub sink. Jimmy, you scrub in, too. Once we see the condition of the bodies, we can figure out when to implement Plan B."

As they gathered around the morgue's massive stainless-steel sink, Jonathan looked at Jimmy. "I know this isn't your first rodeo. But repetition and practice make perfect. School's back in session. No medical books here. Time for some down and dirty nitty-gritty."

"I'm ready, Doc. Autopsy 101." Jimmy grinned. "By the time I hit med school, I'll be a pro."

"Robby taught me that attention to detail is crucial. Washing hands before an autopsy isn't as rigorous as before surgery. In an autopsy, you don't have to worry you'll infect a living patient. But, God, he was a stickler. I remember the first time I scrubbed in with Robby at the helm."

Jonathan transformed his voice into the familiar drawl affected by his mentor.

"It's real simple, Gray. You must be careful to avoid contaminating the cadaver to ensure any foreign substances do not influence test results. Protocol in my morgue calls for a three- to five-minute scrub from elbows to fingertips. Then it's into our surgical battle armor: gowns, gloves, caps, and masks. Dirty hands and a stray hair or two won't kill a corpse, but they might ruin an investigation and jeopardize a criminal trial."

Jesus, how could Jonathan make it without Robby? Cletus Robillard O'Malley, MD, what a character. He came armed with stories of New Orleans in the '60s and '70s and about how things were changing for the better. His flowing silver hair, neatly trimmed beard, and round tortoiseshell glasses made him look like what he was: an old Cajun Flower Child. He had a knack for getting you into his corner.

But Jonathan had to get past it all. Robby was gone. No time to mourn, at least not right now. He poured surgical cleanser on his hands and scrubbed his fingernails with a brush. He bore down extra hard, as if it would allow him to wash away the grief and move forward—out from under his mentor's shadow.

Susan cleared her throat. "So, you thinking murder-suicide?"

Jonathan nodded. Returning to his own voice, he replied, "Seems to be where the evidence is pointing us. But I have a lot of questions to answer before I'm ready to sign their death certificates."

Chapter Seven: Maggie

Wednesday, December 24, 2014

"Y ou know," Jonathan said, "I'll understand if you want to sit these two out."

Susan nodded and sighed. "I appreciate that. But I think it's best if I stay on the horse. Like I said, can't quit now. I'd be letting the family down."

"Okay," Jonathan said. "How would you be comfortable proceeding?"

"Well, their deaths seem related. Why don't we tag-team it? I'll be lead examiner for Maggie's autopsy. You observe and make suggestions and comments. After completing her exam, we can switch roles for Bill. Jimmy can be the med tech for both procedures."

"Sounds like a solid plan," Jonathan said. "And we should be especially careful given the identity of the victims and the violence involved." He pursed his lips, then exhaled a loud sigh. "Fastest way to create problems later is to skip a step. We've all seen colleagues squirm on the witness stand during cross-examination as a defense counsel takes them through everything they forgot to do on their way to a sloppy, inaccurate autopsy.

"Robby used to say that it would be a snowy day in Hell before he let it happen to him. Now that he's gone, I suppose I should start my own rule book. Rule Number One: It'll be a *hot* day in Hell for anyone working for me who lets it happen on my watch."

After they scrubbed and dressed in full surgical garb, Susan opened

Maggie's autopsy per standard protocol. She dictated basic information, such as date, starting time, and location, and named Maggie as the subject of the autopsy and herself and Jonathan as the participating medical professionals. She mentioned Jimmy by his given name and official title: "Serving as diener for this autopsy is Mr. Robert Thomas Caplan."

Susan turned off her recorder and looked at Jimmy. Jonathan waited for the fireworks that were about to follow.

"Jesus, I hate that word. I wish I could have a long talk with the Nazi rat bastard who came up with it."

Susan smiled at Jonathan. Jimmy had often expressed his dislike at being referred to as the diener, a German word meaning *servant*.

"You know, Jimmy," Susan said, "the formal term is *Leichendiener*, which is usually translated as 'servant of the *corpse*.'"

"Right," Jimmy said, "and it's why I'd like to tell whoever came up with it to go fu—"

"Come on, Jimmy," Jonathan said. "Rumor on the circuit is that your nickname in theater was 'Corpsman Caplan, the Cleaner, Meaner, Devil-Dog Diener.'"

"Geez, Doc. You know better than that. No autopsies in the field. Couldn't have been a diener." Jimmy changed into an exaggerated backwoods accent. "Besides, I'm just a country boy from Natchitoches. So, why don't you just run my ass up a flagpole and shoot me?"

"Fair enough." Jonathan smiled. "But that nickname—even if not true—makes more sense than someone named Robert Thomas Caplan being called Jimmy."

"I know." Jimmy's voice returned to his normal, crisp Southern accent. "Comes from when I was a kid. Momma locked herself out of our house. I fiddled around and jimmied the lock open. Well, you can figure it out from there."

"Bravo, Jimmy." Susan laughed. "Well done."

"All right, wise guy," Jonathan said. "Let's get back to work."

Maggie's autopsy proceeded methodically. Routine stuff to Jonathan and Susan, but Jimmy, as expected of any premed student, peppered them with questions, and shared comments about his days as a combat medic.

Susan spoke into the recorder. "The only sign of foul play is an entry wound to the top of subject's skull from what appears to be a small-caliber weapon. Interestingly, no burn marks are visible. There is no exit wound."

She paused. "Hmm, what's this?" She looked at Jimmy. "Dim the lights and bring the Wood's lamp."

"The ultraviolet light?"

"Yeah, and hold it over Maggie's head."

"Interesting." Susan spoke into the recorder. "Ultraviolet examination of the wound reveals few bloodstains and minimal stippling—certainly not in a concentration expected of a firearm discharged in such proximity to the skull. Examination also reveals small bits of what appears to be a cloth material."

Susan stopped recording and grabbed a magnifying glass. "Look at that, will you? Those tiny strands. Not hair. Some sort of cloth residue."

Jonathan came closer. "Yeah, interesting. Let's get some samples."

Susan picked up a pair of tweezers, then retrieved several pieces of the strands and put them in a small glass vial for laboratory analysis.

"That's about it for the outside," Susan said. "Let's move on to the internal examination."

Stepping up to the cadaver, Susan raised her scalpel and made a deep incision, starting at the top of each shoulder and running down the front of the chest, meeting at the lower point of her sternum. She then cut in a straight line all the way down the abdomen to the top of Maggie's pubic bone, making a slight detour around her navel. Susan peeled the tissue back enough to expose the rib cage.

"Seems like there ought to be a better term than *Y incision* to describe it," Jimmy said.

"No need for fancy Latin names," Jonathan said.

"Whenever I do this," Susan said, "I feel like a burglar or a safecracker. Jimmy, note that breaking through the protective shell of the sternum and ribs is never easy. But it's critical because it allows us to expose the vital organs for examination without damaging them."

"It's like a little bone basket protecting the internal organs," Jimmy said.

"Good analogy," Jonathan said.

"Hmmm," Susan said. "The bullet doesn't appear to be in the chest or abdomen. Before removing any internal organs, let's look at the oral cavity."

Susan opened Maggie's mouth and shined a light inside. "Look there." She pointed toward a slight bump on the roof of Maggie's mouth. "It's not quite what we expected, but close. The bullet came to rest in the hard palate, just outside the base of the brain. And not in the soft tissues of the neck. Interesting."

With the bullet located, Susan examined each internal organ, to ensure there wasn't any other damage. She gathered appropriate aliquots—samples—for laboratory analysis. As she cut into Maggie's stomach, Susan gagged. "Alcohol was being digested. Smell it?"

Jimmy's wrinkled nose and facial expression showed how he felt. "Oh, God, yes. That definitely wasn't present during the external examination. It's sweet and fruity and gross."

"I can smell it from four feet away," Jonathan said. "Must be pretty bad for you two."

"Of course," Susan said, "lab results will show how much alcohol's in her system, as well as whether she had taken any medication. I suspect we'll find a mixture."

Susan looked toward Jonathan. "How about it? Questions so far?"

"Nope," Jonathan said. "Looks like it's time to crack the skull."

"The last time I saw Maggie," Susan said, over the muted grinding sound of the oscillating Stryker saw, "was a couple of years ago when she and Bill renewed their vows. She still seemed so vibrant, despite being in her nineties. She laughed and joked like someone forty years her junior. But when you hit ninety—the tenth decade of life—each year brings a lot of changes. Maybe I missed the warning signs."

Susan removed the skull cap and turned on the recorder. "Subject's brain shows damage consistent with a small-caliber bullet wound from a weapon discharged at close range from above. In addition, subject's brain shows signs of advanced dementia, possibly Alzheimer's. Overall brain mass appears to be approximately half of normal. Atrophy is especially pronounced in the hippocampus."

She lifted Maggie's brain from its protective shell and placed it in the scale's metal basket.

"Subject's brain weighs twenty-six ounces, over twenty ounces less than the average healthy female brain." Susan took a deep breath. "Jimmy, would you take some photos of the brain before I dissect it for microscopic slides and lab samples?"

"I've never seen an Alzheimer's brain," he said, "except in medical texts. It's very dramatic in real life. The pictures don't capture the starkness of the changes."

"Pictures never do," Jonathan said.

Susan nodded her agreement. "I always think about a light bulb. One minute, it's so bright you can't look straight at it. Then the filament burns out. Only thing left is a darkened shell. You can still see the outline of the filament. But there's no energy or infrastructure to provide light. A bullet might have caused catastrophic physical damage leading to a ceasing of bodily functions and death, but Maggie Haldeman's brain as an intellectual mechanism died long ago."

Susan sighed. "We've done our scientific duty. Now it's time to get Maggie ready for the undertaker—and a proper funeral and burial."

She wrapped the now-mutilated organs in white cloth, placed them in the body cavity, and returned the ribcage covering. Her hands trembled as she reached for the suturing tools.

"Can I suggest something?" Jonathan asked. "I'm curious about what our master diener learned about stitches during his Navy days. I wonder—"

"Great idea," Susan said quickly. "Jimmy, would you like to close?" She folded the chest flaps over, revealing the Y-shaped incision. "A great opportunity to practice your suturing techniques."

"Wow, thanks, Dr. Miller. Sure thing. You have a specific suture in mind?"

"Not really. I most often use a baseball stitch. Why don't you start with that? I don't think Maggie would mind."

Jimmy started on the upper-right arm of the Y using the diagonal over-

and-under technique of a continuous running suture—a baseball stitch—as requested. It was a two-handed process. In his right hand was an aptly named needle holder, a small forceps used to grasp a curved needle and nylon suturing thread. His left held a specialized, tweezer-like forceps designed to provide stability or move the skin, as necessary.

He guided the needle into the skin, applying enough force to penetrate the barrier, but not too much to rip out the hole. With each penetration came a slight popping sound, as he made a hole and pulled the thread through. He then joined both sides of the incision to make the first suture. He tied off the beginning of "the run" with a square knot. Then he proceeded with sutures about every four millimeters. The resultant diagonal pattern—like the seam on a baseball—soon emerged. At the intersection of the two arms and base of the Y, Jimmy completed his task by making another square knot and cutting the remaining ends on the threads.

He looked up. "How am I doing so far, Doc?"

"Good," Susan said. "You're very poised. And your skill level is excellent at this stage of your training. How's your technique for a simple interrupted suture?"

Without missing a beat, Jimmy moved along the upper-left arm of the Y, making individual sutures, closing off each with a square knot before starting the next one.

"You're doing a great job, Jimmy," Susan said.

"Thanks." Jimmy paused before starting the straight line of the Y. "And now the grand finale, a vertical mattress. My favorite. I had to use it on a platoon buddy who had a knife wound in his thigh, almost from his knee to his hip. Saved his life, and his leg."

Jonathan had never seen such suturing skills in someone who hadn't been to medical school. And Jimmy's ability to converse without missing a beat while suturing—amazing.

"Talented hands," Susan said. "Just the right touch. Gentle but firm. And your technique—I guess you got plenty of practice in Afghanistan."

"An unfortunate truth, Dr. Miller. I suppose you could think of it as some good that came from the whole mess, although I hate to think of the human cost of my on-the-job training. But when you're all there is between a shipmate bleeding out or living, you learn to do what's necessary. Emergency stitches were only one service I offered. I was also the closest thing we had to a chiropractor if anyone needed a spinal adjustment or neck manipulation after a full day of carrying fifty pounds of equipment and weapons."

Jonathan nodded. "I guess it's true that necessity is the mother of invention."

Chapter Eight: Bill

Wednesday, December 24, 2014

"Final conclusions will have to wait," Jonathan said, as they gathered around the sink after changing into new scrubs. "But there seems little doubt Maggie is the murder portion of this potential murder-suicide."

"I agree," Susan said. "First, there's clear visual evidence her brain had succumbed to dementia. That suggests she was the victim of a mercy killing. And the bullet wound on top of her head? The location and apparent angle of trajectory mean there's no way it was self-inflicted."

"In other words," Jimmy said, "Mrs. Haldeman's autopsy most likely revealed the means and motive of her murder, but it didn't go far enough to identify her killer."

"Once again, you're spot on," Jonathan said. "And the nature of injuries to Mr. Haldeman—shotgun blasts to the base of his chin upward into his brain—seems to act as the suicide part of the equation. At least, circumstances point that way. From there, it's a matter of linking the two. So, let's see what truth lies with Mr. Haldeman."

Leaving Jimmy to complete the preliminary workup for Bill—as he had done with Maggie—Jonathan and Susan walked around Bill's corpse, stopping often, and talking.

Jonathan pointed to the back of Bill's skull. "See that indentation?"

"Yeah," Susan said. "I see injuries like that all the time in the ER."

"Interesting. We'll take a detailed look later."

Moving away from Bill's head, Jonathan grabbed the Wood's lamp and passed it over Bill's torso and chest.

"Hmmm," he said. "That's strange. Jimmy, come hold this for me, please."

"Sure."

"Hold it right here." Jonathan pulled Jimmy's hands and the lamp closer to Bill's torso.

"Susan, what do you think?" Jonathan asked.

"Looks like a mixture of blood and gunpowder. But the concentration seems off."

"Precisely," Jonathan said.

"I would expect there would be a greater concentration of gunshot residue driven into his chest and torso," Susan said. "But here the concentration seems very light. Lighter than you would expect."

"Interesting," Jonathan said. "Jimmy, let's make sure Mr. Haldeman's shirt gets a full look-see at the lab. Ask them to give us a blood-spatter report and a GSR—that's gunshot residue—pattern analysis."

"Can do, Doc," Jimmy said.

After a few moments of silent observation, Jonathan spoke into the recorder. "I can see several cloth bits on Mr. Haldeman's shirt, neck, and chin similar to those discovered on Mrs. Haldeman's head. And there are cloth bits on the top of Mr. Haldeman's head and his face, as well. We will retrieve some for analysis."

Jonathan asked Jimmy to move the Wood's lamp over Bill's hands.

"The GSR here," Jonathan said, "also isn't very heavy for someone who killed his wife with a pistol and then committed suicide with a double-barrel shotgun." Jonathan turned to Susan.

"I agree," she said.

"The mystery deepens," Jonathan said. "Wonder what it all means."

After completing his external examination, Jonathan directed Jimmy to prepare Bill's body for the next phase. Once he was done, Jimmy looked at Jonathan expectantly. "Okay, Doc, it's show time."

The massive damage to Bill's face and skull was the most notable part of the physical examination.

Jonathan inspected Bill's head and winced. "The shotgun did its job. After a couple of twelve-gauge blasts at close range, there isn't much left of his lower jaw, face, and forehead."

"You know," Susan said, "I hate to say it, but Smitty Hebert's characterization of a snapping turtle's beak—rough, serrated, and pointy on the end—isn't far off the mark."

"Good God, you're right," Jonathan said. "Looks like the shotgun was put against the bottom of his chin. And both triggers pulled. Damage seems too far forward and angled to one side. It's as if he slipped when he pulled the triggers."

Jonathan looked at Susan. "Ready to take a deeper look at that dent?"

"Let's go," Susan said. "Curious, isn't it? A concave depression in the middle of the occiput. This doesn't appear to be from a bullet wound, and I don't see how he could have done this himself. And there's very little hair to hide it. Whoever's responsible wasn't trying to cover his tracks, that's for sure."

"Were the damage caused by a shotgun blast," Jonathan said, "fragmentation should be focused outwardly. But there aren't any buckshot pellets near the depression. And the blast angle appears to be straight up from the bottom of the chin. Or even slightly forward."

"Ball-peen hammer or something similar, I'd bet," Susan said. "I've seen too many like this one in the ER for it to be anything else."

Jimmy put the X-rays he had taken earlier on the light board. As Jonathan and Susan approached, Jimmy pointed. "It's defined even better on film."

"Wow, it really is clear," Jonathan said, turning on the recorder.

"Plainly visible on the X-ray is a curved indentation most likely caused when something pounded the scalp and bony layers of the skull and pushed them inward. Minimal amount of bone fragmentation suggests a small object. To do that much damage with such a focused impact site, *whatever* was used must have been very solid. An iron or steel ball-peen hammer certainly fits the description."

"Seems pretty clear," Susan said. "Someone must have come up from behind and—"

"Right," Jonathan nodded. "Now the authorities just have to figure out who—"

"And why," Susan said.

This newest twist was like a jolt of adrenaline laced with caffeine. Time to dig deeper into Bill's violent and as yet unexplained death. The telltale buzz and crunch of the Stryker saw again pierced the air as Jonathan cut into Bill's cranial cap and removed his brain. Except for damage from the shotgun blast and the round object striking the back of the skull, the brain was intact. In stark contrast to Maggie's autopsy, it didn't appear to show deterioration or other signs of dementia.

"I'll be very interested to learn what our lab results tell," Jonathan said, as he handed the samples to Jimmy. "Okay, Jimmy, you know the drill. Plan B. Commence Operation Deep Freeze. Dr. Miller and I will suture Mr. Haldeman back together."

"Got it, Doc. Thirty pounds of ice per adult cadaver, for a total of sixty pounds of cubes. That's a dozen five-pound bags. And I already turned our A/C down to fifty degrees."

Chapter Nine: Betsy Sprance

Wednesday, December 24, 2014

Betsy Sprance arrived at the morgue just after 5:00 a.m. Observing coroners at work in their natural habitat was a grizzly, albeit necessary part of her job. She had been on her feet for most of the night. She'd welcome a break from the brisk, predawn chill—even if she had to put up with a cadaver or two. Betsy entered the building through the loading dock.

"*Soc au' lait.*" Betsy shuddered. "It's like a glacier in here."

To her right, two gurneys sat in the hallway near the cold-storage lockers. Each gurney had the outline of a human body on it, lying stiff and lifeless under the standard white cloth sheet often used to cover and protect cadavers. Jimmy wrapped a bag of ice in a towel, put it in a plastic garbage bag, and placed it on one of the gurneys. The ventilation system roared as frigid air rushed through the ducting. Despite the strength of the airflow, her nostrils stung from the sharpness of the metallic smell from the volume of blood released by the autopsies and the pungent odor of the bleach used to clean up afterward.

"Plan B, huh?" She spoke loudly enough for Jimmy to hear over whatever he was listening to on his headphones. "I'm guessing you're overbooked."

Jimmy looked up and removed his headphones. "Detective Sprance, good to see you. Dr. Gray hoped you could make it earlier so you could observe part of the Haldeman autopsies. Must be some crime scene."

"Yeah. And something's out of whack. Not sure what, exactly. Anyway, thought I should cut it short at the crime scene and chat with Doc. See if the stiffs—I mean, corpses—have any secrets they're willing to share. Left Mitch Broussard at the house to wrap things up. Keeping my fingers crossed y'all can shed some light. I'd love to crack this case wide open and get back to Ranger and Brandon in time for Christmas."

"Your two dogs?" Jimmy asked.

"Hubby and son." Betsy rolled her eyes. "Dogs are more obedient."

Jimmy smiled. "Is Investigator Rabideau coming?"

"Not yet. Sonny wanted to talk again with a couple of family members. And then walk the area one more time with Detective Broussard. I think he planned to stop for a bite on his way here. You know how Sonny is about his shrimp and grits for breakfast."

"Yes, ma'am, I do." Jimmy crinkled his nose. "I know many people consider that combination to be a Southern delicacy, but I can't stand it. Shrimp's meant to be eaten alone or in a variety of dishes, but grits isn't one of them—and surely not for breakfast."

Betsy laughed. "You *sure* you're from Louisiana?"

Jimmy turned off his music and grinned. "Speaking of food, can I offer you some coffee and a fat pill?"

He pointed to the desk next to the examination room. "When I was picking up the ice, I added a Cube-O'-Java to Dr. Gray's bill. And I had them throw in some beignets and frosted Long Johns. I hope the Parish doesn't look too closely at our request for reimbursement."

"Thanks, Jimmy. I'm happy to help you eat the evidence."

Jimmy opened the pop-up spout of the Cube-O'-Java and poured some coffee into a mug. The morgue's coffee mugs were a wonder. No two alike, they seemed to appear magically and reproduce through some sort of ceramic mitosis. As she accepted a steaming cup of coffee from Jimmy, Jonathan and Susan came into view, arguing over what sounded like the relevance of small cloth fibers.

"Betsy, long time no see," Jonathan said. "What was it, yesterday morning, about this same time?"

"That soon?" Betsy said. "So much's happened since then. Seems like it's been days, not hours."

"Agreed," Jonathan said. "A lot *has* happened."

"Good to be here. It really has been a long day. Longer than anything I remember from my military police days in Afghanistan working for NCIS."

Jonathan and Susan poured themselves cups of coffee.

"Do you have Sonny Rabideau in tow," Susan said, "or did he drop by Momma Mae's for shrimp and grits?"

"You know Sonny well," Betsy said. "He wanted to clean up a couple of loose ends. But I suspect he plans to visit Momma's once he's done."

"Sonny Rabideau is a creature of habit," Jonathan said. "Any day he doesn't visit Momma Mae's is a day to avoid him like the plague. Shrimp-and-grits deprivation seems to bring out his inner grouch. And it's been a long day *and* night. Standing here drinking coffee is likely as relaxed as any of us has been in several hours."

"Now I'm really tired, Doc." Betsy chuckled. "Let me get some more joe."

"Before we go through details of our autopsies," Jonathan said, as Betsy reached for a refill, "I'm interested to hear your impressions from the crime scene."

"Yes, right away," Betsy said as she sat down in one of the morgue's heavy aluminum chairs and groaned. "Man, that feels good. Cold as a block of ice and hard as hell. Except for time in the car, I've been on my feet since receiving the police dispatcher's call about the Haldemans."

"A well-deserved sit-down," Jonathan said. "So, relax. And start at the beginning."

"Jimmy and I talked right after I arrived," Betsy said. "There's more to this case than meets the eye. It just seems too easy. Preliminary evidence points in one direction, toward one conclusion. Something tells me it just fits together *too* nicely."

Jonathan and Susan looked at each other as if recognizing a dark secret Betsy had just uncovered.

"Yeah," Jonathan said. "Aspects of the autopsies struck us as out of the ordinary as well. What's your gut telling you?"

43

"I arrived just before ten p.m. Uniformed officers had been there long enough to confirm the Haldemans were dead and to clear the premises. They did a good job protecting the evidence. Once the scene was stable, they notified the dispatcher to send the CSTs. I directed them to call your office. The bodies looked like they'd been dead for not much more than an hour."

"Sounds about right," Susan said. "Rough estimate of time of death is between eight and nine o'clock."

"The CSTs told us where the corpses were." Jonathan glanced at Susan.

"Do you think the location of the bodies is significant?" Susan asked.

"I do." Betsy nodded, looking at Susan. "Mr. and Mrs. Haldeman seemed so dedicated to one another. The people I've interviewed have told me about their seventieth wedding anniversary and how they renewed their vows in front of families and friends."

"I was there," Susan said. "I remember it well. You could tell they were destined to be together."

Betsy nodded her acknowledgment and studied Susan. If she had known the Haldemans that well, she had to be grieving, yet she was doing a damn good job of maintaining her professionalism.

"A year ago," Betsy continued, "Maggie started deteriorating physically and mentally. Their children talked about bringing in a caregiver to help, but Bill would have nothing of it. The worse she got, the more dedicated he became."

"Our autopsy confirmed Mrs. Haldeman suffered from advanced dementia," Jonathan said. "It takes a special patience and love to deal with what Mrs. Haldeman must have been experiencing."

"Exactly," Betsy spoke, her passion building. "And that's why placement of the bodies is so unusual. There are a couple of types of murder-suicide, depending on the parties' relationship."

"Interesting," Jonathan said. "Tell us more."

"The first type is what we call a true murder-suicide. It's usually motivated by anger or revenge, like when a divorced couple is fighting about custody and one ex-spouse kills the other one to keep him or her from getting the kids. We expect to find the suicide victim a greater distance away from the one they killed. It's as if they want to underscore they were apart in life and would be apart in death."

Betsy yawned. "Excuse me." She pressed on.

"The second type is where the killing's done out of love, perhaps misguided, but love nonetheless. Where there is a couple so dedicated to one another, we typically see their bodies as close together as they can be. It's as if they're starting their journey to the afterlife together.

"So, if Bill shot his wife to put her out of her misery, then shot himself to be with her…it doesn't fit the profile. I mean, shooting your wife, putting the pistol down, walking around to the other side of the table, and then shooting yourself? It's off the mark. Might make sense if he had been on the floor right next to the couch. But not so far away."

Betsy trailed off in thought before snapping herself back to the present. She softened her voice as she continued.

"Then there's Bill Haldeman's body stretched out on the floor, neatly, with the shotgun propped up against his chin and his thumbs on the trigger. Too neat. If he had pulled both triggers simultaneously, the recoil would make his weapon come loose. And even if he had only pulled one trigger, the shotgun should have been askew. Or even at his side. In either scenario, it shouldn't be tight against his chin."

Betsy looked into the distance. "Often, we find triggers wired in such a way that it takes a single yank to make both move simultaneously. Here, they weren't wired."

"Sorry to interrupt," Jonathan said, "but if this is a murder-suicide, why do you think Bill Haldeman used a shotgun when the pistol proved sufficient for his wife?"

"His motivation?" Betsy shrugged. "Who knows what someone's thinking at a time like that." She shook her head and sighed. "A couple of scenarios could have been playing out. Bill might have wanted to punish himself for killing his wife. Or he wanted the love of his life to remain as beautiful as possible in death. So he used a small-caliber weapon that would cause very little disfigurement. There was nothing she had done wrong; she was a victim of the dementia. And by disfiguring himself so completely, Bill might have wanted to show his shame for the murder.

"Another, more practical, reason is that he wanted to guarantee he completed the job. The pistol was such a small caliber. So there's always a chance a bullet would do insufficient damage, resulting in severe injury but not death. I've seen many suicides where a victim ends up paralyzed or brain-damaged but alive. All because the weapon slipped at the last second."

"I see." Jonathan stifled a yawn as he rose, then topped off his coffee. He caught Susan's eye, then turned back to Betsy. "How was the shotgun placed in relation to Bill's torso and chest?"

"Excellent question. My experience is that a suicide will put the top of the shotgun against his chest. With the triggers pointing upward."

As she spoke, Betsy stood and drew an imaginary line up the center of her torso and chest with two fingers. When she reached her neck, she put her fingers against the bottom of her chin.

"At that angle, the explosive blast travels in a more direct path straight to the brain. And with the barrels so close to the chin, it adds to the impact. It also helps keep the shotgun from slipping out of nervous hands."

Jonathan and Susan nodded, seeming to agree. Jimmy stood nearby, sipping his coffee.

"But to answer your question, we found the shotgun in the opposite orientation. The trigger side was toward his torso. This should have made for a blast angle more to the back of his head."

Betsy exhaled loudly. She had been practically holding her breath while she was talking. "Of course, we can't form a solid picture of what happened until we put all the evidence together."

Relieved she had made it through her observations and opinions, Betsy sat down again. "Any clues from your autopsies?"

"Absolutely," Jonathan said. "Your description brought it home. We also found some things that didn't quite fit."

"Interesting," Betsy said. "I'm curious. Do tell."

Jonathan motioned to the gurneys outside the cold-storage lockers. "Let's go to Bill Haldeman's cadaver, and I'll show you what we found."

"Excuse me, Doc," Jimmy said. "Before you start, I need to take our samples to the lab so they can get started before the holiday. They're down to the emergency crew until after Christmas, so if we have any hope of speeding the results along, I need to get moving."

"Right you are. Thanks for keeping us on schedule. Let's take a break. We can run through our evidence list again before you go. Given the number of samples and other items, it'll take you quite a while to transfer custody. That all right with you, Betsy?"

"Sure. It'll give me a chance to make a pit stop."

"On your heels," Susan said. "After so much coffee, I'm headed in that direction too."

Chapter Ten: Sonny

Wednesday, December 24, 2014

The team, absent Jimmy, assembled to continue the debriefing. They seemed energized after their brief respite.

"Morning shift reports in about an hour," Jonathan said. "So we need to take full advantage of our time together. And I've worked with Betsy enough to know that each tick of the clock affords anyone who might be involved a chance to wash gunshot residue down the drain, bury sullied clothes, and work on developing an alibi."

"Amen, Doc." Betsy nodded. "Let's get after it."

"You know what?" Jonathan said as they walked toward Bill Haldeman's cadaver. "I think the most profound revelation so far is fairly obvious. The most solid conclusion we can draw is that Maggie's death was a homicide. Location and angle of her wound make it impossible for her to have shot herself."

"Even if she was a contortionist with rubber arms and a mirror?" asked a booming voice coming from the direction of the loading dock.

Jonathan turned toward the voice, already knowing the source: Coroner's Death Investigator Bartholomew Augustus Rabideau Jr. Following a well-respected Southern tradition usually reserved for a male child, his family had named him after his father, then referred to him as Sonny.

A medically retired Louisiana state policeman, Sonny wore jeans and a purple polo shirt with "LSU" embroidered in small gold letters on the upper-left side of the front. He stood exactly six feet tall, unless you included his flattop haircut, which seemed to add an inch or two. Slim and muscular, Sonny walked stiffly, with military bearing, grimacing as if in pain, likely because of the reason for his retirement: a bullet lodged dangerously close to his lower spine.

"Sonny," Jonathan said. "Welcome back. We've been hoping you'd drop by. How's Mae?"

"Momma's doing tolerably fine, Doc. She sends you her best. And she asked when you and the Mrs. will be by for some gumbo."

Jonathan smiled at the mention of his favorite restaurant. Momma Mae's—the best-kept secret in Orleans Parish, perhaps in the entire state. "Mae's place *is* a treasure. And she's right. Emma and I are overdue for a visit. So maybe we'll try to make it before New Year's." Jonathan grinned. "But tell us about Miss Corrine. I assume she was about the premises."

Sonny's otherwise stoic demeanor softened, and his cheeks flushed. You didn't have to be Sherlock Holmes to solve this puzzle. Sonny frequented Momma Mae's for breakfast at every opportunity because he was "sweet" on Corinne Mayweather, a server at Mae's place.

"Miss Corinne was there." Sonny cleared his throat, his face now undeniably crimson. "I hoped I would catch you and Detective Sprance before your shift change so I could bring you the latest and see what the autopsies revealed. Any conclusions yet?"

"Yes, and we only just started going over them," Jonathan replied. "You're here just in time. I was telling everyone the only certainty is that Mrs. Haldeman's death was a homicide. We were just about to show Betsy something we found during our external examination of Bill Haldeman that might or might not have played a part in how he died."

They gathered near Bill's head. Jonathan pulled back the white covering, exposing Bill's body to the middle of his chest. Susan positioned a magnifier over the indentation, then put X-rays on the light board. Jonathan described Susan's ball-peen hammer theory.

"Do you think this injury was the cause of death?" Betsy asked. "Or only a contributing factor?"

"Neither one looks likely," Jonathan said. "Given enough time, he might have bled out, but it appears the shotgun blasts are the cause of death."

"In the short term," Susan said, "using the ball-peen hammer was probably meant to disable him."

Betsy and Sonny looked at each other. Their eyes reflected surprise—shock, even. Sonny spoke first.

"Jesus, Mary, and Joseph. Who would want to incapacitate Mr. Haldeman? And why? It doesn't look like a robbery. Not a stick of furniture out of place. Judge Haldeman told us where to find critical documents, jewelry, and other valuables. Everything checked out."

"How did Judge Haldeman get notified?" Jonathan said. "I forgot to ask the CSTs."

"I understand Polly Bondurant called him," Betsy said. "Not too long after we discovered the bodies, I think."

"Got it," Jonathan said. "Probably wouldn't be unusual for the super-intendent of police to be monitoring such a high-viz crime and call the family."

"Especially someone of Judge Haldeman's standing," Betsy added.

Sonny glanced at Betsy, then at Jonathan. "I'm not sure what Betsy told you, but this, bar none, was the cleanest murder scene I've ever visited. It's as if angels carried bodies to their final resting places and touched nothing else. So if nothing is missing and someone was there to club Mr. Haldeman, it means…"

His words simply stopped. Closing his mouth, Sonny raised his right hand toward his face, made a fist, and tapped his chin gently as if he were sending his brain a message in Morse code. His silence spoke volumes.

"Got it," Betsy said. "Double murder, not murder-suicide. Where should we go from here?"

"We need to wait for the ballistic analysis and other tests," Jonathan said. "But we can go through some highlights, then talk about the way ahead."

With the rapt attention of the two investigators, Jonathan reviewed salient findings: lack of significant gunshot residue on Mr. Haldeman's hands; unusual juxtaposition and angle of the shotgun; small amount of blood and gunshot residue on Mr. Haldeman's shirt; odor of alcohol being digested in Mrs. Haldeman's stomach; and the small bits of cloth.

At his mention of cloth bits, Betsy jumped as if she'd had an electric shock to her system. "Soup to nuts. Why didn't I see it before? Their killer was trying to muffle gunshots with a towel or blanket or something similar. No wonder the initial police call didn't mention any shots fired."

"Wrapping a towel around a shotgun would reduce residue on Mr. Haldeman's shirt, wouldn't it?" Sonny's statement was more a declaration than a question. "And covering Mr. Haldeman's head might explain a lack of blood spatter as well."

"A-plus to you both," Jonathan said. "Once we get lab results, we'll know if Maggie had taken any sedatives. In the meantime, I suggest locating any bottles of alcohol in the Haldemans' house and taking prints, if there are any."

"I'm making a list, Doc," Betsy replied. "Time to revisit the crime scene with a fresh perspective."

"Detective," Susan said, "sorry to ask this so late in the game, but I'm curious. Did you find a note?"

"No, but we seized the Haldemans' computer hard drive. We also found hard copies of their wills and some insurance policies and mortgage documents from a loan Judge Haldeman made to his parents. The DA's determining whether they give any clues about who would profit from Bill and Maggie's deaths.

"Of course, that was when we thought this was a murder-suicide. Now it seems they're even more important. I'd best call in some extra help and get back to work. If we're lucky, Old Saint Nick will have left a present or two at the crime scene."

"That *would* make it a merry Christmas." Jonathan smiled. "But my money's on the Homicide Squad."

Chapter Eleven: St. George's

Wednesday, December 24, 2014

By shortly after 9:00 a.m., Jonathan had finished his administrative duties, allowing him to bid the morgue adieu. His nose crinkled as he walked across the parking lot toward his car. There was no residual dampness. The storm brewing when he drove to the morgue last night must have stayed north of the lake.

Soon, he turned his car onto Earhart Boulevard and headed home. The past day and a half had been draining, physically and emotionally. Now was an excellent time for a detour through the Garden District. Surely, he'd find a midmorning Christmas Eve service. After last night's shift, a peaceful sanctuary full of live people might be just what he needed.

Heading down Martin Luther King Jr. Boulevard toward St. Charles Street and the center of the Garden District, it seemed like there was a house of worship every block or two—in all denominations except his, Episcopal. It made sense, being an Episcopalian. He'd been raised as a Methodist, Emma as a Catholic. The Anglican liturgy and rituals landed about in the middle—more structured than he'd grown up with, but without the need for the priestly intercession demanded by the Catholic faith. It might not be the right path for everyone. But he had to follow his heart.

Trinity's single bell tower came into view. The church looked deserted, though a sign outside invited him to "Join Us for Midnight Mass, Christmas Eve at 11 PM." Disappointed to see a similar greeting as he approached

Christ Church Cathedral, Jonathan continued along St. Charles toward Tulane University. Surely, St. Andrew's in Carrollton would have a midday service.

Well before reaching Tulane, the stone edifice of St. George's loomed ahead. He had forgotten about St. George's. Great. Its big wooden doors stood open, and organ music resonated from inside. Jonathan pulled into the only parking space he saw—on St. Charles, within view of the church. This must be his lucky day.

As he reached for the ignition to shut off the engine, the car's interior vibrated with a telltale ring—a call coming in via his iPhone sitting on the passenger's seat. Given the name displayed by the Caller ID, this wasn't one to let roll over to voicemail.

"Good morning, Mr. Mayor." Jonathan took the call with a mixture of surprise, curiosity, and humor. "How may I be of assistance this Christmas Eve morning?"

"Dr. Gray, I hope this isn't a bad time."

"Not at all, sir." Jonathan wasn't sure how to tell their city's sober-sounding chief executive he was tired and had better things to do.

"Dr. Gray, please call me Max. I'm truly sorry to interrupt your holiday. I just hung up from talking with Polly Bondurant at police headquarters."

Jonathan relaxed. "Is this about Mr. and Mrs. Haldeman?"

"It is, Doctor. You're very perceptive. I've already heard from Judge Haldeman, some of his siblings, and several other influential citizens. The children, of course, are concerned about what happened to their parents. They were grieving when they believed this was a mercy killing and a suicide. Now NOPD acts as if it's a double murder. Judge Haldeman's beside himself in disbelief."

"I can imagine their shock," Jonathan said.

"And others outside the family have been vocal in reminding me that homicides, much less *double* homicides, *do not* happen in the Garden District. I've assured everyone that our Superintendent of Police and our Coroner are doing everything in their power to solve this crime and bring whoever's responsible to justice."

Jonathan closed his eyes before he spoke. He needed every bit of self-control he could muster to avoid telling Max that, for several hours, these two prominent citizens were lying lifeless in a hallway, covered with sheets, and surrounded by ice from a convenience store. Maddening. All because the politicians wouldn't provide him with sufficient cold-storage facilities. He took a deep cleansing breath, then opened his eyes.

"Max, you have my word. My office has allocated every appropriate resource to investigate their tragic deaths."

"Thank you, Doctor, that's all I can ask. If there is anything your office needs to ensure a full, *expeditious* investigation, please let me know."

"Very kind of you, Max. With budgets what they are these days, we're struggling. I'll review the matter with my staff and contact your office if necessary."

"Excellent, Dr. Gray, I knew you would understand. Robby O'Malley picked the right man to follow in his footsteps. I hope you and Mrs. Gray pass a wonderful Christmas."

The mayor ended the call before Jonathan could extend his own wishes for the holiday. No matter. No doubt, he would hear from Max again if the police, with support and cooperation from his office, couldn't solve the Haldeman murders soon. An abrupt end to the conversation also meant Jonathan had said nothing he might regret later. He exited his car and hastened toward the now-closed doors of St. George's.

Chapter Twelve: Maison Gris

Wednesday, December 24, 2014

Despite his physical exhaustion, his detour to St. George's had been time well spent. What a contrast between the stainless-steel efficiency and stark odor of death permeating the morgue and the ethereal hopefulness of the church's sanctuary and homily. His mind no longer raced with thoughts of cadavers and autopsies. More relaxed and calmer, emotionally, he'd soon be home, ready for much-needed sleep.

Jonathan exhaled as he approached the intersection of St. Charles and Canal, signifying he was on the edge of the French Quarter. Navigating the Quarter's maze of one-way avenues and streets, like Bourbon, often blocked to create pedestrian malls, presented a challenge. Over the past few months, detours around repairs to the antiquated water and sewer system transformed each trip via car into an adventure. And today, the GPS satellite must be taking a holiday, because Google Maps didn't track some changes. Regardless, by memory of the traffic patterns, some guesswork, and a bit of luck, he wound up on Bienville, headed away from the river. The move put him on his final approach to Maison Gris, his nickname for their home, which occupied two floors above the street-level shops below.

Jonathan turned into the internal courtyard of their building, pushed a button in his car, and lowered the metal door covering the entryway. He stepped out of his vehicle and proceeded up the stairway leading from the courtyard and entered their foyer. What a magnificent sight: Fen, his nickname for Emma since their first date at a baseball game when they were in college, standing there to greet him. Her shining eyes signaled he was once again in his safe place. No cadavers or police here.

"Been expecting you," Emma said. "From the news reports, it sounds like you had a busy shift last night."

"Haldeman killings?" he asked, as he put his coat in the closet.

"Yeah. There's one clip of Max Jamerson saying he had spoken to both the Superintendent and the Coroner and offered whatever resources they needed. And I can't believe Judge Haldeman is so poised, especially this soon after his parents' killings. He made a statement and answered questions. Very impressive. And surreal at the same time."

"Well, he's used to controlling his emotions in court," Jonathan replied as they walked out of the foyer toward the living room. "I guess it stays with you, even under trying circumstances."

"I suppose. You know, I nearly cried. There's crime-scene tape plastered all over Bill and Maggie's beautiful home in the Garden District. It's such a tragic sight, especially for an architect. I recorded it all for you."

"Thanks, that's very helpful." Jonathan answered slowly, almost like he was in a trance, as the fatigue finally hit. "I'll watch it later." He yawned. "Past day and a half's been worse than med school. I've only had a brief nap in thirty-six hours. Washed up quickly at the morgue. But I need a proper shower—and a shave. And I'm hungry… maybe we can grab a quick lunch at Felix's before I crash for a few hours."

"Don't worry about lunch. I'll put something together. Now drag your smelly backside upstairs and get in the shower."

Chapter Thirteen: The Gallery

Wednesday, December 24, 2014

Jonathan joined Emma on their second-story gallery overlooking Bienville Street. She was setting out lunch: her special Cajun chicken salad nestled on a bed of lettuce and mixed greens with fresh Rio Grande tomatoes. Next to the salad was a small wedge of freshly baked mirliton pie, Jonathan's favorite dessert.

The ongoing gumbo ya-ya of voices, traffic noise, and jazz notes from the street below served as a reminder of how much he and Emma loved living and being property owners in the French Quarter. Bon Jovi, a calico cat belonging to one of their retail tenants—proprietor of a shop on the ground floor of their building—sauntered along the wrought-iron railing like a king watching over his fiefdom. He plopped down in a sunny spot as if *he* were the landlord. Despite the cool December temperature, the winter sun rendered their space heaters unnecessary.

He sat down and they ate lunch, talking and enjoying their time together. Despite his fatigue, the food and conversation energized him. He revealed what few details he could about the Haldemans. And although he told Emma about the infant he'd autopsied during his shift, he didn't mention his nightmare. He spent most of his time complaining about the mayor's call. He just couldn't get it out of his mind.

"Jesus, Fen, after all the times we asked for Max Jamerson to support budget increases, it took murders of two prominent citizens to get any reaction."

"Must be infuriating." Emma sipped her wine. "I'm sure I'd feel the same way in your shoes. But you can't control everything."

"I know. But still..." He drank the rest of his wine and then poured himself some more.

"I got a text from Abby today," Emma said. "The triplets decided to meet in Paris to celebrate the holidays."

Jonathan smiled and nodded. It was so like their kids—Peter, Abigail, and Marjorie—to take full advantage of their sophomore-year study-abroad options, bankrolled by the First National Bank of Mom and Dad. Each had chosen a different city—not too near one another, but not too far, either.

"Which means," Emma said, "we can video-chat together on Christmas morning before we visit Beatrice."

Jonathan took a bite of pie and stared into space. Beatrice. Their oldest child, a daughter. The reason for the nightmares. Twelve years since the school shooting. Thank God for her brother and sisters.

"I guess Paris is the most central location between Oxford, Paris, and Milan." He shrugged, still looking past Emma, blankly, into the Quarter. "I'm irritated, and a little hurt, they didn't want to come home for a few days." He again looked at Emma. "And now, with Robby's death... It was so unexpected. I mean, he was almost seventy-five, but so healthy—"

"I know how hard it is," Emma said. "But we have to let go of our kids *sometime*. This is a once-in-a-lifetime adventure for them. Besides, it gives us more time together."

"I suppose you're right. I guess I just worry too much." Jonathan sipped his wine.

"I made reservations at your favorite place for a late dinner tonight."

"Bourbon House?"

"You guessed it." Emma smiled. "Nine o'clock."

"Merry Christmas to me." Cajun chicken salad. Mirliton pie. The Bourbon House. Talking about the kids. Fen was pulling out all the stops. Must be trying to keep his mind off work. What else would she try?

"And I set an alarm for eight," she said. "Should give us plenty of time for a nap."

"Sounds good." A nap. That's what else. His heart beat a little faster at Emma's suggestion. Jonathan nodded his approval. No matter how exhausted he was, he always had enough energy for Emma's style of napping.

Emma extended her hand to Jonathan and smiled. "So why don't we get started?"

Chapter Fourteen: The Reporter

Thursday, December 25, 2014

With no children at home demanding his presence while they tore through wrapping paper to uncover their gifts, Jonathan took a run through the French Quarter. Afterward, in the kitchen, he found Emma enjoying her Christmas morning by sipping coffee, perusing her laptop, and eating a bagel with cream cheese and homemade mirliton jelly.

"Good run?"

"Oh, yeah. Only one block smelled like urine this time. Thank God for the cool weather."

"Definitely true." Emma winced. "At least we haven't had a BWA in a couple of months."

Boil Water Advisories. Part of what made New Orleans great. Between BWAs and streets smelling like pee or vomit, living in the Quarter had its disadvantages. What a unique place to call home.

"Let's talk about something more pleasant, like yesterday afternoon." He smiled.

"It *was* nice, wasn't it?" Emma smiled and looked up from her laptop. "We should take naps more often. And it's already afternoon in Paris. I'm about to dial up the kids."

As Emma's laptop rang their video call through, Jonathan poured himself a cup of coffee, then spread cream cheese and jelly on a freshly toasted bagel.

"Hi, Mom," a trio of voices called out in unison. Jonathan rushed to Emma's side, carrying his bagel and coffee. Peter, Abby, and Margie filled the computer screen. "Hi, Dad. Merry Christmas!"

"Greetings," Jonathan replied. "Merry Christmas." What a relief to see their shining, cheerful faces. They were safe. And together. It had been too long since they last talked.

They spent the next half hour catching up on the latest news of their studies and other activities. Then, Jonathan held back tears as he told them about "Uncle" Robby and how he had died.

"I'm so sorry, Dad," Margie said. "We know how close you were with him."

They talked with the trio for nearly an hour. Emma drew the call to a close, telling them she and their dad needed to get ready for Mass. The kids said their goodbyes and promised to send pictures of the three of them together.

* * *

As Jonathan and Emma neared Jackson Square and their destination, St. Louis Cathedral, someone called, "Excuse me, Dr. Gray."

The voice came from off to his right. A silhouetted figure stood near the corner of the square, shaded by an ancient live oak. Shriveled brown patches of resurrection fern clung to its trunk and branches, a reminder of the long dry spell.

"I'm Bryan Whitcomb from the *Times-Picayune*."

A tall, lanky man in his early thirties with neatly organized beaded hair braids emerged from under the tree. Jonathan stopped, annoyed that a reporter was already hounding him for an interview.

"Apologies to you and Mrs. Gray for the timing. And please accept my sympathy for Dr. O'Malley's death. But I called, and it rolled over to voicemail."

"Well, yes," Jonathan said, "thank you. It *has* been a shock."

"Especially just before Christmas," Emma added.

"Sir, our paper is planning an extended feature on Dr. O'Malley's life and long service as Coroner. They pulled me off my current story to assist. Might I trouble you for a brief remembrance?"

Jonathan frowned. What a terrible time and place for an interview. He glanced at his watch, then at Emma, who raised her eyebrows. Barely a few minutes to give Robby justice. "Okay. But please make it brief. Mass is about to begin."

The inquiry was general. How was Dr. O'Malley as a boss? What is your fondest memory of him? Softball stuff, really. But Jonathan complied, answering the reporter's questions about Robby and their time together. He emphasized Robby's role as a mentor and friend.

The cathedral bells rang the hour.

"Mr. Whitcomb, here is where I leave you. I hope I provided some insights for your story." Jonathan extended his hand to the reporter, who didn't reciprocate.

"Yes, you've been very helpful, Dr. Gray. But before you go, I have one more question."

Jonathan retracted his proffered handshake and shoved his hands into his pockets. What else could there be?

"As you begin your duties, are you concerned you'll uncover irregularities in finances or other shady dealings, like those that put the Coroner of St. Tammany Parish in prison? Some people believe being in office as long as Dr. O'Malley leads to complacency and corruption."

Whitcomb might as well have slapped him in the face. A brief remembrance? Like hell. No doubt, he hoped to catch Jonathan off guard. Act friendly, build rapport, then lob a hand grenade. But it wouldn't work. Despite how much he *wanted* to respond, and no matter how much he felt like punching the reporter, he refused the bait. Faking a smile, Jonathan took a deep breath.

"As you pointed out, I'm just beginning my tenure. So, it would be premature for me to comment. And now, if you'll excuse us, Mrs. Gray and I are late."

He turned to Emma and, together, they walked up the steps toward the open doors welcoming the faithful to worship.

Chapter Fifteen: Sanctuary

Thursday, December 25, 2014

The Cathedral-Basilica of St. Louis, King of France, with its triple spires standing watch over the French Quarter, had long been a familiar image of the Crescent City. Yet, as a fully functioning icon of the Catholic Church, St. Louis was much more than a postcard picture. Jonathan always entered the magnificent nave, with its vaulted arches and richly adorned ceilings, awestruck as if he were seeing it for the first time.

But he questioned the grandeur. How much did it cost to maintain the facade and interior? Surely the money could support the poor and homeless. Valid concerns, perhaps, but he kept them to himself, never daring to say anything to anyone—not even Emma. Especially not Emma.

Church doctrine meant that Jonathan, as a non-Catholic, arrived as both a welcome guest and an outsider. Although forbidden to take part in Holy Communion, attending Mass with Emma brought them closer together. Emma drew strength from the liturgy and rituals—that's what counted. Her faith sustained her through the hardships they'd faced during their nearly thirty years of marriage.

Thankfully, they hadn't attended Midnight Mass. There were always too many people. Smaller congregations were quieter and allowed him to meditate and think. Despite the number of worshipers, today's eleven o'clock service met his criteria for orderliness and contemplation.

When Mass ended, Jonathan and Emma filed out with the rest of the congregation. As they neared the door, the familiar voice of Monsignor Daniel Rossignol, Auxiliary Bishop of New Orleans and Rector of the Cathedral, caught Jonathan's attention.

"Excuse me, Dr. Gray. May I have a word with you?"

Curious, Jonathan escorted Emma toward the cleric, who stood at the rear of the nave, partially hidden by one corner of the confessional.

"Of course, Monsignor, how can I help?"

"Merry Christmas." Rossignol smiled at Emma. "We had hoped to see you and the good doctor today."

"Thank you, Monsignor," she said. "Today's sermon was rewarding, as always."

"I'm very sorry to disturb your Christmas Day together, but Archbishop Fontenot wishes to speak with Jonathan on a matter of considerable sensitivity and urgency. Jonathan, we'd be grateful if you would accompany me to the archbishop's office. And Emma, while the archbishop and the doctor are meeting, I'd be honored to show you a couple of our architectural secrets I believe will be of interest."

"I'd enjoy your special tour very much." Emma's quick glance at Jonathan reflected both pleasure and puzzlement.

Jonathan shared her curiosity. Must be something very important if the archbishop's involved. He nodded his approval. "Please lead the way, Monsignor."

Compared to the nave, the spaces used by Archbishop Fontenot—the city's first African American archbishop—when he visited St. Louis were plain and businesslike. When Father Gregory Nguyen, his assistant, announced Jonathan's arrival, he expected to be ushered into an inner office and formally introduced. Jonathan flinched when the office door opened, and out came a tall, muscular gentleman dressed in the black suit and white tab-collar of a parish priest. He looked more like a linebacker in the NFL dressed for a night on the town than a senior representative of the Catholic Church.

"Good afternoon, Dr. Gray. I'm Phillip Fontenot. Thank you very much for speaking with me." He extended his right hand to Jonathan.

Jonathan accepted the handshake. "Of course, Archbishop Fontenot. And congratulations on your new post."

"Please. Call me Phillip. May I call you Jonathan?"

"By all means."

"And thank you for the recognition. These past weeks have been a real eye-opener. I pray I will be worthy."

Jonathan smiled. Perhaps he should invite the archbishop to witness an autopsy. Blood and guts might be a real eye-opener, too. "Believe me, I understand fully about taking on new duties."

"Ah, yes, Dr. O'Malley. What a shock. Circumstances often leave us with so little time to grieve."

Archbishop Fontenot gestured toward a closed door with his right arm. "I think we'll be more comfortable in our conference room. It's right through here. But first, may I offer you a drink? The strongest beverage we have is coffee, although you might need something more potent after we finish our discussion."

As Jonathan sat down at a massive mahogany conference table, his curiosity grew. His face flushed with anticipation. What sort of secrets was the archbishop about to reveal?

"Thank you. A cup of coffee would be great. Though, I have to say, now you have my complete attention."

"Jonathan," the archbishop said, "are you familiar with sanctuary?"

"Somewhat. Although, because of my Navy days, I'm more familiar with claims of political asylum from defectors who turned themselves in at an American embassy or individuals who gained access to a Navy ship and then requested the same protection."

"Of course." The archbishop seemed solemn and still rather official. "The two concepts are very similar. Sanctuary's an ancient and revered tenet of the law of the Church—Ecclesiastical Law. When the Church grants sanctuary, it includes physical asylum in the edifice itself as well."

"I see—but I don't understand how this relates to me or my office," Jonathan said.

"I'm sharing this information because not quite forty-eight hours ago, a

Guatemalan couple came to the cathedral and requested sanctuary. The husband is here legally, but his wife has overstayed her visa."

A request for sanctuary? Interesting, but disappointing. A simple request for sanctuary shouldn't require something stronger than coffee, much less demand the Orleans Parish Coroner's involvement.

"As you might imagine," the archbishop continued, "we often deal with similar situations. When one spouse is here legally, we can usually work behind the scenes to obtain the proper paperwork for them both to stay. We handle these requests with little fanfare, and the public never hears of them. However, our grant of sanctuary is illusory. We have no guns or fortresses to keep out civil authorities. We simply hope to provide a place of safety while we negotiate an acceptable solution."

Jonathan leaned forward in his chair. "But you didn't ask to see me because this is a routine request for sanctuary."

The archbishop pursed his lips and nodded. He flashed a barely noticeable smile, as if to signal that Jonathan had caught him trying to avoid an uncomfortable subject.

"That's correct. This situation has some complicating factors. First, we believe the couple's employer is a highly placed official or perhaps a business executive. It appears he's holding the husband's passport and threatening to prosecute him and have his wife deported. We also suspect there was inappropriate physical contact. The couple guard their privacy—and the details—rather tightly."

"In all candor, it sounds like a police matter. Unless..." Jonathan paused. "Unless the police are already implicated."

Archbishop Fontenot put his fingertips together in a steeple formation and rested his chin on them, his smile more noticeable. "You're very perceptive."

The archbishop's hands spread apart as he gestured openly. "But I must answer you in an admittedly circular manner. The Church is concerned primarily with matters not of this world. Yet we must operate daily in the secular parish, so to speak. And sometimes the two clash. Wherever possible, we try to avoid confrontations with worldly institutions. As I said, we're a place of peace without firearms."

"I see," Jonathan said. "And I apologize. I interrupted before you could tell me the entire story."

"Yes, thank you. And once you hear the other complicating factors, I think you will have a greater appreciation for our dilemma. The woman has a younger sister who came to the United States recently and disappeared under mysterious circumstances. The woman cannot get any information from the authorities. The couple desires to avoid deportation. Since the wife's visa expired on the first of this month, they've been on edge. And when her sister went missing, they became even more scared."

"So they came to the cathedral for sanctuary?"

"That's correct."

"But no one's dead, as far as we know, right? So, how's this a matter for my office?"

The archbishop's hands came together. He closed his eyes, as if in prayer. After what felt like an eternity, his hands relaxed and his eyes opened.

"Your office also conducts sexual assault examinations, doesn't it, Jonathan?"

"Yes, of course," he replied. "But you've said nothing about a sexual assault."

"The couple has been tight-lipped about the details. But our people, mostly our nuns, have an unfortunate amount of experience dealing with these matters. They've almost developed a sixth sense to know when something's amiss."

"I see," Jonathan said. "And they don't want to go to NOPD because the wife's visa expired?"

"Exactly. The couple's in a very sensitive position. The wife's here illegally, and her sister disappeared under mysterious circumstances. They are wary of the police."

"I understand," Jonathan said. "So, you would like me, as Coroner, to look into the matter without raising any alarms."

"Yes, as a favor to the Church."

"Okay." Ironic. A favor for the organization that treated him as an outsider, ineligible to receive Communion. But Emma would expect him to help. He nodded. "I'll see what I can do. But no guarantees."

"I understand, Jonathan."

"And I will need to speak with the husband and wife to get affidavits. I'll also need to take specimens of blood, saliva, hair, and so forth."

"Of course. Regrettably, they are not presently available, but we will set up a meeting. Here's my card. When you're ready, please call Father Nguyen, and we'll make the arrangements. We have Sisters who are fluent in Spanish. They can translate. And, if you approve, some of them have medical training and are certified as Sexual Assault Nurse Examiners."

"Thank you, Phillip. That will prove helpful. And I also need to know who the couple is working for. Like you, I wish to avoid any unnecessary entanglements, and I must know whom I can trust as I investigate this unfortunate situation."

"We're not positive." Archbishop Fontenot hesitated. "But I'll tell you our suspicions and why we believe them to be true. Please take the information in that vein. The Church does not wish to defame or slander anyone."

"Yes, of course."

"The husband and wife seeking sanctuary are Eduardo and Josefina Diaz. By all appearances, Mr. and Mrs. Diaz are working for someone high in business or perhaps government. Mr. Diaz refers to their employer as El Patron and El Jefé, which is translated in various ways as "boss," "chief," or "employer." Regardless, it implies someone of importance, an authority figure. We surmise Mr. Diaz was a gardener or handyman, and Mrs. Diaz was a domestic."

"All very circumstantial," Jonathan said. "But it tells me of the sensitivities and potential roadblocks. It'll take me a day or so to think this through. But I'll be in contact with your office soon."

"Thank you, Jonathan. I had faith that the Church could count on your discretion and your diplomacy."

"And what of Josefina's sister?"

"Oh, yes, of course. Her name is Esperanza. Esperanza Morales."

As the pair spoke their goodbyes, Archbishop Fontenot clasped his left hand on top of their handshake, cementing a newly forged bond between them.

* * *

Father Nguyen escorted Jonathan back to Emma and Monsignor Rossignol. They were drinking tea and chatting as if they were the only two people on the planet. Emma seemed engrossed in the conversation and didn't react as Jonathan approached.

"Dr. Gray." Rossignol rose to greet Jonathan. "I trust you and Archbishop Fontenot had a productive meeting."

"Yes, we did, thank you." Jonathan smiled at Emma.

"Excellent." Monsignor Rossignol nodded. "I was just telling Emma how much I admire her work in the architectural field and in the community. If her forward-thinking designs for upgrading residential structures in New Orleans to be more wind- and water-resistant had been more readily accepted before Katrina, one can only wonder how many homes and how many lives might have been spared."

Emma blushed. "You're too kind. And I appreciate the personal tour of this magnificent cathedral."

"Thank you, again, Monsignor, for your hospitality and time," Jonathan said. "Emma and I should continue with our plans. We're overdue for a visit with our daughter."

"Yes, Emma mentioned your visit. Beatrice. What a lovely child. I remember her First Communion as if it were yesterday."

Chapter Sixteen: A Reminder

Thursday, December 25, 2014

After leaving the cathedral, Jonathan and Emma walked briskly along Chartres Street toward the nearest streetcar stop on Canal. Though neither the most comfortable nor the speediest mode of transportation, a streetcar would provide them quiet time together on their way to see Beatrice. Well, not exactly *quiet* time, to the uninitiated. But to people living in New Orleans, the metallic clang of the wheels on the tracks and the pops and grinds from the intermittent starts and stops provided white noise, background sounds. A soothing mantra to those riders who had "been there, done that."

"I have to send a quick email to Sonny and Jimmy," Jonathan said as their streetcar departed. "We need to figure out how to deal with some new information."

First Robby. Then the Haldemans—and political pressure from the mayor. Now, a personal request from the Catholic Archbishop of New Orleans. Resources were already strained. His office couldn't afford to spend time on wild goose chases. But there was no reason to burden Emma with his latest challenge of dealing with yet another high-visibility situation.

"Got it," Emma said.

Jonathan nodded, absorbed in typing on his phone's keyboard. He looked up briefly. "Sorry for the interruption."

She smiled, but only with a slight upturn of the corners of her mouth.

"I'm not going anywhere."

After about a half-dozen blocks, Jonathan put his phone away.

"So," Emma said. "You going to help the archbishop?"

"Sorry?"

"With the Diaz mess."

"How did you—?"

"And her sister's disappearance?"

Jonathan shook his head. "How—?"

"You need to pay better attention, Gray." Emma peered at him as if she were a school teacher ready to lecture a daydreaming student. "People talk. Even priests."

Jonathan exhaled a loud sigh. "I don't quite know what to say."

"A simple yes would be good. Who do you think suggested to Monsignor Rossignol that you might be willing to get involved?"

"Okay. Right." Jonathan's face warmed. "I should have guessed."

"So?"

"I told the archbishop that I'd do what I could. No guarantees. Our office is overwhelmed with Robby and the Haldemans. We don't really have the assets."

Emma nodded. "You'll find a way."

The streetcar lurched to a stop.

"Here we are," Emma said. "End of the line."

Jonathan and Emma had made the fifteen-minute journey from the end of the streetcar line along City Park Avenue and under the I-10 interchange to the massive marble and granite structure so many times. By now, it must have been dozens. No, likely well over a hundred. They hadn't visited every month for the past twelve years, but nearly so. No two trips were the same, emotionally, although the destination seemed etched in history. The grounds were immaculate, with stately magnolia trees to provide shade and—along with clusters of camellias and jasmine bushes— aromatic harmony, especially during warmer months.

Emma inched closer to Jonathan as they entered the vestibule, her arm wrapped through his. Immersed in the solitude of All Saints' Mausoleum, neither spoke. They stood together in silence, separated from their oldest child and her tiny coffin by an engraved bronze marker identifying Beatrice and heralding her brief life and premature death to the world. The memories clawed at Jonathan, welded into his psyche as if they'd happened yesterday.

Every day for the past twelve years, the school shooting haunted him. Stark images of the young victims delivered to the morgue during Jonathan's shift, without warning of what he was about to see. His own nine-year-old daughter, cold on a stretcher before him, suddenly, disbelievingly. In the chaos, no one had called the morgue with the details.

The horror had softened over the years, but the bitterness remained. Bitterness about an obviously disturbed man being released from the hospital by the Coroner of St. Charles Parish gnawed at him. Bitterness about a coroner who was a minister by training, who ran for office and was elected when no physician was willing to serve—as allowed by Louisiana law. "The Lord guided me," the Reverend-Coroner had told reporters. "How could I know he'd do such a thing?"

Beatrice. *She* was why they had to reform the system. And he could no longer hide behind Robby's promises to bring change. Jonathan was Coroner. The mantle had shifted for everything. Looking into the mystery surrounding Robby's untimely death, the Haldeman murders, investigating the archbishop's information, and implementing reforms—all was in his hands. If Jonathan didn't make it happen, no one else would.

An elderly white-haired man shuffled toward them.

"Merry Christmas, Arthur," Jonathan said.

"Merry Christmas to you and Mrs. Gray, Doctor. I'm sorry to interrupt your visit with Miss Beatrice, but we're closing early because of the holiday. I'm afraid I'll have to ask you to pay your last respects."

Chapter Seventeen: Dim Sum

Thursday, December 25, 2014

"I had forgotten how popular this town is during the holidays," Jonathan said, as they emerged from their streetcar on Carondelet, near Canal Street.

Bands of miniature, sparkling white lights adorned the trunks of the palm trees along the expanse of Canal Street. And the varying green, gold, and red color combinations on wreaths and other ornaments on the streetlamps added just the right yuletide touch. Pedestrians strolled along the avenue, as if it were just another pleasant winter afternoon.

"You can hardly tell it's Christmas Day," Jonathan said, "with so many restaurants and other businesses open."

"Speaking of proper nutrition," Emma said. "I'm famished. We haven't eaten since this morning."

Jonathan looked at Emma, puzzled at first. He hadn't been thinking about food. Amidst the day's distractions, he had forgotten about being hungry.

"Wow, you're right. But after the day we've had, I'd rather stop by the Roosevelt for a Sazerac. Maybe more than one. Even if the bar's closed, the restaurant must be up and running for the guests."

"How about some brandy later?" Emma said. "But I need food *right now*. I wonder if Golden Tower's open. It's been a while since we've had dim sum."

Two blocks up Canal, they approached the purple, gold, and green neon "Open" sign of the Golden Tower, their favorite place for Chinese. The aromatic orchestra of soy sauce, rice, ginger, and myriad Asian spices invited them to enter. Jonathan's stomach growled as the hunger pangs finally arrived.

Their early dinner provided an opportunity to decompress. What started out as a family-centered day had morphed into something different after Mass. And now that Emma knew about his not-so-secret request from Archbishop Fontenot, Jonathan needed an emotional break from the added pressure. Tomorrow he'd begin the effort in earnest. Now was his chance to relax, at least a little, and get ready for the battle ahead. And to think about his personal mission to reform the Louisiana coroner system.

Jonathan dipped his *cha siu bao* in spicy chili sauce and devoured the barbeque-filled roll. "On top of everything else, I have a lunch meeting with Paul Nichols next week to discuss legislative reforms."

"You mean Paul Nichols, our state senator?"

"The same. When he's not serving in the legislature, Paul's an attorney with one of the old-money law firms in the One Shell Plaza complex, representing the shipping industry. Several years ago, when he was just out of law school, Paul lived in Jefferson Davis Parish. When no physician ran for Coroner, Paul stood for election and won. He ended up suing the Police Jury due to lack of funding and other issues."

"But isn't Paul exactly what you're working against, a coroner without medical training?"

"Well, yes. And I think Paul would agree it was not an ideal situation. He eventually resigned and returned to New Orleans, partly because the parish government wouldn't let him hire trained personnel."

"Right." Emma looked away briefly, then returned her gaze to Jonathan. Her eyes moistened. "And I'm sure our visit with Beatrice reminded you how important this is."

Jonathan nodded. "All we can do is our best. I just hope I don't let everyone down. With over three years remaining in Robby's, I mean *my*, term of office, pressure and stress will only get more intense."

* * *

Jonathan and Emma paid their bill and began their short walk home. Late afternoon had turned into evening. As the sun disappeared, the temperature dropped significantly. Jonathan's phone vibrated.

"Sorry. But I have to take this."

Emma nodded.

"Betsy, Merry Christmas."

Jonathan motioned to Emma. They could continue walking as he talked.

"Oh, that's okay," Jonathan said. "Don't worry about it." He listened. "Okay, where would you like to meet and when?" Jonathan nodded. "Nine o'clock tomorrow morning at my administrative office in city hall is fine. See you then."

Jonathan pushed End Call, just as they reached the street-level entrance to their home. Upstairs, Jonathan unlocked the door. They entered the foyer, then hung their coats in the front closet. Cascading light from the gallery window landed on Emma's face as they proceeded into the living room. She was as beautiful as Jonathan had ever seen her, despite their emotional roller coaster of a Christmas Day. Jonathan brushed his hand against Emma's waist and the curve of her hip. Turning, Emma responded by touching his face as he drew her toward him. He kissed her softly and slowly.

Emma pulled back and looked at Jonathan. "It's been a long day." She smiled. "Why don't we have that brandy now?"

Chapter Eighteen: Pappy

Friday, December 26, 2014

Neon-blue digits on Jonathan's bedside iPhone docking station flashed "4:45." Awake thirty minutes and still unable to fall back asleep. His autopsy on the eighteen-month-old female was nearly three days ago. She shouldn't still be on his mind. Yet, there she was, in the storage locker. The image jogged his memory, reopened old wounds. He was back at that day twelve years ago. In the early afternoon. Beatrice carried into the morgue without fanfare or warning—in a body bag.

Often, he could fight off the memories. But this morning, nothing seemed to take his mind off Beatrice—and other events. The Ninth Ward drive-by. The myriad other death investigations heaped on his plate. Pressure from the mayor and the archbishop. Half an hour was his unspoken demarcation. Unable to clear the emotional clutter, it was time to get out of bed and start his day.

By half past seven o'clock on the morning after Christmas, Jonathan had already been at his desk in their downtown administrative office in city hall for almost an hour, slogging through email and reviewing various summaries and reports filed by the deputy coroners. He had a small window of quiet time before diving into nearly wall-to-wall meetings and other commitments. Betsy was due to stop by at nine o'clock. And then he needed to brief Sonny and Jimmy in anticipation of their as yet unscheduled interviews of Eduardo and Josefina Diaz.

Jonathan shook his head as he reviewed a report submitted by Dr. Cassandra Melançon. The sexual assault figures were unbelievable. Cass, a descendant of the politically powerful Boudreaux family, was Deputy Coroner for Physical Examination Services—a euphemism for the emotionally draining work of conducting medical examinations in sexual assault cases.

It was as if people had no fear of any repercussions from their actions. The residents were bad enough. But the bad conduct seemed to be worse among the visitors. New Orleans was the Wild West. What happens in NOLA, stays in NOLA. What a line of bull. Where had their humanity gone? A report in their hometown newspaper might make them think twice. Or maybe he should start an official social media page: Perverts and Rapists of the Big Easy. Let the wife and kids see what their husband or father had been doing while on that "convention" for work.

Despite his irritation, or perhaps because of it, he couldn't concentrate fully. Along with everything else, his confrontation with Bryan Whitcomb in front of the cathedral kept nagging at him. What was Whitcomb getting at, asking if he was concerned about uncovering any irregularities? As Chief Deputy, Jonathan had been in charge of day-to-day finances. So he knew everything was in order. And what were the "shady dealings" the reporter mentioned? Comparing Robby with that crook in St. Tammany? Ludicrous. There was no complacency or corruption in the Orleans Parish Coroner's Office. They were too damned busy.

How in hell could anyone challenge Robby's integrity after fifty years of public service? Regardless, he had to find out if there was any basis for Whitcomb's accusations. Doing so would require invading the inner sanctum: Robby's office. It was technically *his* office now, but it still felt like trespassing. Oh, well. Probably best to get it over with.

He stood just inside Robby's office door, embarrassed to be there. He fidgeted like a teenager who worried his parents might come home early. If Robby was a criminal mastermind, as Whitcomb intimated, certainly he wouldn't hide the evidence in his office. Couldn't hurt to look, though. Maybe there'd be a hint. Something out of order. But what? Where?

A series of clean spots surrounded by dust provided mute testimony that Verniece Jackson, their office manager, had performed yeoman's work in putting away Robby's personal effects. But there was still much to do. Sorting through the flotsam of a fifty-year career would take a while.

Verniece hadn't touched any of Robby's filing cabinets or his desk. His LSU Conference and National Championship banners still hung on the wall. The guitar Robby often played to relax after a stressful day rested in its stand between his desk and credenza. With an adrenaline rush of recognition, Jonathan focused on his target.

Robby's desk. That was it. Robby's special drawer. Where he kept his negotiating whiskey. He should look there first. Moving behind Robby's desk, Jonathan grabbed the handle of the deep drawer on the right side. Locked. Damn.

Jonathan sat in Robby's leather chair and searched for something suitable to pry the drawer open. He sure could use Jimmy's lock-picking skills about now. He grabbed a letter opener and inserted the thin stainless-steel blade into the crease between the drawer and the desk. He increased the pressure with his right hand, keeping his left hand on the upper drawer for stability. The lower drawer separated slightly, then a little more. Success seemed close. Jonathan gritted his teeth. Just a little more pressure. The letter opener snapped. Its remaining piece, the handle, collided with his left hand.

"Damn it." A small trickle of blood appeared on the top of his hand. Jonathan applied pressure to the wound with his bandana and searched for something else to use in opening the drawer. He picked up a pair of scissors next to Robby's inbox. A much sturdier tool.

He wedged the tip of the scissors into the small opening between the upper and lower drawers. His left hand throbbed. No use risking his surgical skills more than he already had. There had to be a better way. He returned the scissors to the desk, then removed the bandana. At least he had stopped the bleeding. Something as easy as opening a desk drawer shouldn't be so difficult.

He closed his eyes. They flashed open a minute later when an idea came to him. Surely, it couldn't be that easy.

Jonathan pulled on the upper drawer, which slid out without effort, and exposed the contents of the drawer below it. He sighed, irritated with himself for not seeing the obvious sooner. He reached into the darkness, flipped the lock from the inside, and pulled on the handle of the file drawer. It opened easily, as if to mock how thickheaded he had been. He removed a half-empty bottle containing a dark amber liquid and smiled. Booker's. Nice. Robby really liked his small batch.

He put the bottle of Booker's on the desk and retrieved a long, narrow brown-paper bag from the drawer. Most likely more liquor, given the shape and heft of the package. Jonathan freed the bottle from its paper cocoon. Pappy Van Winkle. Twenty-three-year-old Family Reserve. Impressive.

He and Robby had sealed many late-night discussions with a jigger or two of Booker's. But he had never been treated to the expensive stuff. Robby must have saved it for the really important people. The nuclear option of negotiating. And what sort of deals did Robby make over shots of Pappy's? The old hippie knew how to schmooze.

Jonathan again reached into the drawer. Bingo. He pulled out an expandable file and put it on the desk. Hidden in plain sight. That was just like Robby. Now for a look-see.

He unwrapped the elastic fastener, opened the portfolio, and removed its contents. Interesting, certainly unexpected. One manila file folder marked in pencil with the letter *J*. The folder contained five pieces of paper: five original death certificates, apparently never filed at the Vital Records Registry. Each certificate listed the sex as female. The surnames sounded Hispanic, like Gutierrez and Escobar. He recognized one name: Morales, Esperanza.

His stomach sank as he studied Esperanza's death certificate. She'd died in a car bombing a few weeks before. He wouldn't be able to bring good news to the archbishop—though at least he could tell him what had happened to her. But not yet. There had to be more to the story. Why had Robby kept these certificates? And who, or what, was *J*? What had Robby gotten himself into?

He returned the documents to the manila folder, then placed the folder in the portfolio and closed it. Bryan Whitcomb's last question played repeatedly in his head. He had to find answers before that son-of-a-bitch nosy reporter did. The next step came to mind. The working papers. Of course. He needed to review the working papers from the five autopsies, and soon.

Chapter Nineteen: The Tontine

Friday, December 26, 2014

Jonathan returned to his old office carrying the five death certificates. An alarm on his computer chimed, breaking the almost deafening silence of the empty space. Betsy would be there in fifteen minutes. Time enough to see what's new in his inbox. Jonathan sat in his chair and clicked on his inbox with his mouse. Some lab results had just arrived.

"Betsy will be *very* interested to see these," Jonathan said, talking aloud to himself.

"Do tell, Doc."

Jonathan's head jerked up from his computer screen toward the voice coming from his left, and his heart seemed to skip a beat. He had been so lost in his own thoughts. Thank God it was only Betsy.

"I let myself in because Vern wasn't there. You should be more careful about locking doors around here."

"Betsy." Jonathan stood. "I suppose security is lax over Christmas. But here you are, one of Crescent City's finest, to protect me."

"At your service." Betsy laughed. "But I'm surprised you're still here. Figured you would have moved into the new forensic center up on Earhart Boulevard."

"They didn't design the new morgue to replace this office suite entirely, just our interim morgue on MLK Boulevard. And we're finding we've outgrown our new facility even before we've fully moved in."

Jonathan sat and motioned toward a chair. "Make yourself comfortable."

"You don't have to ask twice," Betsy said.

"Besides," Jonathan said, "the spaces here at city hall aren't extensive enough to fit everyone. In addition to my office, we have individual offices for each of my deputy coroners. And there are a couple of conference rooms and shared workstations for assistant coroners, investigators, and other staff when they're not in the wards executing their duties. It's good to have a central location where we can meet."

"Well, I'm not complaining. This office is convenient for me, seeing how it's just a quick ride from the Sixth District."

"So, how was your Christmas?" No use talking about the new morgue facility, at least not right now. "Hope you didn't lose your entire holiday investigating the Haldeman case."

"Thanks, Doc. I chiseled out a few hours to celebrate with Ranger and Brandon."

"How *is* Ranger? I haven't seen him in I don't know how long. Certainly not since he retired."

"Better. It took him a while to work through some issues, especially from his time in the anti-narco-terrorism unit in Central America. It's got to be hard coping with memories of killing people using your bare hands. Ranger just shrugged it off. Said it was his job. No big deal."

"Right," Jonathan said. "His job. The job taxpayers, like you and me, gave him." Jonathan rolled his eyes. "We demand so much of our military. Kill or be killed on a daily basis. And then come home and be normal. Like watching *Wheel of Fortune* was the most controversial thing you've been dealing with." He shook his head in disbelief. "You know, Ranger's a lot like our lab assistant, Jimmy, in some ways."

"Yeah, I know." Betsy exhaled, and her voice lightened, still serious but not as foreboding. "Quality time with Brandon since retirement has helped him adjust. Still, it has to be difficult. I mean, fearsome Green Beret one day, civilian the next. But he's picked up some work on the side as a security consultant. Whatever *that* means. Between his part-time work and getting used to no longer being Sergeant Major Sprance, things are calmer with him. Besides, as long as there's a football game on television, they don't seem to miss me much."

"Speaking of football, has Brandon decided on a school yet?"

"He's pretty settled on Auburn. You know he wants to be a large-animal veterinarian, right?"

Jonathan nodded. "Sure."

"Auburn has a great program. Even as a pre-veterinary student, he'll be in the field, mentored by a licensed practicing veterinarian. LSU doesn't have a similar program. Brandon likes the thought of the hands-on experience. And they offered him a full ride. Seems like Auburn needs a good fullback."

"Makes the decision easier, doesn't it?"

Betsy nodded and smiled. "Easier on the pocketbook, too."

"Well, I wish him the best of luck, whatever he decides. Just don't let Sonny find out he chose Auburn instead of LSU."

They both laughed.

"Listen, I know you didn't drop by just to chat—as nice as it is. Yesterday you said there were some recent developments. What's going on? How can I help?"

"Well, I told you Superintendent Bondurant has been bird-dogging this investigation like crazy," Betsy said. "Usually, she stands back and lets us do our job. I wonder where the pressure is coming from."

"Keep this close hold," Jonathan said. "As I was going home on Christmas Eve, Max Jamerson called. He'd been hearing from the Haldeman family and from other concerned citizens. Max said he'd just finished talking with Polly."

"That explains it." There was a definite tone of relief in her voice. "Makes the pressure more understandable. Does nothing to advance our investigation. It just makes me wonder why the politicians want us to close this one out so quickly."

"Yeah," Jonathan said, "makes me want to press even harder to see where the evidence leads."

Betsy nodded. "We learned that Mr. and Mrs. Haldeman had been at a family gathering at Judge Haldeman's house. All four children—Henry,

Constance, Benjamin, and Evelyn—and all eleven grandchildren were there, along with about twenty great-grandchildren. With spouses and significant others, it was quite a crowd. Here are some group photos they took. We gathered tons of photos and some video footage as well."

"What a great-looking family," Jonathan said.

"Exactly. And everything was going fine until Judge Haldeman and his youngest child, Joe, had a fight. Joe's the black sheep of the family. At least, that's what Judge Haldeman says. Joe's been in and out of trouble, though nothing major—mostly matters related to drug and alcohol abuse. But he can't seem to keep a job and apparently doesn't have a permanent residence. He certainly hasn't lived up to Judge Haldeman's standards."

"Do you know what they fought about?"

"Alcohol. Apparently, Joe had something to drink despite telling his father he was clean and sober. And there was a claim that Joe was giving one of the teenagers stuff to drink. Anyway, one thing led to another. Some wine got thrown. Judge Haldeman got angry. Told Joe to 'Get the hell out of my house.'"

Jonathan nodded. "I see."

"Not long after, Maggie said she wasn't feeling well, so Bill took her home. About an hour after they left, police received a call complaining about a domestic disturbance at Bill and Maggie's house. Like I told the group the other night, when the officers arrived, the Haldemans were already dead."

"Have you spoken to Joe Haldeman? Heard his side of the story?"

"No," Betsy said. "Seems like he's dropped off the grid. But he can't hide for long. And we took your suggestion to look for a ball-peen hammer. We never found one. But we discovered Bill Haldeman had taken up watch and jewelry repair as a hobby several years ago. He was even teaching one of his great-grandchildren, Hunter Dejarnette, about his hobby. There's a small workshop in a corner of the family room. Among the tools he often used was a jeweler's chasing hammer. It helps shape metal. And it looks like a ball-peen hammer, only smaller."

"Did you find one?"

"No, but we located a tool kit with several chasing hammers of various sizes. The largest one was missing. The toolkit wasn't out in the open. So someone knew what they were looking for. Or it was a damn strange coincidence they found it.

"We also found an almost full bottle of brandy. Judge Haldeman advised us that his parents usually had a bottle or two of bourbon or brandy in the house, but that they didn't drink very much. He wasn't positive. But his mother might have had a glass of wine at the party, he said."

"Very interesting," Jonathan said. "I just got the tox screens from the Haldemans' autopsies. Maggie's results confirmed there was ethyl alcohol being digested. And there was also a sedative. I believe it was one of the prescription medications you recovered at the scene. So, by all indications, Maggie Haldeman had something to drink, in concert with a sedative, and fell asleep on the couch, where police found her with a bullet hole in her skull."

He paused. "You have a theory?"

"Well, it's speculative, but here's a scenario that fits. Bill and Maggie Haldeman live a few streets away from Judge Haldeman. After arguing with his father, Joe went to his grandparents' house, knowing he could probably find something to drink. When his grandparents returned home early, it threw off his plans. Either their arrival startled him, or he was waiting for them. Regardless, after Maggie fell asleep, Joe hit Bill with the jeweler's hammer to knock him out. Then he completed his deadly work with the pistol and shotgun and placed their bodies to make it look like a mercy killing followed by a suicide."

"Sounds *more* than speculative," Jonathan said. "You think the district attorney will prosecute on what you have? And what about a motive?"

Surely, Betsy wasn't so desperate to build a case based on a damn near a blind guess.

"Wait for it," Betsy said, "there's more. The Haldemans' estate plan set up an elaborate series of trusts and bequests designed to minimize inheritance taxes. They left their assets in trust—not to their children—but to benefit their grandchildren by providing a college fund for them. Each grandchild had access to $250,000 for his or her college or postgraduate education. If they didn't use everything, they would get what's left.

"Any grandchild not using their funds toward college would receive a full payout of his or her designated $250,000 upon Mr. and Mrs. Haldeman's deaths. Ten of eleven grandchildren used their college trust funds and have an insignificant balance. Upon disbursement of the basic $250,000 to each grandchild, any remaining money went to various charitable foundations. So there is no personal motive beyond the basic amount."

"Excuse me if I steal your thunder," Jonathan said, "but I'll bet their only grandchild not to graduate college is Joe, so he's looking at inheriting $250,000."

"Oh, it gets even more interesting. Along with the trusts, both Mr. and Mrs. Haldeman were participants in a variation on a life-insurance collective called a tontine. Tontines were popular among military personnel, like the Haldemans, who couldn't get insurance during the war. Their particular tontine agreement involved a limited number of participants who paid premiums into a collective pool for up to thirty years, assuming they were still alive. Then they stopped paying premiums. The fund was invested and managed. As members died, their designated beneficiaries received a portion based on their original payment and an agreed-upon interest rate.

"This tontine had a termination date: December 31 of this calendar year. Anyone who died on or before New Year's Eve would receive the payout set out in the tontine agreement. On January 1, they would pay out the rest of the tontine in equal shares to surviving members."

Jonathan crossed his arms. "Why do I think you're going to tell me there's a difference in the payouts before and after New Year's Day?"

Betsy smiled and her eyes twinkled, in a cat-ate-the-canary sort of way. "We ran the numbers. If Bill or Maggie were alive on January 1, their combined payout would translate to around $300,000 for each grandchild. If, however, they both died before the New Year, their eleven grandchildren would receive about $650,000 each. There was a condition. The funds had to be placed in a trust for the Haldemans' great-grandchildren's college education. If any grandchild didn't have children on the date of death, then the entire payout went to that grandchild, with no requirement to put it in trust."

"Another guess," Jonathan said. "Joe isn't married and doesn't have any children."

"Winner, winner, chicken dinner," Betsy said. "And, if my arithmetic's correct, between the two payouts, he's about to inherit around $900,000 free and clear of any educational obligations. But the case is still very circumstantial. Until I talk to Joe Haldeman, I'm not about to ask the DA to go before a grand jury or even make an arrest."

Jonathan smiled. What a relief. Betsy had more evidence. With her years of experience, he shouldn't have doubted her. But past events had planted a seed of mistrust—skepticism. Bryan Whitcomb's question about shady deals. Finding hidden death certificates in Robby's desk. Judge Haldeman's sterling reputation as a jurist and family man. Betsy had clearly been doing what she was supposed to do: investigating, digging for truth. Still, all she had were gossamer strands. No clear picture yet. But at least she had a vision of the way ahead. Hopefully, she would connect the dots with some more digging. Yet, it didn't seem to fit together.

"Sounds like a solid plan," Jonathan said. No use raising questions, at least not yet. He needed to let Betsy do her job.

"Thanks. I was hoping your test results might provide some additional evidence. Anything help my case?"

"Not all results are back. But what I've seen supports your current theory—or, at least, there's nothing to contradict it. Ballistics analysis seems especially relevant. The twenty-two you recovered from the scene fired the bullet that killed Maggie Haldeman. Shotgun pellets came from the twelve-gauge. Registration forms list Mr. Haldeman as owner of both weapons. Each had Bill's prints on them.

"Along with the clues we've already discussed, test results on Maggie Haldeman showed negligible GSR. The amount on her hands was consistent with ambient GSR landing on her hands. GSR on Bill Haldeman's hands was not very heavy. So he might have touched a weapon after it was fired or was in close contact with a weapon. The amount, however, isn't consistent with someone firing a pistol and later a double-barrel shotgun."

"How about the cloth fragments found on the Haldemans?"

"They matched a standard terry cloth bath towel. And they were consistent with the towels you seized from their linen closet."

"Hmm," Betsy said. "Appears everything's connected with the Haldemans' house or their family. Joe's our current person of most interest. But we need to focus on others in the holiday party picture to rule them out as suspects."

"Given Bill and Maggie's visibility and social standing, you've got your work cut out for you," Jonathan said. "Listen, if you get any more pressure, let me know. I can provide some top cover. I want to make sure this one is squeaky clean before I declare cause of death."

"Will do, and thanks. Well, I better get to it."

"Say, Betsy, before you leave, can I ask you something in confidence? I know I can count on your discretion."

"Sure thing, unless you confess to being a serial killer—or a 'Bama fan."

Jonathan smiled. "Nothing quite so serious. But I'm working on one case potentially involving some highly placed individuals, and I need to tap your experience on how best to proceed."

"Okay, let me have it."

"Suppose you were aware of an allegation against a senior member or members of the administration or a powerful business executive with political connections. Is there someone in the police department you would go to? Someone you would trust with your career or even your life?"

"*Soc au' lait.* Kind of a heady question for the day after Christmas."

"You're right, it *is* a bag of milk—*sour* milk at that. And it's a heady question for any day. But I know you'll come through."

"Well, within the department, of course, I trust my partner, Mitch Broussard, but he's only a sergeant. You want someone higher up, right?"

"Yeah."

"Well, I would turn to Deputy Chief Jacob Landry. Jake's a senior career civilian in the department. He has been with NOPD for nearly forty years. He's a cop's cop. If you can't trust him, then God help us.

"And I would trust Assistant US Attorney Mandy Simpson. I knew her first when she was a major and then as a lieutenant colonel before she retired from the Corps. She is not in the department, but I've seen her stare down Afghan warlords twice her size. And if she can keep her calm amid roadside ambushes, she can take anything thrown at her."

It was as if he had just been hit with an ice-cold bucket of water. How could Betsy operate if she trusted only one person in her chain of command? He had damn well better be careful to ensure he was on solid ground before he accused anyone, especially a public figure, of being involved in the Diaz matter.

Betsy pulled out a business card and wrote on the back. "Here are names and phone numbers."

"Okay. Thanks. I've worked with Jake for years. It's good to hear your confirmation. I don't know Mandy Simpson, but I trust your instincts. Hope I don't need to contact either of them. At least I'll be ready if I have to go down that road."

Chapter Twenty: Hunter

Friday, December 26, 2014

The next step involved talking to Eduardo and Josefina Diaz. Using the speakerphone, Jonathan called the number on Phillip Fontenot's business card.

"Good morning, Archbishop Fontenot's office. Father Nguyen speaking. How may I be of service?"

"Good morning, Father. This is Jonathan Gray. I'm following up on my meeting with the archbishop."

"Yes, Doctor. We've been expecting your call."

They arranged for an interview of Eduardo and Josefina that afternoon at the Convent of St. Helen's, a consecrated facility in Orleans Parish where they were staying. Jonathan accepted Father Nguyen's offer to have two nuns available to assist with any necessary physical exams.

He hung up the phone and heard someone whistling "Deep in the Heart of Texas," punctuated by a repetitive electronic hum. Jonathan rose from his desk, peeked into the previously deserted common area outside his office, and confirmed his suspicion.

"Leo. I didn't realize anyone else was in today."

Dr. Leo Pearlman, Deputy Coroner for Mental Health Services, hunched over the copy machine. Texas-born, Leo was a forensic psychiatrist trained at the University of Chicago. Hired two years ago, he was the newest of the deputy coroners. He looked up from the copier.

"Howdy, Jonathan. Christmas isn't a big holiday in the Pearlman household. So I thought I'd take advantage of the calm to catch up on this week's mental status evaluation reports, Physician's Emergency Certificates, and such."

"Well, I salute your dedication."

"I'll send you a reminder when it's time for giving out bonuses." Leo smiled. "So, what brings the boss to work on the day after Christmas?"

"You know what they say: 'No good deed goes unpunished.' Those autopsies from the other night seem to have taken on lives of their own."

"Haldeman killings, right? Local news stations are obsessed with them. You must be exhausted."

"Does it show?"

"Well, to use the technical psychiatric term, you look like you've seen a ghost."

"Remind me why I hired you again?" Jonathan chuckled.

"Sorry, Boss. Gotta call 'em like I see 'em. You look exhausted."

"Fair enough," Jonathan said. "I *am* tired. And the Haldeman killings have only added pressure. I had to conduct an autopsy on an eighteen-month-old female killed by a stray bullet in a drive-by shooting. Infant and child victims get to me more than adults."

Jonathan paused, then shifted to a more upbeat, businesslike voice. "But that's *my* tale of woe. I've been keeping up with the summaries you submit, and I know they're only part of the story. So, tell me about your workload, any issues you've been facing, and any hurdles. I think we're finally in a position to influence changes, and I want to make sure I account for our full list of issues."

"Glad to bring you up to speed. But let me warn you to put on your seat belt. Dealing with people and their mental health issues can be a bumpy ride."

Jonathan smiled. "Got it. I'm buckled up."

"The period between Thanksgiving and New Year's Day is fraught with highs and lows for nearly everyone," Leo said. "For individuals who are already vulnerable emotionally, holidays are especially bad. Probably eighty to ninety percent of people we examined this past week wouldn't have been on our radar in June or July. Society puts so much pressure on people around Christmas. It's supposed to be all 'happy, happy, joy, joy.' But when things don't work out as planned, some people lose it."

"That makes sense, as it touches on something in the Haldeman investigation," Jonathan said. "I'll share it with you because I think you can help, but I need you to keep it close-hold."

"Okay, Boss, I'm on board."

"I saw a picture of the Haldeman family taken during a holiday get-together. They looked like a classic television family from the '50s. But not everything was perfect in paradise. One of Bill and Maggie Haldeman's children had a falling-out with his son—one of their grandchildren—and now police are focusing on the grandchild as a person of interest in what they suspect is the Haldemans' double murder."

"Do you remember his name?"

"Joe. Judge Haldeman's younger child. His son, Joe."

"Hmmm. Interesting. I hadn't thought it was relevant then, and I'm not sure it's relevant now. One of my assistant coroners signed an Order of Protective Custody for one of the Haldemans' great-grandchildren last night based on an application submitted by his mother. Anyway, I examined him at Riverview Children's Hospital and issued a Physician's Emergency Certificate committing him involuntarily for further observation."

Jonathan held his tongue. Protocol was for a physician at the hospital, not a third party like Leo, to conduct the initial examination and issue a PEC if necessary. Leo should have known better. "Report filed yet?"

"Yep. Finished my supervisory review of the paperwork and uploaded our final report into the central tracking system about an hour ago."

"Can you give me some highlights?"

"Sure thing. If I recall it right, the kid's fifteen or sixteen. He's the grandson of Constance Haldeman and her husband, Michael Jennings."

"So his last name isn't Haldeman?"

"Right. It's Dejarnette. Hunter Jennings Dejarnette."

"Which means," Jonathan said, "police might not pick up on it after a simple review of names on a list of exams conducted."

"Most likely. Hunter's mother, Grace Dejarnette, brought him to Riverview because she was worried. Her son spent a lot of time with his great-grandparents. He was very close to them. He was at a Christmas party at Ben Haldeman's house on the night his great-grandparents died. He left the party early, saying he was going to walk home. Later, he was found lying on his bed, curled up in a fetal position, crying. His mother became more anxious when he didn't move for a full day. He wouldn't eat. Apparently, he loved his great-grandparents more than anything. Called them Gram and Pap. He hated to see his Gram suffer."

"Sounds like he was grieving," Jonathan said. "So soon after their deaths, his reaction doesn't seem completely out of the ordinary—not worth committing someone to a psych ward over." He paused. "I've known people who've lost loved ones, especially children, who act much the same way..." His voice trailed off as he thought of Beatrice and the nightmares.

"For most people, I'd agree." Leo's voice seemed more serious, with no hint of his normal, jovial asides. "But we're not dealing with just anyone. Hunter's on the autism spectrum. He's high functioning, but numerous studies support increased suicide risk for autistic youths and adults."

"Got it," Jonathan said. "Better safe than sorry. I understand."

"Then there was an escalating event. Hunter's mother said she left him alone for a few minutes, and when she returned, he was coming out of the bathroom, putting what looked like a medicine bottle in the pocket of his hoodie. His mom gave him some Benadryl, telling him it would help his runny nose. When Hunter fell asleep, she grabbed the bottle—prescription sedatives issued to his great-grandmother."

"I see. Must have taken them from his great-grandparents' house at some point." Jonathan paused. "But it doesn't fit. The pills were much-needed medicine for the great-grandmother he loved so much."

"Right," Leo said. "And the combination got her so concerned, she took Hunter to the hospital right away. She woke Hunter up and tricked him into coming along with her to the hospital, as if she needed help. There, they got one of the assistant coroners to sign the OPC."

"I'm following so far," Jonathan said.

"I know Grace and her husband, Tom, from our Mardi Gras Krewe and charitable work. So when she contacted me to examine Hunter for the PEC because I have admitting privileges, I obliged."

Obliged? Like hell. Jonathan gritted his teeth in anger at Leo's disregard for proper procedures. What if some fast-talking attorney discovered Jonathan's employees didn't pay attention to the rules? The office didn't need a multimillion-dollar lawsuit for an invalid commitment. Or another killing spree by someone released improperly from the psych ward, not to mention the bad press that came with it. And if by-the-book Leo was so careless, what other protocols had his team ignored?

He took a breath and remembered his go-to calming technique from Mark Twain. What had he said? Something like, "When angry, count to four. When very angry, swear." It always made him smile, defusing his anger just enough for him to respond more calmly.

"Seems like," Jonathan said, still somewhat stiffly, "we should have given him a shot and let him sleep off his grief and anxiety. I'm not convinced he was enough of a danger to himself or others to warrant a PEC."

"I understand, but like you said—better safe than sorry." Leo exhaled a loud sigh. "I was in the middle of a mess. Once our office acknowledged there was cause to issue an OPC, I couldn't exactly cut him loose. Besides, he needed to be in a facility for monitoring. There were too damn many what-ifs to do anything else. It's better to be sued by an angry patient than attend the funeral of a patient who committed suicide because he didn't receive proper treatment."

"Of course." Jonathan remained concerned that Leo had broken strict protocol. But he paid Leo to be his psych guru. Maybe he should let him do his job. "But, from now on, stick to proper procedure, unless you check with me first. Those rules are in place for a reason—for your protection and the patient's."

"Got it, Boss," Leo's face flushed.

"What happens with Hunter next?" Jonathan asked.

"Further commitment requires a Coroner's Emergency Certificate, so

I deputized Janine Dubois, Chief Psychiatrist at RCH, to conduct the required exam and issue a CEC if necessary. The second examination is to be conducted within seventy-two hours of the initial commitment. I explained the situation to Janine, so I'm sure she'll wait the full seventy-two hours before conducting another exam. Earliest he'll be released is Sunday evening. Plenty of time to figure out what's going on with him."

"Thanks, Leo," Jonathan said, calmer now, but still nervous. "I suppose you made the right move."

Jonathan's cell phone signaled an incoming call. "Excuse me. I need to take this. Can you send me Hunter's full name and case number so I can review your report?"

"Sure thing. Will do. Right away."

Chapter Twenty-One: Po' Boy Surprise

Friday, December 26, 2014

"Two Brothers'?" Jonathan looked at his watch while he talked on the phone. "Both you and Sonny?" He paused as he listened to the response. "Outstanding. I had forgotten it was so close to lunch. A Sausage Surprise sounds good. Make it a Full Boy, dressed. See you soon."

Sonny and Jimmy arrived within a few minutes, a half hour before the originally scheduled 1:00 p.m. Along with them came lunch from Two Brothers' Trolley Stop Café, a sandwich shop down the block. Jonathan paid Jimmy for his po'boy. They moved into the conference room and took seats around the table.

Today's po'boy featured mild Cajun andouille sausage—ground, mixed, and put into casings at the café—placed on a crusty sandwich roll, then "fully dressed" with lettuce, tomato, pickle slices, and homemade mayonnaise, or *my-nez*, as the brothers pronounced it.

"Okay, Doc, we're intrigued," Sonny said. "I've been turning it over in my mind ever since your email. I assume it's about the Haldemans."

"Eat your lunch and I'll explain."

While Jimmy and Sonny dug into their sandwiches, Jonathan told them about his Christmas Day conversation with Archbishop Fontenot. As he delved deeper, Sonny and Jimmy were eating less and listening more. By the time Jonathan related Archbishop Fontenot's speculation about someone highly placed in politics or business, Jimmy and Sonny seemed frozen, unable to move. He told them about Esperanza Morales and her sudden disappearance, but not about finding the death certificates in Robby's drawer. Best not to confuse circumstances too much. At least not right now.

For several seconds after Jonathan stopped talking, the loudest sound came from the banging and whirring of the air ducts. Sonny broke the silence.

"Hang on. First it was a switch from murder-suicide to double murder for the Haldemans. Now you hit us with this latest info about a potential sexual assault and a mysterious disappearance. You got any more secrets? I'm not sure I can stand much more excitement right now."

"Listen, you know what I know. For what it's worth, you could have knocked me over with a feather when I heard the story."

"Well," Jimmy said, "I'm thinking that might be the understatement of the week. I'm afraid the next thing you're going to tell us is the Pope's not Catholic."

They laughed. Jimmy's sense of humor was welcome at a time like this. After their laughter subsided, Jonathan continued.

"We're due at St. Helen's in about an hour and a half. So let's review our plan and what equipment we need. I've already alerted Emma I'll be late for dinner. If either of you has a hot date tonight, you might want to let them know."

"Do Mr. and Mrs. Diaz speak English?" Sonny asked.

"They do," Jonathan said. "But English is their second language, and there might be some comprehension issues. Father Gregory Nguyen, the archbishop's aide, promised to have two interpreters available just in case."

"I'm not sure Sonny or I are qualified to conduct a sexual assault examination, let alone comfortable with it," Jimmy said. "What's our plan?"

"Father Nguyen offered to have a nun at the convent who's a Sexual Assault Nurse Examiner available," Jonathan said.

"Peculiar, almost weird," Sonny said. "Nuns have been in nursing as long as there've been nuns, I suppose. Even so, seems a goddamn shame that it's come to this."

"I'll drive," Jimmy said. "If that's okay."

"Thanks, Jimmy." Jonathan nodded.

"We should take one of the unmarked vehicles," Sonny said. "They have city plates but shouldn't draw too much attention."

"Good idea," Jonathan said. "And Jimmy, we need to take extra samples. Enough to support sending a second set to a private lab for testing, and even some for potential retesting. We want to cover all our bases. Leave nothing to chance. Let's also see if we can use the Rapid DNA Testing protocol at each lab. We'll have to wait for the Combined DNA Index System results. But the Rapid DNA will at least let us know if we're headed in the right direction."

"Sounds like," Jimmy said, "this case is likely to get a lot of attention. So the quicker we get results, the better. But they need to be perfect."

"Amen," Jonathan said. "We don't just need to be *perfect*. We need to be perfect beyond a reasonable doubt."

Chapter Twenty-Two: The Blue Acura

Friday, December 26, 2014

With Jimmy driving, their white unmarked Ford Explorer proceeded out of the city hall complex and turned right onto Poydras Street. Jonathan rode shotgun, and Sonny sat in the back seat. The Superdome loomed on their left, just before they passed into the maze of concrete pillars and steel columns supporting the highway above them.

"Something wrong, Sonny?" Jonathan turned around to look at him.

"Not sure. But that blue Acura's been behind us ever since we left the parking lot."

"Think we're being followed?"

"Let's find out, Doc," Sonny said. "Jimmy, act like you're getting onto the interstate toward the airport. When I say so, veer right. Keep going on Poydras."

Jimmy nodded. "Got it."

Jimmy turned on his directional signal. He eased their Explorer left, into the lane leading to the I-10 entry ramp. The Acura stayed about a half block behind them. It moved into the left lane as well. Jimmy glanced in the mirror at Sonny and then back toward the on-ramp. They were almost at the point of no return.

"When—"

"Now."

Jimmy veered sharply to the right. He crossed the white dividing line onto Poydras, just feet away from the concrete curbing. The Acura followed, seconds behind them.

"Piss." Sonny hit the car seat with his hand.

As their Explorer proceeded on Poydras under the interstate, the blue Acura stayed about half a block behind them.

"Still there," Sonny turned forward. "Let's give him another test." Sonny paused. "We're approaching South Galvez. Speed up into the intersection. Take a left without signaling. Run the light if need be. But watch traffic. And don't get us killed."

Jimmy did as Sonny directed, turning left just as the light switched from yellow to red. Jonathan's heartbeat moved into his throat as their bulky Explorer executed a maneuver more suited to a sports car. The Acura fishtailed behind them, forcing oncoming traffic to stop quickly. Squealing tires and honking horns signaled the chase was on.

"Okay, Jimmy." Sonny leaned toward the front seat. "In a couple of blocks, make another left."

Jimmy executed another quick left turn, this time onto Julia Street.

Sonny pointed to his left. "Turn in there."

Jimmy pulled into a parking lot between two aging warehouses and, at Sonny's direction, turned their vehicle around, allowing them to observe the street. Within seconds, the Acura zoomed past.

"Anyone get the license?" Jonathan asked.

"Too damned fast," Sonny said.

"Same," Jimmy said.

As they waited for the Acura's next move, Sonny removed their portable printer from its metal suitcase in the cargo area.

"Put your cell phones in here to shield any tracking via the GPS locators embedded in them."

They did so without question. Jonathan's heart pounded hard. What in hell was going on? Thank God for Sonny.

After a few minutes, Sonny told Jimmy to pull their Explorer out of its hiding place onto Julia Street and head back in the same direction they had just come from.

"Pull over there," Sonny said. "Into that parking space on the right. Let's make sure we gave him the slip."

Jimmy complied. Jonathan sat silently along with the others, switching between looking at his wristwatch and peering over his shoulder down Julia Street. Thirty seconds passed. Nothing unusual happened. Forty-five seconds. A minute and a half. Still nothing.

"Okay," Jonathan said. "Shouldn't we get moving? We'll be late."

"Not yet," Sonny said. "Let's give it a bit longer. We need to be sure."

Three minutes since they pulled to the curb on Julia Street. Then, a blue Acura came into view and stopped about one hundred feet in back of their vehicle.

"Shit." Sonny gritted his teeth. "Everyone duck."

Jonathan did so, his heart still racing, but he maintained his view of their apparent adversary.

The Acura drove past their Explorer, slower than the posted speed limit of twenty-five miles per hour, and pulled into a lot about one hundred feet ahead of them across the street. Their game of cat and mouse lasted less than a minute longer, when the passenger window on the Acura lowered. A black cylindrical object poked out of the open passenger window.

"Gun it," Sonny said. "Get us out of here."

The Explorer again challenged the forces of physics as Jimmy accelerated out of the parking space, executed a quick U-turn, and sped away.

"Did you see that?" Sonny said.

"See what?" Jonathan said.

"A flash. I didn't hear a shot... Were they taking photos of us?"

"Don't know." Jonathan slammed the dashboard with his palm. "And don't care. Jimmy, get us the hell out of here."

Chapter Twenty-Three: Across the Net

Friday, December 26, 2014

J immy drove their SUV through the gates of St. Helen's about fifteen minutes after the appointed time of 3:00 p.m. and pulled into a space behind the convent office marked *Official Guest*. Though not hidden, they were more secluded from view from the street. For the last ten minutes or so, they hadn't seen the blue Acura.

As the trio exited their vehicle, Father Nguyen emerged from the office door. "Dr. Gray, good afternoon. Thank you very much for coming."

Grasping Father Nguyen's hand, Jonathan returned the welcome. "My pleasure, Father. I apologize for being late." Jonathan paused and glanced at his companions. "We hit some unexpected traffic."

"Don't give it another thought," Father Nguyen said. "We're pleased you made it."

"Thank you, Father," Jonathan said. "Now let me introduce my team."

Father Nguyen shook Sonny's hand. "Excuse me, Inspector Rabideau, but I must ask you to leave your handgun outside."

Jonathan nodded his approval and reached toward his waist to remove his own sidearm and holster as well.

"You sure, Doc?" Sonny again looked at Jonathan. "We just—"

"It's fine," Jonathan said. "What could be safer than a convent?"

"All right, you're the boss," Sonny said. "I'll put them in the lockbox in the trunk." He looked at Father Nguyen. "Apologies, Father, I forgot where I was."

"Thank you for honoring this holy place, Inspector, and you as well, Dr. Gray."

As Jonathan followed Father Nguyen to the convent's main conference room, a pungent blast of French roast, almost strong enough to taste the caffeine, wafted past. Upon entering the conference room, two nuns, both appearing to be in their late twenties, huddled next to a coffee maker. An older nun stood nearby.

"Mother," Father Nguyen said to the elder nun, "allow me to introduce Dr. Gray and his team."

After acknowledging them and introducing herself, the Mother Superior spoke softly, but with authority.

"Mr. and Mrs. Diaz have been here only a few days. But they have earned our love and affection. Mr. Diaz insists on working on the grounds, and we cannot keep Mrs. Diaz out of our kitchen. It is as if they express their anxiety and grief through work and service to others."

"We understand," Jonathan said.

"And..." the Mother Superior paused and pursed her lips. "They should be treated with kindness and respect."

"Yes, of course." Jonathan nodded.

"Thank you, Doctor." The Mother Superior gestured to the two nuns standing behind her. "Please let me introduce you to Sister Miriam and Sister Mary Esther. Both are fluent in Spanish. They will be your interpreters. Sister Mary Esther is a Sexual Assault Nurse Examiner and will assist you in any physical examination of Mrs. Diaz."

The nuns smiled, though seemingly more out of polite recognition of their duties than of happiness. The team members introduced themselves.

"We've prayed with Mr. and Mrs. Diaz," the Mother Superior said. "They know they are facing difficult circumstances, and they have both put their fate into the Lord's hands. They understand that truth is the pathway to their salvation, and they are ready to tell you everything they know."

"Thank you, Mother," Jonathan said. "I know having Sister Miriam and Sister Mary Esther present will be a comfort, especially since we will need to interview Mr. and Mrs. Diaz separately. Please rest assured, we are here to learn the truth and nothing else. Investigator Rabideau will interview Mrs. Diaz. I will interview Mr. Diaz. Medical Technician Caplan will collect blood samples from the couple and coordinate gathering other physical evidence from Mrs. Diaz, with Sister Mary Esther's help."

"Yes, of course," the Mother Superior said. "Sister Mary Esther, please escort Mr. Rabideau to the room with Josefina. Sister Miriam, please accompany Dr. Gray and Mr. Caplan to see Eduardo. I will be here in the conference room or in my office if you need me."

"I, likewise, will be available either here or in Mother's office," Father Nguyen said.

Eduardo Diaz was taller than Jonathan had imagined, probably five feet ten, and wiry and muscular. Not a giant. But certainly not a shriveled, malnourished weakling, either. He wore a clean and pressed semi-uniform of dark-green work pants and a matching long-sleeve shirt. He had a firm handshake. The clothing and handshake were likely related to his occupation as a gardener. Eduardo spoke English well, though with an accent and often in a stilted, memorized manner, as they exchanged introductions and pleasantries.

Most striking was the contrast between Eduardo's overall demeanor and his eyes. He seemed calm, but his eyes betrayed worry.

Jonathan explained the purpose for their visit, particularly the need for drawing Eduardo's blood. Ruling out suspects was an important part of identifying the perpetrator or perpetrators.

"Excuse me, Mr. Diaz," Jimmy said, "Would you please roll up your sleeves so I can check your veins and draw a blood sample?"

Eduardo's eyes grew large as Jimmy removed the phlebotomy equipment from his medical kit. Eduardo looked at Sister Miriam.

"It's okay," Sister Miriam said in English. Then she spoke in Spanish, apparently telling Eduardo everything would be fine.

"Bueno," Eduardo said. "I understand." He rolled up his sleeves.

As the interview proceeded, Eduardo acted as if he didn't understand the questions when they touched on sensitive areas, such as the potential sexual assault of Josefina and the disappearance of her sister. But, with Sister Miriam's help, the truth came, albeit slowly.

Eduardo's experience in the United States had started well. He had arrived, legally, about five years ago. He found work as a gardener in New Orleans. After about a year of working for various prominent families, Eduardo landed a job at the mayor's personal residence. He seemed most animated, happy, in describing Josefina's arrival.

"With the help of El Jefé and his wife," Eduardo said, "I brought my beloved from Guatemala. It was about two years ago."

"El Jefé. That's Mayor Jamerson, right?" Jonathan asked.

"Sí," Eduardo said. "Josefina worked as a maid in El Jefé's house. Everyone liked her. She earned a lot of overtime."

"Tell me," Jonathan said, "what caused you and your wife to leave your jobs and come to the church for sanctuary?"

Eduardo hesitated. He spoke with Sister Miriam in Spanish and then responded in English. "After a while, Josefina seemed distant, and cold to me in bed."

He looked at the floor for several seconds, then at Sister Miriam. She nodded, as if signaling to Eduardo that he should continue.

"I thought it was because of the long hours she was working. She often worked very late at night and on weekends."

"I see," Jonathan said.

But Eduardo seemed too overcome with emotion to go on. He stared at the floor and appeared near to crying. Best to change the subject. Avoid unpleasant memories, for now. Building rapport with Eduardo might draw him out more.

"Tell me about Josefina's sister."

Eduardo's demeanor brightened noticeably. His eyes sparkled. "Sí. Esperanza."

"Yes," Jonathan said, "tell me about Esperanza Morales."

"Sweet Esperanza. Josefina was so happy to see her. No one told us she was coming north. She appeared as if by magic."

"Do you know why she came?" Jonathan asked.

"Esperanza told us," Eduardo said, "that she was here to be a fashion model."

"A model?"

"Sí," Eduardo said. "She met a lady who said Esperanza was pretty enough to be one."

"A lady?"

"We don't know who she was," Eduardo said. "The lady brought her to this country and was teaching her English. And how to walk like a model."

"What was Esperanza's arrangement with this lady?"

"We don't know that either," Eduardo said. "Esperanza never told us exactly. But she seemed happy, and it made Josefina filled with joy."

"How often did you see Esperanza?" Jonathan asked.

"We didn't see her very much," Eduardo said. "But the lady gave Esperanza an expensive phone. At least we could send her text messages."

"So," Jonathan said, "tell me about when Esperanza disappeared."

"A few weeks ago, Esperanza stopped visiting, and she didn't answer our texts."

Eduardo paused and again looked at Sister Miriam. She nodded and raised her eyebrows. He continued.

"We argued. I wanted to go to the police. Josefina said no. She seemed scared. I asked her why."

Eduardo's eyes moistened, and his jaw quivered. Sister Miriam placed her hand on his.

"My beloved told me she was alone in the storeroom at El Jefé's house when someone came up from behind and pressed against her and pulled up her dress. She couldn't move because she was afraid."

"Did she say who—"

"Josefina wouldn't tell me who did it. Perhaps she didn't know. But she was scared. I could see it in her eyes. And it scared me, too."

Eduardo wiped his eyes with a red bandana. "Whoever it was told Josefina he would ruin us if she said anything. We kept it to ourselves. This was wrong, but we were afraid."

"But something must have changed," Jonathan said. "You came to the church."

"Sí. We didn't hear from Esperanza. Many days passed. So we went to the Tulane Emergency Room to see if she had been there. I got scared. I saw two policemen from El Jefé's security escort talking to the front-desk nurse. By then, Josefina's papers had expired. We knew no one would believe us over El Jefé. That's when we sought protection of the Holy Church."

"I see," Jonathan said. "Thank you, Eduardo. I understand how hard this must be for you and Josefina."

"Yes, sir."

Eduardo looked Jonathan in the eyes. Much more direct than before. A vote of confidence in Jonathan, perhaps. No doubt, Eduardo was wary of anyone connected to the city. But what would Eduardo say once he learned Jonathan was already aware of Esperanza's fate? A cruel decision, perhaps, not telling Eduardo. Certainly, an unfortunate circumstance. But keeping the secret for now might lead to discovering more information about the identity of her killer.

"What will happen now?"

"Right now," Jonathan said, "we need to type up an affidavit for you to sign. It should only take a few minutes. Then we will see where the evidence leads us. In the meantime, you and Josefina will be safe at the convent."

Jonathan left Eduardo and Sister Miriam together and returned to the group's original meeting room. He poured a cup of coffee and sat down. Eduardo's written statement would add granularity. But questions remained, especially regarding the five death certificates. What path led to Esperanza dying in a car bombing? Despite knowing what had happened, they still didn't know why. He would have to tell Eduardo and Josefina the truth. But not yet.

Sonny wasn't there. Josefina's interview must still be going on. Perhaps he should go listen. Before he could decide, Sonny and Jimmy walked into the conference room. Jimmy carried a small cardboard box, likely containing vials of blood and tissue samples from Eduardo and the clearly marked standard sexual assault kit from Josefina. They looked tired. By his lowered eyes and the downward slant of his mouth, Sonny appeared more than just exhausted. He seemed despondent.

"Why the sad face, Sonny?"

"That was rough, Doc."

"Okay. Tell me about it."

"I was out of the room when Sister Mary Esther conducted the rape examination, of course. But the rest of the interview? Didn't go well."

"How so?" Jonathan asked.

"It was difficult because of the language problems." Sonny shook his head and sighed. "And what happened to her was awful."

"I see," Jonathan said. "Tell me more."

"My impression," Sonny said, "is that Josefina knows how to speak English better than she lets on. But the whole thing resembled a verbal game of volleyball in English and Spanish. Sister Mary Esther played on both sides of the net. I presented a question in English, which Sister Mary Esther translated into Spanish and sent across the net to Josefina, who would answer in Spanish. Sister Mary Esther translated her words and sent the answer back across the net in English. The same pattern of question, translation, answer, and translation played out over and over again. We finally cobbled together an affidavit."

Jonathan and Sonny compared notes about their respective interviews.

"Sounds like their stories track with one another," Jonathan said. "But did Josefina say who—?"

"No, she wouldn't crack. Sister Mary Esther confirmed Josefina didn't see who it was."

"Did she share anything else about her sister Esperanza?"

Sonny opened his file folder, put a photograph on the table, and pushed it toward Jonathan. "There's this. She gave it to Sister Mary Esther."

"Esperanza?"

"Yeah, said it was a photo from her sister's work as a model. And there might be more photos on their phone. Eduardo has it."

"Wow," Jonathan said. "Esperanza's quite a beauty."

"Yeah, very pretty," Jimmy said. "Young and innocent. Let's hope modeling's all she's wrapped up in."

Thank God he had said nothing about the death certificate to Sonny or Jimmy. They could carry out their duties without worrying—or lying.

"Guess we need to keep digging," Jonathan said. Jimmy was right. Being a "model" was often just a euphemism for something darker and more dangerous. "Let's split up and get the affidavits signed. We need to make sure no one claims they coordinated their testimony."

"Got it," Sonny said. "See you in a few."

Within fifteen or twenty minutes, everyone was back in the conference room, with the sworn statements prepared and signed by Mr. and Mrs. Diaz. Jonathan herded his companions toward the exit, though first he thanked everyone for their courtesy and assistance.

"Dr. Gray," Father Nguyen said, "to you and your team, on behalf of His Excellency, please accept our appreciation for your professionalism and compassion. Allow me to escort you to your car."

Sonny and Jimmy walked ahead, carrying their equipment, as Jonathan and Father Nguyen lagged behind, talking.

"Dr. Gray, did you have a successful visit?"

"Yes, Father. We learned a lot today. We'll need to see test results. But we're in a better position than before. Please thank Archbishop Fontenot for his courtesy and cooperation. I'll keep you informed as circumstances warrant."

"Yes, I shall." Father Nguyen reached into his suit coat. He pulled out an envelope and gave it to Jonathan. "And His Excellency asked me to give you this. It's an invitation for you and Mrs. Gray to join him Sunday after next at his St. Louis Cathedral study for wine and cheese."

Jonathan accepted the envelope. "That's very thoughtful. Please tell the archbishop that Emma and I are delighted to accept." Jonathan moved closer to Father Nguyen. "Father, I suggest you keep Mr. and Mrs. Diaz secluded and out of sight as much as possible. My hunch—"

"What in blazes?" Sonny dropped the equipment cases and rushed toward their Explorer. "Hey, Doc. You need to see this."

Sonny knelt along the right side. Jimmy walked around to the left, looking at the lower half of the vehicle.

"The tires." Sonny gestured toward the wheels. "Both of them are flat. Slashed. You can see the cuts."

"Same over here," Jimmy said.

Jonathan pointed to three black pieces of wood under the wipers. "Hand-carved wooden coffins. Someone's trying to send us a message. Sonny, get our weapons. We need to search the area. Father, please call the police."

As Jonathan, Sonny, and Jimmy fanned out and moved toward the convent's entrance, a blue Acura pulled out of a parking space on the street, its tires squealing as it sped away. Sonny ran forward and brought his handgun into firing position.

"Damn it." Sonny returned his pistol to its holster. "Too far for a clean shot." He pulled out his notepad, scribbled something on it, and walked back toward the sedan. "At least I got the license plate number."

Father Nguyen came out of the church office. "I asked Mother to report the vandalism to your vehicle. I'm sure the police will be here soon."

"Thank you, Father. Someone from our office will pick us up. Sonny and Jimmy will take pictures. We need a complete visual record."

Jonathan retrieved his cell phone from the equipment case. He pressed Betsy's speed-dial number, but the call went straight to voicemail.

"Betsy. Jonathan Gray. Following up on our talk this morning. Someone is tailing my team as we investigate the high-level lead I mentioned. The car is a blue Acura sedan, Louisiana license number...hang on a second..." Sonny showed him the notepad "...9X-48TPQ. Someone slashed our tires and left us what seems to be a rather crude voodoo death threat. Call me and I can provide details."

He hung up the phone and stared at the slashed tires. "Gentlemen, it looks like someone's trying to intimidate us. I don't know who or even really why. But we all need to be watchful." He turned toward Father Nguyen. "Father, as I said earlier, I suggest you keep Mr. and Mrs. Diaz secluded and out of sight as much as possible. I need you to call me immediately if you notice anything suspicious."

"Yes, of course, Dr. Gray. We will be ever vigilant."

Jonathan nodded, not really paying attention. Their slashed tires and the hand-carved coffins signaled that their ostensibly discreet investigation was no longer a secret. Someone was watching. But who? And what did Eduardo and Josephina—and Esperanza—have to do with it? Each day seemed to end with more questions than answers.

Chapter Twenty-Four: Don't Shoot

Friday, December 26, 2014

"Don't shoot," Jonathan said, as he walked through the front door at Maison Gris. "It's only me."

"Okay, Me." Emma's voice resonated from the living room. "I put my Glock back in the drawer. You're safe this time."

She wasn't joking about having a pistol. And she was trained to use it. Though violence wasn't common in the French Quarter, it wasn't exactly rare either. Jonathan was happy she was so prepared, especially considering someone might be stalking him and his team.

He walked into the living room to find Emma sitting on their oversized sofa in flannel pajamas, an open novel next to her.

"Tough day at the office?" she asked.

"And then some." He kissed her. "I'll go change, then tell you what I can."

Soon, Jonathan emerged dressed in his pajamas and robe, ready to relax and share some time with Emma. She presented him with a glass of Knob Creek, neat.

"Very nice, thank you."

"So what's going on?"

"I can't give you many details. But the Haldeman case seems to have taken a dark turn. And someone might be following me and my team. Sonny, Jimmy, and I went to St. Helen's to interview witnesses. On the way there, we spotted a blue Acura tailing us. Thought we had outfoxed them. But when we finished, the Acura was parked just outside. It drove away quickly."

"Could be a coincidence. I'm sure there are a lot of blue Acuras in town."

"Possibly, but this blue Acura kept after us pretty intensely. Doubt it was just someone out for a leisurely drive. And Sonny seemed pretty convinced. Also, someone slashed our tires while we were inside. I don't think they will try anything here. But you need to be aware."

"I understand. Forewarned and forearmed." Emma smiled and pointed to the open drawer. "I'll be on my guard."

The grandfather clock in the foyer chimed the hour.

"It's ten already," Emma said. "Let's check the news."

She turned on the television. The Haldeman killings were the lead story, but there was a breaking development. Joe Haldeman had been taken into custody earlier, about the time Jonathan had called Betsy. No wonder he got her voicemail.

The story included an official comment from the police. Joe wasn't being charged. He was merely a person of interest. Finally, the report referred to a "highly placed source." Joe was in line to receive an insurance payout of nearly one million dollars after the death of his grandparents. Judge Haldeman read a statement before a bank of microphones, with reporters taking notes or straining to record events on their phones. News cameras clicked and whirred in the background.

"Mrs. Haldeman and I are deeply concerned to discover our son, Joseph, has been implicated in his grandparents' deaths. We cannot accept he would be involved in such a heinous offense. Kathleen and I love our son unconditionally. We will always be here for him. Finally, we ask you to respect our family's privacy in this time of reflection and prayer as we deal with this tragedy."

Emma pressed the remote control, and the screen went dark. "How sad. Having your parents murdered and then learning your son's a suspect. I can only imagine what they're going through."

Jonathan's cell phone vibrated. He looked at the caller ID and answered it.

"Evening, Detective Sprance." Jonathan used Betsy's title and said it loud enough to make sure Emma knew it was official business and, especially under the circumstances, an important call. "Yes, Emma and I just caught the news. It appears you've had some interesting developments in the Haldeman case within the past few hours."

Jonathan nodded as he listened.

"Okay, would you like me to come to the office?"

Upon hearing Betsy's response, Jonathan looked at Emma and raised his eyebrows. He mouthed one word: *visitor*. Emma nodded and replied with a silent *okay*.

"No, we wouldn't mind at all. Of course, you might see us in our pajamas. Buzz when you get to our street-level entrance, and we'll unlock the door. In the meantime, we'll put on some coffee."

Chapter Twenty-Five: It's Not What Changed...

Friday, December 26, 2014

Jonathan and Emma greeted Betsy as she walked upstairs shortly before 11:00 p.m. "Listen," Betsy said, "sorry for barging in so late."

"Detective Sprance—" Emma said.

"Betsy."

"Betsy, you're most welcome, no matter the time. Something tells me you and Gray are two peas in a pod when it comes to your cases."

"You've got me there, Mrs. Gray."

"It's Emma."

"Thank you, Emma. I appreciate your understanding."

"We have some hot coffee," Jonathan said. "I'll bet you could use a cup right now."

"I'd love some coffee. And not to be pushy, but do I smell mirliton pie?"

"Reheating some leftovers," Emma said. "Hope you don't mind. Some people prefer theirs cold."

"Not at all. Can't think of a better thing right now, warm or cold."

Jonathan and Betsy sat down at the kitchen table. Emma brought a tray with coffee and wedges of mirliton pie. She handed the first plate to Betsy, who took a bite and closed her eyes.

"Emma, this is delicious." Betsy opened her eyes.

"Thank you."

"I recall spending summers with my grandparents on their farm in Iberia Parish," Betsy said. "My *grandmère* was a master gardener and executive chef with mirlitons. She grew them on a big trellis in the backyard and made them into all sorts of dishes. I think one of my favorites was parmesan-crusted mirliton stuffed with shrimp."

"Sounds wonderful," Emma said.

"Oh, it was." Betsy closed her eyes. "Mmmmm." When she opened them again, they looked misty. "And my grandparents argued about whether mirlitons were a fruit or a vegetable. They finally agreed that if a recipe called for sugar, it was a fruit; otherwise, it was a vegetable. I think the compromise might have saved their marriage."

They shared a quick laugh.

"It feels good to relax," Betsy said. "So much has happened since this all started. And especially in the past twenty-four hours. I needed some balance."

Emma smiled. "Mission accomplished. Now it's time for me to leave you two to your work. I'll be in our front room reading if you need anything."

Jonathan and Betsy poured themselves more coffee.

"Sorry you're going through this, especially during the holiday season," Jonathan said.

"Goes with the territory, Doc. You know how important it is to jump on every lead as soon as possible."

"Yeah. The first forty-eight hours, right?"

"You got it." Betsy shook her head. "We're past that, but still..."

Betsy smiled. How could she possibly be happy? Certainly, her holiday was shot all to hell.

"But there's at least one silver lining," Betsy said. "When a fresh homicide comes in, they let us jettison all our nonessential assignments."

"Like?"

"Like participating in the Algiers Point Exercise."

"Okay," Jonathan said. "Don't be so mysterious."

"Yeah, sorry. It's a terrorism thing. Named after Algiers Point. Suppose there's a threat on the river. Like a freighter smuggling in the plague or something. We send a couple of police boats out to intercept."

"I see."

"The boats will carry weapons, have divers, that type of thing. It all depends on the threat presented." Betsy shook her head. "We practice it every few months. Why in God's name they scheduled one during the holidays, I'll never know."

"Like you said, a silver lining."

"Right. I guess that's something." She sighed. "Not that homicide's a silver lining." Betsy sighed again. "Anyway, back to work. This morning, Judge Haldeman's son was number one on our radar. Now I'm not so confident he's even a person of interest."

"What changed?"

"Not what. Who."

Jonathan canted his head slightly to the side. "Go on."

"Remember our talk this morning about photos from the party?"

"Yeah." Jonathan nodded.

"Well, we've interviewed almost everyone. And we're continuing to gather photographs and videos, including images taken by television news crews."

"Sounds logical and very thorough. I can understand why you're so tired."

Betsy removed a tablet computer from her briefcase, powered it on, and turned its screen toward Jonathan. "Got some photographs I want you to see. First one is a family photo taken early in the Haldemans' holiday party the day before Christmas Eve. I've circled Judge Haldeman and his son. Notice they're standing at opposite sides of the photograph, almost as if they were trying to keep their distance from one another."

"I see what you mean." Jonathan nodded.

Betsy tapped on the screen, shifting the image. "We isolated Judge Haldeman and Joe. Here are photo enhancements with close-ups of them. Note what they're wearing."

"Got it," Jonathan said, a note of doubt in his voice. What was Betsy going for? He didn't see how clothes mattered in this case. But he'd already learned his lesson that Betsy knew what she was doing. There must be a logical explanation. "Judge Haldeman's wearing a pair of dark gray slacks, black shoes, a white shirt, and a red Christmas-themed sweater. His son's wearing khaki pants, a blue button-down shirt, a blue sweater, and brown shoes. They look like Doc Martens."

"Good eye. Next is a photo of the clothes we seized when we took Joe into custody."

"Looks like the same as in the group photo."

"You get the blue ribbon, Doc." Betsy pointed to the image of the outfit that had been laid out on a steel table for the photo. "See the dark spots on the right pants leg?"

"Yeah."

"Our current theory is that it's a wine stain he got at the party. We don't believe it's blood. We sent his clothes for analysis."

"Seems a little strange that Joe didn't wash his clothes if there was a wine stain—or any stain—on them."

"That's not the half of it." Betsy's brow wrinkled. "What's really strange is that officers found the clothes on a chair near the bed in the place Joe was staying. They were folded neatly."

Jonathan tipped his head, considering. "As if Joe wanted you to find them."

"You catch on fast."

"But why would—?"

"Stand by. First, let's concentrate on Judge Haldeman."

"Fine," Jonathan said.

"Not long after the group photograph, Judge Haldeman and Joe exchanged words. Joe left almost immediately. Ten or fifteen minutes after their argument, Bill and Maggie Haldeman left." Betsy tapped on her tablet again. "One grandchild took the next photo after Joe left. It shows Judge Haldeman saying goodnight to his parents. Note what he's wearing."

"Looks like the same outfit as in the group photo," Jonathan said. "And now I have a better view of that interesting Christmas sweater."

"Yeah, *interesting* is one word to describe it. Just wait. This next photo shows Judge Haldeman talking with some of the family as the party was winding down. That's almost two hours after Bill and Maggie left."

Betsy looked away from the screen. She tapped on the table as if to emphasize an as yet unrevealed fact. "Assuming the time stamps on the pictures are correct, that would make it almost sixty minutes before police called the judge from his parents' house."

"Wow." Jonathan pointed to the computer screen. "Judge Haldeman's wearing a different outfit. Now he's wearing khaki pants, a blue shirt, cordovan tassel loafers, and a plain red sweater."

"The last image is from the crime scene," Betsy said. "See Judge Haldeman in the background?"

"Yeah."

"We haven't enhanced the photo yet, but it looks like Judge Haldeman is wearing the same khaki pants, blue shirt, cordovan tassel loafers, and plain red sweater; the only change is that he's wearing a blue blazer."

"So between when he said goodbye to his parents and when the party ended, Judge Haldeman changed clothes," Jonathan said.

"Perhaps more important," Betsy said, "there's a two-hour window during which Judge Haldeman disappeared. From talking to family members, I gathered the judge said he was upset because of his argument with Joe and needed some time alone."

"Can you establish an exact time when he left?"

"No. The closest we can tell by family members' accounts is that it was 'quite a while' before he reappeared. We haven't found any photographs with Judge Haldeman in them during the two-hour gap."

"It certainly points a finger at Judge Haldeman. But it's still very circumstantial."

"You're right. It might not be enough to convict him. But the photographic evidence *is* enough to cast doubt on Joe's involvement."

"Yeah, I can see that."

"Oh, I forgot to tell you the details of how we arrested Joe. We located him based on a tip from Judge Haldeman. Joe was staying with his girlfriend, Molly Westcott. She's an artist who has a workshop and studio in the old Warehouse District. Between eleven and eleven-thirty on the night the Haldemans died, he showed up at her place. He had been drinking. She took away his bottle of whiskey and put him to bed. He slept for over twelve hours. And she swears he never left the studio until police came to get him."

"How did Judge Haldeman find him?"

"Molly says she doesn't watch television very often because she's so busy in her studio. But when she finally turned on the news and saw reports about the killings, she became worried and called Judge Haldeman. He told her he would take care of everything. Within minutes, police showed up and took Joe into custody."

Betsy tapped at her tablet. "Here's an image from one of the officer's body-worn camera showing Joe."

"I see," Jonathan said. "And the woman in the coveralls is Molly Westcott, right?"

"Yeah, you know her?"

"Sort of. Emma and I met her a few weeks ago at the New Orleans Museum of Art. Her pottery was part of an exhibit. *Rising Local Artists*, or something like that."

"I see."

"And she must really work at the wheel a lot. Her handshake was like iron." Jonathan pointed to Molly. "See the back of her hand? Looks like tattoos of two snake heads, one on each hand."

"Yeah," Betsy said. "I see them."

"Well, at the museum, she had on a muscle shirt, you know, a wifebeater."

"We prefer 'A-shirt,' if that's okay," Betsy said.

"Sorry. I didn't mean—"

"Understood. So many people call them that, like being a wife beater's somehow macho. Anyway, I didn't mean to get us off track. You were talking about Molly Westcott—"

"Right," Jonathan said. "At NOMA, you could see almost the entire tat. It was a two-headed snake, running up both arms and across her back. It added to her artistic mystique, I suppose."

They were both silent a moment, looking at the image on the tablet.

"You know," Jonathan said, "we can't tolerate murder, but what sort of father abandons his child in the middle of a personal crisis? I would have at least gone with the police to be there when they arrested my son."

"I have conflicting emotions as well."

"It's as if we're witnessing a family coming apart at the seams. One of my assistant coroners signed an Order of Protective Custody the other day for the Haldemans' fifteen-year-old great-grandson. Later, one of my deputies signed the PEC."

"Not proper protocol, is it?" Betsy asked.

"Not technically. But the kid was so distraught, the deputy believed he might do himself harm."

"Do you recall which great-grandchild? I don't remember interviewing anyone like that yet."

"His name is Hunter Dejarnette. He's at Riverview Children's. His seventy-two hours is up Sunday evening. Let me know, and I'll tell the chief psychiatrist you'd like to talk to him."

"Okay, thanks," Betsy said.

"You're welcome. And back to your pictures...it looks like we have ourselves a full-fledged mystery again."

"You're right on that score. I guess our next step is to see what Joe has to say tomorrow."

"Didn't you talk to him tonight? Aren't you afraid he'll decide to lawyer up by morning?"

"Figured it wouldn't do any good," Betsy said. "Didn't want to give him a chance to claim that he was tired and confused. So we put him in an isolation cell." Betsy raised both hands and formed air quotes. "For protection." She lowered her hands. "And to let him sleep. By the time we talk to him, he should be fresh as a daisy."

"Do you have a game plan for his interrogation?"

"Nothing special, just our standard protocol. We're looking to start at ten tomorrow if you don't mind stopping by. I'd be interested in your perspective on what he says."

"Sure thing, I'll be there." Jonathan looked at his watch. "Jesus, it's almost one."

"Man, I apologize again for barging in so late."

"Don't worry about it. You need to crash in our guest room so you can sleep before you go back to work?"

"Thanks, but I can't. I need to check a couple of things before Joe's interview. And I'm hoping our trace on the blue Acura came back. I'll grab some shuteye in the duty room. We have a couple of bunks set up for occasions like this."

Jonathan escorted Betsy downstairs and locked the door behind her. He felt overwhelmed by the progress of the case and all the new details to think about. But it could wait until morning.

He went upstairs, where Emma lay curled in the fetal position on the oversized couch in their living room, sleeping. A still-open novel sat on the coffee table nearby. Jonathan bent down and kissed Emma on the forehead. "It's only me," he said.

Emma's eyes opened. She smiled, pulled Jonathan toward her, and kissed him on the lips. "Come here, Me. I've been waiting for you."

Chapter Twenty-Six: C. Bosworth Tipton, Esquire

Saturday, December 27, 2014

J onathan dragged himself off the living room couch just after 8:00 a.m. Still half asleep, he lumbered toward the heavenly scent of freshly brewed coffee—maybe Sumatra Dark or an East Africa blend— signaling to him like a liquid alarm clock.

"Hey there, sleepyhead." Emma grinned, a touch of mischief in her demeanor. "How late did you and Betsy work? I didn't check the clock when you woke me up."

"She left about one." Jonathan yawned and poured himself a cup of coffee. Sumatra Dark. Good. He needed an extra jolt of caffeine. "I offered to let her stay in the guest room. She declined. Had to take care of something at work."

"Well, I'm glad you offered. She must have been exhausted."

"Definitely, but Betsy's a tough old Marine. She had to get ready to interview Joe Haldeman at ten this morning. I hope she got some sleep at the station. At least, that was her plan."

"Okay, good."

"Betsy asked me to be there."

"*That* should be interesting," Emma said. "If news reports are correct, it sounds like Betsy's about to break the case wide open."

"We'll see." Jonathan buttered a piece of toast and sprinkled it with cinnamon sugar. "I think Betsy's confirming what experienced investigators know—not everything is as it appears at first glance. She's uncovering new evidence as she digs into the case. Not sure how confident she is about identifying the killer yet."

Emma's brow furrowed. "You're having something more nutritious for breakfast, right? Our city needs its Coroner in top form."

"Very funny. I thought you knew cinnamon toast is the breakfast of champions."

Emma shook her head and sighed. "Promise me you'll have a healthy lunch, at least."

"Tell you what," Jonathan smiled. "Why don't we visit Momma Mae's tonight? I promise to get the healthiest thing on the menu."

"Sounds nice. It's been a while since we've talked to Mae. It'll be good to see her."

"Great. Think you'll have a chance to call ahead and make sure they have some CPR available for us?"

* * *

Just after nine-thirty, Jonathan weaved between four mobile television-broadcasting trucks, their associated equipment, and several support vehicles as he pulled off Gravier Street into a parking lot across from police headquarters. Technicians were setting up microphones and a podium on the steps leading up to the entrance. The commotion outside added to the organized chaos in the squad room, where Betsy sat at her desk drinking coffee—an oasis of calm amid tumultuous surroundings.

"Betsy, good morning. Hope you got some sleep."

"Ended up crashing in the bunk room for almost six hours. I feel refreshed enough to run a marathon."

"Always this hectic on Saturday mornings?"

"Not usually. Today's special. Max Jamerson, with Superintendent Bondurant in tow, scheduled a press conference today at one o'clock to

125

discuss developments in the Haldeman investigation. They believe Joe Haldeman's about ready to pop with a confession. Max wants to declare our manhunt over and the case closed. Said he wanted to show solidarity by having his press conference here at headquarters and not at city hall."

"*Is* Joe ready to confess?"

"Not likely. About twenty minutes ago, Judge Haldeman showed up with C. Bosworth Tipton."

"Tipton? As in the high-powered society divorce lawyer?"

"Affirmative," she said. "Judge Haldeman told us their family hired Tipton to represent Joe. Judge Haldeman's been in with Joe for around ten minutes. That's Tipton—the guy in the expensive suit with the alligator-skin briefcase—waiting in the chair outside."

"Wonder why they didn't hire a criminal defense attorney?" Jonathan asked.

"Expert watercooler opinion is that all local criminal defense attorneys conflicted themselves out because they represented people put away by Judge Haldeman or they have appeals pending before him."

"Makes sense."

"Even money says this is just a delaying tactic to give the family long enough to locate a big name from Houston or Memphis. You know, someone like Dakota Bouvé or Jim Farrell. Either way, it probably means we won't get anything else out of Joe."

"Jim Farrell," Jonathan said. "Nickname's Whiskey Jack. Out of Memphis, right? I remember when he defended ex-governor Longfish Collins about ten years ago against charges that Collins allegedly ordered his mistress killed in a murder-for-hire scheme. Some thought Farrell bribed the jury. But those who followed the case'll tell you that Whiskey Jack out-investigated the police and ran circles around the DA."

Jonathan paused. He took a deep breath and sighed. "What's more interesting, guess who the trial judge was?"

Betsy's forehead wrinkled. "Ben Haldeman?"

"Yep. Small world, isn't it? And guess—"

The rattle of the interview room door opening interrupted Jonathan's question. Judge Haldeman's raised voice resonated from inside. The judge emerged, turned back toward the room, and yelled.

"You always were a stubborn, ungrateful kid. It's obvious you won't let me do anything to help. At least I can tell your mother I tried."

Judge Haldeman slammed the door and gestured to Tipton. The pair approached Jonathan and Betsy. Tipton introduced himself. They exchanged social pleasantries, except for Judge Haldeman, who still hadn't offered to shake hands or even wish them good morning.

Stern-faced, the judge said, "I promised my wife I'd do my best to hire legal counsel for our son." He paused. "Now that he's rebuffed my efforts and declined Mr. Tipton's services, my job here is done. Dr. Gray, I'm disappointed to see you socializing, sipping your coffee, and distracting Detective Sprance from her work. Perhaps you should become more engaged in investigating my parents' murders and not just sitting in your office playing guitar and drinking bourbon like your predecessor."

Jonathan and Betsy remained silent. Tipton blushed.

"Charles, if you please. We'll be going now."

After Judge Haldeman and Mr. Tipton left the squad room, Jonathan looked at Betsy. "What just happened? Seems like Judge Haldeman thinks it's an open-and-shut case because his son decided not to lawyer up."

"Far be it from me to disappoint," Betsy said. "Given this latest turn of events, let's see if we can coax a confession out of Joe so His Honor the Mayor can avoid looking silly at his press conference."

Chapter Twenty-Seven: Joe

Saturday, December 27, 2014

Shortly after ten o'clock, Betsy grabbed her case file and winked at Jonathan as she headed into the interrogation room. Betsy's partner, Detective Sergeant Mitchell Broussard, escorted Jonathan to an adjacent room, where a technician operated recording equipment and where they could observe Joe's interrogation through a one-way window. Betsy entered the room, where Joe Haldeman sat at a desk in handcuffs. A uniformed officer stood guard next to the door.

Broussard sat down near Jonathan. Barely out of his twenties, he had a solid reputation as a homicide investigator. His trademark was chewing on a cheroot he cut in half. Then, he could work on it from both ends and not waste any good tobacco. It was a cliché, but it fit him to a T.

"All right, Doc." Mitch nodded toward Jonathan and spat small pieces of his stogie into a nearby wastebasket. "This ought to be quite a show. Sorry I can't offer you some popcorn. How about a cigar to chew?"

Jonathan smiled and shook his head. "Maybe later."

Betsy introduced herself to Joseph Lewis Haldeman, who was tall and thin, with a neatly cropped beard.

"Seems harmless enough," Jonathan said. "Looks more like a college professor than a cold-blooded killer."

"Be careful, Doc. Can't judge a book by its cover."

"True." Jonathan shifted himself, now almost sitting on the edge of his chair.

"Morning, Joe," Betsy said. "I'm Detective Sprance."

Through the recording system, her voice had an offbeat quality to it: muted and tinny, with a slight echo.

"Sleep well?" Betsy asked.

"All right, I guess," Joe said, "considering the surroundings."

"I understand. You were out of it last night. You need some coffee or something?"

"Well." Joe shifted in his seat. "Coffee would be great. Black, no cream or sugar." He held up his shackled hands. "And can you do something about these?"

Betsy nodded toward the guard, who removed the cuffs and exited the room.

Joe rubbed his wrists. "Thanks for this."

"Don't mention it," Betsy said. "The jail has certain protocols. You know how it is."

She stood, moving her chair to the side of the interview table, putting herself on Joe's right. "I hate these tables," she said. "They seem so impersonal."

Joe shifted in his seat.

"So. We're just here to talk," Betsy said. "To get your perspective on things. No need for restraints."

"Okay." Joe again shifted in his chair as if he were trying to scratch an itch on his buttocks. "I know I'm here because of what happened to Bill and Maggie."

"Exactly. But let me emphasize that you aren't being charged with anything. The DA's still reviewing the evidence, and you're just a person of interest, a potential witness."

"Got it," Joe said. "So you're not going to read me my rights?"

The guard returned with a cup of coffee. He put it on the table in front of Joe.

"Well, we are," Betsy said. "We have to advise you of your right to an attorney and all that, since you're in custody. But this is more of a conversation. An interview about what happened."

"Fine. I see."

Joe was polite, articulate, and cooperative. Unusual behavior for someone who might have been involved in such gruesome killings. Betsy read Joe the standard Miranda warning, emphasizing his right to have a lawyer of his own choice or one appointed for him if he couldn't afford it.

"Okay," Joe said. "Give me a pen. I'll sign. Got nothing to hide."

"Before we talk about the other night," Betsy said, "can I ask why you declined your father's offer to pay for an attorney?"

Joe nodded, as if he'd expected the question. "I know it seems weird. I'm a judge's son. So I grew up around lawyers and legal stuff. My sister's a lawyer too. And what I learned is that people should hire lawyers, whether they're innocent or guilty. Could be even more important to hire one if you're innocent, like me."

Joe paused, then nodded to the guard. "Thanks for the coffee." Joe blew on the cup and took a sip. "That hits the spot." He took another drink.

"I might be foolish for not accepting his offer, but I didn't *kill* Bill and Maggie. After my father told me to leave his house, I saw them briefly when they returned home. They were alive last time I talked to them."

"Fair enough. And if you're familiar with lawyers and legal stuff, you know I need to ask where you went and what you did after you left. But before we go there, I'm curious about why you call your grandparents by their first names."

"You know, I never thought about it. I started calling them by their names a long time ago, when I was a teenager. My father and I kept fighting, and I would run away to their house. They talked to me like I was an adult, and it seemed so natural to call them Bill and Maggie."

"Sounds like you were very close to them."

"I guess they were the parents I never had, or at least ones I always wanted. My mom was okay, but she couldn't protect me from my father."

"Did he abuse you?"

"Not physically. He just wouldn't stop pushing me toward being a lawyer or something else I didn't want to be. But I don't know where we got off track. I remember when I was younger how much I enjoyed listening to him tell me about his cases and how inventive criminals were in covering up their crimes."

Betsy didn't look away to take notes. She stayed engaged with Joe.

"And I enjoyed riding along with him on the Algiers Ferry, where he often went to think about his cases. It was special to him. He even made us promise to throw flowers off the ferry into the Mississippi when he died."

Joe sighed and rubbed his eyes. He took another sip of coffee before continuing.

"But the control was just too much. It even included what we wore. Our clothes had to be from Banks Brothers, or he had a conniption. Hell, I can predict my Christmas presents each year: socks, belts, or neckties—all from Banks Brothers. But Bill and Maggie encouraged me to pursue what I wanted: being an artist. I could come dressed in paint-stained coveralls from Molly's studio or even rags from a thrift store. They wouldn't care."

"Hmmm. I didn't realize you painted."

"I've had a modicum of success. It's how Molly and I got involved. She paints and does pottery. Molly helped me with gallery showings in Houston and Memphis. My only real exposure in New Orleans has been a couple of paintings I sold to Bill and Maggie."

"Haven't I seen some of your work at city hall and police headquarters?"

"Well, yeah." Joe's face flushed. He shifted in his chair again. "Molly's the mayor's niece."

"Oh, I see."

"But it's not like that." Joe, still a little red-faced, seemed nonplussed. "A panel of artists chose my paintings in a citywide contest. She just helped me prepare the entry paperwork."

"Got it," Betsy said.

"And Molly doesn't need her uncle's help." Joe's voice was more animated than before, almost angry. "Besides being an accomplished artisan and businesswoman, she's an expert on ancient Central and South American pottery. Molly travels there a lot. And she's fluent in Spanish."

"Wow," Betsy said. "Molly really has her act together."

"She does. But for me, there were always roadblocks when I tried to get a show here."

"Your dad?"

"Could be. Or maybe I'm not avant-garde enough for this town."

"I see. Thanks for adding some background. So, where'd you go after the holiday party?"

"Well, I walked toward St. Charles to pick up the streetcar to head back to Molly's. After the fight with my dad, I needed a drink. Since I was only a few blocks from Bill and Maggie's, I thought I'd see if they had anything in their liquor cabinet. I know where they hide an extra key. So I figured I'd let myself in, take some booze, and then leave with no one knowing I was there."

"But something or someone interrupted your plans?"

"Just as I reached their house, Bill and Maggie were getting out of their car. I tried to turn away, but Bill saw me. He called and asked me to come inside.

"I helped them into the house. Maggie was tired, and I helped her to the couch. Bill went to their liquor cabinet and poured them each a drink of brandy. Maggie took a sip and lay down, still in her clothes from the party. Bill took off her shoes and massaged her feet."

"Did she fall asleep?"

"I think so. I know she closed her eyes."

"What happened next?"

"Bill and I talked about the argument. I told him why I was near their house. Bill went to the liquor cabinet and pulled out a fifth of bourbon. He found a bag, put the bottle in it, and gave it to me. He said, 'Here, you need this more than I do right now.' I took the bottle and gave him a hug. Bill asked if I wanted to spend the night. I thanked him for the offer but declined. Then I told Bill I loved him."

Joe paused and exhaled. He looked around the room and blinked.

"How long were you there?"

"Twenty minutes, max."

"And after?"

"I went to Lafayette Cemetery Number One and sat under a tree just outside the wall. I was swigging from the bottle of bourbon. Some guy came over from Commander's Palace and said I should leave.

"Figured I might as well take the streetcar back to Molly's. So I headed to the stop near Christ Church Cathedral. I crossed over St. Charles and sat down on the church steps. I felt drowsy. I figured it was because I haven't had much to drink lately. I might have fallen asleep. I'm not sure. It took all my concentration to get up and get on the car and make it back to Molly's place. I slept a long time and then just hung around Molly's doing holiday stuff. And then the cops came. You know the rest."

With the basic chronology of events established, Betsy took Joe back through his story, asking questions in different ways, probing for inconsistencies. Joe stuck to his version of events.

"Tell me about the stains on your clothes we seized at Molly's studio."

"Just after our group photograph, I caught one of my cousins with a glass of wine. I got on him about it, and he dumped his glass on me. Then the little prick told my father I gave him wine and was encouraging him to get drunk. He said he threw it on me to get me to stop."

"Is that what you and your father fought about?"

"Yeah. I got into trouble when I was younger, partly because my parents didn't crack down on my underaged drinking. I accept responsibility for what I did, but I don't want others making the same mistakes, especially if it's a family member. But my father didn't seem to believe me."

"Which kid was it?" Betsy pulled out her tablet computer and displayed the family group photo. "Can you show me?"

"My cousin, Hunter Dejarnette." Joe's upper lip curled upward, almost imperceptibly, not quite a snarl, but certainly not a smile. "He's about fifteen. He's right there, standing next to me, grinning."

"Is Constance Rose Jennings his grandmother?"

"Right, Aunt Connie. His mother is Grace Dejarnette. Hunter's my first cousin once removed or something like that."

Betsy looked at her watch. "It's almost noon. I don't have any more questions. So we should get you back to your holding cell for lunch. I'll review my notes, and we might need to talk again later."

Betsy stood. The guard handcuffed Joe and escorted him out of the room. Betsy motioned for Jonathan and Mitch to join her.

Chapter Twenty-Eight: Don't Let 'Em See You Sweat

Saturday, December 27, 2014

"*That* was enlightening," Jonathan said as he entered the interview room and sat down. "Joe doesn't seem like someone who would shoot his grandparents and stage the crime scene to look like a murder-suicide."

"I'm with you," Mitch said. "Listen, Betsy, I need to go write up my notes, if it's okay with you."

"Fine by me, Mitch. Catch you later."

"Betsy," Jonathan said, as the door closed behind Mitch, "I'm curious about how you conducted the questioning."

"Okay. Shoot."

"Why'd you move your chair? Don't you want to have something between you and a suspect? After all, Joe's accused of some pretty violent behavior."

"Well." Betsy sighed and nodded. Her forehead furrowed, indicating she was in deep thought. "Interrogation's a form of communication. And effective communication's an art. But it's not something they teach at the Academy."

"Okay..."

"Over the years, I've formed some conclusions. I'm still not as good at it as I would like."

"And?"

"In every form of interpersonal communication, even a criminal interrogation, you're trying to connect. You want the suspect to feel like it's okay for them to confess. They don't want to do it. So you have to break down the barriers. You want them to trust you."

"But Joe didn't confess," Jonathan said. "And you didn't seem to press him very hard in your questioning."

"All part of the dance," Betsy said.

"Okay, don't keep me in suspense."

"This morning was the foundation. I just wanted to probe. The primary emphasis was on letting Joe tell his story and start getting comfortable talking to me."

Betsy paused and grinned. Her eyes sparkled.

"But next time I talk to Joe, it'll be a lot different."

"How so?"

"Today was an interview. Next time will be an interrogation. We know a lot more than Joe probably believes we do. And even if we *don't* know something, we'll play on Joe's anxiety that we *might* know. The more nervous he is, the more tells he displays. Once we see what makes him nervous, we can focus on the details."

"Sounds effective."

"Incredibly so," Betsy said. "And instead of staying at the table next time, I'll sit face-to-face with him. Almost touching knee to knee."

"Why?"

"Well, we're asking Joe to reveal the most intimate of personal details—that he murdered his grandparents. If you were Joe, would you rather confess to some impersonal police asshole sitting across a table yelling at you? Or would it be better to tell someone close to you? Someone who makes you feel like they won't judge you if you told them the truth, regardless of how horrible the truth is?"

"Jesus, Betsy, now you've got me scared. You could probably get me to confess to anything."

Betsy laughed. "Oh, come on, Doc. It's not that bad. Besides, you've got nothing to hide, do you?"

"Guilty," Jonathan said. "Or, not guilty."

They laughed.

"Say, Doc, I'd like to hear what you thought about Joe's interview."

"Well, Joe looked more like a straitlaced college professor than a cold-blooded killer."

"I know," Betsy said.

"As I watched, Joe expressed some emotion when you mentioned his dead grandparents, but his actions were consistent with someone who had learned of their deaths a short time before. I didn't notice any micro-expressions or side glances—nothing to indicate deception. The only thing I noticed out of the ordinary was when Joe smirked as he mentioned Hunter. Not sure I'd read too much into it under the circumstances."

"I picked up on the same vibe," Betsy said. "But I didn't delve into it too much because his description of events at the party tracks what most family members say happened."

"Except for Judge Haldeman, I take it?"

"Affirmative. But Joe's story checks out from Molly Westcott's vantage point, too. And the streetcar driver remembers Joe getting on at Sixth Street, near Christ Church Cathedral, around 10:30 p.m. She saw him carrying what appeared to be a bottle in a bag. She was afraid she might have to say something. Joe looked woozy. But he could show his fare card and seat himself. So she let it pass. She recalls letting him off at Lee Circle, around 10:45."

"Security camera footage on the streetcar?"

"Negative," Betsy said. "System glitch."

"If I heard everything correctly," Jonathan said, "there was a window of around two hours, perhaps more, from when Joe left the party until he got on the streetcar."

"Exactly. So he had plenty of opportunity to kill his grandparents and still make it to Christ Church Cathedral. Although, if we try to prove it was Joe, we'll have to explain why his clothes don't have blood stains or any gunshot residue."

"What I hear," Jonathan said, "is that Joe Haldeman has reasonable doubt written all over him. So Max Jamerson has some verbal dancing ahead of him if he continues with a press conference as planned."

"To complicate matters, there'll be a probable cause hearing on Monday. That's the first day a magistrate's available. Fortunately, we have some time to develop additional evidence before we have to let him go."

"What's next?"

"I think the road just got bumpier. We've intensified our search of dumpsters in the Garden District, looking for the towels and hammer. We're checking for other security camera footage. Two detectives are on their way to the hospital to visit Hunter Dejarnette. I'm on my way to meet with Judge Haldeman at his home. I'll ask him to explain his change of clothing and his two hours missing from the party. And I'd dearly enjoy taking custody of that tacky red Christmas sweater."

Jonathan smiled. "I don't envy you telling a sitting appeals court judge you suspect him of murdering his parents."

"What will piss him off even more is that we convinced one of his former colleagues on the trial bench to issue a search warrant. We'll bring the dogs through to his house to sniff for any buried evidence. It should prove to be a very exciting evening."

"There's not much I can do to help you on either score. Because one of my assistant coroners issued the original mental health paperwork on young Hunter, we can't do anything to make it look like we're interfering in an independent review by hospital staff. We're already out on a limb." Jonathan thought of Leo's break of protocol in issuing a PEC. He wanted to curse but held his tongue. "Remember about one of my deputy coroners with admitting privileges at Riverview?"

"Yeah," Betsy said. "He signed the PEC—the initial commitment papers—and breached protocol."

"And I'm hoping it won't cause problems. But we need to be squeaky clean from here on out." Jonathan paused and sighed. "As for your visit with Judge Haldeman, well, just know you have my moral support."

"I understand. I appreciate all you *have* been able to do. You've gone above and beyond."

"Thanks."

"So, how *do* you plan to spend the rest of your Saturday?"

"Another lesson I learned from Robby. Citizens need to see their Coroner out, glad-handing when high-visibility cases are being investigated. They understand we have to work late occasionally. But when we disappear from view too much, they invent conspiracies."

"Don't let 'em see you sweat, right?"

"Something like that." Jonathan smiled. "So while you and your team are out doing your investigative work, Emma and I will be at Momma Mae's talking about old times and eating some phenomenal South Louisiana cuisine."

Betsy laughed. "I'm definitely jealous. Say hello to Mae and have some extra CPR for me."

Chapter Twenty-Nine: The Riverfront Run

Saturday, December 27, 2014

Jonathan arrived home just after 2:00 p.m. A handwritten note on their refrigerator advised:

> Gray—
> No one around to row;
> went for a riverfront run.
> Fen—2p.

He had just missed her.

The first time Jonathan saw Emma, she was rowing with the varsity team in college, her long legs and arms moving in perfect unison with her crewmates. It was her outlet, her serenity. And while New Orleans wasn't Cambridge, and the Mississippi wasn't the Charles, there were certainly enough canals and lakes and bayous around to provide adequate opportunities to row without challenging the mega-tankers on the river. But today her usual partners from Crescent City Rowing Club or the Tulane Crew must not be available.

Jonathan hurried to their bedroom and changed into running clothes. Emma had a head start. But if she stuck to their normal riverfront run, he should be able to catch her—if he cheated.

Their usual route paralleled the Riverfront streetcar line, from its beginning near the old US Mint, then along Decatur Street to North Peters and up Canal. Sometimes they would run as far as the biomedical district before turning around. Their course was somewhere between five and seven miles. If they wanted a shorter run, they would turn back into the French Quarter at Rampart Street and head home. So, if Emma stuck to the plan, he should catch up with her by running down Bienville toward the river.

Success. As Jonathan neared North Peters, Emma ran perpendicular to him from left to right. Everything—traffic, pedestrians, and so forth—seemed normal. Nothing out of the ordinary. Turning right, he was behind her by a hundred yards. He picked up his pace and closed the distance. A car—a blue Acura—swerved out of a parking spot, sped to just a few feet behind Emma, and pulled over to the right side of the street. Jesus. A blue Acura? This couldn't be happening—but it was. He was too far away to read its license plate. Tinted windows. He couldn't see inside. His gut tightened. He sprinted toward Emma.

Any doubt Jonathan had that the car was following Emma evaporated when she crossed the street and angled left down Iberville. That route would take her around the Westin to the foot of Canal Street. The car, after waiting a few seconds, followed her. Emma and the Acura disappeared on the other side of the hotel.

Still too far away to read the plates, Jonathan proceeded directly to Canal Street and stopped. What if something happened while he was out of sight? Too late now—he just needed to wait and hope. So, he stepped into an alcove, remaining hidden as Emma ran past, with the Acura continuing its stealth maneuvers a short distance behind. Jonathan breathed in deeply and exhaled. He repeated the cycle several times, to calm himself.

Whoever was in the Acura better not do anything to hurt Emma. He put his hand into the pocket of his running jacket. Why hadn't he thought to bring the Glock? But, hell, why would he? He was just out for a run. How could he know what would happen? And he couldn't prove the Acura was up to no good. Besides, there were too many people around for him to use a pistol. His face warmed, partly from the excitement and partly from the sun breaking through the clouds.

Jonathan hastened to a nearby building renovation site. He picked up two shards of brick and an old nail. He put them in his pocket, not sure what he was going to do with them. He turned around and scanned the street, hiding partially behind a palm tree.

As Emma and the Acura proceeded up Canal Street, Jonathan ran as near to them as he dared. With so many people around, he couldn't take a chance on a confrontation. He needed to see the license plate, but couldn't get close enough to read it.

Emma turned right on Burgundy, a block earlier than Rampart. The Acura turned right as well. Crap. Why Burgundy? Why now? Rampart was more out in the open. More people around. Less likely for anything bad to happen. As Jonathan rounded the corner, the car halted a few feet from Emma. No longer jogging, Emma was bent over, hands on her knees, most likely catching her breath. The car's passenger side window opened about six inches. A dark, cylindrical object emerged, just as it did when he and Jimmy and Sonny were being chased on their way to St. Helen's.

Enough was enough. Emma had nothing to do with any of his investigations. Jonathan dashed ahead and hurled the bricks in rapid succession. One after the other, they hit the window and the cylindrical object.

Emma sprang upright, her eyes wide.

"Run." Jonathan lunged forward and scratched the right rear quarter-panel of the car with the nail.

Emma bolted around the corner onto Iberville Street, out of sight. The passenger's window closed, and the Acura sped away from the curb, continuing along Burgundy. The car didn't turn down Iberville. He could see only the last three digits of the license number: TPQ. Damn, same as on the Acura at St. Helen's Convent.

Jonathan stumbled and tripped. He fell in a heap onto the sidewalk. Glass and plastic crunched under him as he rolled over. Some of the small, curved pieces of plastic had white numbers and tick marks. A broken camera lens.

Thank God—the cylindrical object hadn't been a gun.

Dizzy from his fall, Jonathan stood up slowly, struggling to regain his breath. Had Emma gone back home, or was she hiding somewhere? He walked onto Iberville Street. Emma was nowhere around. She must have ducked into one of the shops. His temples throbbed.

Jonathan proceeded toward the river, looking down streets and alleyways and into the varied storefronts. Maybe he'd get lucky. Within a couple of blocks, he spied her sitting in Addiction, a local coffee house, though she wasn't drinking coffee. Jonathan sighed with relief. She'd chosen to hide in plain sight. Smart. If the Acura returned, other people around—potential witnesses—should deter another attack. His respiration and pulse finally settling down, Jonathan entered Addiction.

"Thank God," Emma said. "Are you okay?" Her tone seemed both angry and bewildered. "What was *that* all about? Why was that car following me?"

"Let's get an espresso and talk. Maybe some caffeine will calm us down." Jonathan smiled and rolled his eyes. He patted himself on the back, mentally, for remembering to bring a credit card on his run.

After placing their order and finding a table where they could have some privacy, Jonathan moved closer to Emma and whispered, "That's the car I told you was following my team when we went to interview witnesses. I need to call Betsy."

Emma nodded and sipped her espresso. Her cup swayed in her still-shaking hands. Jonathan called Betsy and left a voicemail describing what had just happened.

"When did you figure out you were being followed?" Jonathan said.

"As I approached Canal, I could sense a car was following me closely."

"Is that why you ran down by the Westin?"

"Yeah. And when it followed me around the hotel and up Canal, I took a right on Burgundy to throw them off. Where did *you* come from?"

"I got home not long after you left. Read your note and thought I could catch up."

"Shortcut?"

"Yeah."

"What happened? I heard a crashing sound, and the car drove off."

"I saw the passenger window open, and something come out," Jonathan said. "I was afraid it was a gun. But all I had was two pieces of brick and a rusty nail. I threw the bricks. I think I broke the window. Or at least cracked it."

"Well, no one shot at me."

"Yeah, about that." Jonathan's face warmed. "It turned out to be a camera lens."

Emma tilted her head. Her forehead wrinkled. "Why would anyone want to follow me or take my picture?"

"Like I said, someone is worried about one of our investigations, and they're trying to intimidate my office. Or maybe they were just gathering intel on us or something. Regardless, they just crossed the line."

"Honestly, Gray, sometimes you can be such an ass. Why didn't you do something earlier?" She sipped her espresso. "I don't know whether to kiss you for warning me or slap you for waiting so long."

Jonathan smiled. "Let's go with the first choice."

Emma returned his smile, moved closer, and kissed him on the cheek. "Let's go home."

Jonathan and Emma hastened to their house without incident. Once inside, Jonathan emailed Sonny and Jimmy. He told them the car had been following Emma and warned them to be on the lookout for the Acura or any other suspicious vehicles or people.

"I called Mae before I left for my run," Emma said. "She's excited to see us. I told her we'd be there around seven-thirty."

"You sure? After what just happened?"

"I am. I'm looking forward to talking with Mae. And I've learned something from you. At times like these, it's best to be out in the open. Cowards like dark corners, away from the public eye."

"So true." Jonathan smiled. "But I'm bringing my Glock, just in case."

"An excellent idea. I'm thinking I should bring his little brother along to keep him company."

Chapter Thirty: The St. Charles Line

Saturday, December 27, 2014

The streetcar would drop them two blocks from Momma Mae's. Leaving home at around six-thirty, a ten-minute walk took them out of the French Quarter and across Canal Street to its intersection with Carondelet. There, the formerly designated Stop Zero signaled both the end and the beginning of the St. Charles Line. It should be slightly over thirty minutes to their destination—Riverbend—where their antique, green Perley Thomas streetcar would make a sharp right turn from St. Charles onto South Carrollton.

Almost immediately after stepping into the car, Jonathan removed his vibrating cell phone from his coat pocket. Not recognizing the number, he activated the RecordMe app on his iPhone as he moved to the rear, out of earshot of other passengers.

"Jonathan Gray."

"Dr. Gray. This is Bryan Whitcomb with the *Times-Picayune.*"

"Mr. Whitcomb. I didn't expect any calls from you after our discussion on Christmas Day."

"Well, this isn't about Dr. O'Malley. It's about something else."

"Oh?"

"I already called the Police Department Public Affairs Office about it. They weren't very helpful."

"Not surprising, if you were asking for information about an active investigation. My office is not at liberty to divulge details about ongoing cases either. Investigations take time. The answers you seek will come in due course."

"Dr. Gray, look. I don't have the luxury of waiting any longer. My paper is running a story tomorrow about the Haldeman killings. Highly placed sources tell us that police placed Judge Haldeman's son, Joe, at his grandparents' house shortly before their murders. And we have reason to believe that authorities knew of his whereabouts for several days before arresting him."

"Reason to believe. Does that mean the paper has actual evidence? Or are you just assuming?"

"We protect our sources. First Amendment and all that."

"Sure. Freedom of the Press." Jonathan shook his head. "Very patriotic, but—"

"Dr. Gray. I want to be fair and give you an opportunity to comment and provide your side of the story."

"Mr. Whitcomb, there is no *my side* of the story. There is only evidence, and where that evidence leads us. Like any other autopsy, my office is committed to investigating the deaths of Mr. and Mrs. Haldeman in a complete and thorough manner. That is what our state constitution, our state legislature, and the people of Orleans Parish expect of my office. Commenting on the evidence at this stage is premature and unproductive."

"Okay. If you won't provide input for my story, will you at least tell *Times-Picayune* readers why their Coroner and two of his staff spent several hours at St. Helen's Convent on the day after Christmas?"

Jonathan's jaw tightened. Why their Coroner spent several hours at St. Helen's? What a bastard. He must have been following them. How else could he have known? Jonathan's response had to be measured, considered, and reasonable—but to the point. He counted to four, exhaled his anger, and drew a deep cleansing breath.

"Mr. Whitcomb, for me to comment on where my staff and I may or may not have traveled as part of our job duties, or otherwise, isn't productive. I can assure you there is nothing sinister afoot, as your question implies. And

146

your question also suggests you're having me and members of my office followed. If so, I demand you cease and desist from any further stalking. Of me. Of my staff."

Jonathan paused and glanced at Emma.

"And of my family. Good evening, Mr. Whitcomb. This call is finished."

Jonathan ended the call and rejoined Emma.

"Fen, I might have figured out who owns the blue Acura."

Emma nodded. "I heard."

"I need to send a quick email to Betsy to let her know."

Chapter Thirty-One: Momma Mae

Saturday, December 27, 2014

Jonathan and Emma's streetcar ride provided an excellent opportunity to observe Joe Haldeman's route between Lee Circle, where he exited the streetcar on the night of his grandparents' murders, and the stop near Christ Church Cathedral, where he entered. Jonathan had traveled it hundreds, perhaps thousands, of times before. Now he needed to pay attention to every detail. But Whitcomb's unexpected call agitated him so much that he abandoned his plan.

He sighed. Saturday night in New Orleans. Their destination was one of the city's most unique restaurants. He wouldn't let some reporter ruin his evening with Emma.

Minutes after leaving the streetcar at the Riverbend stop, they arrived at Momma Mae's 24-Hour Gumbo and Poultry House. Before entering, Jonathan stopped to leave his handgun in a locker just outside its main entrance. Emma followed suit.

"Well, Lawdy, Lawdy." Mae's voice was loud and boisterous. "If it ain't my favorite Dr. Sawbones and his lovely wife, the Builder Lady. You chil'ren come here and give Momma a hug."

As Mae approached Jonathan and Emma, she winked. First hugging Emma and then Jonathan, she greeted them again in a much lower tone and different voice entirely. "How have you two been? It seems like forever."

"You're right, Mae," Jonathan said. "It's been much too long. I don't think we've been here since summer."

"Doesn't matter how long it's been—you're here now. It's a relief to talk to friends in my own voice. Seems like in between Christmas and New Year's Day, we get almost as many out-of-towners as we do during Carnival. And you know me, always marketing the atmosphere. The tourists seem to expect the Cajun accent." She paused. "Now let's get you seated so we can talk. I reserved one of our private rooms."

Mae escorted them toward a room off the main dining area, away from the band scheduled to start in about an hour.

Along the way, Emma interlocked her arm with Mae. "How have you been? You look fantastic."

"Well, dear, I've been hanging in there. Our other restaurants and children and grandchildren keep me busy. And we're still foster parents, though not as active as we used to be. Our youngest daughter's a full partner in Pinky's orthodontic practice, so he's been cutting back on work, and we've been traveling a fair amount. But there are good days and bad."

Most of Mae's offspring were scattered to the four winds this holiday season, much like Jonathan and Emma's triplets. Emma and Mae commiserated about wanting their kids at home, especially at Christmas.

Jonathan and Emma had known Mae for what seemed like forever. But their bond went deeper, firmly rooted in shared tragedy and heartache. Mae's daughter Annabelle and granddaughter Sophie Louise died together, arm in arm, in the school shooting twelve years ago, alongside Beatrice. The families understood each other's anguish, the way it ebbed and flowed as time passed. But over the years, the pain softened into acceptance. Best to think about the here and now. No reason to dwell on what they'd lost.

"Oh, Jonathan, I almost forgot," Mae said. "Anthony's in town for the holidays. He'll be along after a while."

"That's great, Mae. I'd love to see him. Ask him to stop by and talk when he gets here. Is Pinky around?"

"No. He's at home watching whatever football game's on TV. And probably sipping one too many glasses of Moscato." Mae laughed. "But I bet you two are starving. I'll get the kitchen working on your CPR. And how about two bottles of Sam Adams for starters?"

"Thanks for remembering the Sam, Mae," Emma said. "You know what they say about taking the girl out of Boston. But we're going to pass on the beer tonight. Just bring us a couple of glasses of unsweetened iced tea."

"Okay, dear. Two glasses of unsweet tea, it is."

Chapter Thirty-Two: The Quarterback

Saturday, December 27, 2014

Any other physician might not be amused. But Jonathan always chuckled at the irony of Mae's culinary invention: her Cajun Poultry Rounder, or CPR. The concoction combined boudin—a sausage made of various meats, often with rice as a binding agent and filler—and deboned duck, chicken, and turkey stuffed together, with each successive bird wrapped in a layer of Louisiana pepper-cured bacon. It was like a Cajun combination of turducken and haggis, literally rolled up into one.

After roasting and being basted in its own juice and some of Mae's secret spice mix, the finished sausage-bacon-poultry roll was sliced and served in portions about as large as a cut of prime rib. Probably a coronary waiting to happen—thus requiring real CPR—but it sure as hell tasted good.

As he and Emma enjoyed their CPR, each other, and the atmosphere in the ramshackle restaurant, a familiar face approached, greeting Jonathan by his Navy Reserve rank.

"Captain and Mrs. Gray, my goodness. How are you on this fine, crisp Louisiana evening?"

Jonathan stood up and offered his hand to Tony, who, at thirty-eight, was one of the youngest full-bird colonels in the United States Air Force.

"And a good evening to you, Colonel Taliaferro."

Tony shook Jonathan's hand. "So, with military protocol out of the way, why don't we go back to being just plain old Tony and Jonathan?"

Jonathan nodded. "Done."

"And how's my favorite architect?"

"I'm well, Tony. It's been a long time. Please join us."

Tony waved to the server to bring his first course, a bowl of his mother's famous gumbo, to his new table. Their conversation touched on many topics. They talked about Mae and her work supporting the community. Tony regaled them with stories about his time as a fighter squadron commander in Afghanistan and Iraq and his impressions of life in Washington, DC, where he was a military aide to the president—the officer assigned to carry the briefcase with missile launch codes.

"I'm not sure I'm made for a desk. Or to be a bag man, even for our president," Tony said. "It's an honor to serve, but I'm eager to get back in command. I hope to be in line for an Air Wing during the next selection board."

"Best of luck," Emma said. "We'll keep you in our thoughts."

"You able to make it to tomorrow's game?" Jonathan shifted the discussion from work to pleasure—football. "We'd love to invite you to Emma's luxury suite."

"Thanks, but no. I have to return to the White House. Duty calls."

"The Air Force Academy did well this year," Jonathan said. "The Falcons might have a shot at the Commander-in-Chief's Trophy next year, *if* they can get past Navy, of course."

"Which may happen," Emma said. "The mayor's son looks like he's coming into his own as quarterback, and he's only a freshman. Maybe next year, when he's a sophomore, he'll step up his game."

"True dat," Tony said. "For what it's worth, we call sophomores Third Class Cadets. Juniors are Second Class Cadets. Anyway, Beau Jamerson has made a real difference. We were pleased, but surprised, to get him."

"Surprised?" Jonathan asked. "Why?"

"Beau Jamerson signed a letter of intent to play up in Baton Rouge. And at the last minute, he received an appointment to the Academy. I understand the Tigers' coach was pissed off beyond belief. But LSU didn't want to look bad by criticizing someone for choosing to carry out his patriotic duty, so there weren't any issues raised with the NCAA. Long story short, they allowed Beau to play without sitting out a season."

"I recall a small controversy, but never gave it much thought," Jonathan said.

"Well, a couple of friends in a place to know let it slip that Beau's choice wasn't influenced by patriotic zeal. At least not as much as the press reported."

"How so?" Emma asked.

"It's no secret Max Jamerson has his eye on being governor and even a U.S. senator someday. Let's just say Max must have been worried that something Beau had done would come back to haunt the family, politically or otherwise. So he pulled some strings. Got Beau appointed to the Academy. Swept him out of Louisiana. You know, out of sight, out of mind. Rumor is Max took care of the situation once Beau reported for duty."

"Hmmm." Jonathan chewed over Tony's thought-provoking revelations. The timing of Beau Jamerson's sudden burst of patriotism was curious. What was the situation Max Jamerson had taken care of? How had he taken care of it? He lamented that there had been no media coverage that he could recall. This was the story Bryan Whitcomb should pursue, instead of bothering Jonathan.

Jonathan and Emma talked, ate, and laughed with Tony, enjoying the atmosphere provided by the zydeco tunes playing in the other room. How tempting it was to lose himself in the good times. But his current investigations still pulled at him. Someone grabbed his shoulder. He flinched. Mae.

"Excuse me, Jonathan. Betsy Sprance is here to see you. She didn't want to interrupt, so she asked me to pass you a message. I put her in my office. It's the most private space I can offer."

Jonathan thanked Mae and stood, apologizing to Tony and Emma for the interruption. Before leaving, he bent down and whispered in Emma's ear. She nodded and went back to her conversation with Tony. Mae joined in and made it a threesome again. As Jonathan left the dining area, their laughter continued, as if his presence didn't matter.

Chapter Thirty-Three: The Guardian ad Litem

Saturday, December 27, 2014

Jonathan walked through the kitchen but hesitated as he approached Mae's office. Betsy, visible through the large window next to the door, glanced at her watch as she paced back and forth. After four nights with probably very little sleep, she must be exhausted. Staying in motion, no doubt, kept her blood flowing and helped keep fatigue in check. Perhaps the investigation was getting the best of her. She probably needed a break, and soon.

Jonathan opened the door. Betsy jerked her head around. Her eyes darted back and forth. Her hand dropped toward her holster. Then she exhaled and smiled.

"Evening, Betsy."

"Doc, I'm sorry to interrupt your dinner, but I'm damn glad I found you. We need to talk."

"Sure thing." Jonathan sat down. "It must be serious. But I need you to stand by while I take care of something. Tony Taliaferro gave me an idea. I need to email my office. It shouldn't take long."

"Got it. Let me know when you're done."

Betsy stopped pacing. She closed the blinds on the office window facing into the kitchen.

Jonathan focused on his iPhone as his thumbs tapped on the screen. He stopped typing and looked up.

"All done. Thanks."

"Not a problem. Do you remember C. Bosworth Tipton?"

"Yeah, he's the lawyer Judge Haldeman hired to represent Joe, before Joe turned him down."

"Right. And just a few hours after Joe Haldeman declined to meet with him at the police station, Tipton showed up at Riverview Children's Hospital with two court orders. One declared Hunter Dejarnette a temporary ward of the state. It appointed Tipton as guardian ad litem to evaluate him and report back to the court with his findings and recommendations on whether commitment proceedings should go forward.

"A second order directed Riverview to present Hunter in district court for an emergency hearing tomorrow morning at ten o'clock to show cause why he shouldn't be released. As you might imagine, Tipton declined to allow Hunter to talk to my detectives when they showed up at the hospital earlier today. Claimed Hunter wasn't ready, emotionally."

"At least," Jonathan said, "Janine Dubois has another night to observe Hunter. That should help at a hearing."

"I wish it were so simple."

Betsy closed her eyes. She massaged her temples and forehead with her left hand for a couple of seconds before reopening her eyes.

"This damn case gives me a headache. We just received word that Dr. Dubois conducted a follow-up mental status examination. She decided he was no longer a danger to himself or others. So she rescinded the PEC and directed Hunter's release into his parents' custody. That was about eight p.m. today, a full day earlier than he was supposed to be released. And she recommended they keep him sedated. Of course, this latest development makes tomorrow's hearing unnecessary."

"How convenient," Jonathan said. "I don't suppose Judge Haldeman was involved."

"Not directly. A district court judge—not Judge Haldeman—signed the court orders. Besides, we had Haldeman tied up all afternoon as we executed our search warrant on his house and grounds. But you know what *is* convenient? Judge Haldeman's wife, Kathleen, is on Riverview's Board of Directors. Hell, it's not just my head. This case makes my hair hurt."

Jonathan exhaled noticeably and shook his head. "This political crap burns me up too. Our legislature provided a specific procedure for mental status examinations and reviews of preliminary commitment orders. That Dr. Dubois sped up her mental status review and released Hunter Dejarnette must have been in response to legal pressure and political influence. We need reforms to take nonmedical considerations out of the equation."

Betsy nodded. "I agree." She shook her head. "Politicos pulling strings. Just another day in my world." She sighed. "Everyone's equal under the law. But *some* are more equal than others."

"You know," Jonathan said, "seems unusual for Judge Haldeman to take such an interest in Hunter's release. Hunter's mother was worried enough to bring him to the hospital. Why would Judge Haldeman go through the effort of hiring an expensive mouthpiece and exerting influence through his wife's position against the obvious concern and wishes of Hunter's parents?"

"Does seem out of the ordinary. I don't have a logical explanation. What I have is another mystery."

"Okay," Jonathan said. "You've got my attention."

"All the statements we've collected from the kids at the party are consistent on Hunter's whereabouts, initially. Hunter was playing video games in another area of the house with his cousins. But he left for several long periods of time. They assumed he had gone to get food and talk to their older cousin, Joe. Apparently, Hunter had been hanging around with Joe a lot over the past few weeks. Hunter had been moodier. More withdrawn than usual. Joe might have been giving Hunter alcohol."

Betsy paused. "And, at one point, Hunter left, and none of the other kids saw where he went."

"Must have been after Joe and his father argued," Jonathan said. "Hunter's mother told Leo Pearlman that Hunter left the party and said he was going home. They found him in his room, curled up in a ball, crying."

Betsy nodded her understanding. "And the other kids might not have witnessed the argument if they were playing video games. But they all reported that Hunter left and didn't return. So we can't account for Hunter during the critical time frame."

Betsy paused. "And Hunter's extreme reaction to his great-grandparents' deaths and Judge Haldeman's apparent influence in his release only adds to the strangeness."

"You can't mean...Hunter's fifteen. Hell, he's on the autism spectrum. He was probably just internalizing Maggie and Bill's deaths."

"But you know age isn't always a determinant," Betsy said. "Hunter is a *big* kid, so he's physically capable of being involved. And who knows what his emotional state might have been?"

"My God. Do you really think Hunter could have killed Bill and Maggie?"

"I don't want to get ahead of the evidence. It's still very circumstantial, but I can't rule him out yet."

Circumstantial didn't begin to describe it. How could Betsy possibly believe that a fifteen-year-old who loved his grandparents with such intensity could kill them? Maybe Betsy was just doing her job, leaving no stone unturned. Perhaps the lack of sleep clouded her judgment. Regardless, with the mayor and superintendent crawling up her backside demanding closure, Betsy must be feeling extra pressure to move her investigation off dead center.

"Judge Haldeman's house reveal anything?"

"We're still searching," Betsy said. "But so far, we haven't found the hammer. Or whatever was used to muffle the gunshots. One thing we *have* discovered: the Haldeman family seems to be clumsy around wine."

"Oh?"

"We showed Judge Haldeman the photos indicating he had changed. We asked him why, and to provide the clothes he was wearing in the first photo."

"And?"

Betsy rolled her eyes. "Judge Haldeman said he had to change because he spilled wine on his pants and his sweater, and it soaked through to his white shirt as well."

"Now I see your point."

"Next, Judge Haldeman produced a button-down Banks Brothers white shirt very similar to the one in the photo. Judge Haldeman said he had tried to wash it, but the entire stain didn't come out. We took custody of his shirt and sent it to the lab. I'll bet my next paycheck the analysis will reveal residue of red wine on it in exactly the right spot."

"What of his pants and sweater?"

"That's where the story gets more interesting. Judge Haldeman took the pants and sweater to the dry cleaner yesterday. He gave us a couple of receipts. Mitch Broussard went to the dry-cleaning shop and retrieved them. They had just cleaned them earlier in the afternoon."

"Why not do the same thing with the shirt?" Jonathan asked.

"Not sure, but it's likely because his shirts all have his initials monogrammed on his left cuff, and it would take too long to get a new one."

"And," Jonathan said, "it would look suspicious if all his shirts but one had the monogram."

"Bingo, Doc," Betsy said.

"So, you suspect his sweater and pants will have residue of wine and not blood, I take it."

"Right. It seems the good judge has an answer for everything else. Why shouldn't he have an alibi for his clothes, as well?"

"You sound skeptical, Betsy, but it also sounds like you don't have a lot of evidence against him. Perhaps Judge Haldeman is telling the truth."

"Perhaps, but it's not what my gut says. So I dug deeper. Doc, do you buy any clothes over the internet?"

"Sure."

"Well, the slacks from the dry cleaner were ordered from the Banks Brothers website. And the critical thing? Each pair of pants has a unique code number reflecting location and date of manufacture. The number helps trace defects back to the factory—"

"And links the pants to who ordered them," Jonathan said.

"Affirmative. Records from Banks Brothers reflect that Judge Haldeman ordered those slacks, the same kind he was first wearing the night of the murders, online early Christmas Eve morning—day after the murders—

with a request for rush delivery. They arrived on the day after Christmas at around ten a.m. Judge Haldeman took them to the dry cleaners in the afternoon, about one o'clock. He could have stained the clothes with wine to prepare his alibi."

"I see," Jonathan said.

"Banks Brothers is a very high-end men's clothier," Betsy continued. "I can understand sending an expensive pair of slacks out for dry cleaning. The red Christmas sweater is another matter. Ugly holiday sweaters are a dime a dozen. Personally, I'd be thankful for an excuse to throw it away."

"Sentimental value?" Jonathan rolled his eyes.

"Which is exactly what he told us. Judge Haldeman received the sweater last year in a family Secret Santa exchange from his grandnephew, Hunter Dejarnette. He wore it because of the family connection."

"So you think Judge Haldeman rush-ordered a pair of slacks the morning after the party and sent them to the dry cleaners almost immediately once he got them because he wanted everyone to believe those were the pants he wore at the party?"

"Precisely. The pants he actually wore could have been soaked with blood. But for now, we're leaving it alone. No use giving him another opportunity to bolster his story."

"Well, this certainly is an interesting turn of events," Jonathan said. "I know the search has been disappointing. But now you have even more reasons to turn things upside down. You need to find the pants the judge was wearing at that holiday party, if they still exist."

"We've already started. Judge Haldeman and his wife checked into a hotel today. He's irritated because we inspected and photographed what they packed. We have a team scouring a ten-block radius of their house. They're looking in dumpsters and trash cans, canvassing for witnesses who might have seen someone coming from the house. And we're still checking for security camera footage. Not all home cameras are on the NOLASafe Network."

Betsy's cell phone rang. "Excuse me a minute. I need to take this call."

Jonathan nodded.

"Sprance." Betsy's raspy voice underscored her exhaustion.

"Where? When?" Betsy scribbled on her notepad. "Okay, I'll be there as soon as I can."

She turned toward Jonathan. "Doc, you might want to settle up with Mae. And I think I should drive you and Emma home. That was Mitch Broussard. Looks like we found your blue Acura."

Chapter Thirty-Four: The Turning Basin

Saturday, December 27, 2014

Betsy spoke first as her unmarked police SUV turned onto South Carrollton.

"I assume there's a connection between your blue Acura and your autopsy work. Anything you can share?"

"Remember when I asked about people you would trust with a high-visibility case?"

"Yeah. This related?"

Jonathan nodded. "Sonny, Jimmy, and I were on our way to interview a couple of witnesses when Sonny noticed a blue Acura following us. We thought we had eluded the tail, but it was there when we finished our interviews. Our tires had been slit. That's when I first phoned in the license number to you. You're already aware of Emma's incident earlier today."

"I see." Betsy looked in her rearview mirror, perhaps checking for traffic, but more likely trying to see Emma, who sat in the back seat in silence. "We probably shouldn't go into too much detail. I know you're already involved enough, Emma. But I don't want to reveal confidential information. It might jeopardize our investigation in the long run."

"I understand," Emma said.

"We can talk later," Jonathan said.

"Sure. But I *can* say one thing, even in front of Emma. NOPD found out who owns the Acura. It's one reason I came to see you at Mae's place.

Someone reported the car stolen over in Biloxi on Christmas night. Didn't hit our database until this afternoon."

"Which means," Emma said, "we don't know who was using the car to follow Jonathan on the day after Christmas or me earlier today, do we?"

"Affirmative."

"Who's the owner?" Jonathan asked.

"It's registered to Bryan Whitcomb from the *Times-Picayune*, at an address in the Bywater. Whitcomb was working on an article about the Haldeman killings scheduled to run in tomorrow's morning edition. We sent a detective by his house, and no one was home. We didn't have a search warrant, and there weren't any signs of a struggle, so we didn't have probable cause for an exigent circumstances entry."

"Whitcomb," Jonathan said, "called me as Emma and I were on our way to Mae's. That was the recording I emailed you earlier."

"I saw your email," Betsy said, "but couldn't open the attachment. I sent it to our computer techs but got wrapped around the axle with the search warrant and haven't followed up on it."

"He was trying to get me to tell him why a team from my office visited a particular destination yesterday. Whitcomb seemed convinced that it was connected to the Haldeman matter. And he believes we're protecting the judge or his son. He wanted to give me an opportunity to tell my version of events so he could put it in his story."

"Based on what you said, there doesn't seem to be any connection."

"Absolutely. And I tried to tell him he was barking up the wrong tree in trying to find some sort of conspiracy. But he had a source, or sources, feeding him different information."

"We talked to the managing editor," Betsy said. "Whitcomb called the editor around six-thirty. He had one more lead to check out. Said he would be in to review the final copy around eight o'clock. Must have called his editor just before he called you."

"And I suppose he never made it to the *Times-Picayune* office," Emma said.

"Affirmative," Betsy said. "Which means he must have gone missing somewhere between seven and eight. Not long ago, we received an anonymous call about a blue Acura plunging into the Industrial Canal, just up from the Turning Basin, over by the Broh Brothers' complex."

* * *

Betsy's SUV bumped along an unpaved driveway leading from France Road toward the Industrial Canal, past a couple of abandoned brick buildings with rusty tin roofs. She parked near the edge of the canal slightly after ten-thirty. Floodlights illuminated the area, revealing a police department tow truck dragging something from the water.

The trio exited Betsy's vehicle as the tow-truck winch emitted a high-pitched whirr, straining as it pulled the weight of the object. A blue Acura emerged from the dark expanse.

"Excuse me while I speak with Mitch," Betsy said.

"We'll be right here," Emma replied.

After exchanging a few words with Detective Broussard, Betsy motioned for them to come forward.

"Is this the blue Acura?" Betsy asked. "License plate, Louisiana 9X-48TPQ. It's the same one you phoned in from St. Helen's."

"Looks like it," Jonathan said. "Passenger window's cracked because I threw bricks at it earlier today. And there are marks on the right rear quarter-panel from where I scratched it with a nail."

"Bricks and a nail," Broussard said. "Sometimes low-tech is the best approach."

Betsy pursed her lips and glared at her colleague.

"I saw it in my peripheral vision," Emma said. "But it looks the same to me, too."

"No corpse, Mitch?" Jonathan asked.

"Not yet, Doc."

Broussard removed what remained of his cheroot, looked at the tiny nub of tobacco, and pitched it into the Industrial Canal.

"Standard protocol in a vehicle submersion is for divers to check for a body in the car first. Then they search the immediate vicinity, up to fifty yards away. Depending on water conditions, they might dredge a wider area. Wouldn't hold my breath, though. If there *was* a body, likely it's drifted away by now. Some of these big-ass tankers cause a shitload of prop churn. So we'll be watching for a floater in the river over the next couple of days."

"Betsy, you have a theory about what happened to Whitcomb?" Jonathan said.

"We'd be guessing. But I'll say one thing. Seems like your autopsies have been producing a bit of mayhem since you worked the night shift this past week. You should consider riding a desk for a while."

Jonathan smiled and nodded. "You've got me there. A desk job sounds very restful. For now, how about a ride home for your favorite coroner and his wife?"

Chapter Thirty-Five: Jonathan's Secret

Saturday, December 27, 2014

Betsy turned into the French Quarter and approached Bienville Street.

"Betsy," Jonathan said, "why don't you stop up for a few minutes? We can turn on our heaters and sit on the gallery."

"I've imposed too much this week. And it's already after eleven."

"We won't take no for an answer," Emma said. "You look like you could use some coffee. I know I could."

"Thanks, Emma. I guess Jonathan and I do need to talk."

The trio entered the foyer and removed their coats. Jonathan pulled his sweater down, covering his holster.

"You know," Betsy said, "I forgot you had a concealed carry permit until I saw you retrieve your handgun at Mae's."

"Actually, I'm allowed by statute to carry a gun, as Coroner. Of course, I had a permit long before that for my personal weapons."

"Same as me," Emma said. She removed her Glock and its holster from her purse. "We rarely take them to dinner. But after what happened earlier with the blue Acura, well, you know..."

"Good on you," Betsy said. "I understand."

"You two head to the gallery," Emma said. "I'll bring some fresh brew."

"Thanks, Fen. Come on, Betsy, let's listen to the boss."

Outside was cool, but bearable. Jonathan turned on both space heaters and sat down. He described the archbishop's request for a favor.

Emma reappeared with coffee and a small tray of pastries.

Betsy smiled. "Wow, this is great. I've been so busy I forgot to eat dinner. Sugar and caffeine. Just what I need to keep going."

"I'd offer to make yours an Irish coffee, like I plan for mine," Emma grinned. "But I know you have business to discuss. I'll let you get back to it."

"Thanks, Fen," Jonathan said.

After Emma departed, Jonathan outlined what he had learned about the apparent sexual assault of Josefina Diaz and the disappearance of her sister, Esperanza Morales.

"Do you think Max was trying to make political capital out of helping immigrants, by hiring them?" Betsy asked.

"Not sure. Could be. But Mrs. Diaz claimed someone snuck up from behind and assaulted—raped—her. First in a storeroom at the mayor's house. Maybe other times, too. She's very closed-lipped and vague about the details. She hasn't told her husband who it was, assuming she even knows. She's scared to death. I'd be scared, too."

"But how will you get a sample from Mayor Jamerson and his staff? I assume that's the next step."

Jonathan smiled. "Actually, getting their DNA is the simple part."

"How?"

"After Katrina, there were so many bodies we couldn't identify. There was a big push for people to give DNA samples."

"I remember."

"Well, one of the loudest voices was a state senator representing Orleans Parish, one Theodore Maximillian Jamerson."

"You're right," Betsy said. "When he ran for mayor, one of his campaign slogans was 'Only Criminals Fear DNA.' Do you have any results?"

"Not yet. I sent an email to Sonny asking him to put in a rush request. But I don't expect anything back until at least Monday. And even that'll be a minor miracle."

"Aren't you afraid the DA will charge you with concealing a felony?"

"I haven't given it much thought. All I'm doing is investigating a potential sexual assault. The evidence isn't strong enough to charge anyone yet."

"True," Betsy said. "You're investigating a potential crime, just like NOPD does."

"Except, oddly enough, concerning Esperanza Morales."

"What do you mean?" Betsy looked at him, her forehead wrinkled.

"NOPD opens investigative cases on all assaults, even those that lead to an autopsy by my office, correct?"

"Affirmative. Probably more so where your office is required to conduct an autopsy."

"Josefina hasn't reported the sexual assault yet, so I can understand why NOPD has no file on it." Jonathan cleared his throat. "But Esperanza's different. To date, no one from NOPD has asked me or my staff about her."

"Why would they, unless something was reported?"

Jonathan paused. He looked to his left, then to his right. He lowered his voice almost to a whisper. "This is very close hold. I found five autopsy reports Robby hadn't filed with the Vital Records Registry before he died. Esperanza Morales was one of them."

"She's dead? Why would Robby—"

"Well," Jonathan said, "you've asked the million-dollar question, haven't you? I don't know the answer yet. Regardless, dead bodies don't magically appear at the morgue without some level of police knowledge. The police are *always* interested to the nth degree, at least in the early stages, after a death under mysterious circumstances, before the trail goes cold."

"I understand why you don't want to involve the department. Too many suspicious...well, too many coincidences."

"I figured you'd get it once I started painting a picture."

"Give me the names and death info about those five autopsies. Let me do some snooping."

"Will do."

"And it might be time to speak with Mandy Simpson in the US Attorney's Office. Unless you have a strong objection, I'm going to talk with her about Esperanza Morales."

"Okay. But aren't you concerned about your police chain of command if you contact the Feds?"

"I don't think they'll find out. I talk to Mandy all the time, so it shouldn't raise any eyebrows. Besides, if this cover-up goes as high in the administration as we fear, the Feds might be our only option."

"Okay," Jonathan said. "But I hate to add anything else to your plate. You look beat."

Betsy closed her eyes and rubbed them. "You're right, Doc." She opened her eyes and blinked. "I'm pretty damned tired." She drank some coffee. "And maybe this is the lack of sleep talking." She yawned. "But I've got this feeling."

"Okay," Jonathan said.

"It's almost like a premonition."

"Go on."

"Like something bad's about to happen."

"Like what?"

"Not sure. It's just—"

"You having nightmares?"

"Sometimes." Betsy took another swig of coffee. "I don't actually sleep much, though. Every minute I sleep is a minute I hold up the investigation."

"Late-night caffeine probably doesn't help either," Jonathan said. "Can't you crash for a while? Let Mitch carry the load?"

Betsy looked at the floor, then back at Jonathan. "Right. Wish I could. Department's slammed as it is. Mitch has other alligators snapping at him."

"Fair enough. How can I help?"

"Listen. I know this sounds paranoid." Betsy exhaled. "But if something happens to me, promise you'll step in to guide Mitch. He's good, but he just can't give this case the attention it needs. Now that I've updated you, you know the evidence nearly as well as he does. Hell, probably better."

"Well," Jonathan said. "Not sure what to say."

"I know, Doc. You probably won't have to do anything. It's just a feeling I have. But I'd sleep a lot better if I knew I had you as backup."

"Don't give it another thought. I'm sure everything will be fine. But if

169

something happens, you know I'll be there."

Chapter Thirty-Six: Sunday Morning Puzzles

Sunday, December 28, 2014

Sunday mornings. Jonathan's favorite time of the week. Even more so during the waning days of December, when sunrise graces New Orleans a few minutes before seven. He could sleep in but still wake up in time to see the first amber rays peel back the darkness. And it was early enough for him to ease into the rest of his day, without feeling guilty for taking a break to enjoy nature's beauty.

This Sunday morning, almost midway between Christmas and New Year's Day, was no exception. Jonathan sat in the kitchen sipping coffee as the soft, warm hues of first light spread over the French Quarter's historic buildings and the broad expanse of the Mississippi. What a peaceful way to start *any* morning. Especially on a day capping such an eventful week.

Emma entered, wrapped in her bathrobe. The unmistakable scent of warm cinnamon and hot java must have been too inviting to resist any longer.

"Coffee smells delicious."

"Morning, Fen." Jonathan poured her a cup. "Here you go."

"Did you make cinnamon rolls?"

"Yeah. They're done. Warm oven's just what the doctor ordered. Let the icing melt to perfection."

"This is excellent coffee. Been up long?"

"A little more than an hour, I guess. I didn't notice. I wanted to read Whitcomb's article about the Haldemans as soon as possible. *Times-Pic* wasn't here yet. Figured I'd take advantage of the wait."

Emma sipped her coffee and eyed him warily. Getting up early and making breakfast on Sunday morning had long been one of Jonathan's favorite activities. But it had been quite a while since he'd baked anything. She probably realized that making cinnamon rolls from scratch took him a lot longer than the hour he claimed.

"How'd his article turn out?" Emma drowned a yawn with more coffee.

"Not bad. It focused on their family history and accomplishments. There's a lot about Bill and Maggie Haldeman and their association with the Navy when they first met. And it hinted about some still unanswered questions. The investigation's ongoing, and there hasn't been a final autopsy report. But it didn't get into details or pose any theories about what happened."

"Which may mean Whitcomb listened to you when you told him there wasn't a conspiracy. At least not one involving the coroner's office."

Emma took a bite of her pastry. She paused, a puzzled look on her face. Maybe it was the orange icing. Beatrice's favorite: cinnamon rolls with orange cream cheese icing. He hadn't made that combination in the twelve years since her murder.

"I'd feel better if we knew where Whitcomb is," Jonathan said. "I suspect the paper was reluctant to go with a more controversial story without him there to vouch for his sources."

"Good point," Emma said.

"And there's a sidebar noting that Whitcomb's missing under mysterious circumstances and that police pulled his car out of the canal last night."

"You think the *Times-Pic* is dropping hints that his disappearance is related to the article?"

"Could be. Maybe they see an additional mystery as a benefit to paper sales."

"How so?"

"Even if his article on the Haldeman killings named names, I'm not sure it would get much play because of the timing. Between today's football game and the holidays, people focus on other things. Whitcomb's sudden and mysterious disappearance adds more thrill. It gives the Haldeman killing additional legs without making the *Times-Pic* look like it's desperate for news."

"If you're right, Bryan Whitcomb's probably alive and well."

"And enjoying this magnificent sunrise, I hope," Jonathan added.

Emma took another bite of her cinnamon roll. She looked pleased but still seemed skeptical. Time to change the subject.

"Sounds like fans are already getting wound up for today's game," Jonathan said. "And with the Bucs in the running for a Wild Card slot—not to mention the Saints playing for home-field advantage—it should be a good one."

"Are you up for a run before Mass?"

"Sure. I need to burn some extra calories before the game. I always eat too much food and drink too much alcohol. But we'll have to make it a quick one."

Chapter Thirty-Seven: Haunting Thoughts

Sunday, December 28, 2014

Though less crowded than Christmas Day, St. Louis gloried in the significant number of parishioners and tourists listening to Monsignor Rossignol and his comforting message of peace and redemption.

When Emma stepped forward, along with others in their row, to accept Communion, Jonathan sat down to wait for her. He bowed his head. Images of recent events rushed through his mind: Robby's unexpected stroke and the five death certificates; revelations about Esperanza Morales; Josefina Diaz's potential sexual assault; Bill and Maggie Haldeman. And now, their great-grandson, Hunter Dejarnette, released from the hospital after possible political pressure from Judge Haldeman.

It didn't make sense. Why would anyone want him released early? Most of the possibilities were unpleasant, horrific even. But Hunter was sedated at home and vulnerable. *Vulnerable*. Why had that word sprung to mind? A cold sensation spread through Jonathan's face as if he were about to faint. Was Hunter in some sort of danger? Who would want to harm him? And why? Surely, Hunter's parents could protect him. Still, his accelerated release from the hospital didn't add up. Something was wrong.

Despite his attempts to focus on the church service, Jonathan couldn't get Hunter off his mind. After Beatrice's murder, he had felt so helpless. He had thought that if only he had known what was going on, he could have done something that might have saved her. He could have stormed that school, his own safety be damned, and shot down that shooter himself. He could have tried to rescue his little daughter from the terror she must have felt in the minutes before her death.

If he had any power to help Hunter now, even if it just meant checking that he was safe, he had to do it.

Emma sat down and smiled. The warmth returned to his face. But he still couldn't shake his feeling that something was terribly wrong.

"Sorry," Jonathan whispered, "but I need to step out."

"Should we leave? Would you like me to come along?"

"No. Don't worry. I need to make a quick phone call. I can take care of it before the service finishes."

Jonathan made his way to a side aisle and exited. Moving away from the cathedral entrance, he dialed Betsy. He ducked into a semi-secluded archway at the centuries-old Presbytère, a former courthouse and administrative center now part of Louisiana's State Museum. His call rolled over to voicemail.

"Damn it," he muttered through clinched teeth. "Betsy, this is Jonathan Gray. I think we should check on Hunter Dejarnette. Perhaps Hunter has changed his mind about talking to police and providing a statement. I think he knows something, and he's keeping it to himself. There's nothing concrete I can point to, it's just a hunch. You know how these things are. Maybe we can just check that he's back home safe since being released last night."

Jonathan dialed Sonny Rabideau. Voicemail again. "*God* damn it." Jonathan glanced toward the cathedral. His face flushed with embarrassment. Turning away from St. Louis, he lowered his voice and left a message. The warm feeling from his embarrassment moved into his gut. He gagged but didn't throw up.

What else could he do? He didn't know where Hunter lived. Even if he did, he couldn't waltz up and tell Hunter's parents about his premonition that their son was in danger, could he? And what would he say the danger was? If he dialed 9-1-1, the operator would trace his call and send police to arrest *him*. Maybe the operator wouldn't trace his phone. But his voice would be on a recorded emergency call, raw and unedited. And waiting for Bryan Whitcomb, or some other journalist, to discover it. Then they'd expose the Coroner of Orleans Parish for relying on feelings and premonitions to make recommendations for police action.

Frustrated that all he could do was to wait for Betsy or Sonny to call him back, Jonathan reentered the cathedral. His head pounded, and his stomach filled with butterflies. He slipped into a seat in the back, bowed his head, and tried to calm down. He took deep cleansing breaths and imagined a successful outcome. Hunter would wake from a long nap and thank everyone for their concern. As Jonathan's heart rate and breathing returned to normal, a shadow fell over his meditation. Now what? He couldn't stand any more bad news. Jonathan opened his eyes and exhaled a sigh of relief.

"Fen. Sorry. Wasn't paying attention. Didn't hear you coming."

Mass had ended, and celebrants were filing out. Jonathan stood and grasped Emma's hand.

"Everything all right, Gray?"

"I thought of something Betsy Sprance needs to know. Thought I'd speak to her before the info got stale."

"I figured it must be something important. You still clear for this afternoon?"

"Absolutely." Jonathan hoped he sounded confident. "You know how these investigations are. Taking a few minutes now might avoid a big headache later."

"I'm glad," Emma said. "Let's hurry home for a quick change and then get to the skybox. Might as well take full advantage of the tax deduction."

Chapter Thirty-Eight: The Superdome

Sunday, December 28, 2014

One perk of being married to the owner of a successful architecture and design firm was a luxury skybox leased by Emma Gray and Associates Limited as a combination business expense and client-development tool—something Jonathan could never afford on his salary as Coroner. But today's timing was not the best. The Saints had drawn the early TV game. With the difference in time zones, it was noon in New Orleans. So they couldn't dawdle as they changed and headed out of their house in order to have time to check on the caterer and greet their guests.

"Should be a great game today," Emma said as they neared Canal Street. "I can't believe Tampa Bay has a shot at a Wild Card. And our streetcar ride should be something else."

But everything *wasn't* great. Jonathan hadn't heard from Betsy or Sonny. His mood turned somber. "Actually, would it be okay if we took a cab today?"

Emma slowed her pace and looked at him. "Sure. We can drop by the Marriott and get in line. It's always easier than flagging a cab on the street." She paused. "Something wrong? You look worried."

"Nothing's wrong."

It was a lie. He *was* worried, very worried. But there wasn't much he could do about it. At least not right now. No use dragging Emma into his angst. He tried to look nonchalant but wasn't sure he could make her believe him fully. So he downplayed the situation.

"I'm waiting for a callback, and a noisy streetcar isn't an optimal place to talk. Once we're at the Dome, I can find some privacy if necessary."

Located on the Superdome's 300-Level, Emma's luxury suite had sixteen seats overlooking the field, with a large bar and lounge area behind them. The suites offered opportunity for business development and networking and, from a social vantage point, a place where one could see and be seen.

As Emma mingled among her clients, Jonathan surveyed the common area outside the suites. Max Jamerson was there, backslapping with his right hand and holding a daiquiri in his left. Max always seemed to be accompanied by very attractive, very attentive young women. Today was no exception. His escort was young enough to be Max's daughter. There were rumors that Max liked to keep the company of paid young escorts. Jonathan could believe it. For what other reason would attractive young women fawn over an old sot like Max?

Jonathan scanned the area and focused on Judge and Mrs. Haldeman, thinking that it was incongruous—almost eerie—for them to be there. The judge's parents had been murdered days ago, their bodies released to a funeral home just over twenty-four hours earlier. They were still living in a hotel because of the investigation at their house.

The couple didn't seem entirely present, at least emotionally. Judge Haldeman, with Kathleen's arm intertwined in his, moved zombie-like toward a luxury suite leased by his former law firm. Their path brought them within a couple of feet of Jonathan.

"Good afternoon, Your Honor, Mrs. Haldeman. Please accept my condolences."

"Yes. Thank you very much, Doctor." Mrs. Haldeman's gentle demeanor served as a poor mask for the sadness in her eyes. "This has been a...a difficult few days for us."

"I can only imagine what you're going through."

"Yes, thank you." Though Mrs. Haldeman looked straight at Jonathan, it was as if she was speaking to someone else, someone who wasn't there. "And we thought perhaps young Hunter might wish to join us for the game."

She sighed, staring past Jonathan. "He was devoted to Benjamin's mother and father. Hunter's been through so much, especially for a teenager."

Judge Haldeman remained silent. He glowered at Jonathan.

Mrs. Haldeman dabbed her eyes with a tissue. "But he's at home under his parents' care. He's not at all well."

An awkward situation all around. Jonathan coughed and cleared his throat as if to hide his discomfort.

"Yes, I understand." Jonathan searched for a way to end the conversation. "Well, I hope you get some enjoyment from the game." There wasn't much else he could say. But it worked. Mrs. Haldeman nodded and led her husband away.

He lingered in the common area well after Judge Haldeman and his wife disappeared. They must have a unique set of priorities. If Jonathan's parents had died under mysterious circumstances, could he take time out to go to a football game? Distraction from their pain? Puzzling. Something wasn't right.

Nearing halftime, the Saints were three points ahead. Everyone else in Emma's suite, and most in the stadium's partisan crowd, seemed enthusiastic and involved. But Jonathan's mind drifted to a list of unanswered questions—the death certificates from Robby's special drawer primary among them. Five young women, most likely from Central or South America, all dead under mysterious circumstances. And in such a short time frame. It couldn't be a coincidence.

Then there was Hunter. Jesus Christ. Why couldn't he think of something more effective than waiting for Sonny and Betsy? Surely with the resources at his disposal, regardless how strained they might be, he could do *something*. But what?

He went to the wet bar and pretended to pour a drink. He waited for an exciting play to distract everyone's attention, then ducked out of the suite. He found a relatively quiet corner near a trash receptacle. He sent a text to Susan, who was acting as the duty coroner on the afternoon shift. He asked her to research Hunter's home address. It was something. A start. Why hadn't he thought of it before? Time was of the essence.

179

He next looked through the Received Calls queue in his phone until he found the number he wanted. He needed help in figuring out the connection between Robby and the five death certificates. Despite his previous reluctance, Jonathan hit Call Back, hoping his hunch was right.

"Yes, Mr. Whitcomb." Jonathan breathed a sigh of relief. "Thank you for taking my call."

Silence. Had Whitcomb heard him? There wasn't a dial tone, so Whitcomb must still be on the line. Time to double down.

"I believe we got off on the wrong foot," Jonathan said. "I'd like to meet with you to discuss a couple of thoughts about your inquiry. Are you familiar with Two Brothers' Trolley Stop Café?"

Jonathan nodded. Good. Whitcomb had been there before.

"Great. Tomorrow afternoon at two. Meet me at one of the benches in the small park just up the street. Bring a copy of the latest *Times-Picayune*. Sit down and start reading. After I sit down, fold your copy and put it on the bench between us."

Whitcomb acknowledged the appointment.

"Thanks again," Jonathan said. "See you tomorrow."

Jonathan returned to the suite but was unable to concentrate on the game. Nearing the end of the third quarter, his phone buzzed, signaling an incoming text message. Hunter's home address. Screw his reputation. So what if Hunter's parents thought he was crazy? Like Leo had said: Better safe than sorry. He had to know Hunter was okay.

Jonathan sent a text to Emma, who was sitting a few seats away, surrounded by people. *Sorry, Fen. Something's come up. Gotta go. Later, Gray.*

As he raced toward a taxi stand on the Poydras Avenue side of the Superdome, the return call he'd been waiting for finally came.

"Sonny. Where are you?" He listened, nodding at the information. "Great. I'll meet you and Betsy there as soon as possible."

Chapter Thirty-Nine: Broken Clues

Sunday, December 28, 2014

On the low-rent side of Magazine Street, just a couple of blocks from the much more affluent Garden District, Tom and Grace Dejarnette's two-story modified double-shotgun house— a camelback—and front yard appeared well-kept and orderly, but nothing like the Haldemans' mansion. Maybe they had moved there to be near Bill and Maggie and other family members, but in a home they could afford without breaking the bank. Maybe being within easy walking distance was how Hunter had grown so close to his great-grandparents.

Jonathan exited the cab, paid the driver, and hurried along the brick sidewalk toward the front porch. Betsy and Sonny were already there, along with the cavalry: two uniformed NOPD officers.

"Hey, Doc," Betsy said, "we barely beat you here." She pointed at her police colleagues. "And I brought a patrol unit to leave behind as a protective detail once we're done."

"Good thought," Jonathan said. "Have you talked to the Dejarnettes yet?"

"No," Sonny said. "We knocked just as you pulled up."

The front door opened, revealing an attractive woman in her late thirties or early forties. A tall, dark-haired man of about the same age stood behind her.

"Good afternoon, officers," the woman said, a tremor in her voice. "May we help you?"

"Mrs. Dejarnette?" Betsy asked.

"Yes," she said. "Grace Dejarnette. And this is my husband, Tom."

Betsy displayed her badge. "I'm Detective Sprance from NOPD. And this is the Coroner, Dr. Gray, and Investigator Rabideau from his office."

"Is something wrong?" Mrs. Dejarnette turned pale and stepped back toward her husband. She looked at Jonathan. "Is someone else in the family dead?"

Betsy glanced at Jonathan. "Well, no, Mrs. Dejarnette—"

"I'm afraid," Jonathan said, "this is my doing."

Now everyone's eyes were trained on Jonathan.

"When I learned they had released your son from Riverside Children's Hospital early, I grew concerned someone might be out to do him harm. So I called Detective Sprance."

"Who the hell would want to harm Hunter?" Mr. Dejarnette stepped in front of his wife. "It's that no-good Joe Haldeman, isn't it?"

"Oh, Tom," Mrs. Dejarnette said, "they're cousins. And they're such friends." She turned toward Jonathan and Betsy. "Joe visits here all the time. They love video games."

"What would make you say that about Joe, Mr. Dejarnette?" Betsy asked.

"That son-of-a-bitch was here this morning, wanting to see Hunter. I think he blames Hunter for his arrest. I don't know why the cops released Joe from custody last night."

"Oh," Betsy said, "did he see Hunter?"

"Of course not," Mr. Dejarnette said. "Joe's father wouldn't let him. Said he would call the police if Joe didn't leave. It's all such a shame."

"Judge Haldeman was here?" Betsy asked.

"That's right," Mrs. Dejarnette said. "He offered to watch Hunter while Aunt Kathy took Tom and me to Mass."

"What time was this?" Betsy asked.

"Around eight-thirty, as we were leaving for church," Mrs. Dejarnette said.

"What did Joe do?" Betsy asked.

"What his old man told him to do," Mr. Dejarnette said. "He got in a

BMW driven by Molly Westcott and left."

"What happened afterward?" Betsy asked.

"Well," Mr. Dejarnette said, "we left Hunter with Ben and went to services. We got back just before eleven."

"They probably went straight to the game," Jonathan said. "I ran into Judge and Mrs. Haldeman at the Superdome around noon."

"How was Hunter when you returned home?" Betsy asked.

"Ben told us Hunter slept the entire time," Mrs. Dejarnette said. "So we left him alone."

"Have you checked on Hunter since you got back?" Jonathan asked.

"No," Mrs. Dejarnette sounded tentative, as if she wasn't sure she'd done the right thing. "Like I said, we let him rest."

"I wonder," Betsy said, "if we might convince you to check on Hunter." She looked at Jonathan. "I mean, just to be sure he's all right."

"I don't know," Mrs. Dejarnette said. "The doctor told us he really needs his rest. He's under sedation, you know."

"Of course," Jonathan said. "And we'll respect your decision. But perhaps just this once—"

"Damn it," Mr. Dejarnette said. "This isn't a good time. For us *or* for Hunter. Just pack up your bags and—"

"Tom." Mrs. Dejarnette tugged at her husband's arm. She spoke softly, her voice cracking. "It'll be okay. They're here because they're concerned about Hunter."

Her husband nodded, obviously still perturbed. "Okay. Follow us."

The inside of the house was well furnished, but not overly fancy. Mr. and Mrs. Dejarnette led the way through the front parlor toward Hunter's room. One of the uniformed officers accompanied the group, leaving the other standing guard at the front door. Mrs. Dejarnette knocked lightly on the door and whispered.

"Hunter, dear, it's Mom and Dad. We've come to check on you."

No answer. Mrs. Dejarnette knocked again, this time raising her voice.

"Hunter. Are you okay? We need to come in."

Tom Dejarnette turned the doorknob. Locked. He looked at his wife and then at Betsy and Jonathan.

"Do you have a key?" Betsy asked.

"A key wouldn't work." Mr. Dejarnette pushed on the doorknob again. This time, he used greater force. "Deadbolt's turned from inside."

Betsy motioned to the uniformed police officer who had accompanied them into the house.

"Excuse me, Mr. Dejarnette, let Officer Friedrich try it."

First, the officer repeated the simple effort—turning the doorknob. No movement. Then he tried leaning into the door with his shoulder. There was a crunching sound, and the door moved slightly.

"Detective," Friedrich said, "something's in the way. Like a chair propped under the doorknob. We'll need to force it."

Mr. and Mrs. Dejarnette hugged each other. Mrs. Dejarnette buried her head in her husband's chest. Mr. Dejarnette nodded.

"All right," Betsy said. "Do what you need to do."

Friedrich spoke into the radio handset clipped to his vest. "Goncalves. It's Friedrich. Bring the ram."

Within a minute, the second patrol officer appeared. He carried a large, cylindrical piece of iron with handles and a flat metal plate on each end. Standing to the left of the door jamb, Officer Goncalves twisted the ram to his rear and then brought it forward.

BAM. The door didn't budge.

"Up a little and to the right." Friedrich held his sidearm in a high-ready position.

BAM. The wooden door frame cracked. The door moved slightly.

"Again," Friedrich said. "You're almost there."

BAM. The door frame cracked. The door opened about two feet. The furniture, or another large item made of wood or metal, scraped across the floor inside the room. But something else was preventing the door from opening completely.

Friedrich shouldered his way past his colleague and entered the room, his pistol positioned to meet any threat. Two steps into the room, he lowered his weapon.

"Sweet Jesus," he said.

Mrs. Dejarnette rushed through the doorway, then halted.

"Hunter? My God. What have you done?"

Chapter Forty: Out of the Closet

Sunday, December 28, 2014

Sitting at the morgue alongside Betsy and Sonny and watching Susan and Jimmy conduct the autopsy on Hunter Dejarnette was like being at a funeral home waiting for the memorial service. Betsy and Sonny sat on the hard metal chairs, drinking coffee, stern, sad looks on their faces. Jonathan's hunch had been right—Hunter *was* in danger. Maybe he should have been more insistent that Hunter needed protection. But that Hunter would wrap a belt around his neck, attach it to the doorknob, and hang himself? Unimaginable. God, the kid was only fifteen.

"Looks like we have our A-Team assembled again," Jonathan whispered to Betsy and Sonny. Silence and blank stares greeted his comment. His attempt to lighten the dark mood fell flat. Finally, Betsy spoke.

"We're at a loss with what happened to Hunter. It's really thrown us for a loop. Whatever he might have done, for a fifteen-year-old kid to have his life end like that—that's a tragedy."

"I can't get over it either." Jonathan kept his voice low. "But we have the right team to figure out what happened."

There likely was something more profound bothering Betsy and Sonny. And he couldn't blame them. They couldn't have foreseen that Hunter would know how to wedge his desk chair under the doorknob enough to require a forcible entry. Or that Hunter was hanging on the doorknob with a belt wrapped around his neck. Regardless, the pair no doubt feared the

186

autopsy would show that the brute force of the ram against the door broke the teen's neck.

"I understand you two are upset," Jonathan said. "But we haven't completed processing the crime scene. Until the CSTs locate more evidence, we won't have any additional granularity. And Dr. Miller and Jimmy still haven't completed Hunter's autopsy."

"You're right," Betsy said. "We should be patient. No conclusions until we have more facts."

As though she had overheard their conversation, Susan left the autopsy table and approached Jonathan, Betsy, and Sonny. "I think a couple of aspects of Hunter's autopsy will intrigue you. Come to the examining table. I'll show you what I mean."

As they gathered round, Jonathan was struck by the solemnity of the moment compared to other autopsies, when he and Susan and Jimmy would chat sociably as they worked. But Sonny and Betsy seemed so down, and Susan and Jimmy matched their mood. No doubt, the days since the Haldemans' cadavers arrived at the morgue had been stressful on everyone. That a teenager had apparently killed himself was bad enough. That the teenager might have murdered his great-grandparents and then himself? Unthinkable.

"Before we get started," Susan said, "I can confirm Hunter's neck was broken, as Sonny and Betsy predicted."

Sonny and Betsy looked at each other, then back at Susan. Their eyes spoke volumes about their regret. Killing a perpetrator during a crime was one thing. But the guilt they must be feeling over the tragedy, whether or not Hunter had committed murder, had to be overwhelming.

"But," Susan continued quickly, apparently sensing their regret, "I don't think his broken neck had anything to do with his death. In my medical opinion, Hunter Dejarnette had been dead several hours before his neck broke."

Betsy and Sonny stared at each other, then at Susan. Betsy placed her hand on Sonny's arm.

"Are you sure?" Betsy said. "What—"

"I estimate Hunter's time of death at between eight and ten this morning, about five hours, and as many as eight hours, before you arrived at the Dejarnette residence," Susan said. "It's clear his cause of death was asphyxiation due to ligature strangulation and not hanging."

"I'm not sure I understand," Betsy said.

"It's a simple difference," Jonathan said, "but it's graphic and not very pleasant. In death by hanging, the weight of a dropping body pulling against a ligature, classically a rope, provides enough force to break the neck at a level that will snap the spinal cord and cause death in a few seconds. When hanging's done incorrectly, the force of the drop doesn't break the vertebrae, and the rope squeezes the neck arteries and windpipe, which results in death from asphyxiation. Death may take several excruciating minutes. Of course, strangulation can occur from anything that disrupts air or blood flow in the neck."

"What do you think happened here, Dr. Miller?" Sonny asked.

"Hunter," Susan said, "was strangled by a ligature being pulled tight around his neck. If you come closer, I can show you what we discovered."

Susan focused a light on the area around Hunter's neck, pointing to a continuous, linear discoloration around the full circumference of his throat.

"Detailed examination," she said, "revealed ligature marks around the neck from what appear to be two separate sources. The most noticeable one is about two inches in width. The pattern marks are consistent with the belt we removed from Hunter's neck—the belt Mr. and Mrs. Dejarnette identified as his favorite. We labeled this as Ligature Mark A. Lack of hemorrhaging leads me to conclude that Ligature Mark A was made postmortem."

Moving the magnifying lens, Susan pointed to another discolored area, this one narrower and showing a crisscross, or woven, pattern. The wider ligature mark, Ligature Mark A, masked the narrower one, but a crisscross pattern was plainly visible.

"As you can see, this second mark, referred to as Ligature Mark B, differs from the first," Susan said. "It's only about half as wide. And subcutaneous bleeding in a petechial pattern indicates Ligature Mark B formed while blood was still flowing. The pattern is consistent with many belts with a woven design. The kind without holes in the leather. That square mark on the side of the neck is most likely from the buckle. Whatever caused Ligature Mark B is what strangled Hunter Dejarnette."

"Dr. Miller," Betsy said, "are you telling us someone strangled Hunter Dejarnette and then tried to make it look like he hanged himself with his own belt?"

"I'm just presenting the autopsy results. But that is what I believe the evidence shows," she replied.

"I agree with Dr. Miller's assessment," Jonathan said. Someone wanted you and Betsy to think exactly what you were thinking earlier—that you broke Hunter Dejarnette's neck and killed him when you forced your way into his room."

Betsy stood, her expression still pained, and grabbed at her side. Jonathan exchanged a quick glance with the others. The tension evaporated when Betsy removed her now-vibrating cell phone and excused herself to take a call.

"So it appears we're looking for a real sick bastard," Jonathan said, as Betsy disappeared around the corner. "Susan, did Hunter's autopsy reveal any clues about *who* might have strangled him?"

"Not directly," Susan said. "There are some missing pieces. We can't make accusations at this point."

"Okay," Jonathan said, "what's missing?"

"First, we collected tissue and fluid samples for a tox screen. I'm most interested to see how much sedative was in his bloodstream. His level of sedation will help determine whether he would have been capable of hanging himself. Assuming Hunter was as heavily medicated as his parents say, someone else must have been involved.

"Second, we removed small pieces of leather from his neck. If we can locate the belt, perhaps we can make a match. Finally, there should be pieces of Hunter's skin in the belt used to strangle him. We took DNA samples from Hunter and can compare them with the belt, if we find it."

Betsy returned just as Susan mentioned, taking DNA samples. Betsy had a glazed, stunned look about her.

"Sonny, we need to return to the Dejarnettes'. It was Mitch Broussard on the phone. They just uncovered a garbage bag from Hunter's closet. Inside were a hoodie, a pair of jeans, and several towels, all covered in blood."

The group was silent for a moment. Jonathan looked at the face of the boy before him.

"I'm wondering whether we underestimated our fifteen-year-old." Sonny's voice was sad, tenuous.

"Regardless," Betsy said, "looks like we'll need to buy a Cube-O'-Java on the way. It's going to be another long night."

Chapter Forty-One: An Unannounced Visitor

Sunday, December 28, 2014

Jonathan exited the cab near the street-level entrance of their home on Bienville Street. Probably shouldn't rely on his usual "don't shoot" greeting. Best not to appear too flippant, given recent events. His call to Emma on their landline rolled over to voicemail. He speed-dialed her cell. Same result.

Perhaps she had gone to bed. But it was barely past nine o'clock. And all the lights were on. If Emma wasn't at home, where could she be? She was always so good about marking their family calendar, but there wasn't anything noted last time he checked. It wasn't the monthly Bingo Night for their Mardi Gras Krewe. No one would be there on a Saints game day, anyway.

Jonathan hadn't received any communication from Emma—not even a text—since he left the Superdome. Other possibilities? Not too many. But most were worrisome and foreboding, especially after what happened to Hunter. There was a killer on the loose. And what about whoever was in the blue Acura?

"Gray." The voice, almost a whisper, came from a dark area a few feet away.

"Fen." Jonathan matched the voice, speaking in a whisper. "Is that you?"

"Gray, thank God." The voice, still soft, was clearly Emma's. "Don't move. And don't look around. I think he sees you."

"Who? What?" Jonathan stood as still as possible. His heart almost stopped with worry. What in hell was so important that he couldn't move?

"I think it's Joe Haldeman," Emma said. "I recognize him from TV news."

"But how—"

"I went for a walk. On my way back, I saw him go into the street-level entrance. So I waited here. Then I saw him sitting at the bottom of the stairs like he was waiting for us to come home. I forgot my phone on the kitchen counter."

"How long has he been there?"

"About five or ten minutes."

"You armed?"

"Yeah," Emma said, a hint of sarcasm in her voice. "Learned my lesson with the blue Acura the other day."

"Okay, we can't just stand here. But if we leave, Joe might panic, and the police will never find him."

"So what do we do?"

"I don't want to show my pistol in public. Cover me with yours. But stay hidden. Don't let any pedestrians see your gun if you can help it."

"Okay. Be careful."

Jonathan moved closer to their door, leaving Emma a clear shot. "Who's there? What are you doing here? I'm Jonathan Gray, and this is my home. I'm going to call the police."

Slowly, the door opened, and Joe Haldeman emerged with his hands stretched out in front of him.

"Look, I'm not armed and I'm not here to hurt you. I'm Joe Haldeman. I'm here because I don't have anywhere else to go. I heard about my cousin, and I'm scared. Someone got to him. That same somebody can get to me."

"Fair enough." Jonathan studied him. "But why come here? You don't know me."

"I was too afraid to go to the cops. I don't know who to trust. And talk in the cellblock was that you were there when police questioned me. I don't know if I can trust *you*, either. But I had to do *something*. So I came here."

"How the hell did you find out where I lived?"

"Well," Joe said, "this town's not that big. And you're a public figure. It wasn't hard."

As Jonathan approached Joe, Emma emerged with her Glock visible at her side. "Stay where you are, Joe," he said.

Jonathan patted Joe down. No weapons.

Emma and Jonathan looked at each other. Without speaking, they seemed to agree.

"Upstairs," Jonathan said. "You first."

They proceeded with Joe in the lead. Once out of the public eye, Jonathan unholstered his handgun.

"Sorry if I startled you," Joe said. "All I ask is that you listen to what I have to say."

Jonathan directed Joe to their sofa. He sat down across from him—close enough to talk but far enough away so he'd have time to pull the trigger if Joe tried anything foolish. Emma left the living room but remained within view.

"Okay, Joe, let's have it. I'll warn you, I'm very skeptical. I'm aware you tried to visit Hunter after your release from custody."

"I understand, Dr. Gray. I don't blame you. But I just wanted to check that Hunter was okay. When I learned he'd been let go from the hospital, I got worried. Hunter had some problems and should have remained in protective care. I wish I were still at the jail. I don't know why they released me when they did. As much as I hated it, I was safe—or, at least, I thought I was."

Jonathan softened. He could understand that Joe would want to make sure his cousin was okay. Hadn't Jonathan felt the same urge earlier?

"Do you think he could kill your grandparents?"

"Never," Joe said. "I mean, physically, maybe. And Hunter's smart as a whip, in his own way." Joe stroked his beard. "But I've known him all his life. He's not violent, and he loved my grandparents. Maggie called him her Special Angel. I can't believe he would hang himself, either—especially with my father just downstairs."

"So what do you think happened?"

Joe looked straight at Jonathan. "Despite how the evidence might appear, I didn't *kill* my grandparents." He hesitated. Then it was as if a linguistic dam burst. His words came rapidly, gushing out, more stream of consciousness than organized discourse.

"It makes no sense. I mean, look at it. Someone diagnosed as emotionally disturbed. Then, suddenly ruled completely stable. He killed himself—but was calm enough to leave a suicide note? And under sedation? Me being released on a weekend? Why not wait until Monday morning, just before my probable cause hearing? It makes no sense."

"Perhaps," Jonathan said, "the district attorney wanted to do the right thing. You know, not hold an innocent man any longer than necessary."

"Or," Joe said, "someone with enough legal clout pressured him. You know, someone who might sit in judgment of future criminal cases on appeal."

Jonathan looked at his watch. "It's almost ten p.m. I didn't realize the details of Hunter's death were public knowledge."

Jonathan turned on their television. Text scrolling across the screen presented an ongoing message: "Exclusive...Breaking News...Exclusive..."

"In tonight's lead story," the announcer said, "we bring you grim news about a fifteen-year-old boy, who might have played an alleged role in his great-grandparents' deaths and who was found dead in his room this afternoon. Did he commit suicide, or was he a victim of a homicide himself? We take you live to the scene, where our investigation is unfolding."

With the Dejarnettes' camelback as a backdrop, a reporter described the same basic events Betsy Sprance had relayed earlier. But the reporter didn't interview any of the investigators or the official spokesperson for the police department. Rather, she referred to "highly placed persons" as her sources. She talked in vague generalities, without concrete details. Perhaps the most bizarre development was a news clip of Judge Haldeman standing next to his wife, reading a statement on behalf of his family.

"Hunter's death is a sad and shocking development for our family, as we still mourn for my mother and father. Hunter held a special place in their hearts. We're deeply saddened to learn the circumstances of his death. We ask you for your forbearance and to respect our privacy as we continue to mourn. Mrs. Haldeman and I appeal to our son, Joseph, to contact authorities as quickly as possible. Regardless of the circumstances, we love our son."

After Judge Haldeman finished his statement, he hugged his wife.

Jonathan turned the TV off. "Joe, I understand your concern. But I'm not sure what I can do for you."

"Dr. Gray, I have to trust you. You must have the right connections in the police department—connections that can keep me safe."

"I know a couple of people to call," Jonathan replied. "I'll do what I can."

Chapter Forty-Two: In the Bag

Sunday, December 28, 2014

Betsy and Sonny arrived together approximately twenty minutes later, along with two uniformed NOPD officers—Corporal Jividen and Officer Michaud from the night Robby died. After directing the quartet to the living area, Jonathan and Emma retreated to their kitchen to make coffee as the two investigators sat with Joe and questioned him about Hunter's death. Though he couldn't hear everything, Jonathan caught enough to confirm that Joe was repeating the same basic chronology and details he had related earlier.

"Joe, I'm not going to take you in for questioning," Betsy said. "But I want you to stay in town and keep us apprised of your whereabouts and how we can reach you. Here's my card and contact information."

"Can't you take me into protective custody?" Joe seemed near panic. His eyes darted around until they landed on Jonathan, who had returned to the living room. "Come on, Dr. Gray, talk to her. Please."

"Joe," Jonathan said, "this is a police matter now. And you're in excellent hands."

"I don't believe you're in any real danger," Betsy said, shooting a quick glance at Jonathan. "But I'll have Corporal Jividen and Officer Michaud drive you home and remain outside overnight. And if we get *any* inkling someone is trying to do you harm, we'll reconsider."

As the officers guided Joe toward the stairs, Betsy, Sonny, and Jonathan sat down.

"Jesus, Betsy." Jonathan sipped his coffee. "Can you tell me what I just lived through?"

"We don't think Joe Haldeman is a viable suspect," Betsy said. "Based on the autopsy results, we believe Hunter was strangled and his hanging was staged to cover up his murder, just as Dr. Miller suggested. From talking with Hunter's parents, we're aware of his sedation schedule. It seems highly improbable he had enough strength or mental acuity to hang himself or even to type a suicide note."

"What about the bag with clothing and towels?" Jonathan said.

"We're having it tested now," Sonny said, "but I'm still suspicious. Why would Hunter hide such damning evidence where it was certain to be found? And there's something very important missing."

"What?" Jonathan asked.

"If Hunter killed his great-grandparents," Sonny said, "there probably would be blood or gunshot residue on his hands, even this many days later." He paused. "But he had neither. Which means, if he was the killer, he must have worn gloves. We didn't find any gloves—or the jeweler's chasing hammer. Why would he keep the other clothes but not the gloves?"

"Perhaps," Jonathan said, "because they can lift fingerprints or locate DNA from inside the gloves—depending on the type. But it still seems odd that he would get rid of that damning evidence, but not the clothes."

"Exactly," Sonny said.

"Here's something else," Betsy said. "His door was locked from the inside. And we initially didn't notice it, but a pane of glass in his window had been cut. There was a circular pattern in the right area and dimensions to allow someone to reach through and unlock his window. Then they could exit when the job was done and lock the window. The glass was removed, and then the piece replaced and covered with a clear plastic film to make it appear intact."

"Footprints?" Jonathan said.

"It's been so dry lately, finding footprints wasn't easy. Thank goodness the Dejarnettes watered the flower beds around their house. We located a couple of very light prints and took molds," Betsy said. "They were common athletic shoe soles. We traced them to a pair of shoes tucked away behind some bushes in the Dejarnettes' backyard. Mr. and Mrs. Dejarnette identified them as Hunter's."

"So what you're telling me," Jonathan said, "is that someone wearing Hunter Dejarnette's shoes broke into his room, killed Hunter, planted a bag full of evidence, set the stage for a false hanging, and then exited, covering their tracks by repairing Hunter's window on the way out?"

"Something like that," Betsy said.

"Planning and execution seem too precise for an amateur," Jonathan said. The clock chimed eleven.

"Man," Betsy said, "looks like I imposed on your home and your hospitality once again."

"Don't give it another thought," Jonathan replied. "Say, do you have your tablet with the Haldeman family photos on it?"

"Yeah."

"Mind powering it up? There's a website you and Sonny might want to check. And I have some thoughts on the photos as well."

Chapter Forty-Three: The Floater

Monday, December 29, 2014

On Monday after Christmas, the city government complex was like a ghost town.

"Good morning, Vern," Jonathan said. Their office manager usually greeted him with enthusiasm and a broad grin. Today, she seemed less than happy. "I forgot how quiet it gets over the holidays. How was your Christmas?"

"Good morning, Dr. Gray." The corners of her mouth turned upward—almost a smile. "Christmas? Exhausting. All seven grandbabies visited. I had to come back to work for some peace and quiet. I need to rest up for New Year's Eve."

"Seven? I'm surprised you're still alive."

"Amen. Thank you. And Dr. Gray, did you hear about the shootings up in Gentilly?"

"Yeah. I caught the tail end of a radio report on the way to work. Any details?"

"Just what the scanner said. A drive-by on Franklin Avenue, just off I-10. Police think it's gang-related. They called for paramedics. There were two victims. Probable fatalities, but no confirmation."

"Thanks, Vern. Looks like we might have some more customers soon. I guess there'll be no rest for the weary this week either."

Jonathan moved past Vern's workstation and hastened to his office. Time to catch up on what he'd missed. Jonathan reached into his inbox and removed a single piece of paper with the heading "Coroner's Activity Report—12/27–28." The numbers seemed unbelievable. Over the past weekend, his office had performed two additional death investigations, responded to eight reported sexual assaults, and conducted nine mental health status examinations. If media reports about shootings in Gentilly were accurate, they could expect two more cadavers by noon.

But he couldn't lose sight of the big picture. The 10:00 a.m. meeting with the deputies—his first in his new leadership role—was more important than ever. As Coroner, he was the senior medical examiner for the city and parish. But his deputy coroners coordinated day-to-day operations: the autopsies, mental health commitments, and sexual assault examinations forming the three-pronged primary mission of the coroner's office. Without their cooperation and support, he would fail. Eventually, he would select another chief deputy—his old job—but not yet. It had been less than a week since he'd taken over. He needed to give it more thought. Still, the meeting loomed large.

So, shortly before 10:00, he headed for the conference room, thinking about all that had happened since Robby's death and worrying again about the deputies. Would they have the same affection for him as they'd had for Robby? Would he live up to Robby's example or fall flat on his face? Would they try to sabotage his efforts so they could lay the groundwork for their own election campaigns three years down the road?

Jonathan swallowed, though his mouth had suddenly gone dry.

Reaching for the doorknob of the conference room, he took a deep breath. He couldn't worry about those things. After all, he knew these deputies just as well as Robby had. Robby might have signed the final paperwork, but as chief deputy, Jonathan advertised for job vacancies, interviewed candidates, and recommended who should be hired. His concerns subsided at the sound of laughter from inside the conference room. High spirits—a good sign. As Jonathan entered, the conversation stopped.

"Good morning, all. Don't let me interrupt the revelry."

"Howdy, Jonathan." Leo Pearlman greeted him. "We've been discussing who got the worst of the holidays."

"How uplifting."

"Oh, it gets better," Leo said. "By unanimous vote of all present, we decided the award goes to you, with a score of four probable murders, two faux-suicides, one pissed-off appellate court judge, and a missing newspaper reporter."

Jonathan paused and stared at his three colleagues. He scowled, then broke into a smile.

"Of course, this means I have a bunch of underachieving med-school dropouts working for me. Once again, your boss has set the pace."

The group enjoyed a good laugh. They kidded him about what he had been through, but his entire office was busy and facing challenges as well. After the initial round of laughter subsided, Jonathan brought them back to their purpose.

"I know you all have plenty to do. And a couple of you took time out of your leave to be here. I appreciate the dedication. Especially with the extra turmoil over the holiday and Robby's death."

"Any word on his funeral?" Dr. Melançon asked.

"Good question, Cass. Jacki wants to wait until after the New Year. That way, as many of their children and grandchildren as possible can attend the service. No specific date yet. But I'm guessing this week on Friday. Or maybe over the weekend."

"Thanks."

"I wish I had more definitive news. But I know we'll send Robby off in style. He'd want it that way."

"How about Robby's replacement?" Cass asked. "Newspaper says there should be an election held this coming March." She hesitated, glancing at the other deputy coroners but never making eye contact with Jonathan. "But I thought the chief deputy took over for the balance of the term."

"Me too," Leo said. "But I'll bet you didn't call this meeting to talk about elections, did you?"

"Right." Jonathan glanced at Leo and nodded—a silent way of saying 'thanks for keeping things on track.' Why would Cass care? Especially now?

Perhaps it was starting already. Did she want his job? Her maiden name was Boudreaux, after all. She probably inherited her political savvy from her father. So much for a peaceful transition. For now, though, he couldn't worry about it. He had an office to run, murders to solve.

"I have two things I want to cover," Jonathan said. "First, as you so eloquently noted, my autopsies from last week have become a huge time drain. So I want to make sure I'm aware of what you're handling and that I'm providing whatever support you need. Second, I want to review our legislative proposal. I'm scheduled to meet with Senator Nichols tomorrow, and I want to send him a final draft today, if possible."

With that, they discussed completed and pending cases. Except for work on the Haldeman killings, it was routine fare for the busiest coroner's office in Louisiana.

"Ronnie," Jonathan said, "I see you followed up on the dead body in Old Muddy."

Dr. Rajamahendri "Ronnie" Mohan, Deputy Coroner for Forensic Examinations—the autopsies that were the bread and butter of their office— was the longest-serving of the three deputies.

"Correct," Ronnie said. "Police pulled a floater out near the Domino Sugar facility in Arabi."

"Arabi's in St. Bernard Parish," Jonathan said. "Did they give you any grief over taking jurisdiction?"

"Not really. There were questions about the exact location of the corpse and its origin. Our friends in St. Bernard were more than happy to let us take lead."

"Good," Jonathan said. "Any findings?"

"Cause of death, drowning, was easy enough to ascertain. But the body's swollen, and it also appears marine life nibbled at it, all of which makes visual identification more difficult. Police speculate the floater was a merchant seaman who fell overboard, and they're checking usual sources, like missing-persons reports, fingerprint databases, and port authority manifests."

"Interesting," Jonathan said. "Any first impressions?"

"I'm not convinced the floater engaged in manual labor, as a merchant seaman would've. Musculature and hands are more indicative of someone in a less physically demanding profession."

"Like a doctor, lawyer, or writer?" Jonathan asked.

"Perhaps." Ronnie shrugged. "Also, we just received a report of two corpses incoming from a drive-by shooting in Gentilly. Should be an eventful day in the morgue."

Leo Pearlman's case load was heavy but routine. He spent a fair amount of time complaining about Janine Dubois's decision to release Hunter Dejarnette from the hospital and advocating legislative changes to allow coroners to direct longer-term involuntary commitments.

"How about you, Cass?"

"Not much to report beyond the usual stuff. I've seen some positives from the use of certified Sexual Assault Nurse Examiner personnel and standards. I think we'd do well to talk about ensuring that our legislative package includes requirements for all personnel conducting sexual assault investigations and examinations to have some very basic training and, whenever possible, certification."

"Thanks. Your reports and recommendations provide an excellent transition to a quick discussion of our latest draft legislative proposal. My hope is for this legislation to strengthen our statewide coroner system. I included most of your comments in earlier drafts. I'll make a few adjustments based on today's inputs, then send the final version to Paul—Senator—Nichols."

Chapter Forty-Four: The Potter's Wheel

Monday, December 29, 2014

Jonathan sat at his desk proofreading what he hoped would be the final drafts of their legislative submission and his testimony before the Louisiana Senate Judiciary Committee "A." The work, though tedious, was important because it represented progress—baby steps, perhaps—toward his goal of improving the system. After what seemed like his millionth time poring over the words, Jonathan typed a brief forwarding email to Senator Nichols and his chief of staff, Elaine Devereaux, and hit Send.

It was a major item he could check off his to-do list. Yet it seemed that for each task he completed, two more appeared. There was so damned much to accomplish.

He had a couple of hours before his two o'clock meeting with Bryan Whitcomb. Plenty of time to swing by the Warehouse District. Then he'd grab a quick bite before his tête-à-tête with the reporter. He picked up his briefcase and inventoried the contents before walking out of his office toward the reception area.

"Vern, I need to check something out, and then I'm headed for Two Brothers'. I have a meeting right after. I should be back by three."

"Okay, Dr. Gray. Enjoy your lunch."

* * *

Molly Westcott's studio seemed unassuming enough. The only features distinguishing it from the other businesses in the block of refurbished brick warehouses on Constance Street were a storefront window displaying various pottery pieces and a large wooden sign announcing "The Potter's Wheel" in gold letters. An oval neon sign in the display window flashed the bright-red declaration: "Open."

As Jonathan walked through the door, a bell chime on the door tinkled. The structure's plain facade had belied the interior, which looked like a museum. Terra-cotta vases and other items of pottery lined nearly every available space. A cash register sat on a counter about twelve feet from the front door. Despite the cool late-December temperatures outside, the room was warm and smelled of clay curing in a kiln. An opening, covered by multiple strings of ceramic beads, masked what must be Molly's studio beyond.

"I will arrive to greet you momentarily." The voice, which came from the other side of the beads, sounded female, with a definite Hispanic accent. "Kindly make yourself comfortable, like you were at your home."

"Take your time," Jonathan said. "I'm in no hurry." Quite a falsehood given his upcoming lunch and his meeting with Bryan Whitcomb.

Some of the pottery appeared to be contemporary—or at least made within the twenty-first century. Other items, a fair number of them, were older. Much older. They looked like the ancient Mesoamerican pottery— Aztec, Incan, Olmec, and others—he had studied in college archaeology classes. God, that was over thirty years ago. Regardless, best not to touch anything. If he broke it, he probably couldn't afford to buy it.

An attractive girl, probably in her late teens, pushed the ceramic beads aside. She had jet-black hair. Given her physical features, she looked more like a model than the hired help in a pottery studio. No visible tattoos. It wasn't Molly.

"Good morning, señor. I am called Consuela. Señora Molly will appear to you soon."

"Thank you, Consuela. Are you a potter?"

Consuela blushed, her olive complexion darkening, especially her cheeks.

"Oh, no, señor."

She looked at the floor. "I help Señora Molly clean. Señora Molly, she teaches me English and manners."

"Oh, I see." Gray paused. "Where are you from?"

Consuela didn't make eye contact. Now she looked at the ceiling.

"I am from—"

"Thank you, Consuela." Molly entered the room. The beads in the doorway rattled as they parted, then came back together. "You may finish your work now."

"Yes, Señora Molly."

Consuela bowed her head, turned, and walked through the beads, into the other room.

"Hello, Dr. Gray," Molly said. "What brings you to the Potter's Wheel?"

Jonathan's face warmed. "Oh, I didn't realize you know who I am."

"Well, I might work with clay, but I read the news. And we met a few weeks ago at NOMA." She paused. "Besides, Joe's mentioned your name. I believe he came to see you earlier. Yesterday, wasn't it?"

He nodded. "Sounds about right. And I also recall seeing you at NOMA. *Rising Local Artists* exhibit."

"So, Dr. Gray, what brings the Coroner of Orleans Parish to my humble establishment?"

"I promise you, it's not about Joe."

"Oh? Perhaps you would like to buy a vase or a jug. Perhaps a set of coffee mugs?"

Damn it. He hadn't expected her to recognize him, so he hadn't come prepared with an explanation for being there. He couldn't exactly say that he was looking for clues in three murder investigations. Time to think on his feet. "Well, Miss Westcott—"

"Molly. Please call me Molly."

"Yes, of course. Well, Molly, Mrs. Gray, and I have a New Year's tradition."

"Oh, I see."

"We exchange presents at Christmas, of course. But our tradition is to greet the New Year with a gift as well. Something small, but meaningful

206

enough to remember the occasion. Nothing elaborate. Unfortunately, I've been so busy at work, I haven't had time to shop."

"I understand. How may we be of service?"

"You see..." Jonathan paused, as he searched for the right words, some nugget of truth to blunt his lie about what he was doing there. "I remembered your showing at NOMA a few weeks ago. I wondered whether you might have any handcrafted jewelry for sale. Earrings and such."

"No," Molly said. "I haven't branched out into jewelry. At least, nothing for commercial sale."

"Oh, okay. I figured as much once I saw your impressive display."

"Thank you, doctor. My collection is very extensive. I travel often to Central and South America to round out my inventory. Perhaps Mrs. Gray would enjoy an Aztec bowl."

"Perhaps another time." Jonathan pursed his lips, then smiled. "For the New Year, I should keep with something smaller, less expensive."

"Sorry, I can't help, Dr. Gray. Please have a wonderful New Year."

Jonathan turned and left the Potter's Wheel, hoping Molly hadn't caught on to his ulterior motive for dropping by. Adding two and two together—especially Molly's trips to Central and South America, bringing back ancient pottery and young, impressionable "models"—pointed to an uncomfortable conclusion. Regardless, he needed to be more inventive in covering his tracks. Maybe he'd do better at his two o'clock meeting.

Chapter Forty-Five: The Bench

Monday, December 29, 2014

His visit to Two Brothers' for lunch proved productive and delicious. A warm bowl of gumbo hit the spot. He said goodbye to the brothers and exited the café. He exhaled a slow, cleansing breath. "God, Robby, I hope I'm doing the right thing," he said softly to himself.

He neared a bench where a man wearing a baseball cap sat reading a newspaper. Whitcomb was apparently trying to hide his face. It wasn't much of a disguise, but it signaled that the reporter was worried about being recognized. Jonathan sat down, pulled out his phone, and acted like he was thumbing an email.

Whitcomb glanced up from his paper. "Good afternoon, Dr. Gray." He folded the paper and placed it beside him on the bench, as Jonathan had instructed him earlier. "I had hoped you would end up giving me a call. It means you've been doing some digging on your end."

Jonathan peered at him sideways. "When I called, I wasn't positive I wanted to talk with you or be seen with you. The more I've thought about it, the more I've convinced myself I should at least give you a chance. I have a lot of questions, and I think you're one of the few people who can help me get answers.

"I want to know why your car was following me and why it was following my wife—who has nothing to do with any of my official business. Also, I wanted to confirm you were alive—especially since the police pulled your car out of the Industrial Canal and because the *Times-Pic* says they haven't seen you."

Whitcomb nodded. "Got it. Well, here's my side. Frankly, I need your help. For eighteen months, I've been compiling evidence linking city hall to an ongoing criminal enterprise involving the importation of young females, mostly from Central and South America. The scheme involves holding their passports and threatening them with deportation until they pay back exorbitant customs fees, often by working as a maid or a hooker."

Jonathan bit his lip to avoid showing his surprise. He listened without comment or question and didn't interrupt. It sounded as if he might finally get the rest of the story.

"About two months ago, I finally felt I had enough information to write an article. I just needed some quotes from the victims. So I contacted the women. Every time I convinced one of them to come forward, she disappeared. It happened five times. Five women, all connected to the prostitution ring, all disappearing within hours of when they planned to make a formal statement."

Jonathan nodded. "And?"

"Let's start with Josefina Diaz. She's disappeared, too, along with her husband, but she's the only one who didn't seem to be involved in the human-trafficking operation. I believe she is still alive, and I've been hoping to talk with her."

"And you think I'm the one who can arrange an interview."

"That's right. I believe Josefina Diaz was the reason you visited St. Helen's Convent last week."

Hmm. Maybe Whitcomb *was* the one in the blue Acura.

"Why do you assert she isn't involved in the prostitution ring?"

"As far as I can tell, the mayor and his wife took an interest, an actual humanitarian interest, in helping Mr. Diaz bring Josefina from Guatemala. Everything was legitimate. She worked as a domestic in the mayor's home."

"So, all was going well in the mayor's house," Jonathan said. "But then something changed, I gather."

"And that something was Beau Jamerson," Whitcomb said. "Apparently, Beau believed part of his family privilege included carnal pleasure from their hired help. Beau is the mayor's son, and Josefina must have been afraid to say no to his advances. No doubt he threatened she'd lose her position and be deported."

Passports. Prostitution. The mayor's son was unable to keep his pants zipped around the domestic staff. Perhaps Whitcomb had additional evidence to bolster Josefina's claims.

"So it's entirely possible the mayor's son is guilty of rape?"

"That's right," Whitcomb said. "Beau somehow kept it from his parents for several months. But the mayor must have found out. I suspect Beau first showed an interest in playing football at the Air Force Academy shortly after his father discovered what had been going on."

"Interesting." No need to let Whitcomb know about the sworn declarations Eduardo and Josefina had signed at St. Helen's Convent. At least not yet.

"Very."

"At the risk of sounding callous," Jonathan said, "how does this theory relate to my office? And what of your blue Acura, which someone used to follow me, my colleagues, and my wife?"

"I'm convinced," Whitcomb said, "everything was fine until Mrs. Jamerson found out about her son and Josefina. She must have been afraid Josefina might expose her husband—and the family—to a scandal. I'm sure she didn't want her precious Beau behind bars. How else to explain Beau's last-minute acceptance to the Air Force Academy?"

"Again, very interesting. I assume you have evidence to back up your theory. And don't think I haven't noticed you've neglected to tell me who was tailing us and why."

Whitcomb sighed. "Two goons from the mayor's police detail stole my car from outside my place in the Bywater. I have photos of them doing it. I think they took my car to intimidate me."

"And pretended to be you when they reported it stolen?"

"That's right."

"And they would do that, why exactly?"

"Does it matter?" Whitcomb shrugged. "Maybe to make it look like I was in Biloxi all along. What matters is that they didn't realize I had my Acura rigged with a GPS transmitting device. I have an electronic map of where they drove my car. For example, I knew my car went from near your office downtown to St. Helen's on the day after Christmas."

"And you just assumed—"

"I'm an investigative journalist. I get paid to put two and two together." Jonathan nodded.

"So I made an educated guess that you and your staff must have gone to the convent. And it's why I didn't report the theft. I wanted to see why they took my car. There's the story."

"Yes, I see. And we were being followed because Max Jamerson wanted to keep tabs on us?"

"That's my guess. Perhaps they wanted to flush me out as well. When the car got stolen, I went underground as much as possible."

"Well. I can understand why you haven't gone to NOPD. What I don't understand is why you haven't broken the story about the mayor in the *Times-Pic* yet."

"It's scheduled to run in this Sunday's broadside, but I think management's been getting pressure, so they're holding off until we can tie up a couple of loose ends."

"Like DNA evidence from Josefina?"

"Correct."

"In the meantime, you're on the run from the mayor's goons."

"Yeah." Whitcomb glanced around as if checking for surveillance. "Exactly. But I'm desperate for a breakthrough. Now you know why I took a chance when you called."

"Mr. Whitcomb, before I agree to help, I insist on two promises. You can't publish anything I tell you until at least Saturday, and you can't divulge your source."

"Okay, Dr. Gray. You have my word."

Chapter Forty-Six: The List

Monday, December 29, 2014

Jonathan reached into his briefcase and pulled out a copy of the current edition of the *Times-Picayune*. Tucked inside was a single file folder. He put the newspaper on top of the one already on the bench. Jonathan then removed the newspaper left on the bench by Whitcomb and put it in his briefcase. Finally, he took a single sheet of printer paper out of his briefcase and placed it on the bench.

"Recognize the names on this list?"

Whitcomb's forehead wrinkled, and his eyes narrowed. His head shook back and forth, signaling what must have been his internal debate about the document's contents. He exhaled loudly. Then his eyes widened and his face lost color, as if he had seen a ghost. After several seconds of silence, his lips moved, but no words came out. Finally, Whitcomb looked up and stared at Jonathan.

"How the hell did you know?" Whitcomb pointed to the list. "These are the women I talked to who went missing."

"Inside the newspaper I just put on the bench," Jonathan said, "is a file folder with copies of five death certificates. One for each name on the list. I haven't established why, but it appears no one filed them at the Vital Records Registry. Don't read them now. But when you do, you'll see that four of the women died from strokes allegedly induced by a cocaine overdose. All four within the past sixty days."

"Seems like a rather strange coincidence. Whitcomb sounded sarcastic. "What about the other one?"

"The fifth woman," Jonathan said, "the most recent victim, died just a little over a week ago. A bomb exploded in her car. Robby O'Malley performed autopsies on all five."

"This is all very disconcerting, Dr. Gray."

"You don't know the half of it yet," Jonathan said. "Brace yourself."

"All right. Let's hear it." Whitcomb leaned toward Jonathan.

"Let's talk about our four stroke victims first," Jonathan said. "A cocaine overdose can cause a stroke. So I pulled the working papers. Cause of death in each was a stroke—that's one fact I can confirm with confidence. And there was cocaine in each woman's blood. But not as much as expected. Usually, much higher amounts are required to cause a stroke. Or, at least, much higher amounts are usually associated with causing a stroke.

"There's something else I found in all four cocaine-related autopsies. Each cadaver had faint contusions in the upper chest, upper back, and neck. In any individual case, the marks might not get much notice. Especially considering the cocaine. But four together reveal a pattern not to be ignored."

"Okay, Dr. Gray, you've got me hooked."

"Mr. Whitcomb. Have you ever heard of stroke by chiropractor?"

"Are you saying a chiropractor killed these women?"

"Not exactly. A stroke results when an artery to the brain ruptures after the artery stretches too much or becomes blocked by a blood clot. But several studies show a causal connection between strokes and certain types of neck manipulation, whether done by a chiropractor, an osteopath, a physical therapist, or anyone else with the right skills and knowledge— though the science isn't fully accepted. The mechanism is simultaneously basic and complicated.

"Go online and find a video showing how chiropractors manipulate the upper neck. They place their hands on the patient's head and rotate the skull to adjust the cervical spine—and they do so with extreme caution because too extreme a movement can damage the patient's blood vessels.

"The vertebral artery is most susceptible because of how it winds around the upper cervical vertebra. Any abrupt movement, even a gentle rotation, can stretch an artery or tear its delicate lining. If a blood clot forms, it may dislodge and flow into one of the smaller blood vessels, stopping blood from getting to the brain. What can also happen is that an artery gets blocked, forming a pool of blood. Stress eventually causes the vessel wall to weaken and burst, resulting in a massive hemorrhagic stroke."

"So," Whitcomb said, "you think someone manipulated these four women's necks and caused them to stroke out? And they killed the last one in her car?"

No longer leaning toward Jonathan, Whitcomb sat silently. His dazed look left little doubt—he wasn't sure what to make of this fresh evidence.

"Because each of them had been talking to you, Mr. Whitcomb, I surmise it was someone who wanted to prevent their statements from coming to light."

No reaction yet. Whitcomb stared into the distance, his eyes fixed on something that only he could see—or maybe nothing at all.

"You need to be *very* careful." Jonathan lowered his voice and slowed his pace to emphasize the seriousness of his revelation. "The strokes didn't result from a medical examination gone awry... Someone who is extraordinarily skilled and well-practiced made them happen...purposefully."

Finally, Whitcomb looked Jonathan in the eyes.

"Just think," Jonathan said, "about how much self-discipline and strength it takes to move the vertebra just far enough to stretch an artery without breaking the neck. All while subduing the victim, who was probably fighting for her life. That's the complicated part."

Jonathan leaned closer to Whitcomb. Time to hit him across the forehead, figuratively.

"As for our last victim, Esperanza Morales? The bomb was very small, like someone designed it personally for her."

Jonathan paused, waiting for a reaction. Was it possible Whitcomb hadn't connected Josefina and Esperanza after such a long investigation?

"There was very little collateral blast damage. So whoever is directing these actions—assuming it's just one person—has stopped trying to mask their intentions by killing in a way that could be interpreted as an accident. Could be a sign of desperation. Or, confidence no one will care."

After so many dead ends, the wealth of information Jonathan shared should have had Whitcomb turning cartwheels. Yet he simply sat there, again staring into the ether. Perhaps he was still in shock. Or perhaps he was afraid to tackle the story now that he knew the women he thought had disappeared had instead been murdered. And that in four cases, the killer was savvy enough to stage the deaths to appear like drug overdoses. Still, his lack of a stronger reaction was unusual.

"Dr. Gray." Whitcomb head canted to his left, and his lips moved, without saying anything, as if searching for the right words. After several seconds of silence, he spoke. "I'm not sure how to respond to all this."

"Well, Mr. Whitcomb, I assume that after I leave, you'll take the *Times-Pic* from the bench and move to a safe location. Once you're where no one can see, you'll open the folder and read the death certificates. Armed with this new information, you will, I hope, follow your training and instincts as an investigative journalist."

Jonathan stood. The reporter looked up at him, clearly overwhelmed.

"Good afternoon, Mr. Whitcomb. And good luck. Remember, nothing before Saturday."

Chapter Forty-Seven: Switching Gears

Monday, December 29, 2014

Jonathan moved away from the park, still perplexed about Robby's connection to the five death certificates and Whitcomb's investigation. He hadn't told the reporter Robby had similar marks on his chest, back, and neck. Perhaps now was his opportunity to revisit his autopsy findings and go public. But Jacki and the children didn't need the additional pain of a murder investigation or political scandal. Jonathan should leverage Whitcomb's desperation for a story to see what he could uncover.

Jonathan's cell phone vibrated. "Good afternoon, Betsy. How are you?"

Betsy cleared her throat and sniffled as if she had a cold. "Fine."

"Speaking as a physician, you sound less than fine. Did you get any sleep after we talked last night?"

Betsy tried to justify her exhaustion by noting that Sonny had been up all night, too. "Well, I hope you know you can't keep up this pace."

"Got it," Betsy said. "That's a big reason I called. Sonny and I think we're close to having enough to present a case and obtain an arrest warrant in both the Haldeman and Dejarnette murders."

"Outstanding," Jonathan said. "How can I help?"

"I'm reluctant to say anything else over the phone. Can you come by the Sixth District so we can run some ideas past you? We want you to be our sounding board to review test results and other evidence."

"Fine," Jonathan told her. "Let me call Jimmy and have him gather our files. We should be there around three-thirty."

Chapter Forty-Eight: The War Room

Monday, December 29, 2014

Now came Jonathan's turn to venture into Betsy's natural habitat, the Sixth District Police Station. Not very appealing, architecturally. A drab exterior, nothing fancy. Certainly not a waste of taxpayers' dollars. Emma might make up a description like "a prime example of the Neoclassical Cinderblock School of Design" to add a splash of culture. Regardless, the building seemed right at home in the working-class neighborhood surrounding the intersection of Martin Luther King Boulevard and South Rampart.

The desk sergeant appeared calm, almost blasé, as if a visit by the coroner and one of his assistants was an everyday event. He nodded and spoke, even before Jonathan and Jimmy could introduce themselves.

"Second floor, Doc. Stairs are on the left past the vending machines. They're waiting for you in Conference Room Two."

Conference room wasn't an appropriate description. *War room* might be more accurate. It looked like something between a noir detective thriller and the Fifth Fleet's high-tech Combat Information Center from Jonathan's Navy deployments. There were charts, diagrams, photographs, and assorted other documents attached to the walls or on whiteboards scattered at various locations. Three whiteboards labeled "Judge," "Joe," and "Hunter" occupied the wall to the right of the conference table. They each had three subcategories describing standard investigative areas: "Motive,"

"Opportunity," and "Physical Links to the Crime." Each category had lines of text. Some had more text than others.

"Man, oh, man," Jimmy said. "You two have been busy beavers."

"No shit, Sherlock," Sonny said. "Someone's got to do the work."

"All right, you two," Betsy said. "One team, one fight—right?"

No response from either Jimmy or Sonny, except for some silent nods and reddened faces. Betsy shifted her attention to Jonathan.

"Thank you two for coming so quickly, Doc. We think we're at critical mass, and we want your input."

"We're here to do what we can," Jonathan said. "But it looks like you've done a lot of work on your own. This is a pretty sophisticated setup."

"Superintendent Bondurant opened the checkbook," Betsy said. "I think she heard the mayor loud and clear: solve this one quickly, or else." She sighed. "Much of what we've done is compile the evidence you provided from the autopsies. A lot of what we think might lock up the case is based on the suggestions you made last night."

"So where do we begin?" Jonathan said.

"As you can see," Betsy said, "we decided not to narrow our field of suspects, despite Hunter's death."

"Hunter was never a strong suspect," Sonny said. "And his death seemed to validate our conclusion. But we're concerned the case against Hunter was *too* easy. So we want to see how the evidence against him holds up when compared to other suspects."

"Fair enough," Jonathan said. "Let's get started."

They turned their attention to the whiteboards with summaries of evidence under each category and suspect. The smallest amount of writing was associated with Joe Haldeman.

"Joe's the perfect suspect in a lot of ways," Betsy used a laser pointer to highlight his name and the text under each column. "But the evidence is too indirect, too circumstantial. Sonny, you mind giving us the full skinny on Joe?"

"Sure." Sonny accepted the laser pointer from Betsy but didn't use it. "Joe had a powerful motive to kill his grandparents. Jesus, nearly a million bucks from the trust fund and tontine at stake. Seems pretty damning, if you ask me. And we know he was angry with Hunter for causing the fight with Judge Haldeman."

Sonny pointed his finger at the "Opportunity" column on the whiteboard dedicated to the evidence against Joseph Haldeman. "Joe had obvious opportunities to kill his grandparents and his cousin. Joe admitted he was in the Haldemans' house before the murders. And we have eyewitnesses who saw Joe come to the Dejarnettes' house on Sunday morning, not long after Hunter was released from the hospital. Maybe Joe waited until the Dejarnettes left for church, then broke into Hunter's room and strangled him."

"Sonny," Jonathan said, "I see one thing I haven't heard about before. Under all three names it says, "Surveillance Camera Footage." What's that? I mean, I know what surveillance camera footage is. But how's it relevant here?"

Sonny placed the laser pointer on a table. "We retrieved footage from forty-eight surveillance cameras covering likely routes from Judge Haldeman's house to his parents' and between there and the trolley stop at St. Charles and Sixth Street that seemed connected to our investigation."

"Thought there'd be more," Jimmy said.

"You'd think," Sonny replied. "We also checked for footage between Molly's studio and the Dejarnettes' house. So far, we've located a few of interest, six or seven, I think. And we're still canvassing the area."

"And I take it the footage either exonerates Joe or at least doesn't incriminate him," Jonathan said.

"True dat, Doc," Sonny said. "That's our conclusion, anyway. One camera was on Commander's Palace, near one route between the judge's house and Bill and Maggie's place. It had two clips. First one shows Joe walking toward Bill and Maggie's. Second one, about forty-five minutes later, shows Joe walking back carrying a brown-paper bag."

"Probably the whiskey Joe said Bill Haldeman gave him," Jonathan said.

"Most likely," Sonny replied. "Timing fits with Joe's story. Camera footage also shows Joe across the street from Commander's Palace, sitting against the cemetery's wall, drinking from whatever was in the bag. Then a security guard came and talked to Joe. He got up and walked away."

"We interviewed several people at the restaurant," Betsy said. "They confirmed they often find people lingering nearby and ask them to leave. They also confirmed the second person in the footage was an employee. Unfortunately, he couldn't provide a conclusive ID on Joe. Said they get a lot of drunks sleeping along the cemetery wall."

"Next images are from cameras at an apartment building across from Christ Church Episcopal," Sonny said. "There's a figure on the steps to a side entrance. Same stature and clothing as Joe. And it's about the same time Joe said he was there. The figure appears to fall asleep, wake up, and then walk toward the streetcar stop on St. Charles. Finally, here's footage showing Joe, or someone of similar build and clothing, near the front entrance of Molly's studio."

"Everything seems to support Joe's version of events," Jonathan said. "And he certainly has a knack for being in range of security cameras at critical times. I assume the tests you performed were not incriminating."

"That's right, Doc," Sonny replied. "Lab results confirmed the stains on Joe Haldeman's clothing were wine and not blood. And there wasn't any gunshot residue on his clothes or his hands."

"Seems pretty airtight in Joe's favor," Jimmy said, "at least for the Haldeman killings. How about for Hunter Dejarnette?"

"Other than Hunter's parents and Judge and Mrs. Haldeman saying Joe was there," Sonny said, "we can't link Joe to Hunter's murder. We don't have *any* physical evidence."

"And the video evidence isn't conclusive," Betsy said. "There's video footage showing Joe and Molly in front of her studio just before ten a.m. Molly's BMW must be in back. We didn't find any working cameras covering the rear entrance."

"Peculiar, don't you think?" Jonathan said. "Convenient as hell, anyway."

"I suppose," Betsy said. "Given drive time from the Dejarnettes' house to the Warehouse District and estimated time of death, Joe could have killed Hunter and made it back to Molly's. But the footage doesn't show anyone leaving Molly's studio until late afternoon, when it looks like Joe bolted, almost at a run."

"Which is around the time Joe heard about his cousin," Jonathan said. "At least, according to Joe."

"Right. So I figured we should look at Hunter Dejarnette next." Betsy retrieved the laser pointer. "His death seems both the simplest and the most mysterious. The question, of course, is whether it was suicide or murder."

"I thought the evidence pointed to murder and not suicide," Jonathan said.

"It did and still does," Betsy said. "Along with what we knew last night when we talked, we've developed a couple of other pieces of evidence shoring up our view about Hunter's murder. This latest evidence also gives us additional clues about the weapon and the killer. First, his tox screen."

Betsy aimed her laser pointer at the results of the blood analysis.

"A pretty high level of sedation," Jonathan said. "But probably not enough to incapacitate him. Most likely, he wouldn't have been able to hang himself, though we can't rule it out."

"Exactly," Sonny said. "Our conclusion as well."

"Still, I guess the numbers surprise me," Jonathan said. "I thought surely, he'd be incapacitated. Still, when coupled with the ligature marks Dr. Miller showed us, I think the most probable conclusion is that Hunter Dejarnette was strangled and then set up to look like he hanged himself."

"And your hint last night might have led us to who killed Hunter," Betsy said.

Jonathan's cell phone chirped. He looked at the caller ID. "Gotta take this." He put the phone to his ear as he opened the door and exited the room. "Jonathan Gray." The door closed behind him.

Chapter Forty-Nine: Occam's Razor

Monday, December 29, 2014

"Sorry," Jonathan said as he reentered the room after about two minutes. "I guess Max Jamerson's getting heat." He rolled his eyes. "Needed some assurance that the investigation's moving forward."

Betsy exhaled. "Bet I'll be getting a call from Polly Bondurant soon."

"Probably," Jonathan said. "Wouldn't worry too much. I think I talked Max off the ledge."

"Great," Betsy said. "I'd suggest giving him a push next time, but—"

"Tempting." Jonathan smiled. "Now, where were we?"

"Well," Betsy said. "As you suggested, we magnified the family photos from the Haldemans' holiday party. We can show Judge Haldeman was wearing a belt with the same pattern as the ligature marks Dr. Miller identified as the mechanism of strangulation. The buckle's the right shape. Then, we checked the Banks Brothers catalogue, as you suggested. We located a similar belt, so we contacted them. They provided a printout of items bought through their online or call-in ordering systems.

"The list showed various purchases of ties, belts, and such the judge sent as gifts. But most relevant here, we confirmed Judge Haldeman ordered belts matching the ligature pattern online about six months ago, and again just a few weeks ago. We also picked up one at the Banks Brothers on Canal Street. The pattern and buckle are identical to the ligature mark."

"Did you find any similar belts at the judge's house?" Jimmy said.

"No," Betsy said. "We were still conducting our search, so we seized all the belts we could find. There were a couple that were close. But neither matched the ligature marks. And neither had any skin or other DNA on them, which we believe should be the case if they were used to strangle Hunter."

"Have you allowed the Haldemans to go back home yet?" Jonathan said.

"Not yet, Doc," Betsy said. "But we catalogued everything they packed for the hotel. There weren't any belts, except for the one Judge Haldeman was wearing."

"Which might be the murder weapon," Sonny said.

"And that," Betsy said, "is why we haven't released the house and still have crews there digging up the yard. We want him to believe our search is still active. If we can make a strong enough case, we plan to arrest Judge Haldeman tomorrow, before he can get home and find out we're looking for his belt."

"Aren't you afraid he'll just get rid of his belt and buy a new one?" Jimmy said.

"It's a concern," Betsy said, "but we believe he's worried we have him under surveillance and won't want to risk ordering one online or going to the store where someone might recognize him."

"Okay," Jonathan said. "And we know Judge Haldeman had an opportunity to kill Hunter, because he was alone in the house with him for two and a half hours while Kathleen Haldeman accompanied the Dejarnettes to church. But if you can't connect his belt to the crime, what other evidence do you have to link Judge Haldeman?"

"We researched the cases Judge Haldeman prosecuted, defended, or presided over as a judge," Sonny said. "We identified several involving techniques similar to Hunter's murder. While he was a district attorney, Judge Haldeman prosecuted four murder cases where means of death was strangulation using a belt or similar item. And one murderer tried to cover his tracks by making it look like his victim hanged himself. The jury bought it and acquitted the defendant."

"Which would embolden Judge Haldeman to try a similar trick, I assume,"

Jonathan said.

"Affirmative," Sonny said. "And we found several cases involving thieves breaking into homes with glass cutters and patching windows so no one would notice."

"I can see a circumstantial case building against Judge Haldeman," Jonathan said, "but what about the footprints outside Hunter's window? Don't the footprints point to someone breaking *in*?"

"There are a couple of things to know, Doc," Betsy said. "In our experience, thieves often put tape or other polymer film on the window to hide the entry hole. More and more, they've figured out how to cover both the inside and outside to make it look consistent.

"Here, the covering was only on the outside. That points to a less practiced burglar. And from the plaster casts we took, it appears whoever made the prints put a lot more weight on the heels. Which likely means that the perpetrator backed out of the window. We also found indentations consistent with a small bag being placed on the ground. But, like I said, the impressions weren't deep."

"So," Jonathan said, "your theory is that Judge Haldeman killed Hunter, cut the window to make it look like a break-in, left through the window, and then repaired it to appear as if the burglar was covering his tracks. And the bag was where he kept his tools."

"Bingo." Betsy's face contorted into more of a frown than a smile. "Of course, it's circumstantial unless we can connect Judge Haldeman's belt to Hunter's neck. But it's one of the stronger circumstantial cases I've had. I've seen our DA win with a lot less. Then again, those cases weren't against a sitting judge from a well-known family. And there are other pieces as well, like the judge's apparent involvement in getting a guardian ad litem for Hunter and the potential influence of his wife in getting Hunter released early."

"So," Jonathan said, "Hunter would be out of the hospital and sedated at home when the judge offered to babysit while his wife went to church with the Dejarnettes."

"Right again," Betsy said.

"But I didn't hear any mention of motive, Detective Sprance," Jimmy said. "You've shown Judge Haldeman had the opportunity, and you've linked him to the murder, sort of. But why would Judge Haldeman kill his parents? And why would he kill his nephew? We know the judge won't gain from the insurance payoff like Joe will."

"Very astute, Jimmy," Betsy replied. "The more we've peeled back the onion on our good judge, the darker it gets."

"Okay," Jimmy said. "And?"

"We have two potential theories on motive," Betsy said. "First, Hunter knew Judge Haldeman was culpable in his parents' death, and Judge Haldeman was afraid Hunter would turn him in. The other, and more plausible, one deals with the value of real estate in the Garden District."

"Very interesting," Jonathan said. "How so?"

"Bill and Maggie Haldemans' house is one of the bigger, fancier ones in the area. The most recent appraisal was slightly over two million dollars. Garden District houses often sell for far above their appraised price.

"Not quite five years ago, Judge Haldeman loaned his parents $250,000 and in return received a right of first-refusal option to purchase their house for another $250,000 if they sold it anytime within the next five years. At the end of the five years, he could buy the house for an additional $250,000. The only condition was that his parents could stay in the house rent-free for as long as they lived.

"But if they died before the option ran out, Judge Haldeman's loan would get paid out of the estate, and he'd lose his option to buy. He would get his loan paid, with interest, but it would shoot his potential profit to hell."

"Let me guess," Jimmy said. "The five-year period ends soon."

"January fifteenth," Betsy replied. "About two weeks away."

"So," Jimmy said, "Judge Haldeman lost his opportunity to make over a million and a half dollars on the net proceeds because he wasn't able to exercise his purchase option."

"Affirmative," Betsy said.

"Which means," Jimmy said, "he had a vested interest in his parents staying alive—at least for the next two weeks—and would have been upset at anyone who killed them and messed up such a sweet deal."

"Correct again," Sonny said. "That's the view we're leaning toward. But there's also a sinister twist we've been considering."

Betsy picked up the video player's remote control.

"Look at this security footage from about four blocks away from Bill and Maggie's residence," she said. "According to the time stamp, it's very close to the probable time of their murders. It's grainy, but it's the best we've got."

Several vehicles appeared on the screen, traveling in front of the camera. Betsy stopped the video. "See the SUV moving left to right?"

After an affirmative response from the group, Betsy hit the slow-motion button. "And here comes a BMW toward the camera from right to left. And now, a pickup following from the same direction as the SUV—left to right."

Betsy paused the video again. "Okay, focus on the upper-right corner. That's where the sports car just came from."

A figure wearing a hoodie and carrying a shoulder bag entered the frame from the upper-right corner, moving from right to left.

"Jesus," Jonathan said. "Is that Hunter?"

"We can't be sure," Betsy said. "We haven't been able to enhance the image enough. Could just be coincidence. Lots of people wear hoodies. But the time stamp is within the two-hour window after Hunter left the party."

The figure stopped at a dumpster, barely within the camera's field of view. The figure reached into the shoulder bag and dropped a couple of small packages into the trash. The figure, head down, moved out of view.

"Package doesn't look large enough to be clothes or towels," Sonny said. "We believe it might be gloves and the jeweler's chasing hammer. We've already contacted the sanitation company to see if we can find out where they took the dumpster's contents."

"And it might be nothing," Betsy said. "But we at least need to run it to ground."

"So let me understand this," Jonathan said. "You're suggesting that Hunter killed his great-grandparents? What the hell, Betsy? Multiple people have said that Hunter adored them."

"Who knows how susceptible the kid was?" Sonny said.

"Still," Jonathan said. "I mean—"

"Well, we don't think he acted alone," Betsy said. "What we're suggesting is that Judge Haldeman enlisted Hunter Dejarnette to kill Bill and Maggie. Then the judge was angry because Hunter acted too soon, before the judge could benefit from the loan. So he killed Hunter, not only to cover up the conspiracy and crime but also to punish Hunter for the real estate deal gone bad."

Jonathan shook his head. "That would also mean that the judge was willing to throw his own son under the bus to take heat off himself. Right?"

"You catch on quick, Doc." Betsy's voice was tired but determined. "We plan to make our formal presentation to the district attorney tomorrow."

"I don't know," Jonathan said slowly. "Still sounds far-fetched to me. You ever heard of Occam's razor?"

"Yeah, maybe…" Betsy's eyebrows peaked, and her forehead wrinkled.

"Well," Jonathan said, "it's a scientific principle called the Law of Parsimony. We use it in medicine to help us figure out a diagnosis when presented with multiple symptoms."

"Come on, Doc," Sonny said. "In English."

Jonathan smiled and nodded. "Yeah, okay. It means you shouldn't overcomplicate things. When faced with competing explanations, the simplest answer is likely the most accurate."

"So, we're overthinking Judge Haldeman's involvement?" Betsy asked. "And Hunter's?"

"It just seems like such a stretch," Jonathan said. "Especially given Joe's motive from the tontine payout. And have you given much thought to Molly Westcott?"

"Not really. What about her?"

"Not sure I can say, exactly." Jonathan shrugged. "It seems like she's hovering out there on the edges. Not a suspect. I visited her pottery studio and—"

"Okay. So you visited her studio—" Betsy's voice sounded distant, as if she couldn't fathom Jonathan's meaning.

"Well, I just thought we might want to talk more about her—"

"Later. There's a lot on my plate right now."

Betsy seemed rather dismissive.

"On another note," Betsy said, "the DA let it slip that he has a critical piece of information from a report filed by C. Bosworth Tipton. Didn't mention Molly's involvement."

"Does it concern his involvement with Hunter Dejarnette as his guardian ad litem?"

"I believe so," Betsy said.

"Hmmm," Jonathan said. "I guess it would change things if Hunter knew who killed his great-grandparents and told Tipton."

"Definitely," Betsy said. "But the DA didn't provide any details, so we're presenting our case based only on the evidence our two offices have developed. If the DA approves, we'll issue our arrest warrant on Wednesday and bring the good judge in for questioning. I'm sure the DA wouldn't let us proceed if Tipton's evidence didn't implicate Judge Haldeman."

"Makes sense," Jonathan said.

"So," Betsy said, "we might find out what tune His Honor sings once he understands he's facing indictment for three capital offenses."

"Pretty high stakes," Jonathan said.

Betsy nodded, then looked at Jimmy and Sonny. "Say, Doc, you think I could chat with you alone for a sec?"

Sonny and Jimmy exchanged glances, then quickly exited and closed the door.

"Okay, Betsy," Jonathan said. "What's up?"

"I contacted Mandy Simpson in the US Attorney's Office. She's agreed to talk with us Friday morning at ten about the other matter we discussed. I didn't give her a lot of details over the phone. I'll meet you at her office a few minutes before."

"Got it, Betsy. And thanks. I'll be there."

As Jonathan turned to leave, he paused. "Oh, I had another thought about Judge Haldeman. Sorry I didn't mention it earlier."

"That's fine, Doc. What's on your mind?"

"I saw Judge Haldeman at the Saints game on Sunday. Hunter was probably already dead. Given today's discussion, I was wondering whether he might have dumped the evidence somewhere at the stadium. So many people. So much garbage. I can only imagine what gets thrown away."

"Good tip," Betsy said. "Now, if you'll excuse me, I need to call Mitch Broussard."

Jonathan gathered his case file and turned toward the door. On his way, he couldn't hear everything Betsy said to Mitch. One part of their conversation he heard clearly, however, was "—that's right, the Superdome."

Chapter Fifty: Disappointment

Tuesday, December 30, 2014

Jonathan sat on the second-floor gallery just after seven-thirty in the morning and stifled a yawn. Then he blew on his steaming cup of coffee and took a sip. Still hot, almost unbearable, but he needed the caffeine after another restless night. Up early again, he had already completed a predawn run through the French Quarter. Fortunately, there was enough light—from streetlamps and glowing neon signs—to illuminate the maze of potholes in the street and portions of the sidewalk that were cracked or buckled, forming trip hazards for inattentive pedestrians and joggers. No need to add a twisted knee or broken ankle to his other problems.

Emma apparently had the same idea about exercising. The steady rhythm of the rowing machine's fan mechanism echoed from their home gym. She was really giving the machine a workout. Surely, she couldn't keep up the pace much longer. At least there was no danger of her falling head over heels after tripping on a pothole.

Another sip of coffee. Cooler now, still hot but drinkable.

It hadn't been the eighteen-month-old drive-by victim or Beatrice invading his sleep. It was everything else. He had so many irons in the fire. So many things coming at him from all directions. The Haldeman murders. Hunter Dejarnette's questionable suicide. Esperanza Morales, one of five unfiled death certificates. Judge Haldeman. Beau Jamerson and his possible sexual misconduct. Crazy. When would it let up? And he was still working to reform the system. Surely his lunch meeting with Paul Nichols would help him turn the corner and gain control over events.

And Betsy. Important matters—critical to solving the Haldeman murders—weighed in the balance. But thoughts of Betsy and the homicide squad dumpster diving and foraging through trash cans at the Superdome presented a humorous image. Unsavory, perhaps, but down-in-the-weeds investigating to locate a piece of critical evidence often meant the difference between a conviction and an acquittal. Betsy's work wasn't much different from his own as coroner in that respect.

Jonathan sipped his coffee. His phone buzzed and vibrated.

"Jonathan Gray."

He listened and nodded.

"Thanks, Jimmy. That's quick. Sounds like concentrating on the Department of Defense DNA database paid dividends. I'll grab a shower and be there as soon as I can."

Shortly after nine, Jonathan was in the conference room in the coroner's administrative office in city hall, sitting across from Jimmy and reading test results. Jimmy sat without comment as Jonathan made notes on his copies. After several minutes, Jonathan looked up.

"Did you read these?" Jonathan asked.

"I did."

"Your interpretation?"

"Things just got muddier."

"Afraid so," Jonathan said. "Given the passage of time, I'm not surprised."

"Right. Seems like a lot of work for nothing." Jimmy paused and exhaled. "Not to mention poor Josefina being put through all that."

"I agree. I'm glad Sister Mary Esther was there."

"And thank God. I sat behind the screen and didn't have to witness the actual procedure. I will say, the nun was very skilled and reassuring."

Jonathan nodded. "I guess we had to try. But it's still goddamn unfortunate. A woman is raped but is afraid to go to the police. By the time we do a legally sound sexual assault exam, all the evidence has washed away, disappeared down the drain."

"So, where do we go from here?" Jimmy asked.

"I don't know Max Jamerson very well. But he doesn't strike me as a rapist. And I don't think he would dip his wick into the hired help, even if he thought it was consensual. Judging from what I've seen, Max is more of a high-end escort kind of person."

"Well, we know something happened. Josefina doesn't seem to be lying. She's hiding in a convent trying to be as quiet and inconspicuous as a mouse, for Christ's sake."

"Right. But gut feelings and supposition won't pay the freight. Not against a sitting mayor—or his son. It galls me that someone can take advantage of their position like that and get away with it."

An alarm on Jonathan's iPhone chimed.

"The meeting with Senator Nichols you mentioned?" Jimmy asked.

"Yeah, still a couple of hours away. I need to do some prep, though."

"Got it." Jimmy stood but didn't move. His brow wrinkled.

"I know that look, Jimmy. Like something's eating at you."

"You know, Doc, something's been nagging at me. You have a few minutes to talk?"

"Of course. Have a seat. Take a load off." Jimmy always seemed so carefree, so for him to ask to talk must be important. "Let me have it."

"Doc, you familiar with the Elysian Fields?"

"I assume you're not talking about Elysian Fields Avenue in the Marigny." Elysian Fields was a boulevard in central New Orleans stretching from the Mississippi River to Lake Pontchartrain. The New Orleans version was a pale imitation of its Parisian inspiration, the Champs-Élysées.

"That's right."

"Well, if I remember correctly, the Elysian Fields were part of Greek mythology, where heroes went after they died."

"Good start." Jimmy pursed his lips. "We had a lot of time on our hands in between missions overseas. I read tons of books. Some pretty deep stuff. You know, like how different cultures view Heaven and Hell. I guess when you're so close to death, it makes you think. Anyway, at first, only warriors and other heroes were allowed in the Elysian Fields. After many generations, the myth was that anyone deemed worthy could go there as well."

Jonathan nodded. Perhaps Jimmy's devil-may-care attitude was a facade—a defense mechanism. This was a side of their diener he hadn't seen before.

"As we examined Mr. and Mrs. Haldeman, I wondered whether they would have earned passage. They certainly are worthy, given their military service and their goodwill to the community. And the infant shooting victim you examined, shouldn't she be there as well? She didn't live long enough to make her mark, but wouldn't her innocence make her deserving of a spot?" Jimmy hesitated. "And your daughter, Doc. Beatrice. I have to believe she's there too."

Jonathan blinked, hoping to hold back tears. It was nice to see that someone else on his team thought about cadavers as more than just lifeless flesh and organs. Memories of Beatrice added to his angst. He exhaled a cleansing breath.

"Jimmy, I think you're right on all counts. It's an intriguing concept, one I would like to believe in. Wouldn't it be great if Bill and Maggie were there, cuddling the child as we speak? That my daughter is up there playing tag with the others who died with her? It's a comforting thought."

Jimmy smiled, or at least he seemed to try to smile. But it faded. His eyes fixated on something beyond Jonathan.

"Say, Doc, I hope this won't seem too personal...but have you ever killed anyone?"

Jonathan's face warmed as he contemplated the question. This conversation was going deep and dark. "It's sad, but doctors lose patients. It's one reason I prefer being a pathologist. Nothing I do will kill anyone."

"Yeah, but I mean, you ever had to shoot another human being? Anything like that?"

"Well, no." Jonathan paused. "Have you?"

Jimmy trained his eyes on Jonathan.

"I became a corpsman because I wanted to fight terrorists, but didn't want to kill. I wanted to save lives."

"I can appreciate that. And from what I saw of your suturing techniques, you'll make an excellent surgeon. You'll save plenty of lives."

"But there were a few times on patrol…" Jimmy paused. His eyes moistened. "Had to react immediately. Hand-to-hand stuff."

Jonathan's stomach twisted with sorrow. "I can only imagine what—"

"No matter how much I accomplish," Jimmy said, "I just can't forget the feeling. It's like I can't do enough good to offset the bad."

"That was then. This is now. You can't fix the past. You just have to learn from what happened and move forward."

"I suppose." Jimmy exhaled, as if to cleanse himself of the negative memories. "Thanks. I needed to get that off my chest."

"Sure. I understand being in combat and being in medicine may not seem like a good fit. But for a future physician—"

"You're right," Jimmy said. "I guess I'm luckier than most."

"Yeah, well." Jonathan searched for the words. "It's difficult. But you're not alone. If you ever need an ear—"

Jimmy nodded. "Thanks, Doc. Not much else to say." He looked at his watch. "Jesus. Where'd the time go? I need to get on the road. Hope I didn't make you late for your meeting."

Chapter Fifty-One: Café Luke

Tuesday, December 30, 2014

O n sunny days, shadows between the towering office buildings around One Shell Plaza offered a welcome reprieve from the heat. But today, with rain in the forecast for later in the evening, clouds intervened. Jonathan hastened along Perdido Street toward the Hilton St. Charles and its restaurant, Café Luke. The lack of sunlight magnified the winter chill.

Once inside, Jonathan approached the maître d'. "I'm here to meet Senator Nichols for lunch."

The maître d' pointed Jonathan to a table in a small, semi-private alcove near the back entrance of the dining room, where two men sat talking. One of them—Senator Nichols—Jonathan expected. The other, a complete surprise.

Jonathan approached the table. "Paul, good afternoon."

Nichols stood, and the pair shook hands.

"Jonathan, please have a seat and allow me to introduce Bryan Whitcomb, a reporter from the *Times-Pic*. Bryan and I were just talking about Senate Bill 842 and your critical support. He plans to write an article about our initiative."

"Yes, we've met before," Jonathan said. Whitcomb seemed nervous, and he didn't make eye contact. Given Whitcomb's stated desire to avoid public appearances, his presence seemed especially out of place.

"If you'll excuse me," Whitcomb said, "I'll leave you gentlemen to your business. Senator, I wish you the best of luck on this legislation. Dr. Gray, perhaps I can interview you later to get your perspective."

"I have an even better idea, Bryan," Nichols said. "Dr. Gray's scheduled to testify next Monday afternoon at the state capitol building before Senate Judiciary Committee A.' Why don't you cover the proceedings?"

"An excellent suggestion, Senator. I'll look into it. For now, gentlemen, enjoy your lunch. The shrimp and grits is excellent."

As Whitcomb departed, Jonathan sat. He and Nichols engaged in social banter as they ordered their entrées. But soon, the topic switched to the reason for their meeting: the draft legislative proposal and Jonathan's upcoming testimony. They reviewed the main tenets of the draft and compared notes about lessons learned—those gained by Senator Nichols during his tumultuous time as a nonphysician coroner in Jefferson Davis Parish, and the ones Jonathan collected during his long tenure in the Orleans Parish Coroner's Office.

"You know," Nichols said, "I thought Katrina had put us on the right path when Governor Blanco used her emergency executive powers to designate a state medical examiner. Unfortunately, once the immediate crisis had passed and we dealt with the dead bodies, the legislature lacked the will to make the office permanent.

"Blanco's history, a bad memory. But I'm praying this legislation will be a kick in the pants regarding the need for statewide standards and a coordinated approach toward budgets and review of autopsies."

"At least," Jonathan said, "we can point to the limited but current success we've had and hopefully gain support for creation of a chief medical examiner for the entire state. And the nonsense up in Caddo Parish, where the investigator was signing autopsies for the coroner ought to be another wake-up call for statewide action."

"Yet another argument for a centralized state medical examiner with independent oversight authority," Nichols said. "And movement toward regional forensic labs sets the stage for our draft legislation, which addresses issues with mental health examinations and sexual assault investigations.

Lord knows I could have used the support in Jeff Davis when I was coroner. I loved the public service aspect. But the lack of resources made it an uphill fight. It seemed overwhelming. Impossible to do the good job the citizens in the parish deserved. Eventually, I realized it was time to cut my losses. So, I joined my current firm. I can tell you, without a doubt, defending multimillion-dollar ship collision cases and Jones Act claims is a lot less stressful."

Nichols looked at his watch.

"Speaking of which, I have a client meeting in less than half an hour. Regardless of how much I've enjoyed our conversation and how much I appreciate your hard work and support on this legislation, I need to excuse myself."

Standing, they shook hands.

"Thank you, Jonathan. Elaine Devereaux will be in touch with specifics and next steps."

Chapter Fifty-Two: The Envelope

Jonathan exited the hotel, proceeded across Perdido Street, and turned toward city hall. A familiar voice broke his concentration.

"Excuse me, Dr. Gray, can we talk?"

Bryan Whitcomb emerged from a small alcove in the base of One Shell Plaza. Jonathan studied the reporter. Something about Whitcomb had changed since they had talked in Café Luke. He had seemed a little nervous during their brief conversation in the restaurant, but now his eyes, glazed and watery, darted back and forth between Jonathan and their surroundings. Was he paranoid? Or stoned? Something must have happened in the past few minutes.

Jonathan suggested they move to a sandwich shop on Carondelet within sight of the streetcar line. They ordered coffee and sat at a table as far away as possible from the other people there—the proprietor and an elderly Asian couple studying a tourist map—so they could talk without being overheard. Jonathan could see both front and rear entrances.

"Now it's my turn to wonder about the secrecy," Jonathan said.

"I could be wrong." Whitcomb's tone was serious and lacked the false machismo of previous conversations. "But I think someone might be tailing me."

He stopped talking when the proprietor delivered their coffee. Whitcomb looked—or, more accurately, stared—at him as if watching for any sign of a physical attack. The owner smiled and told the pair to enjoy their coffee before returning to the serving counter. Whitcomb's hands shook as he poured cream into his coffee.

"All right, Mr. Whitcomb," Jonathan said. "I'm listening."

Whitcomb glanced at the elderly couple and the proprietor, who were discussing how the po' boy got its name. Turning back to Jonathan, he reached into his coat pocket, removed a letter-sized manila envelope, and slid it across the table. He leaned forward and whispered. "Don't pick it up. Put it in your pocket discreetly when you get up."

"Why so much mystery?" Jonathan spoke softly but didn't whisper.

"You never know who's around," Whitcomb said, still whispering. "It pays to be careful."

"Won't you at least tell me what's in the envelope?"

"It's a safe-deposit key, along with a piece of paper telling you which bank and its address. There's also a power of attorney to allow you to open the box."

"And in the box?"

"Two big envelopes," Whitcomb said, his voice no longer a whisper, but still subdued. "Each one has a draft of my article and copies of all my notes and evidence I've gathered for my story. If anything happens to me before it hits the news, take one envelope to your law enforcement contacts. Leave the other copy in the box as insurance."

"Why me?"

"Because I think I can trust you, especially after our discussion yesterday. I have a source close to Max Jamerson's inner circle. So if you had leaked any information about my story, I would have heard about it. That you're keeping a lid on things and not informing the mayor must mean you're on the up-and-up."

"Look," Jonathan said, "I want to help. But you need to give me some sort of idea what this is all about."

Whitcomb closed his eyes, his head dropping slightly. He breathed in and out deeply as if trying to calm himself. He opened his eyes and looked at Jonathan. "Okay." His eyes darted around the room. He lowered his voice almost to a whisper. "Here's the deal. My investigation points to the mayor or someone very close to him as being involved in an international human-trafficking and prostitution ring."

"Someone close to him?"

"That's the missing link those five women could have provided before they were killed."

"I see."

"So, if something happens to me before I can solidify the link, I'm hoping the information I have so far will help the cops do something."

"Okay. I'll take your key and safeguard your evidence. But I hope I'll be able to return them both to you soon."

"Me too," Whitcomb said. "Okay, I need to go. We should leave separately. Give me a couple of minutes, and then head out. I'm the one they're interested in, so if someone is tailing me, it might take some attention off you."

Whitcomb wasn't stoned. He was scared. Scared of the mayor and his goons. They had done nothing to harm him, yet. Other than steal his car. But fear isn't always rational. And it can be contagious, so Jonathan needed to be careful not to get caught up in Whitcomb's emotional reaction. Whitcomb exited the café and dodged into doorways every few feet. Perhaps it *was* paranoia. But given the salacious and criminal nature of the subject matter, and the prominence of the personalities involved, he was right to be concerned.

Bravery in the face of personal danger was admirable. Whitcomb deserved respect for putting his own safety at risk to uncover the truth and hold politicians accountable. Even if only half of his story were true, no doubt Bryan Whitcomb was on his way to a Pulitzer.

The late hour meant Jonathan couldn't return to his office and finalize the autopsy reports and death certificates before the Vital Records Registry closed, so he headed home instead. He sat on the hard wooden bench of the streetcar as it jerked along Carondelet, clutching the envelope Whitcomb had entrusted to him.

With his political life, family reputation, and personal freedom in jeopardy,

Max Jamerson had many resources he could use to manage his way through a scandal and limit the damage. His son raping a woman on his housekeeping staff was a despicable crime. Being exposed as the kingpin of an intercontinental prostitution syndicate was a horse of a different color. And if members of the mayor's security detail stole Whitcomb's Acura, then used it to stalk Jonathan's team and Emma, it meant Max knew they were on the trail to blow his operation wide open. Bryan Whitcomb wasn't the only person at risk.

Once the story broke, the public outcry would put Max's administration under a looking glass and give Jonathan and the others a level of protection. If something bad happened, it would appear that Max was behind it. Until then, Jonathan needed to make sure those involved took precautions to protect themselves. And he needed to enter the certificates into the record as public documents. Jonathan stepped off the streetcar at the corner of Carondelet and Canal and opened the speed-dial list on his phone. Time to spread the warning.

* * *

What a strange set of circumstances. Usually, the night before New Year's Eve was light and carefree and filled with joyous anticipation of upcoming parties. But here Jonathan and Emma were, sitting at home, snuggled together on their sofa with the TV on, and he was about to destroy the moment. Noise from the street signaled the city, and its revelers carried on without them.

He had always tried to keep his official business away from the family. But Emma was in danger. It was risky to share the details of the trouble they were in, and he hated to burden her with fear, but she deserved to know. Jonathan turned off their television.

"Emma, I need to tell you something."

"Okay." She remained calm, not reflecting even a hint of fear.

"I know this past week hasn't been easy." Jonathan looked into Emma's eyes. "It's finally time I tell you what's going on. The situation's likely to get more intense. You need to be prepared."

Jonathan told her as much as he could about Bryan Whitcomb, Eduardo and Josefina Diaz, Esperanza Morales, and the Jamersons. He left the Haldeman murders out because they didn't seem related to why she was in danger.

That struck him as peculiar. He had been working on cases not directly related to one another, except by time and place. Each case was important in its own right, deserving of the best he had to offer. That was his job. Follow the truth wherever it led him. What a relief it would be to deal with one death at a time, in a linear fashion, before moving on to the next. Nothing in his world had been easy or linear, especially since taking over for Robby.

It had all come at him at once. And he had to deal with it that way—all at once—while trying to reform the system. A single killer or medical emergency didn't bind any two cases together. Rather, it was a tapestry of inhumanity, corruption, and avarice lying, pall-like, over New Orleans. It threatened to suffocate the last vestiges of civility in the city that care forgot.

Raindrops, the first in over a week, tapped against the windows. They came softly at first, then with increasing intensity. Jonathan hugged Emma. They held one another, as if they were the last two people on earth. Exhausted, they fell asleep together on the sofa. Maybe tomorrow, New Year's Eve, would be better. It had to be.

Chapter Fifty-Three: Old Year's Resolutions

Wednesday, December 31, 2014

Waking on New Year's Eve morning, Jonathan and Emma reviewed their plans for the evening, more as a distraction than anything else. In past years, Jonathan and Emma had hosted a party at their home, but once their children left for college, they fell away from the practice. Their celebration this year would be a réveillon dinner at Napoleon's Rooftop, where they would have a view of the fireworks after the traditional Fleur de Lis drop at midnight from the old Jax Brewery.

Then they would retreat to the sanctuary of Maison Gris. Outside, the city would work through a four-day cycle of parties, recovery, more parties, and more recovery. It would all start on New Year's Eve and continue unabated through the Sugar Bowl—scheduled for New Year's Day in the Superdome. Then, events would flow—or, more accurately, stagger—into the weekend. But before any of their plans could take place, they needed to accomplish a few things.

"You going to the office today?" Jonathan asked.

"No. I have a couple of administrative assistants there until one o'clock to speak with any clients who might drop by. But everyone else is off or telecommuting. I can do what I need to do from here. Don't worry—if I take a walk or go for a run, I'll take my handgun."

"Good." Jonathan breathed a sigh of relief.

* * *

Rather than drive or walk to his office, Jonathan took a taxi. With so many visitors in town, traffic would be horrendous, and streetcars packed. No use being bothered with it. Pay a couple of bucks and let someone else worry. As his driver pulled away from the Marriott's cab stand, he reflected on the state of play in Esperanza Morales's death investigation and where it had led.

Almost certainly, his and Betsy's meeting with Assistant US Attorney Simpson on Friday morning would bring the case against Max Jamerson to a head. The potential charges against Max were serious, so federal authorities were likely the only ones with sufficient legal firepower to pursue them. His cab pulled up in front of the city government complex. Jonathan paid the driver and headed for the coroner's suite of offices.

"Good morning, Vern. Ready for the new year?"

"Good morning, Dr. Gray." Her reply included an enthusiastic smile. "I'm rested and ready to go. Thank you for the half-day today."

"You're very welcome. We could all use a nap right now. You know how this town gets during New Year's Eve. We'll have our hands full come day after tomorrow, no doubt."

"Very true, Dr. Gray," Vern said, as Jonathan moved past the receptionist's counter and into his office.

He dialed Sonny's phone extension and asked him to drop by the conference room for an impromptu meeting.

"Say, Doc," Sonny said, as they sat down. "I checked on Jimmy. He's at his folks' place in Natchitoches and doing fine. I haven't located Dr. Miller yet."

"Susan and her family are spending New Year's with Boris's parents in New Jersey," Jonathan said. "I think they're out of the line of fire. You, however, need to watch your back as long as you're in town."

"Will do. I'll wear my bulletproof skivvies from here on out."

"And Sonny, I want to outline what will happen over the next couple of days. Events are converging. I need to make sure we have a common understanding."

"Sure thing. Let her rip."

Jonathan handed two file folders to Sonny. One contained death certificates for Bill and Maggie Haldeman and Hunter Dejarnette. The second held the five death certificates he had discovered in Robby's office.

"First, I need you to file these death certificates at the Vital Records Registry before noon today."

"Consider it done, Doc."

"That's the easy part. Easy, but important. We need to have the death certificates completed and on record. I think certain powerful interests are feeling the noose tighten, and we don't want anyone to believe they can intimidate this office into changing medical opinions or ignoring evidence."

"Roger that. Can I ask who these death certificates are for?"

Jonathan took a deep breath. "Well, that brings me to the next matter. Without going into details, I have reason to believe Max Jamerson's involvement might go beyond Beau's alleged rape of Josefina Diaz. And I've learned that it wasn't the newspaper reporter Whitcomb who followed us to St. Helen's. It was probably someone from Jamerson's protective detail."

Sonny sat quietly. His jaw tightened noticeably with each additional revelation.

"So," Jonathan continued, "there's a meeting this Friday I would like you to attend with me. At ten a.m., Betsy Sprance and I are meeting with an Assistant US Attorney to outline the charges we have building against Max Jamerson."

"I'll be there," Sonny said without hesitation.

"In other news, we both know Betsy Sprance is about to arrest Judge Haldeman and charge him with murdering his parents and Hunter Dejarnette. My guess is that it might happen as early as this afternoon."

"Well," Sonny said softly, more contemplative than Jonathan was used to, "I see why you warned us to be careful. Things are coming to a head. Next few hours should be fun." He picked up the file folders. "Now, if you'll excuse me, it's nearly eleven o'clock. I need to *laissez les bon temps rouler* with a visit to the Vital Records Registry."

Chapter Fifty-Four: New Year's Eve

Wednesday, December 31, 2014

T he clock chimed one o'clock, as Jonathan dropped his briefcase onto the massive mahogany hall tree in their foyer. He put his coat in the closet and hastened toward their family room. He called out to Emma. She shouted an emphatic reply.

"Hurry. You need to see this."

Jonathan hastened toward the sound blaring from the television screen. He arrived in the family room just in time to see Judge Haldeman, in handcuffs, duck his head as a patrol officer assisted him into the back seat of a police SUV. The vehicle drove away, and the camera focus shifted to the reporter, who outlined the charges facing the judge.

"Did you know Judge Haldeman was going to be arrested?" Emma asked.

"Figured it was coming soon. Betsy said it could be as early as today, but she wasn't sure."

"Surprised?"

"Not really. From what I've seen, Betsy has developed a strong circumstantial case." She might even have more than that, if she found the belt and just hadn't had time to share that information with him. "Surely, the district attorney wouldn't let the arrest go forward if he didn't have confidence in the state's evidence."

"Well, I'm sure it's causing quite a stir in the Haldeman house," Emma said. "Especially since it's New Year's Eve."

"Absolutely. And the police would never admit it," Jonathan said, "but that's the point. Cause a stir. Catch the defendant and his family off guard. Police often orchestrate their arrests to maximize confusion and isolation, hoping to get a quick confession. In our criminal justice system, an ordinarily intelligent and organized suspect—even a distinguished appellate court judge—can become unglued after a couple of days away from familiar surroundings, sitting in lockup, waiting for his attorney to return from a bowl game or a holiday cruise.

"Whether Betsy's decision to accuse Judge Haldeman of a triple murder and cuff him on live television just before a major holiday proves to be a stroke of genius that facilitates his confession remains to be seen. I mean, few people would deny that arresting a sitting appellate court judge, especially one who is politically connected and from a well-respected family, should garner extensive media attention, including front-page headlines.

"But on New Year's Eve, I think people often overlook headlines and don't pay attention to media coverage because they're preoccupied with other priorities. The judge may not get as much flak as Betsy is hoping he will. In a city that knows how to say goodbye to one year and hello to the next, news short of a natural disaster gets buried beneath party streamers and hangover remedies."

Jonathan sat next to Emma. Fulfilling his prophecy, the news report moved seamlessly from the arrest to a segment on preparations for the upcoming Fleur de Lis drop.

Emma hit the power button on their remote. "I hope Betsy can get some proper sleep now. She must be exhausted."

"I can't imagine. I've felt exhausted this past week, but she's undoubtedly putting in more hours than I have. If I had to guess, she'll be sound asleep before dark and stay that way well into New Year's Day. She's earned a break after working so hard."

Jonathan and Emma sat in silence, the reality of the day's news washing over them. How frightening. An otherwise well-respected jurist was arrested for killing three family members, apparently with deliberation and planning. Was Ben Haldeman an aberration? Or was the veneer of civilization so thin that even the people sworn to serve the public were capable of such evil? Jonathan spoke first.

"Are we planning to attend the Vigil Mass today before our réveillon dinner? I could use some comforting words right about now."

"I had hoped to. It's not even two o'clock yet. Mass is at five. Dinner doesn't start until nine. That gives us plenty of time to go for a run. Or take a nap. Or do whatever we want."

"Since we're going to be up so late, I vote for a nap." Jonathan smiled.

"Sounds like an excellent suggestion," Emma replied, her eyes seeming to sparkle with excitement.

As they rose, Emma's laptop chimed with an incoming video call. It was their three children who, they learned, were gathered together in London to experience New Year's Eve in Trafalgar Square.

In an electronic instant, they were a family sharing their holiday together, with no cadavers or gunshot wounds or strangulations to interfere. But all too soon, they said their farewells. Emma disconnected from the call.

"Between the glitz of Paris, Milan, and Christmas lights over Oxford Street," Jonathan said, "I'm afraid that boring old NOLA will never be the same for our kids."

"I agree," Emma said. "But it was great *they* called *us*. I've been trying to avoid nagging them too much. We don't want to seem like helicopter parents."

"Well," Jonathan said, looking at his watch, "I loved hearing from them, too, although it reduced our nap time."

"Which means," Emma said, "we don't have any time to waste. Let's head upstairs."

* * *

Jonathan and Emma arrived at St. Louis Cathedral just as the five o'clock service began. Mass provided Jonathan the uplift he needed, setting a positive tone for the rest of the evening. As they walked home, Jonathan and Emma held hands and talked about the burgeoning revival of the multicourse réveillon dinner, traditionally served after Midnight Mass as a family-centered way to welcome the New Year.

"I'm excited," Emma said. "Restaurants are getting the hang of the old traditions. What I like most is that so many of them highlight Louisiana recipes featuring wild game."

"I bet Napoleon's Rooftop will exceed expectations," Jonathan said. "My mouth's watering already."

Chapter Fifty-Five: Welcoming the New Year

Wednesday, December 31, 2014

Tonight would be theirs, as husband and wife, lovers saying goodbye to the old year and welcoming the new. Emma appeared magnificent in her formal attire. A floor-length black gown and jeweled collar highlighted her athletic frame. Shared life experiences over the past quarter-century added to her allure. Perhaps they should skip dinner and celebrate in a more private setting. Tempting. But that would come soon enough. Now was their time to join other partygoers in drinking and dancing and singing "Auld Lang Syne."

The réveillon and atmosphere at Napoleon's Rooftop did not disappoint. Relaxation and renewal came as hope for the future pushed cares and concerns aside. And all without copious amounts of alcohol, usually associated with the giant party stretching from the French Quarter to the riverfront. There was wine with dinner and, of course, a champagne toast to welcome the Fleur de Lis drop. But the joyous lovemaking sure to follow wouldn't be lost to an alcoholic stupor.

Outside their cab on the way home, music and laughter poured from nearly every doorway and balcony. Pedestrians, many not distinguishing between sidewalk and pavement, staggered aimlessly toward another jazz club or party venue. Inside their cab, Jonathan kissed Emma, and she kissed him back. The passion and anticipation grew as they neared home. They would make love, fall asleep together in each other's arms, and sleep until late morning, after which they'd spend a leisurely afternoon watching the Sugar Bowl from Emma's luxury suite. What a perfect start to the New Year.

Arriving home, they kissed in the warmth of their foyer, not bothering to turn on any lights. Emma slipped out of her heels and loosened Jonathan's bow tie as Jonathan kissed her again. He started with her lips, moved downward to her chin, over to her cheek, and then down to her neck. Emma moaned her approval. Jonathan caressed Emma's shoulders and, continuing to kiss her neck, reached for the clasp on the back of her evening gown.

Emma stood still, then turned her head toward their internal courtyard, where they parked their cars. She whispered, "Did you hear that?"

"Hear what?" Jonathan fiddled with Emma's zipper.

"That bumping. Doesn't sound like street noise. It's coming from our courtyard."

Emma pulled Jonathan's hands away and turned toward the noise.

He dropped his head on her shoulder and groaned. Lovemaking would have to wait.

Just then, he heard something too. Had drunken revelers stumbled onto their property? Or was it something more sinister?

With their foyer still dark, Jonathan stepped to a window. "Grab flashlights, Fen."

Guided by a glowing nightlight, Emma hurried away. When she returned, she had two flashlights and their handguns.

"I don't see anything," Jonathan told Emma as she handed him a flashlight.

"Thought you might need this," Emma said, offering him his holster. "Magazine's full."

"Thanks. When we get downstairs, turn on the floodlights." Jonathan chambered a round. "Let's hope it's nothing."

Jonathan put the holster in his tuxedo jacket pocket. He proceeded down their back staircase with his Glock aimed upward in a high-ready position.

Emma stayed two steps behind. Jonathan's heartbeat pounded behind his eyes and in his forehead. He had shot targets at the firing range, but that he might soon face another human being with his gun drawn worried him. The thought of firing his weapon in anger frightened him even more. His hands shook. He halted near the bottom of the stairs. Emma bumped into him, nearly falling.

"Shh," Jonathan whispered. "I hear something. It's coming from the trash bins."

"I hear it too," she whispered.

"Okay. Hit the lights. I'll go outside for a look."

"Be careful."

Jonathan pushed the door open and stepped outside, his Glock now in low-ready position—the weapon wrapped tightly in his right hand and supported by his left. Their courtyard, illuminated almost entirely by the floodlight, appeared empty. It was silent, except for sounds from the street outside as the Quarter continued to party. The duct tape covering the fuel door on his Blazer had loosened and waved in the breeze. Jonathan exhaled and lowered his handgun to his side, releasing his double grip.

"I think I see the problem." Jonathan laughed, relieved. Another mystery solved. Two glowing eyes stared from under Emma's Lexus SUV. "Looks like Bon Jovi's been digging through our garbage. I guess I need to speak with Morrisette again about keeping his damn cat under control."

Jonathan returned his Glock to its holster. As Jonathan placed the trash bin upright, Bon Jovi hissed, then emphasized his disapproval with a guttural cat growl. Jonathan kicked a crushed aluminum can toward Emma's SUV. Their feline perpetrator emerged from his hiding place and jumped onto Jonathan's car on his way to freedom.

"*I'll* talk to Morrisette," Emma replied tersely. "His precious Bon Jovi just scared me out of ten years of my life. Besides, his rent's due."

Emma's words echoed, but didn't sink in. Jonathan's ear had picked up another sound. Something was still amiss. A noise—slight, but definitely there—came from his left, just beyond the area covered by the floodlights. In the shadows behind Emma's car. Might be wind rustling through their

Mexican fan palm trees. As Jonathan turned his head and stepped slightly to his left, he removed the holster from his jacket pocket.

Emma yelled, "Gray, watch out."

Spinning to his left, Jonathan encountered a figure, dressed in black, face covered by a ski mask, lunging at him. With only a split second to respond, Jonathan squared his shoulders and dove into his attacker, hitting just above the waistline. The collision of bone and flesh hurt like hell. Jonathan fell backward onto the brick and concrete surface. His gun, jolted out of his hand, slid across the courtyard out of reach. His head throbbed and his lungs ached as he struggled to regain his breath.

His defensive move had also knocked the attacker off their feet. Stumbling, the figure careened into Emma, knocking her backward. Emma's head struck the doorjamb, and she slumped to the ground. The figure in black—unbalanced—teetered and fell too.

Seconds, seeming more like minutes, passed before anyone moved. Jonathan, still dazed, and the figure in black dragged themselves upright. Now trapped in a corner, the attacker's only avenue of escape was straight through Jonathan. With a click, a knife appeared in the assailant's right hand. Its serrated blade, designed to inflict maximum damage, emphasized the danger. Emma, now sitting up, supported herself against the door. Blood trickled from her forehead.

When the figure lunged, Jonathan jumped to his right. The blade clipped his jacket, cutting the sleeve. Too close for comfort. As his attacker turned around, Jonathan removed his tuxedo jacket and wrapped it around his left hand and forearm. It was a technique he learned during required Navy self-defense classes. Put as many layers as possible between your skin and the knife. Thank God he had paid attention. He wasn't skilled in knife fighting, but at least he had a better chance than he would have otherwise. The figure in black stood between Jonathan and his pistol.

When the figure lunged at him, Jonathan swatted the blade away with his left arm. The attacker thrust forward again. Jonathan removed the jacket from around his forearm and threw it over the knife to confuse his assailant—a trick he had learned watching TV.

Jonathan dove toward his Glock. With no time to think, he removed the weapon from its holster. His instincts and training took over: position handgun, aim for center mass, pull the trigger. Not a perfect shot, but effective enough. The figure in black dropped the knife and tumbled backward, holding their right shoulder. Jonathan's hands shook. His ears echoed. His head throbbed.

Springing up like a gymnast, the intruder charged Jonathan again. Handgun, center mass, trigger. The attacker collapsed, blood flowing from just above the left kneecap.

"You're not going anywhere." Jonathan exhaled and stared ahead, his mind reeling. His hands shook. He'd just shot another human being. Twice. Not as easy as it seemed in the movies.

Emma. What about Emma? Jonathan whirled around to see her leaning against the door. Keeping his eyes on the figure in black, who remained on the ground writhing in pain, Jonathan rushed to her.

"You okay? Let me look at the bleeding."

"Just a scalp wound," Emma said. "Bleeding's already stopped. I was dizzy for a minute, but I'm fine now."

Jonathan nodded. He could check Emma for a concussion later. He needed to get back in control. "Okay. I'll look around to make sure there isn't anyone else. Stay here and keep a gun on our guest."

"Right."

The revelry in the Quarter continued as Jonathan searched. He didn't find any other intruders, but he found wires, wire cutters, digital watches, and bricks of putty.

"Hmm," Jonathan said, "Betsy will be interested in this."

Satisfied their attacker was alone, and with Emma as backup, he approached their visitor. He bound their hands and feet using some bungee cords stored in Emma's Lexus.

"Time to see our friend's face," Emma said.

"Right," Jonathan said. "I'll do it. You keep us covered."

Jonathan clipped his holster to his waistband and then removed the ski mask. Flowing blond hair spilled from under it, revealing a woman in her mid-thirties. Their assailant's fiery blue eyes darted left and right, as if looking for some avenue of escape.

"I wouldn't if I were you," Emma said. "*You* invaded *my* home. The *next* shot won't be to disable."

"I'm going to check your wounds," Jonathan said. "Do you understand?"

The mysterious woman nodded. She remained mute as Jonathan conducted his examination. "You'll live. The bullet went through your shoulder cleanly, and the other one lodged in your thigh. Neither one hit any major blood vessels. Feels like the second one shattered your femur, though. You might not go bowling for a while, but you'll live."

Bowling? She was lucky to be alive. Thank God his second shot hit the fleshy part of her thigh. Just an inch to the left, and Jonathan would have been dealing with a destroyed femoral artery.

"Damn," Emma said, "I'm bleeding again."

"Take my handkerchief," Jonathan said. "Do you feel well enough to get our emergency medical kit?" He would get it for her, but he didn't want to leave her alone with the attacker.

Emma pressed Jonathan's handkerchief against her head. "Yeah. Back soon."

Jonathan called Betsy, but her phone rang several times with no answer. "Come on, Betsy. Wake up." After a few more rings, the call rolled over to voicemail. Jonathan fumed while the recording instructed him how to leave a message.

"Betsy, it's Jonathan Gray. Emma and I just got attacked in our courtyard. It was a female dressed all in black. She was carrying wires, wire cutters, digital watches, and bricks of putty. I wounded her in the shoulder and thigh. Call me as soon as you can."

He tried Sonny Rabideau. It went straight to voicemail, and his mailbox was full. He must have his phone turned off. Thank God, Susan and Jimmy were out of town.

Jonathan called the 9-1-1 Emergency Operations Center. A recording advised, "Due to excessive call volume, all lines are busy. Please try again later."

Damn it. He stared at their assailant. Right. He'd have to deal with her himself. He should investigate further—take another look at the pile of items she'd brought. Blocks of putty. Putty? C-4? Esperanza Morales had died after a bomb in her car eviscerated her from the waist down, and the fire finished the job. C-4, of course. Why hadn't he realized it before?

"You're here to wire my car, aren't you?" Jonathan took a step toward the woman. Heat spread up his neck. "If I weren't a physician, I'd kick you to within an inch of your life."

As Jonathan moved closer, she struggled to drag herself away.

"What's this?"

Jonathan picked up three black wooden objects he hadn't noticed before. Hand-carved coffins.

He gritted his teeth and glared at his guest. His face flushed with anger. "You bitch."

Jonathan raised his weapon, using both hands to steady his aim. "One bullet to the chest. You broke loose and attacked me. No one will question the Coroner of Orleans Parish acting in self-defense."

His assailant's eyes expanded. She struggled, rolling on her side and kicking toward Jonathan. Blood oozed from her wounds.

Jonathan moved his finger inside the trigger guard. His heart pounded. He took a deep breath and exhaled slowly.

"Here's the medical kit."

Jonathan jerked his pistol upward as Emma's voice startled him and brought him back to reality. He lowered his weapon and closed his eyes a moment in gratitude. Thank God, she stopped him. He hadn't recognized himself in that moment. Could he have really pulled the trigger? Hell, he almost had.

"I'm sure she's here to put a bomb in my car," Jonathan said, tilting his head toward the woman in black. "Probably yours, too. And I couldn't get in touch with Betsy or Sonny. Overloaded 9-1-1 circuits. If the bomber's after *us*, I'm betting she's already wired one or both of *their* vehicles. I left a voicemail for Betsy. Sonny didn't answer, and there's no voicemail. I have to get to his place uptown. And there's no way I'm leaving you here alone."

"Okay, tell me what you need me to do."

"Your Lexus has a remote starter, doesn't it?"

"Yeah."

"Good. Go to the storage cabinet. See if we have any rope left from our last boating trip. Then get your starter. We'll make sure your SUV isn't wired. Once we tie our visitor to a support beam and make sure she won't bleed to death, we'll head for Sonny's house. We can call 9-1-1 on the way."

Chapter Fifty-Six: Beware the Neutral Ground

Thursday, January 1, 2015

A s Emma drove her Lexus SUV through the archway leading from their internal courtyard onto Bienville, she asked Jonathan, not taking her eyes off the road, "Where?"

"Sonny lives on Lowerline Street, just off Nelson," Jonathan said.

"Near St. Rita's School?"

"Yeah."

"Okay," Emma said. "Most direct route would be Dauphine to Canal, across Baronne or Loyola, and up Earhart Boulevard. Should take less than fifteen minutes. But look at everyone still wandering around. After drinking this long, they're probably boozed out of their minds."

Jonathan put a blue emergency light issued to him as coroner on the dashboard. "Maybe this will make people get out of the way."

"Or get police to see us," Emma said, as she pushed on the gas pedal and eased her Lexus up Bienville.

"Still no luck with Betsy or 9-1-1," Jonathan said. "Damn it, there must be someone who can get ahold of Sonny."

Their journey to Bourbon should have taken a minute, two at most. But after almost five minutes of stopping and starting and weaving around inebriated pedestrians, they had made hardly any progress. Their blue light hadn't fazed the drunks at all.

"Look," Emma said. "They've got Bienville blocked at Bourbon."

"Crap," Jonathan said. "We'll never get there."

"Let's see about that," Emma said.

She stopped her SUV and began backing up—the wrong way—along Bienville.

"What are you doing?" Jonathan asked.

"Fasten your seat belt, Gray. I'm getting you to Sonny's."

Inching backward and maneuvering the steering wheel, Emma turned her SUV around. She proceeded slowly toward the river down Bienville—the wrong way. Nearing its intersection with Royal Street, Emma came to a halt, face-to-face with a BMW proceeding in the correct direction.

"Screw this." Emma veered to her right and drove onto the sidewalk, honking.

Jonathan lowered his window and shouted. "Out of the way. Emergency. Move it."

The crowd parted. Turning right on Royal Street, Emma proceeded as rapidly as possible to Canal, stopping briefly at a red light before proceeding across the broad avenue, with its wide neutral ground and streetcar tracks.

"Well," Emma said, "I don't see any police cars. I wonder where they are. Usually, they're all over this part of town."

"Who the hell knows?" Jonathan said. "Sounds like I need to have a chat with Polly Bondurant."

Once across Canal and onto St. Charles, pedestrian traffic lessened. After winding her way through the Central Business District, Emma followed Loyola Avenue toward Earhart Boulevard. At Earhart, she turned right and increased speed. The area was predominantly dedicated to light industry, with some abandoned buildings around. There were no people in sight and almost no cars on the road. In the distance to the right, the Superdome's multicolored floodlights served as an eerie beacon, still visible despite the early morning fog. Emma guided her Lexus through a confusing maze of concrete columns supporting the elevated highway overhead.

"We should be close to Lowerline in less than ten minutes," she said.

"Great," Jonathan continued, his efforts to contact Sonny on his cell phone.

"No luck?" Emma glanced at Jonathan.

"Not yet," Jonathan said, as their SUV continued along Earhart Boulevard. He paused and looked up. A small Toyota pickup swerved out of the oncoming lane onto the grassy neutral ground and was making a full-speed beeline for their vehicle.

"Watch out," he shouted. "We're going to hit."

Emma's last-second evasive maneuver avoided a head-on collision. The precipitous movement locked Jonathan's shoulder and lap belts, pulling him backward against the passenger seat, immobilizing him. Glass crashed and shattered. The bang and scrape of metal on metal added to the horror, as their SUV and the pickup whammed together side by side before each continued along now altered paths forward. A loud bang, followed by a hissing sound, signaled the airbags had deployed and then deflated. A smoky odor, almost like a wood fire, filled the air.

Mortally wounded, their Lexus came to a rest on the right side of Earhart Boulevard against a light pole, tapping it hard enough to pop the hood. Their engine gave one last heroic gasp, then sputtered and died. A blast of steam smelled of antifreeze and motor oil. Pulsating blue beams from their emergency light bathed the inside of their vehicle, softened by a cool mist creeping in through broken windows.

"You okay?" Jonathan exhaled and unbuckled his seat belt.

"Yeah. Shaken. No injuries as far as I can tell. Thank God for airbags. You okay?"

"Yeah, fine. But now my ears are ringing. I'm going to check on the other driver."

Emma must have followed Jonathan shortly after he climbed out. She arrived just as he pulled a woman from behind the steering wheel and lay her on the ground. The woman reeked of alcohol.

"I think she'll be all right," Jonathan said. "Best to not move her. Looks like it's just minor cuts and bruises. This lady's very lucky she's not dead."

"And we're lucky she didn't kill us," Emma said. "Damn drunk. Ought to be in jail."

"Let the police and courts sort it out," Jonathan said. "Right now, I'm more worried about getting to Sonny's house. But looks like our trip has ended."

Emma pointed behind Jonathan. "Take another look. At least *one* business is open this time of day."

Jonathan turned around, greeted by a familiar sign: "New Orleans Coroner." Their new morgue might not have enough cold-storage lockers, but it had a well-stocked motor pool. "Outstanding," Jonathan said. "If we had to crash anywhere, *this* was the place. And thank God I didn't close for New Year's."

Within minutes, Jonathan located keys to one of the morgue's official vehicles. Outside, personnel from the adjacent Emergency Medical Services office hovered around Emma and the driver of the pickup truck.

"I need you to stay here and keep trying to get through to the police. See if the EMTs can contact Dispatch. Tell them about the car bombs. Tell them to hurry. And have them patch up your forehead. You'll probably need a couple of stitches."

"Okay. But you know I'm a much better shot than you are."

"You've got me there." Jonathan nodded and smiled. "But I have to take it from here."

He hugged Emma and got into his new vehicle. Turning on emergency lights in the grille, Jonathan sped toward Sonny's, his ears still ringing.

Chapter Fifty-Seven: Sonny's Place

Thursday, January 1, 2015

Jonathan drove the wrong way on Audubon Street and prayed his emergency lights would protect him from oncoming traffic. This was the shortest route from Earhart to Sonny's house on Lowerline, so he had to take a chance. He turned onto Fontainebleau Drive about four blocks from his destination—now going the correct direction—and switched off his emergency lights. He slowed down, careful not to make any unnecessary noise.

Passing Lowerline, he turned into the neighborhood a couple of blocks later. His radio crackled with news of the suspected explosive devices, dispatching the bomb squad to various locations, including any available units to Sonny's address. Emma must have gotten through. But he couldn't wait any longer. He had to make sure Sonny was okay.

Jonathan parked on Nelson Street, around the corner from Sonny's one-story bungalow, just after 4:00 a.m. The morning sky remained pitch black anywhere not covered by a streetlamp or porch light. The neighborhood slept, blissfully ignorant of any potential threat. Overhead, a faint hum from electric lines and transformers added to an already surreal scene.

Quiet and tranquility—good signs. Apparently, no one noticed his arrival. The element of surprise was an advantage. But he needed to calm down; his heart raced, but at least his ears had stopped ringing. Several more cleansing breaths. Time to go.

He exited his vehicle and edged around the corner, hiding behind trees and shrubbery. He bent his knees and crouched, maintaining a low profile as he headed for Sonny's Toyota pickup parked on the street. He touched the hood. Cold. Sonny had been home a while. Corinne's Honda occupied Sonny's driveway. Another cold engine. Good.

Jonathan pulled out his handgun, stepped onto Sonny's porch, and was dismayed to find the front door wide open. The screen door was shut. With a gentle push, the door opened slowly, accompanied by an eerie creaking sound. He inched into the house, his handgun aimed upward in high-ready position. He squinted as his eyes adjusted to the dim lighting; the room was eclipsed in darkness, except for the faint glow cast by ambient light from outside. Jonathan stepped into the open-concept living, dining, and kitchen area. Curtains fluttered slightly in an open window between the dining room table and kitchen.

His foot bumped against something on the floor. Not hard, like a chair or table leg. Softer. He suppressed a gasp. Corinne lay on the living room floor, wearing a bathrobe, but obviously nude underneath. No blood. No gunshot or stab wounds, even better. He crouched down and touched her neck. A weak pulse. She was alive.

Thumping sounds, soft at first, then growing more intense, resonated from a room toward the back.

Silently, with his Glock ready for action, Jonathan turned toward the noise. He had moved only two or three feet when Sonny hurtled through the air out of the back room. Sonny slammed against the wall and crumpled to the ground. A pistol dropped from his hand. It skidded across the floor out of reach.

An enormous figure dressed in black wearing a ski mask rushed out of the room and stomped toward Sonny. A knife fell out of the figure's boot. The intruder picked up the knife, advancing toward Sonny. Sonny grabbed onto the doorjamb, pulling himself out of danger.

"Enough." Jonathan moved his Glock into firing position. "Stop. I'll shoot."

The figure hesitated, then turned toward Jonathan. "Listen, Doc, you can't find me here. This isn't happening. It's not what you think."

Jonathan blinked. That voice. He had heard it before. Jonathan lightened his grip and lowered his handgun slightly as he cycled through his memory, trying to identify his adversary.

"Put your knife down and we'll talk it through."

Sounds of vehicles screeching to a stop and car doors opening came from outside. The figure raised an arm and propelled the knife toward Jonathan. Jonathan stumbled backward as the knife whizzed past, missing him by at least a foot, and embedded into the wall. As he fell, Jonathan pointed his Glock at the intruder, now running toward the open window. Splinters from a roof beam showered from the ceiling. Two shafts of light shone from behind Jonathan. Then, almost simultaneously, two gunshots. The intruder toppled to the floor. Betsy Sprance and Mitch Broussard advanced through the front door, weapons at the ready.

"Soup to nuts." Betsy switched on a light. "This is one hell of a soiree, Doc. And look at you in your cummerbund and patent leather shoes."

"Am I glad to see you two. The party *was* kind of boring till you got here." Jonathan smiled and shivered in almost equal measure as he pulled himself up from the floor. Who in hell could think it was easy to shoot someone? His heart rate must be two hundred; at least it seemed like it.

"Emma got through to us," Betsy said. "We came as soon as we could."

Detective Broussard checked their man in black. "Two bullet wounds. He's unconscious but still alive. It doesn't look like we hit any major blood vessels, so he shouldn't bleed out on us. I'll call for EMTs."

Sonny stirred. "Corinne," his voice hoarse and weak. "How's Corinne?"

"She's alive, Sonny, and she seems better." Jonathan put his still-shaking fingers on Corinne's neck. "Her pulse is stronger, and she's breathing without as much effort." Jonathan covered Corinne with a quilt from the back of the sofa. Sirens announced ambulances and EMTs approaching.

"Before long," Betsy said, "everyone will be on their way to the ER. And we can figure out what happened. But first, let's look at this dirtbag's face."

Betsy pulled off the ski mask. "Sweet Holy God."

She knelt closer to their assailant. "No."

266

Betsy looked at Jonathan, her eyes wild with disbelief and confusion. "It can't be. This isn't happening. This can't be hap…"

She paused. Her lips moved, but no words came out. Her breathing was heavy, labored. Betsy looked at the figure, then back at Jonathan. She stood quickly, as if she were a marionette jerked upright by a malevolent puppet master. She held onto the back of a dining room chair to support herself. "It's Ranger."

Betsy dropped her head and gagged. She swayed, seemingly about to faint. The color drained from her face, like a corpse exhibiting *pallor mortis*. She stumbled toward the open window near the kitchen. She didn't quite make it before she vomited. Betsy leaned out the window and continued to belch and heave. The stench of bile filled the room. Jonathan and Mitch rushed toward her.

Sonny dragged himself toward Corinne. "Can't move. Feels like electric shocks running down my legs."

Jonathan shifted his attention to Sonny, letting Broussard attend to Betsy. Jonathan knelt to examine Sonny's lower back. "I'll bet the impact when you slammed against the wall moved the bullet from your old injury too close to your spine. Stay still until the paramedics get here."

Broussard approached Sonny. "Can you tell us what happened?" Betsy sat on one of the dining room chairs, her head bowed.

"It was so sudden." Sonny exhaled a deep sigh. "Corinne went to get us something to drink. When she didn't come back, I went to check on her. I saw a big guy in black next to Corinne with a hand on her neck. When I yelled, he came after me."

Sonny paused, wincing in pain. He caught his breath and continued.

"I was unarmed, and the guy was huge. So, I retreated to our bedroom to get my weapon. He kicked in the door, picked me up before I could shoot, and threw me into the hall. Then you came in. Another five seconds and I'd be mashed potatoes. And Corinne—"

Sonny wept. The sirens had stopped, replaced by approaching footsteps and voices.

"It's all right, Sonny," Jonathan said. "Cavalry's here."

EMTs loaded Sonny and Corinne into the first two ambulances on scene, as Betsy watched. Jonathan explained the need to monitor Corinne for a stroke.

Betsy put her hand on Jonathan's shoulder. "I'm sorry this all happened." She looked toward the ambulance and then back at Jonathan. "I don't know what's going on. Or how Ranger's involved. Please tell Sonny and Corinne I had no idea—"

"Don't worry," Jonathan said. "I'll tell them. You take care of your family. We'll keep things moving on this end."

Betsy turned to Detective Broussard. "Mitch. It's up to you and Dr. Gray now. I need to recuse myself from this investigation if…if Ranger is involved. And I need to be with him. I need time to figure out what's going on. Can you go along with Jonathan tomorrow to meet with Mandy Simpson?"

"Will do, Betsy," Mitch said. "Will do."

Chapter Fifty-Eight: Bombshells

Thursday, January 1, 2015

S mall groups of residents congregated at a couple of houses across the street from Sonny's. Uniformed officers spread ubiquitous yellow crime-scene tape, and CSTs gathered evidence. Jonathan called Emma to tell her he was fine and would soon pick her up. Then he returned to his conversation with Mitch Broussard.

"Did police get the intruder in our courtyard?"

"They did." Mitch clamped down on a fresh half-cheroot. "And they complimented your work, with both the rope and with the bandages."

Jonathan shook his head and smiled. "Don't you just love police humor?"

"You weren't the only one visited," Mitch continued. "Just after midnight, an explosive device detonated in a car being used by Bryan Whitcomb. The bomb went off when Whitcomb engaged the remote starter as he approached the vehicle."

"Was he hurt?"

"Yeah. He's in serious but stable condition. Blast threw him into a brick wall nearby. If he had been any closer, he would have almost certainly died."

Jonathan sat on Sonny's front steps, staring at the ground. He clinched his teeth and hit his right thigh with his fist. "Who do these people think they are?"

Detective Broussard spat out a couple of pieces of tobacco leaf. "Before he passed out, Whitcomb told responding officers he had been working on a story and had spoken to you about it. NOPD sent a team to Betsy's house since they knew she had been working with you. They got there about the time you left your message. They found a bomb in her police vehicle and disarmed it.

"Then we figured we needed to reach out to anyone connected with his report. We learned Dr. Miller and Jimmy Caplan left town, so we assume they're safe. We located Dr. Miller's minivan in a parking garage at the airport. It was wired as well. And we sent a lead to the state police field office in Natchitoches so they can check out Jimmy's vehicle. A team should be here shortly to give Sonny's truck the once-over, too. There have been hand-carved wooden coffins on each vehicle the bomb squad has inspected."

Jonathan nodded. So close to disaster. Just a few more hours and people, his friends and colleagues, would have turned their ignition keys and... Unthinkable, the terror.

"And so you won't feel left out, they found a bomb in *your* car, too. Our assumption is that your intruder was getting ready to wire your wife's Lexus when you caught her. The device in your car is being defused as we speak. It should be cleared by the time you get home."

"I'll look forward to it," Jonathan said. "I assume they found the voodoo coffins."

"Affirmative. We'll send the bomb components, *and* wooden coffins, to the crime lab. Of course, we're cooperating with the FBI and the Bureau of Alcohol, Tobacco, Firearms and Explosives. Because there are so many that hadn't exploded before we disarmed them, tracing parts should be easier.

"Initial indications are the bombs are of a similar design and construction, which means the same person probably made them. The bomb squad says the devices are well built, which points to a professional. That should also help to narrow their origin. Each bomb maker has his or her individual style or techniques and materials, almost like the unique chisel marks of a master stone sculptor. That leads to telltale clues."

"Any idea who was behind all this?"

"We suspect the woman you captured planted the devices. And the only person targeted who was not a member of NOPD or part of your office, besides your wife, was Bryan Whitcomb. Which means the bombs are likely related to the article he mentioned. When did you last speak with Whitcomb?"

"A couple of days ago. The day before New Year's Eve. I ran into him when I went for a lunch meeting with Paul Nichols. Right after, Whitcomb approached me and asked to talk. We ducked into a sandwich shop."

"Someone must have seen you together and decided it was time to act. Sounds like we'll have some additional points to discuss with Mandy Simpson tomorrow morning, assuming you still want to go."

"Can't let them get us off the trail that easily." Jonathan gritted his teeth. "Whoever's behind this knows we're getting close."

"True that, Doc."

Jonathan stood. "Now, if you'll excuse me, I need to pick up Emma and see what we can do about her Lexus that got totaled in the pursuit of justice."

"Sure thing, Doc. But before you go, I have to ask you for your handgun so I can put it into evidence. Once the investigation's done, you should be able to get it back."

"But I missed." Jonathan handed over his pistol. "Thank God."

"Got it," Mitch said. "But we'll need to do ballistics, regardless."

Jonathan nodded. "Understood."

Within minutes, Jonathan had returned to his vehicle parked around the corner on Nelson Street, eager to put Sonny's house in the rearview mirror and rejoin Emma. He turned the key in the ignition and released the parking brake, but didn't put the car in Drive. He just sat there, staring. He reengaged the brake, lowered his forehead to the steering wheel, and exhaled. His eyes moistened. The adrenaline rush had ended, and the exhaustion finally hit.

One hell of a way to start the New Year—six hours of absolute chaos. Fending off a knife attack. Foiling an attempted bombing. Shooting at two human beings. Wounding one of them. Totaling Emma's Lexus, and damn near turning their kids into orphans. When would it end?

Jonathan swallowed hard to suppress the bile churning in his throat. And, Jesus, what about Ranger? What was going on with him? Why in the name of God would he attack Sonny and Corinne? Poor Betsy.

He would meet with the US Attorney tomorrow and do what he could to help. But without Betsy and Sonny? He'd be lost trying to navigate these cases on his own. Yet he had little choice, given all the people relying on him now. Archbishop Fontenot, the Haldemans, the Diaz family. He couldn't let them down. But there had been so much violence and death. And so little progress.

Jonathan released the parking brake and put the car in Drive. Maybe tomorrow would be a better day. It couldn't be much worse.

Chapter Fifty-Nine: The Iberia Bank

Friday, January 2, 2015

J onathan completed his stretching exercises to prepare for his Friday
morning run, grateful for the NOPD patrol car parked across the street.
Betsy had thought of everything. Thank God she had enough presence
of mind to arrange for increased security before beginning her leave of
absence. Betsy. What Betsy must be going through, emotionally, after
discovering her husband's apparent double life.

Jonathan jogged toward the cruiser, waving at the uniformed police
officers sitting inside. Two familiar faces greeted him, Corporal Jividen
and Officer Michaud—who had responded to Robby's house the night he
died and who had escorted Joe Haldeman from Jonathan's house the other
night.

"Any word on how Bryan Whitcomb's doing?" Jonathan spoke to Corporal
Jividen, senior of the two. "I hear a bomb blast slammed him against a brick
wall."

"Affirmative, Dr. Gray," Jividen said. "He suffered a concussion, two
broken ribs, and a punctured lung. Report is that he's in protective custody
at a local hospital, heavily sedated and still sleeping."

"I guess it's better than the alternative."

"Right," Jividen said.

Jonathan shuffled his feet and kicked the pavement. "You know, I never
said thanks for the night you and Michaud found Robby O'Malley in his

family room."

"Sorry?" Jividen's forehead wrinkled.

"Well, I know you were just doing your job, but I appreciate your professionalism. Robby meant a lot to me, personally."

"We understand, Doc." Jividen glanced at Michaud and then back at Jonathan. "Must have been really hard losing someone you worked with for so many years."

Jonathan nodded and again looked down at his running shoes.

"Now if you officers will excuse me, I'm going to put in some miles. Otherwise, you two will be giving me CPR when I collapse halfway through the Rock 'n' Roll Half-Marathon."

* * *

At 9:00 a.m., Jonathan entered the lobby of the Iberia Bank at the corner of Camp and Poydras. Within ten minutes, he was sitting in a private room, reaching inside Bryan Whitcomb's safe-deposit box, and removing two large manila envelopes. Their contents appeared identical: duplicate copies of Whitcomb's investigative materials and a draft newspaper article.

Jonathan read Whitcomb's draft, stopping every so often to review a particular piece of evidence referred to or to take a photo of something with his smartphone's camera. Each sentence drew him into the dark world the city's chief executive had apparently chosen. Assistant U. S. Attorney Simpson needed to see what he was seeing. 9:40. Time to go.

Jonathan placed one set of materials in his briefcase, then returned the other to Whitcomb's safe-deposit box, as he had promised. His task complete, Jonathan exited the bank and walked quickly along Poydras Street toward the Federal Building.

Chapter Sixty: Meeting the Feds

Friday, January 2, 2015

J onathan spoke loudly enough to be heard through the bulletproof glass protecting the receptionist at the US Attorney's Office. He asked if his NOPD colleague had arrived. As he retrieved his visitor's badge and identification, the electronic lock on the door buzzed, then clicked. The receptionist pointed to his left. Jonathan entered the waiting room, where Detective Sergeant Broussard sat reading a dog-eared copy of *Sports Illustrated.*

"Morning, Mitch."

"Doc." Broussard nodded and pitched his magazine onto the corner table next to his chair. "For all the taxes we pay, you'd think the Feds could afford more up-to-date reading materials."

Jonathan laughed and sat down. Mitch was right. Surely the budget deficit wouldn't move much with a few current magazine subscriptions.

They recounted yesterday's events, concentrating on news that Sonny and Corrine would be just fine, and before they knew it.

"Mitch, heard anything from Betsy?"

"Yeah, stopped by University Hospital earlier. Ranger was still groggy."

"Poor Betsy," Jonathan said. "Can't imagine what it's like."

"Well," Mitch said, "she seems fine, all things considered. Betsy told me Ranger kept babbling about not really being there. Sounds like he's still really out of it."

A deep female voice interrupted. "Good morning, gentlemen, I'm Assistant US Attorney Amanda Simpson. Please call me Mandy."

Even if Betsy hadn't told him about her, Jonathan still would have recognized Mandy Simpson as a Marine. She was a recently retired Marine Judge Advocate. Marines, even lawyers, are first, last, and always riflemen ready to do whatever is necessary to defend their country and fellow Marines against all enemies, foreign and domestic. Physically fit, with a stern demeanor, Simpson looked every inch the part.

Standing, Jonathan introduced himself, as did Mitch. They followed her through another security door to a nearby conference room. Its sole occupant, a man of medium stature, his black hair graying at the temples, stood up from his chair.

"Good morning," he said, extending his hand to Jonathan. "Special Agent Tom Yarid, FBI New Orleans Field Office."

After introductions and exchanging pleasantries, the four sat down at a small conference table to begin their discussion. Mitch spoke first.

"Thank you for meeting with us. As I believe Detective Sprance explained before she left on emergency leave, Dr. Gray and his staff worked on a death investigation that seems to implicate our mayor in some serious criminal activity. There are also some other peculiarities. After talking with Dr. Gray, Lieutenant Sprance felt it best to bring this matter to your attention."

"Sorry to hear about Betsy's circumstances, Detective," Simpson said. "But I'm glad you decided to meet, even without her here. Dr. Gray, I assume you'll provide your insights."

Jonathan detailed the chronology of events. His narrative discussed Eduardo and Josefina Diaz and the allegations of sexual assault at the house of their boss, who later turned out to be Max Jamerson, and the lack of any inquiry or involvement by the NOPD. Ms. Simpson and Agent Yarid seemed unruffled. They showed more interest when he mentioned that Josefina's sister, Esperanza Morales, had disappeared under mysterious circumstances. Another shift to boredom came as Jonathan detailed the game of cat and mouse with the blue Acura and described rumors of irregularities in Beau Jamerson's Air Force Academy admissions process.

"Dr. Gray," Simpson said, "I can appreciate your concern based on what you've described. But—"

"I understand these revelations don't seem worthy of federal investigation, but there's more," Jonathan said. "I'm not a professional criminal investigator. But I was, and am, convinced something's not right. So I dug deeper. Please bear with me while I tell you what I learned from Bryan Whitcomb of the *Times-Picayune* and by inspecting Robby O'Malley's desk."

"Very well, Dr. Gray." Ms. Simpson exchanged a quick glance with Special Agent Yarid.

Jonathan detailed his contact with Whitcomb, starting with his initial phone calls and ending with the meeting where Whitcomb had provided access to his safe-deposit box. Jonathan retrieved the manila envelope and slid it across the table to Simpson. You didn't have to be an expert in body language to recognize that she was at first surprised and then pleased.

"I wasn't able to look at the CDs or DVDs because I didn't bring my laptop. But I promised Mr. Whitcomb that if anything happened to him, I would ensure the secrets from his safe-deposit box made it to the proper authorities. This is important information, and you need to have it."

After a brief pause, he added, "And this as well." Jonathan reached into his briefcase and pulled out another portfolio. He handed it to Agent Yarid. "When you read through Whitcomb's notes, you'll find the names of five women he convinced to come forward. Before they could give statements, each one disappeared. What I just gave you are five death certificates that weren't submitted to the Vital Records Registry until two days ago. I also provided their supporting autopsy documentation. You'll see that the names on the certificates match the names in Whitcomb's notes. One of them is Esperanza Morales."

Simpson raised her eyebrows, signaling her curiosity, and nodded. "Interesting. Can you explain in greater detail the relevance of this documentation, Dr. Gray?"

"Yes, of course. They list cause of death of four victims as stroke secondary to cocaine abuse. The fifth victim, Esperanza Morales, died from massive trauma caused by an explosive device in her car. All died in the past few weeks. Timing's curious. So is the amount of cocaine involved.

"Cocaine overdose can cause a stroke. But the amount of cocaine present is usually in much higher concentration than in these four. It would be easy to miss on one autopsy. But not four in such a short time. Not to mention the similar contusions each cadaver had on the upper chest, upper back, and neck."

Jonathan explained his theory that someone skilled enough to manipulate the cervical vertebrae and damage the arteries without breaking the neck had caused the strokes. Throughout his explanation, Simpson sat quietly, her hands steepled, as she listened. Agent Yarid took copious notes, scribbling continuously on his memo pad, not looking up very often.

"Robby O'Malley performed autopsies on all five of the victims. So finding these death certificates in his desk was initially very puzzling to me."

"Didn't Dr. O'Malley die of a stroke, as well?" Simpson asked.

"That's right."

"Did he have the same bruising as the four women?"

"He did."

Simpson looked at Special Agent Yarid. "Moon?"

"This is the real deal, Mandy. It's the icing on the cake we've been waiting for, as far as the mayor goes. But Whitcomb wasn't able to identify Madam X, apparently his name for our Dragon Lady. Regardless, we need to get Bryan Whitcomb into federal custody as soon as possible. Dr. Gray, this additional material is dynamite. It moves our case to a different level. I think Max Jamerson is toast."

"Okay," Simpson said. "Make arrangements for Bryan Whitcomb. While you do that, I owe an explanation to our guests, especially Dr. Gray. I promise not to compromise our case. But given what he just went through, I think he deserves it."

Explanation? What did she mean? There must be something else happening. And who the hell was Madam X—the Dragon Lady?

"Very well," Yarid said. "Now, if you'll excuse me, I have some work to do. Dr. Gray, I'll prepare a chain-of-custody document for these items and bring it back to you for signature and transfer of the materials before you leave."

Chapter Sixty-One: Inside Baseball

Friday, January 2, 2015

As the door closed behind Special Agent Yarid, Assistant US Attorney Simpson looked at Jonathan and Mitch before clearing her throat.

"I must ask for your respective words of honor you won't divulge any of what I am about to tell you. It's highly sensitive. But it's obvious you both are in great danger. You need to understand what's happening so you can protect yourselves. That's the only reason I'm sharing this information at all."

"Got it," Jonathan said. "You have my full attention and agreement."

"And mine," followed Mitch.

"Sorry," Jonathan said. "I don't want to get off track, but did I hear you call Agent Yarid 'Moon'?"

"It's a nickname he picked up at the FBI Academy. Middle name's Munir." Simpson smiled. "You can take it from there."

"I see," Jonathan said. "Just curious."

"From what we've learned working in tandem with Jake Landry and his team from NOPD," Simpson said, "this recent round of explosive devices involves a professional bomb maker known only as Simon. Simon's on retainer to a human-trafficking syndicate operating out of Central and South America. We've had to deal with victims of Simon's handiwork in other cities, but this is Simon's initial foray into New Orleans."

"The bombings got little publicity," Jonathan said. "Or, at least, I never heard of them. You'd think the press would play them up as related to domestic terrorism."

"There are a couple of reasons for that," she said. "First, these explosions usually involve criminals killing criminals. So they don't always garner a lot of press attention. Second, Simon is an expert at building bombs that kill the driver but don't create a lot of collateral damage."

"Which," Mitch said, "is why Whitcomb wasn't killed. He wasn't in his vehicle."

"That's right," Simpson replied. "And because no innocent bystanders died, the media let it pass."

Jonathan nodded. Mitch pulled a half-cheroot from his shirt pocket and started gnawing on it.

"We're very interested to learn about the autopsies," Simpson added. "Your predecessor, Dr. O'Malley, contacted Moon a couple of days before he died and said he had found some irregularities of potential interest to the bureau. Dr. O'Malley didn't provide any details, but we figured it must be important, given the source. Moon set up a meeting with him on Christmas Eve." Simpson sighed. "Of course, Dr. O'Malley wasn't available for the interview."

Jonathan sat silently, trying not to show emotion. But inside, he was jumping up and down, elated that Robby wasn't part of the trafficking operation. The pieces were falling into place. Robby's scheduled Christmas Eve meeting with the FBI must be what delayed his trip to his beach house in Florida to be with Jacki.

Simpson continued. "But this new information helps connect the dots. We had been investigating the syndicate's activities in New Orleans for about a year, and then started getting leads pointing to the mayor. Eventually, we connected Jamerson, albeit circumstantially, to the organization.

"We also uncovered some irregularities in how his son received an appointment to the Air Force Academy, as well as potential misuse of the mayor's police security staff. Fortunately, the corruption doesn't appear to go very far into the administration or the police department."

"Sounds like we barely scratched the surface with what we brought you," Jonathan said.

"Well, Moon seems impressed with your evidence, especially the possibility that chiropractic manipulation can induce a stroke."

"Why?" Jonathan asked.

"We've had reports of the syndicate using another method, besides car bombs, to carry out hits. Reports are sketchy, but profilers tell us to be on the lookout for a former military member, someone with a medical background. Or possibly Special Forces, someone trained in hand-to-hand combat. Someone who could kill, leaving no trace, and make it look like natural causes."

Special Forces. Hand-to-hand combat. Chills ran up Jonathan's spine. "My God. You don't mean Ranger Sprance?"

"Well, we have a lot more homework to do, but our profilers are salivating. I mean, unless you can name someone else with medical skills, like a chiropractor, who has a disciplined military background. And the timing coincides with Sergeant Major Sprance's retirement. His stints in Central and South America would have provided phenomenal opportunities to network and grow his contact list."

"Which means he's the most obvious suspect for killing those four women...and Robby," Jonathan said. More chills, now radiating across his shoulders and neck. "Is that what I hear you saying?"

"I'm afraid so, though we can't leap to conclusions. From reports of events at Sonny Rabideau's house, it seems plausible that Sergeant Major Sprance was trying to add your investigator and his girlfriend to his tally when you interrupted him. And given that Dr. O'Malley had contacted us, his death by stroke might bear some additional scrutiny."

Jonathan nodded in agreement. "I'm already considering changing our cause of death determination from natural causes to homicide." Robby's family wouldn't like the switch. But at least they didn't need to worry that Robby had turned to the dark side. He was one of the good guys.

"And the female you tied to the wrought-iron column in your courtyard? She's quite a find as well."

Jonathan perked up. She was a find? Hell, *quite* a find? He exchanged a surprised glance with Mitch. The tension in his head lessened.

"We wonder now whether *Simon* might actually be *Simone.* We'll send her fingerprints for analysis to see if they match partials found at seven bombings throughout the world. The device in your car and the cars of other members of your team are consistent with previous ones associated with Simon, or Simone, as the case may be. So we're optimistic. Your lady in black is potentially the fabricator of the devices, not just the installer. In sum, Dr. Gray, you might have just given us a path straight to the heart of the human-trafficking syndicate. Perhaps Simone can identify the Dragon Lady."

"Wow. And all I did was run my neighbor's cat out of the garbage. I guess I owe the cat a thank-you."

The trio laughed. After all the inside baseball from Simpson, Jonathan needed some levity. He exhaled, much more relaxed now—his headache totally gone.

"Do you have thoughts on why Max Jamerson got involved?" Jonathan said.

"It appears to be related to gambling debts and sex. Our profilers believe Jamerson has an affinity for fast women and slow horses, as the saying goes. We assume the syndicate must have been carrying him along. And when he got into a position where he was of value, they called in their markers."

"Blackmail, the old reliable," Mitch said. "So where do we go from here?"

"We were very close to announcing our indictments and making arrests," Simpson said. "But there's one loose end we haven't been able to tie up." Simpson gritted her teeth and shook her head. "We strongly suspect Max Jamerson is involved in the syndicate." Simpson's brow wrinkled, and she exhaled loudly. "But he doesn't appear to be the actual chief of the operation in New Orleans. We think there is another person, a female, involved."

"I see," Jonathan said. "The Dragon Lady, Madam X?"

"Precisely," Simpson said. "The profilers nicknamed her the Dragon Lady because you would have to be cold-hearted and merciless to treat women as the syndicate does, and this woman is the head. Each time we get a lead on her, it goes up in smoke—as if a dragon had breathed fire on the evidence."

"And Whitcomb called her Madam X," Mitch said.

"Indeed," Simpson said. "So we had hoped to wait a few more weeks to see if we could identify her. But the bombs may mean the syndicate is getting nervous. We can't risk giving them time to find another bomber. Next round might be deadlier. Now that we have this new information, we'll probably go public in a day or two, once we can speak with Bryan Whitcomb, interview Mr. and Mrs. Diaz, and update our warrants as may be necessary. I'll talk with Moon about sending a lead to the FBI field office in Colorado Springs so they can pay a visit to the Air Force Academy. Perhaps Cadet Jamerson can shed some light on the situation."

Mind-boggling—from the archbishop's request for a favor and an unexpected discovery in Robby's desk to the mayor on the verge of being indicted. But that was the coroner's job: follow the evidence wherever it may lead. And there would likely be more to follow as they pursued Madam X.

"So we need to be vigilant this weekend," Jonathan said.

"That's right," Simpson said. "What will likely happen is that we'll bring Max Jamerson in for questioning tomorrow afternoon. Were I a betting woman, I'd lay odds that once he sees what we have, he'll turn on the syndicate to get himself and his family out of the line of fire. Hell, perhaps our mayor will help us finally put cuffs on the Dragon Lady. Good old Max will still face jail time. But it'll be in the federal system, where we can offer him more protection."

"Sounds like the end of his political career, regardless," Jonathan said.

"I hope so, Dr. Gray. God, I hope so."

Chapter Sixty-Two: Mitch Broussard's Request

Friday, January 2, 2015

Mitch and Jonathan exited the federal building. "Five after one," Jonathan said. "Our meeting and document transfer took longer than I thought they would."

Mitch nodded. "Why don't we go somewhere for lunch? We can review the status of Judge Haldeman's case and coordinate plans."

They settled on a nearby restaurant and ordered food. Speaking softly so no one could eavesdrop, Mitch brought him up to speed on developments.

"Judge Haldeman requested legal representation after we booked him. Apparently, most of the Louisiana Bar recused themselves. When it seemed like he might have to accept a public defender, Judge Haldeman waived his right to a preliminary hearing before a magistrate until Monday. Right after waiving the earlier hearing, he retained James J. Farrell from Memphis, but they had already set the hearing date for Monday."

"So he hired Whiskey Jack Farrell?"

"Looks like it. You know him?"

"By reputation, he's one of the best criminal defense attorneys in the Southeast. He does white-collar defense and an occasional high-visibility homicide."

"Is he a drinking man?"

"I don't think so. You talking about the Whiskey Jack part?"

"Yep."

"Farrell got his interesting moniker when he was a Navy officer stationed on the battleship USS *Wisconsin* during the First Gulf War. The crew referred to the ship as Big WisKy after a collision at sea many years ago. The Navy repaired it using the bow of the decommissioned battleship USS *Kentucky*.

"His friends gave him the nickname WisKy Jack, and it stuck. He left active duty and went to law school, but his name followed him. At some point, it changed from the Navy spelling to the regular spelling."

"I see," Broussard said. "Well, we're hosting Whiskey Jack and his client at a clambake tomorrow morning at ten. I'm strapped. I could use your help."

"I'm listening."

"Hell, Betsy's temporarily out of the picture. And Sonny's sidelined, too."

"A real double whammy."

"I've been working closely with Betsy, but I just don't feel as familiar with the evidence as either of them would."

"So," Jonathan said, "you want me to tag along for the meeting with Judge Haldeman and Whiskey Jack?"

"Listen, Doc. I saw how you handled the US Attorney and the FBI agent. You'll be great."

It was an unusual request. Jonathan wasn't a police officer. But Betsy had told him there were few people in NOPD leadership whom she could trust. So Mitch must have felt as if he were between a rock and a hard place. He needed help and had asked for it. Of course, Jonathan would support him—just as he'd promised to be there for Betsy, come what may.

"All right, I'll plan on it. But I'd like to learn more about Tipton's statement that Betsy mentioned the other day—the one he made as Hunter's guardian."

"Fair enough," Mitch said. "Hunter Dejarnette made statements to Mr. Tipton that, according to the DA, implicate Judge Haldeman. The issue being considered by the DA is whether those statements are admissible in court now that Hunter's dead."

"Interesting," Jonathan said. "I'll try to absorb everything so I'll be ready for tomorrow."

Chapter Sixty-Three: Whiskey Jack

Saturday, January 3, 2015

Saturday morning brought with it a complex mix of relief, anticipation, and foreboding. When Jonathan arrived at police headquarters on Broad Street, attention seemed focused on Interrogation Room Number Three. He spoke briefly with Mitch Broussard before they entered the room together, where Judge Haldeman sat next to James J. Farrell, Esquire—the legendary Whiskey Jack.

Though based in Memphis, Jim Farrell enjoyed a reputation throughout the Southeast as a tenacious litigator who also epitomized civility and honor—the legal profession as it's supposed to be. Farrell rose to greet his client's interrogators. He appeared in the battle armor of a high-powered defense attorney: a meticulously tailored navy-blue suit, white button-down shirt, and regimental necktie, perfectly executed with a precisely dimpled Shelby knot, and matching pocket square. Jonathan regarded his opponent. It was going to be a long day.

"Good afternoon, Mr. Farrell. And Judge Haldeman. I'm Detective Sergeant Mitchell Broussard. Detective Lieutenant Sprance, our lead investigator on this case, was called away on a personal matter unexpectedly and can't be here. I've invited our Coroner, Dr. Jonathan Gray, to assist because he's the expert most familiar with the medical aspects of our case. And he's also familiar with our evidence, overall."

"Somewhat unusual," Whiskey Jack responded. "But I'm pleased to meet you both. As you might imagine, we're *most* interested to learn what evidence the State of Louisiana has to prove these serious charges."

Whiskey Jack sat back in his chair and crossed his arms. "Of course, this entire affair is unusual." He looked at Judge Haldeman. "Which is why I agreed for my client to be present. He wanted to hear for himself what evidence the State believes it possesses to prove these unprecedented and heinous accusations."

"Thank you, Mr. Farrell," Jonathan said. "I'm somewhat out of my element here. But Detective Broussard asked me for my expertise, which I'm pleased to provide."

"Yes, Doctor," Farrell said, "I understand. Please proceed."

Proceed? Jonathan's sphincter muscles tightened. Shit. Not literally, though. Just nerves. So much was at stake. Maybe he should do what he had learned from Betsy's interview of Joe and sit next to Judge Haldeman. Make the judge feel more comfortable. Get him to confess.

He took a quick breath and calmed down. They weren't here to interview Judge Haldeman. This was the State of Louisiana sharing with Farrell what the evidence against his client was. Stay behind the table. Keep a safe barrier. Tell them what he knew, what he did. Stick to the truth, and everything would be fine.

As their discussion progressed, Farrell comported himself as a model of decorum and civility. When he interrupted to ask a question or make a point, he was calm but deliberate. Mostly, he listened and watched as Jonathan outlined evidence pointing to his client's guilt. The more damning Jonathan's presentation, the calmer Farrell seemed. The legendary Whiskey Jack was living up to his billing. If anyone could convince a jury to acquit Ben Haldeman, it would be Jim Farrell.

Judge Haldeman was also calm, but while Farrell concentrated on listening and taking part in a dialogue, Haldeman took copious notes on a legal pad. It was as if he were back in law school, trying to record every word his professor said—or preparing legal arguments to overturn his conviction on appeal. Regardless, he didn't act like someone cornered and desperate.

It wasn't time for the State—Jonathan, in this situation—to back away either. Steadily, without a lot of fanfare, he went through evidence supporting each key component a prosecutor would have to prove: motive, opportunity to commit the murders, and links through physical evidence or eyewitness testimony to the crimes. An anomalous, perhaps surreal role for a coroner, but justice required it. The evidence had to be presented. With Betsy Sprance and Sonny unavailable, he was the best one to do it. He felt more comfortable with each passing minute, making it easier to keep up a veneer of confidence. Having truth on your side was a definite advantage.

Whenever Farrell interrupted, it was time to listen and respond. Each question-and-answer session provided another opportunity to show the breadth of the State's case against Judge Haldeman. That Jonathan didn't agree with the State's theory of the case wasn't something Whiskey Jack needed to know.

Jonathan stopped and reached for a bottle of water. Whiskey Jack cleared his throat.

"Detective, I must compliment the New Orleans Police Department on an exceptional job of investigating these killings and compiling an impressive list of facts. And Dr. Gray, you are most knowledgeable and eloquent in your exposition of the evidence as you see it. I will, of course, save my closing argument for a jury, should the proud State of Louisiana determine to pursue this matter further."

Jonathan rolled his eyes, figuratively at least. It sounded as if a closing statement was just about to begin.

"But I *must* say that I fail to see any connections linking my client to this evidence and to the killings. My client loved his parents and would never do them any harm. The very thought he wanted them dead over a loan is repugnant. What I see is a very convincing case that a distraught teenager euthanized his beloved great-grandparents and then, feeling guilt and remorse, took his own life in what must have been a most painful self-strangulation."

With that opening salvo, Farrell picked apart each piece of evidence. He asserted there were several alternate conclusions, each pointing to guilt of a third party and the innocence of his client.

"The bottom line, Detective," Whiskey Jack leaned forward in his chair, "is that you and the good doctor don't have a shred of *direct* evidence contradicting my client's statement that his parents were alive when last he saw them. And you can't show my client was in Hunter's room when the teenager passed—tragically—meaning it's just as likely that he died alone and by his own hand."

"Yes, I know." Farrell paused, and his eyes sparkled like those of a comedian about to deliver a punch line. "You have *the pants* from the dry cleaners." Farrell rolled his eyes, then frowned. "Well, had your detectives thought to ask, my client would have reminded them—as reflected in the receipts he gave you—that he took *two* pairs of trousers to his cleaners. He sent one pair with a wine stain and a second pair he had just received from Banks Brothers. His reason for sending the first pair is obvious.

"The slacks your detectives retrieved were the second pair, the new slacks he had dry-cleaned to get rid of folds caused by packaging and handling when Banks Brothers shipped them. How much did police search for his second pair? Or did they find one pair and stop? Did you even read the receipts he gave you?"

Had they? Jonathan sat, stone-faced, nodding to show he was listening. Mitch Broussard wrote notes on his steno pad.

"And while it may be an interesting coincidence that Judge Haldeman bought a belt from Banks Brothers' website similar to one allegedly used to strangle the Dejarnette boy," Farrell continued, "a jury will believe the denial of a respected jurist over an impersonal and probably defective electronic mail order system. And I suspect you will find hundreds, if not thousands, of belts with the same pattern in Orleans Parish—if you cared to look."

Farrell paused, reaching into his briefcase. He slid some papers across the table to Detective Broussard.

"What I just presented to you are copies of three mail-order receipts from Banks Brothers. You'll see they're for belts of the same pattern, given by Judge Haldeman to his son, Joe, every other Christmas for the past five years. Joe received the latest one about two weeks before Hunter Dejarnette met his untimely end."

Whiskey Jack tapped the table with the fingers on his left hand. "I wonder, Detective, whether the NOPD, in its zeal to focus on my client, even thought to check the closets of other family members."

Jonathan bit his lip so he wouldn't give any clues about how he felt. If only Betsy had been there. But after many years providing testimony in court, he had learned a few tricks of his own. Remaining steady and outwardly calm was one of his most polished skills.

"What's more," Farrell said, "you have a combined confession and suicide note written on Hunter Dejarnette's computer and printed on his printer, both of which are in Hunter's room. The metadata gathered from documents reflect they were typed and printed before Hunter's time of death. And you found bloody clothing and towels linked directly to the murder weapons and crime scene hidden in the boy's closet."

Mr. Farrell paused, as if to assess the impact of his statements on Jonathan and Mitch. Neither so much as raised an eyebrow. Within seconds of pausing, Mr. Farrell continued his non-closing statement.

"It seems painfully obvious that the picture the State has painted differs from what it had hoped to paint. While I appreciate the State's desire to have a living person held responsible, it doesn't change one simple fact: the evidence clearly points to young Hunter Dejarnette and not my client."

Everything Mr. Farrell had said was technically correct, yet he had glossed over several points and interpreted others favorably for his client. Another masterful performance by Whiskey Jack, executing his duties as defense counsel with skill and aplomb. Jonathan again bit his lip. Not a time for him to punch and counterpunch. Thankfully, Mitch Broussard stepped up to take their next jab.

"Mr. Farrell, thank you very much for those observations. And Dr. Gray, thank you for your participation. You know, Mr. Farrell, the purpose of this meeting is not to show you every piece of evidence or assert every potential argument. The district attorney will complete discovery, and as required by the rules of procedure, you will have access to the State's case file.

"We're continuing to follow investigatory leads. Today, our job is to provide you and your client with broad brushstrokes of what our investigation has uncovered and to offer your client an opportunity to give his side of the story. Dr. Gray has well and capably outlined that evidence for you to ensure your client is properly informed."

Jonathan smiled internally. Now it was Whiskey Jack's turn to put on a poker face.

"Of course," Farrell said. "And let me apologize if I interrupted you before you had completed your presentation."

"That's fine, Mr. Farrell," Mitch said, "we're nearly done. But there is one additional matter I wanted to bring to your attention that may be of some interest to you and your client."

Curious. Jonathan raised his eyebrow. Broussard reached into his file, pulled out a multi-page document, and handed it to Farrell.

"This is a report filed by C. Bosworth Tipton. Your client should recall him being appointed as guardian ad litem for Hunter Dejarnette. If you look at what I've highlighted, you'll learn that young Hunter links your client to Bill and Maggie's murders."

Whiskey Jack peered briefly at the report and then at Detective Broussard.

"Hunter," Broussard said, "loved his great-grandparents and was worried when they left the Christmas party. So he checked on them. And what did he see at their home? Let me use his exact words to Tipton: 'Pap was on the floor. And there was Pap's shotgun. Then he looked toward me. I ducked but could see enough to know. Why did they have to fight at the party? Why couldn't Joe just leave it alone. And Uncle Ben? Why? I know that bastard killed Gram and Pap. But why?' Hunter's voice trailed off on the transcript."

Broussard placed the report on the table and looked at Farrell. "I think you probably know the rest. Hunter retreated into himself emotionally so he could internalize what he had seen. By the time he spoke with Tipton, he was coming back to reality. Your client had little recourse but to strangle Hunter once he returned home."

Without batting an eye, Whiskey Jack shoved the report aside with a flick of his fingers. He looked at Broussard, shaking his head. As if to underscore his disgust, Farrell sighed and rolled his eyes.

"Nice ploy, Detective. But this is obviously an attorney-client privileged document. And in Louisiana, attorney-client privilege, with few very limited exceptions not present here, survives death of the client. Because Hunter is not here to waive his privilege or allow the release of this document, it's inadmissible. It can't be used at trial."

Farrell seemed unconcerned, but Judge Haldeman no longer took notes. Almost immediately after the mention of Mr. Tipton's report, he had put down his pencil and watched the others in discussion, his jaw tightening noticeably as they continued.

"Mr. Farrell," Broussard said, "the district attorney had the same thought, initially. After further review of the court order appointing Mr. Tipton as Hunter's guardian ad litem, and additional legal research—including appellate cases your client no doubt is familiar with—the state believes the report will be admissible on the merits to prove your client's guilt."

Judge Haldeman's complexion went pale, and his jaw slackened, as if he knew what Broussard was about to say next.

"They appointed Tipton to interview Hunter Dejarnette and to report back to the court. The court didn't appoint him to be an attorney for Hunter. And Tipton didn't file the court order declaring Hunter a temporary ward of the state or requesting an emergency show cause hearing. Judge Haldeman's old law firm prepared those documents. Neither action had the authorization of Hunter, his parents, *or* Tipton.

"And there was never any legal representation by Mr. Tipton. Riverview Children's Hospital released Hunter on its own accord after an examination by its chief psychiatrist. Therefore, there never was an attorney-client privilege between Hunter Dejarnette and Mr. Tipton. I believe that if you ask your client, he will acknowledge the legal accuracy of our position."

"That's a very interesting analysis," Farrell shot back. "Looks like we'll have dueling legal ethics experts battling about this issue. Except for this nebulous, desperate, hearsay document, there's absolutely nothing to link my client directly to Hunter Dejarnette's tragic death or the tragic deaths of his parents."

Regardless of his attorney's thrust and parry, Judge Haldeman seemed nonplussed. *How ironic*, Jonathan thought. They used Judge Haldeman's own judicial rulings against him.

"I assumed that would be your view, Mr. Farrell," Mitch said.

Whiskey Jack gathered various writing pads and other documents, put them in his briefcase, and buckled its leather straps. "Is there anything else the State wishes to present, Detective?"

Mitch handed his business card to Farrell. "The district attorney authorized me to tell you the state would entertain a plea bargain should your client decide to request one. Your client will plead guilty to murdering Mr. and Mrs. Haldeman as an accessory both before the fact and after the fact. He will also plead guilty to killing Hunter Dejarnette."

"And in return?"

"The district attorney agrees not to seek the death penalty and will recommend a life sentence, without possibility of parole. Should your client choose not to request a plea bargain and instead decide to challenge the State's case, the terms outlined will no longer be acceptable."

"Very well, Detective. We understand the parameters of what the state will view as an acceptable offer. Now, if you'll leave me to consult with my client, we'll discuss what you've told us. And so there's no question our discussions are confidential, I request you turn off any recording devices and clear out any areas that can observe this interrogation room."

"Yes, of course, Mr. Farrell. You have my business card. The guard will be just outside. Let him know when you're ready, and he'll take your client back to his holding cell."

Chapter Sixty-Four: Trial of the Century?

Saturday, January 3, 2015

"Come on, Doc," Broussard said, "you can be my witness to shutting everything down."

Jonathan followed Mitch out of Interrogation Room Number Three. Broussard directed the technician to turn off the recording machines and then locked the observation room's door. The pair waited nearby in the hallway.

"I'm curious, Mitch. What's being done to protect Judge Haldeman from potential harm?"

"Well, he's a pretrial detainee, so there's no contact with inmates serving their sentences. As an extra precaution, in case other pretrial detainees might have been previous inmates or know he's a judge, we put him in a single cell in our increased security wing. Same place we put people on suicide watch.

"There are security cameras in the hallway that show anyone entering or leaving his cell. And we patrol regularly, with a deputy passing by cells every seven to ten minutes."

"What happens next?"

"Bail hearing's on Monday. I'm sure Farrell is certain they will release Judge Haldeman on his own recognizance."

"Do *you* think Judge Haldeman will offer to plead guilty?"

Before Mitch answered, the door of Interrogation Room Number Three opened. Jim Farrell spoke to the guard, who pointed to Jonathan and Mitch. Farrell walked toward them.

"Detective Broussard, as you might imagine, my client and I have a lot to consider, and Judge Haldeman is rather tired. We want to break for the day and meet again tomorrow afternoon at one. If that's acceptable to the State."

"Yes, of course. I'll see to it."

"And my client would like me to leave him some paper and a pen. He wants to make notes overnight. I can provide him with both if that's within proper protocol. After all, Judge Haldeman's a pretrial detainee waiting for his preliminary hearing."

"Yes, of course."

"Finally, Judge Haldeman has expressed a desire to receive Communion and would prefer not to use the police chaplain. I've contacted the archdiocese. I assume there won't be any issue with a pretrial detainee receiving a visitor to facilitate a religious observance."

"Certainly, Mr. Farrell. I'll leave word to expect a priest from the archdiocese sometime later today or tomorrow morning."

"Thank you for your professionalism, Detective. And thank you for your courtesy in allowing my client to meet obligations of his faith."

"It's all part of the job, Mr. Farrell. Now let's go inspect those writing materials, and then I'll escort you to check out."

* * *

Moments later, Mitch came back into view, walking toward Jonathan. Something must be up. Mitch was really giving his cigar the once-over.

"To answer your last question, Doc, I don't believe Judge Haldeman will go for a plea bargain. There's an awful lot of truth in what Mr. Farrell says. We have little to link Judge Haldeman to Hunter's death." He spat some tobacco pieces into the trash can.

"Let's hope we find something in the Superdome's trash or in dumpsters in the Garden District. And if the court doesn't admit Tipton's report into evidence, the DA's job just got a lot harder.

"So, my bet is Judge Haldeman will decide to roll the dice and hope to beat the charges by challenging every piece of evidence and continuing to blame Hunter. If he pleads guilty, he faces life in the Louisiana prison system as a fallen jurist and convicted murderer. If he fights and wins, he goes home a free man. Even if he's convicted, he can appeal and hope there was a legal error somewhere along the way. I don't see that he has much to lose by digging in. This will be a lengthy war of attrition, leading up to the trial of the century."

Mitch shook his head, passing his tongue over his teeth and spitting out a piece of tobacco. "We'll be working this prosecution for months, or years, to come."

"You know," Jonathan said, "I thought I noticed a crack in Ben Haldeman's armor when he learned about Tipton's report. Being in custody must be an emotional challenge. I'll bet he's drained, mentally and emotionally."

"Very interesting. We'll have to wait and see what Sunday afternoon brings. Can you be here again tomorrow?"

"Sure thing, Mitch. I'm a poor substitute for Betsy and Sonny, but I'll see you then."

"Don't worry about it, Doc. You more than held your own. I'm sure Betsy would be pleased with how we did today."

"Perhaps." Jonathan nodded. "I plan to drop by the hospital this evening to see how she's doing with Ranger. I doubt we'll talk much about business, though."

Chapter Sixty-Five: Sin Without Redemption

Sunday, January 4, 2015

Jonathan woke up Sunday morning around 6:00 a.m., started the coffeemaker, and went downstairs to retrieve the *Times-Picayune*. It was still dark outside as he picked up the paper from just inside their storm door. He waved to the officers, a different team than the other day, parked nearby.

He walked upstairs, entered the kitchen, and placed the paper on the table. A banner headline took up most of the top half of the front page, declaring in big block letters "**WHOREMONGER MAYOR SHAMES CRESCENT CITY.**" A subhead demanded, "*Times-Picayune* **to Jamerson: Resign!**"

Jonathan poured a cup of coffee and sat down to reread Whitcomb's article.

"Caffeine. Give me caffeine." Emma shuffled in and headed directly for the coffeemaker.

"Local television news," Jonathan said, "reported that Mayor Jamerson is already in federal custody."

Emma yawned. "A murdering judge and a pimp for a chief executive. We're living somewhere between the Twilight Zone and a bad Gilbert and Sullivan opera."

Jonathan smiled and handed the newspaper to Emma. She sipped her coffee.

"The *Times-Pic* ran Bryan Whitcomb's exposé in its Sunday edition after all. And there's a sidebar detailing the attempt on his life."

Emma sat and read the article, stopping to discuss portions with Jonathan. When she finished, she slammed the paper down on the table.

"Stick a fork in me, I'm done. I'm so disgusted right now, I could explode. I need to work off some of my irritation. I'll be on the rowing machine for about an hour. Then I need to attend Mass. Let's shoot for the nine o'clock service."

* * *

The church service seemed sparsely attended. Traditionally, the sermon on the first Sunday of the year concentrated on the importance of new beginnings and on the underlying message that, soon, the faithful would start their annual journey from Epiphany toward Lent and the Mass of the Resurrection. Today's homily, delivered passionately by Monsignor Rossignol, reflected a decidedly Old Testament view, focusing on family, obedience to a fearsome, almighty God, lessons of Cain and Abel, and the price of sin without redemption.

"New beginnings premised on severing family ties that make those beginnings meaningful are not worthy," the monsignor said. "A society that accepts and accedes to dishonesty and violence against the self and others cannot long avoid the fate of Sodom and Gomorrah."

Jonathan listened but shared side glances with Emma, baffled by the sermon. Yes, their city was suffering from corruption, particularly of late, but these were strong words coming from anyone, especially from Monsignor Rossignol. Based on many raised eyebrows and wrinkled foreheads in the congregation, others struggled to understand as well.

"Seems like a strange way to comment on Jamerson's predicament," Emma whispered.

"It surely does."

With the service completed, Monsignor Rossignol left immediately after the recessional. He didn't follow his usual practice of staying around to greet the parishioners as they exited. Jonathan and Emma looked at each other again, more than a little confused.

"Seems odd, Gray. Don't you think?"

"Very odd. He always lingers after Mass. I wonder what made him so upset."

Jonathan and Emma walked home through an uncharacteristically calm French Quarter. With the Saints having a bye as wildcard teams battled for a spot in the playoffs, there was no pregame throng. The weather was chilly but pleasant, especially for the first week in January. But there should have been more activity. The tourist crowd seemed smaller and more sedate than normal. Perhaps the Quarter had a collective hangover. Regardless, the calm provided a welcome respite. Jonathan looked forward to a quiet brunch with Emma before heading to police headquarters for round two of Judge Haldeman's interview.

Chapter Sixty-Six: Sunday's Interview

Sunday, January 4, 2015

J ust after 12:30, Jonathan stood silently in the vehicle entrance of the Marriott on Canal Street waiting his turn in the taxi queue. It might be a few more days before his near miss with a bomb faded from his memory sufficiently for him to have the confidence to get back in his car. Considering Mandy Simpson's warning to be on his guard, he was carrying his spare handgun, an older model Glock.

In line ahead of him, a husband and wife from New York debated which had the better brunch—Commander's Palace or Emeril's. What a weird juxtaposition of priorities. Tourists arguing about brunch at the same time he contemplated the upcoming interview of a suspected triple murderer. Only in New Orleans.

The driver dropped him on South Broad, in front of NOPD headquarters. Jonathan paid the fare and hastened across the plaza, past the eternal flame honoring fallen police officers. Curious. The only signs of life were a large sedan, probably an unmarked police cruiser, idling, unoccupied, in a no-parking zone on Gravier Street, and a couple of workers on the roof of the adjacent Municipal Court building. They must be working on the HVAC unit. But why on a Sunday? And those things hanging around their necks looked a lot like binoculars. Must be some sort of special diagnostic equipment.

He entered the deserted lobby. There should have been some kind of activity, some sort of movement, even on a Sunday afternoon. A bright blue "3" pulsed on the panels above each elevator. Must be a malfunction. They couldn't all be stuck on the same floor at the same time. He lumbered up the stairs rather than waiting to see if the elevators started working. Exiting on the third floor, he proceeded toward the interrogation rooms. Just as he neared the hallway leading to his destination, Mitch Broussard's voice caught his attention. Jonathan stopped in his tracks.

"Okay, Judge," Mitch spoke softly, but with directness and purpose. "I need you to stay calm." The negotiator's on her way. And we have a car outside, just like you requested. We want to resolve this situation peacefully."

"I'm glad to see you know how to be cooperative, Detective." Jonathan recognized it as Judge Haldeman's voice. "If you continue to play along, no one else will get hurt."

What in hell was going on? Jonathan made himself as much a part of the wall as he could. He inched his way to a position where he could see the passageway leading to the squad room, without exposing his presence. As the scene came into focus, the blood drained from his face. He cursed under his breath.

Backing toward Jonathan, Judge Haldeman had one of the jail attendants in a choke hold and pressed a pistol into the guard's right cheek. Beyond him stood Mitch Broussard, as cool as ice, as he talked and moved forward at the same pace, Judge Haldeman backed away.

Behind Mitch, Jim Farrell lay motionless, with the upper part of what appeared to be an architect's T-Square or broken ruler sticking out of his chest just above his collarbone. Two police officers kneeled beside Farrell, applying pressure to his wound. Jonathan's focus shifted back to Judge Haldeman, who must not have realized he was there.

His heart beat faster than he believed possible—even faster than when he and Emma were fighting off the bomber. Beads of perspiration covered his cheeks. Jonathan shimmied out of his overcoat and gently, quietly laid it on the floor behind him. He removed his handgun from its holster, chambered a round, and flattened himself against the wall.

"Judge, we need to get Mr. Farrell proper medical attention," Mitch said, continuing his steady, snail-like pace toward the judge and his hostage. "The paramedics are waiting by the elevator. Won't you please let them take Mr. Farrell to the hospital? Your parents and grandnephew are already dead. Let's not add to the casualty list and make it worse."

"Screw that shyster. He wanted to sell me out with a guilty plea. Then he was going to write a book about the case. I can't plead guilty to something I didn't do. Once I'm in the car and away from here, you can bring in the paramedics to see if they can help the greedy bastard."

Judge Haldeman moved closer, apparently oblivious to Jonathan's presence.

"And my parents? They were going to die soon. Weeks? Months? Who knows? My mother's brain was half-rotten. She was as good as dead. My father wouldn't have been able to survive ten minutes without her once she was gone. Maybe Hunter did them a favor by ending their suffering. But how was I to know he was going to do it when he did? Hell, maybe he deserved what he got for cheating me out of a million and a half dollars. And my son—"

Jonathan stepped away from the wall and placed his Glock against Haldeman's neck. "Judge, I suggest you do what Detective Broussard has asked."

Haldeman stopped his backward movement, still clutching the guard and the pistol.

"Damn you, you meddling son-of-a-bitch. Can't you leave well enough alone?"

"Judge, let me be clear. My barrel's touching your neck at the C-5 vertebra. My hands are steady, and there's a round in the chamber. If I pull the trigger, you most likely will be paralyzed, assuming I don't send you straight to your maker. I, for one, wouldn't want to spend the rest of my life being unable to feel my legs or use my arms and being fed through a tube by some prison orderly with a grudge against the legal system. So why don't you put your weapon down and give yourself up?"

"And why don't you go screw yourself? The situation was resolving itself fine until you got here and interfered."

"Come on, Judge," Mitch said. "Dr. Gray's right. Let's end this peacefully, with no one else getting hurt. It's obvious you're under enormous stress and not yourself. I can hear it in your voice."

The squad room remained silent, the tension palpable. Except for the officers trying to save Jim Farrell, every ounce of energy and attention seemed focused on Judge Haldeman and his hostage.

"Okay, we'll do it your way," the embattled jurist replied. "It's time for closure."

"Very well, Judge," Jonathan said. "I'm going to move my weapon away from your neck. But I still have you covered."

Judge Haldeman slowly released his grip on the hostage. Jonathan exhaled a sigh of relief, moved his pistol away from the judge's neck, and wiped sweat from his face with his sleeve.

Haldeman whipped around and pushed the jail attendant toward Jonathan. The collision knocked Jonathan off balance. As Haldeman fell forward, he put the pistol against his chin and pulled the trigger, propelling a bullet into the soft tissues of his chin and cheeks. The projectile exited just below the crown of his skull as fragments of skin, bone, tissue, and blood—lots of blood—sprayed in an ever-widening arc of chunky red mist in the hallway and toward the squad room. Judge Haldeman's body, still writhing with life, came to rest within four or five feet from where Jonathan and the jail attendant had fallen. The telltale odor of fresh blood—metallic, like copper or rusty iron—filled the air.

Despite being covered in blood, Jonathan, as a physician, had a higher duty—to save lives. Instinctively, as if on autopilot, Jonathan reached toward the judge and applied pressure to his wounds.

Mitch Broussard lunged ahead and kicked the gun away. "Send the paramedics in here, fast. We need to get Farrell to the ER as soon as possible." He slanted his head toward the judge. "And let's help Doc save this sorry bastard's life so we can put him on trial and get legal permission to put a poison needle in his arm."

Jonathan gave way to the EMTs, watching in gratitude as they worked skillfully and efficiently to stabilize Haldeman and Farrell. Within minutes, they sped away with their patients, headed for University Hospital's Level One Trauma Unit.

Chapter Sixty-Seven: Wine and Cheese

Sunday, January 4, 2015

J ust after five-thirty, Jonathan and Emma left for their six o'clock get-together with Archbishop Fontenot at St. Louis Cathedral. Upon arrival, Father Nguyen escorted them into a small reception room. The archbishop occupied himself by placing a tray filled with crackers and cheese on the table next to an open bottle of wine and three glasses.

Their host looked up from his labor and smiled. "Jonathan. What a pleasure. And Mrs. Gray. May I call you Emma?"

"Of course, Your Grace."

"Oh, please, call me Phillip. That's the name they christened me with in the eyes of the Lord. *Archbishop* is just a title. Please have a seat."

"Thank you, Phillip," Emma replied.

"I'm ecstatic you both are here, and I'm especially thankful you felt comfortable enough to come after what I understand happened this afternoon."

"Not to sound melodramatic," Jonathan said, "but we can't let bad people stop us from enjoying life. I'm thankful no one died today. And I won't let someone like Judge Haldeman rob Emma and me of the honor and pleasure of a get-together with you."

"Well, now *I'm* humbled. I must admit I rarely blush, but I feel beet-red now."

Laughing, the trio sat down and engaged in small talk. After a few minutes,

Phillip changed the subject.

"I almost forgot my manners. I asked you here to share some wine. I chose a cabernet sauvignon. I hope that's acceptable."

Standing, he moved to the table and poured three glasses of wine, delivering one each to Jonathan and Emma and keeping one for himself. He placed a tray with crackers and cheese, along with small plates, on a coffee table. Jonathan concealed his surprise about the informality of their host.

"Would you allow me to say a few words before we enjoy our refreshments?"

Jonathan and Emma nodded and bowed their heads.

"Heavenly Father, thank you for this sustenance and for the fellowship we share. And we ask that, in your wisdom, you will permit this wine and these crackers to represent your love and the depth of your sacrifice by giving us your only begotten Son, as they are consumed by *all* those who believe, regardless of the label placed on their faith. For these gifts, we are truly grateful. In your name we pray. Amen."

With a responsive "amen," Jonathan opened his eyes.

"To your health," Phillip said, raising his glass.

"And to yours," Jonathan and Emma toasted in reply.

Jonathan sipped his wine. Yet another random act of kindness, a well-known characteristic of Phillip Fontenot, even before he'd become archbishop. A graceful gesture to a non-Catholic. Almost Communion, but not quite enough to cheapen the sacrament or be sacrilegious.

Phillip's voice interrupted Jonathan's thoughts. "I've seen the news reports and talked with Father Nguyen and others about the Diaz family tragedy."

"Yes," Jonathan said. "I wish I had brought you the news. You shouldn't have learned it—"

"I understand," the archbishop said. "Many events were happening in short order. No time to cover all the bases."

"That's very kind of you, Phillip," Jonathan said.

Archbishop Fontenot tilted his head and nodded. "So, before we chat, I want to thank you for the sensitive manner with which you handled Mr. and Mrs. Diaz's case. And Esperanza's death—a tragedy, of course. But still—"

"Thank you for that recognition. I was simply doing my job. And I'm blessed with very professional staff members, each of whom recognizes the need for empathy and discretion as well."

"I'm sure they are as much a reflection of you as you are of them. Regardless, your professionalism and discretion brought a grieving family closure."

"Thank you, again, Phillip."

"I would also like to acknowledge what must have been a rather trying few days for the two of you."

Jonathan looked at Emma. She wore a puzzled expression on her face.

"I know authorities are downplaying it, but I understand you both were recently subjects of an attempted bombing. I can only imagine what turmoil envelopes your lives, and I applaud your calmness."

"Ah," Emma said. "Yes, these past few days *have* been trying for us. But when I think about all of those unfortunate women who were taken advantage of, I don't worry so much about us."

"I applaud you both," the archbishop replied. "Of course, in times of struggle, it's important to remember and cherish the blessings you do have. How are your triplets?"

As they enjoyed the wine and cheese, Emma and Jonathan told him about the kids and lauded the seemingly miraculous video-calling capability that allowed them to see and chat with them half a world away. The trio then discussed a variety of topics, ranging from the results of that week's bowl games and the Saints' prospects in the playoffs to the excitement that living near the French Quarter in New Orleans brought and Emma's current projects at her architectural firm. They had been talking for nearly half an hour when there was a knock at the door. Father Nguyen excused himself for interrupting, then proceeded directly to Archbishop Fontenot and whispered.

Jonathan couldn't hear their conversation. But when Phillip closed his eyes as if in prayer, it reminded Jonathan of their discussion about sanctuary only a few days before. Phillip opened his eyes and looked at Father Nguyen.

"Thank you, Father. I will inform Dr. and Mrs. Gray of this development. Is Monsignor Rossignol aware?"

"Yes, Your Excellency." Father Nguyen nodded. "He's rather exhausted after taking Judge Haldeman's confession late last night and has been in prayer since leading nine o'clock services. This latest news has been ever more trying. The monsignor asked not to be disturbed unless circumstances require otherwise."

Father Nguyen glanced at Jonathan and Emma as he turned to leave. Sadness and fatigue blanketed the priest's face. What Phillip was about to tell them wouldn't be pleasant.

"The news just reported that Ben Haldeman was pronounced dead at University Hospital less than an hour ago. Injuries from his self-inflicted gunshot wound caused too much damage, and he couldn't be saved."

Phillip closed his eyes, took a deep breath, and released it, then opened his eyes.

"Our church does not condone taking one's life, nor killing others. This latest event just adds to the tragedies we've seen during this most holy of seasons—murder, a happy marriage interrupted by sexual assault. Sometimes, I fear we live in a world gone mad. Sometimes—"

Jonathan's phone made a strange, almost strident, chirping noise. "I'm very sorry. That's the emergency text message notification on my phone."

Jonathan read the text and then looked at his host. "Phillip, I must both thank you for your hospitality and apologize in one breath. This is from the assistant coroner on duty. Police just cleared Judge Haldeman's corpse for autopsy. It means I need to report for duty as soon as possible so I can arrange for a coroner from another parish to conduct his autopsy, as I'm a witness."

"Yes, I understand. Godspeed to you. Please know that you go with my blessings and admiration."

Chapter Sixty-Eight: Post-Holiday Blur

Monday, January 5, 2015

Monday after New Year's began as a blur. With almost everyone back from holiday leave, the office bustled with activity. Although the staff was physically present, it would take one or two more days before they had completely shaken off the holiday's mental cobwebs and returned to fully functioning levels.

"Good morning, Dr. Gray." Vern greeted Jonathan with her ever-optimistic smile. "How are you holding up? I can only imagine how you must feel after what happened with Judge Haldeman. My goodness, stabbing his attorney with the crucifix Monsignor Rossignol had given him the night before.

"And Judge Haldeman's family. So much tragedy. I ran into Molly Westcott, Joe Haldeman's fiancée, this morning at Rouses on Tchoupitoulas. She was buying flowers for an impromptu memorial to Judge Haldeman. Bless her heart. They still have to grieve for that deranged man, I suppose. How awful."

"Thank you for asking after me, Vern. It surely was an interesting afternoon. But I was just doing my job. I feel for what his family must be experiencing."

"Well, we're all proud to have you as our leader, Dr. Gray," she said.

Jonathan blushed under the praise.

"And thank you for closing the office so we can attend Dr. O'Malley's funeral later this week."

"You're most welcome. I couldn't ask any of the staff to stay behind. I hope everyone will come and say goodbye to Robby. It should be quite a show."

"Yes, sir, it should be." After a slight pause, Vern returned to current events. "But it seems like there's no peace for the rest of us. The TV announced a ten a.m. press conference at the US Attorney's Office. Rumor is they're going to indict Mayor Jamerson. Lord, I don't know if I can accept that he could do what he's accused of. It's just so shocking.

"We've been getting calls from state and national media outlets asking for comments about both the mayor and the judge. Of course, we've been referring them to the city's public affairs officer. We all have her name and number memorized. Oh, and Senator Nichols's office called to remind you of your testimony in Baton Rouge this afternoon."

"Thanks, Vern. You and the others are champions. I'm sorry you're being robbed of what should have been an easy return to duty after the holidays."

Vern nodded and mouthed a silent "thank you," as she picked up her ringing phone. "Coroner's office, may I help you?" Then, after listening for a few seconds, she nodded. "Yes, I understand your request. Let me give you the name and number of the city's spokesperson."

Jonathan smiled and made a hasty retreat to his office.

* * *

Jonathan scrolled through his inbox, reviewing the subject lines before deciding whether to read them. The shortest subject line, on an email from Mitch, stood out: "Pants." He opened the email. "Full inventory of dry cleaner revealed one pair of gray wool slacks (Banks Brothers), unclaimed. Same size as other pants from Haldeman. Checking with BB to trace purchase." What if Whiskey Jack had been right? What if there *were* a second pair of slacks?

A small message block opened in the lower right corner of his computer screen. Another email had just arrived, this one from the crime lab, with the subject "Test Results re: Belt." Jonathan was grateful for the quick turnaround on examining the belt Judge Haldeman was wearing when he was arrested. He clicked on the email and read it. He closed his eyes and shook his head when he was done. No way. It couldn't be right.

Jonathan read the words out loud as if that might change them. "Unable to match substance on leather belt or buckle with DNA from Subject Hunter Dejarnette via rapid protocol. CODIS search pending."

No DNA from Hunter? How in hell could that be? The belt was so deeply embedded into his neck. It was impossible that his DNA wasn't there. Jonathan's mind raced. His head pounded. There was only one plausible explanation. If Hunter's DNA wasn't on Judge Haldeman's belt, it must mean Judge Haldeman didn't...

Jonathan sat up, ramrod straight, as if jolted awake from a bad dream. He whispered aloud to himself.

"Flowers?"

He froze, his mind whirring as he pieced together details that before had seemed random.

"Fiancée?"

He rested his forehead in his hands.

"Fuck."

How could they have missed it? They had been so thorough. He should have pushed Betsy to consider an alternate conclusion, but she was so convinced that the circumstantial evidence was strong enough.

Jonathan rushed out of his office, adrenaline coursing through him. Time to bring real closure to the Haldeman family. Vern looked puzzled as he hurried past without saying a word. He punched numbers into his cell phone.

"Mitch. I have a hunch. Initiate the Algiers Point Protocol. I'll call with details once I'm on the way. I just hope it's not too late."

Chapter Sixty-Nine: Springtime on the Champs-Élysées

Monday, January 5, 2015

J onathan faced a brisk wind coming off the river at the foot of Canal Street, shortly before 9:00 a.m., as he boarded the waiting ferry, M/V *Colonel Frank X. Armiger*. He showed his credentials to the crewmember assisting arriving passengers and asked for directions to the pilothouse. As a forensic pathologist, Jonathan wasn't one to follow his instincts. Long years of training and experience led him to rely on empirical data—provable facts—to come to scientifically based conclusions. But here he was again, acting on a hunch, as he raced up the stairway to meet with the captain.

In the rear of the pilothouse stood the captain, a stocky man in his early sixties with a salt-and-pepper beard. He observed the first mate, a thirtysomething female, as she guided the boat away from the Canal Street dock for the approximately ten-minute trip to the Algiers Point ferry landing. The captain's nametag identified him as M.J. Wheeler.

Jonathan displayed his credentials. "Good morning, Captain Wheeler. Sorry to interrupt your routine, but I need your help."

"Good morning, Doctor," Captain Wheeler said, apparently not fazed by the visit. "How may the crew of the Motor Vessel *Colonel Frank X. Armiger*, Master and Commander of the Mississippi, be of service?"

Jonathan smiled. There was probably a joke he could make, but he'd best stick to business. "Thank you, Captain. I'm working with NOPD. I need to monitor two individuals who I believe will come aboard when the ferry arrives back at Canal Street."

In the background, the first mate gave orders as the boat prepared to dock at the Algiers Point ferry landing. Jonathan glanced at her, then returned his gaze to the captain. "We believe the pair will proceed to the stern of the ship."

"Okay," Wheeler said. "We should depart Algiers Point in just over five minutes for the return trip. That'll give about fifteen minutes to get set before we dock on the East Bank. I'll have First Mate Batson guide you to an aft utility locker. It has access to the two main decks and windows, so you can see around you but stay hidden. That should fit your needs."

Wheeler paused. "Batson. I'll take the wheel. Please assist Doctor Gray."

"Aye, Captain," Batson said. "Consider it done."

* * *

Locker was an apt description for the narrow, closet-like space on the top of the boat's two main decks that First Mate Batson made available to Jonathan. About four feet wide and twice as tall, the utility locker held a variety of items such as tools, spools of rope, and life preservers. Each of the two bulkheads—walls—had small windows he could open and close. The space Jonathan occupied was on the port—left—side. A ladder connected the locker with a similarly sized room on the deck below. Batson explained to him that there was another set of lockers of the same dimensions and design on the starboard—right—side of the boat.

Batson left just as the ferry sidled up to the Canal Street terminal. From the locker, Jonathan watched the passengers walking onto the ferry. Soon, he saw Joe and Molly hasten down the pier toward the boat. Jonathan's hunch had been on point. He wasn't too late.

As they walked aboard, Joe flipped up his jacket collar and huddled closer to Molly. She carried what appeared to be a bouquet—lilies, perhaps—in a cellophane wrapper with the Rouses logo clearly visible. She had a large handbag over her left shoulder. Jonathan captured the scene on his iPhone's video camera.

As he had speculated, Joe and Molly moved toward the stern—the back—of the boat and walked down a stairway to the lower deck. Jonathan turned off his camera and climbed down the ladder through a hatch into the space below. He turned on his video camera and focused on the couple through the small window. The idling diesel engines muted Joe and Molly's voices, but Jonathan could still hear them, mostly. His nose crinkled at the diesel exhaust.

"Can't believe you found lilies so quickly," Joe said, "especially this time of the morning."

The engine revved, drowning out parts of Molly's response. She said something about the great flower shop in the Rouses supermarket on Tchoupitoulas. She also asked about the ferry.

"The Judge—um, my father," Joe said, "used to ride when he needed time to think. He told me being on the river helped clear his mind when he was working on a troublesome case. Until about a year ago, it was free, so he would ride back and forth for hours at a time."

"I didn't realize the ferry was special. I assumed it just fit into our plans."

"Well, it does. But my father's love for the trip to Algiers and back makes it even better. His wish that we throw a bouquet into the Mississippi gives us a cover for being here."

Joe looked into Molly's eyes. Another surge from the engine blocked out most of the words for the next few seconds. The only audible words and phrases between the pair were "honeymoon," "Paris," and "...trees along the Champs-Élysées are especially beautiful in springtime."

The engine noise subsided. Molly's voice was now plain and unmistakable. "The quicker we get married, the quicker we qualify for spousal privilege. Neither one has to testify against the other."

Those last few sentiments would likely serve as the proverbial final nail in the coffin. Molly angling for the spousal privilege sounded like what the lawyers called an "admission against interest." Why worry about the privilege unless you had something to hide?

The ferry's whistle sounded, and the boat jolted as it pulled away from the Canal Street pier. With the vessel moving at such a low speed, the water slapped gently against the hull as they navigated across the river channel. So, the conversation came through clearly.

"Nine-thirty," Joe said. "Right on schedule. We'll be to Morgan Street Landing in ten minutes, which means we have little time. Let's get started."

Joe and Molly moved rapidly to the railing on the port side, near the stern. As the ferry turned toward its destination, the New Orleans skyline formed a picturesque backdrop. Jonathan strained to keep the pair in the camera lens while staying hidden.

"You have it?" Joe asked.

Molly pulled a grapefruit-sized cloth bundle out of her handbag. "I put some of the heaviest pottery shards I could find in it. At least five pounds' worth."

Joe reached into his jacket pocket and pulled out a red bandana wrapped around something. He unwound the bandana to reveal a jeweler's chasing hammer, a glass cutter, and all that remained of a belt: a darkened, mangled buckle.

"I can't believe how quickly the leather part burned away," he said. "And that gullible, little prick Hunter's DNA along with it."

"Wish you hadn't had to do that to your cousin."

"Me too. But he was just too emotionally unstable. How was I supposed to know he would leave the party and come to Bill and Maggie's?"

Jonathan's gut tightened as circumstances proved his hunch was correct. Joe and Molly had planned what they thought was the perfect crime, only to be discovered in the act when Hunter showed up unexpectedly. No wonder Hunter had gone catatonic. He had seen his cousin Joe and Molly murder Bill and Maggie. In his statement to Tipton, Hunter had never named Judge Haldeman. The implication was there, but he apparently meant Joe when he said, "I know that bastard killed Gram and Pap." They'd all misunderstood. Worse, they'd assumed without looking behind the assumption—a fatal flaw in their investigation.

"Besides," Joe said, "once he came out of his funk, he would have given us up in a heartbeat. I had to do it. Thank God, they released him from the hospital when they did."

"Yeah," Molly said. "And thanks to your father for unwittingly teaching us how to break in and cover our tracks."

"Right. Those hours of riding along on the ferry, listening to him describe how inventive criminals were, paid off. And your idea to steal Hunter's jeans and hoodie and bag 'em up with the bloody towels was real genius." Joe kissed Molly on the forehead, then dropped his head to kiss her neck. "I'm getting hard just thinking about how devious you are. Can't wait to get you horizontal."

Molly frowned. "Save it for later, lover boy. We've got business."

"Right," Joe said. He placed the buckle and other items on top of the broken pottery. Then he tied up the bundle.

"You know," Molly said, "My kiln gets hot enough to melt the buckle and the hammer, too. Don't you think *that* would be a better way to get rid of this stuff? Like I did with the leather part of the belt and the coveralls and gloves?"

"I guess. But we'd still have to deal with the metal once it cooled. This way, the Mississippi'll take care of it. No loose ends."

Joe glanced around. "This is about halfway across. Let me have the flowers."

Jonathan stepped out of the door from the utility locker. "Hey."

Joe whipped around toward Jonathan, a "Shit, what in hell are you doing here?" look on his face.

"Not so fast, Joe."

Joe buried the bundle in the bouquet and threw it overboard. The package separated from the flowers, petals, and stems as they scattered in the air on their way to the river's surface. Soon, they would float peacefully downstream, as the bandana and its contents sank ever deeper into the silt below.

Joe wore a Cheshire Cat grin—the look of someone who thought they'd just gotten away with murder. "Oh, hello, Dr. Gray. We didn't expect to see

318

you at our memorial."

"All right, Joe, you and Molly can stop pretending." Jonathan pulled out his phone. "I got your little ceremony on video. And it doesn't seem your package is lost after all. Look."

Joe and Molly's faces dropped. A police boat had stopped near where the bundle had hit the river, and divers were already in the water. A second boat, with Detective Broussard visible on board, pulled up alongside the ferry. Joe swayed, slightly off balance, as the ferry reversed its engines and slowed.

"Listen," Joe said, "I told you *I* didn't kill my grandparents." He looked at Molly. "Talk to the Dragon Lady."

"Shut up, idiot," Molly said. "They've got nothing on us. And when we're married—"

"I don't think you'll have time for a wedding ceremony any time soon," Jonathan said. "Even if the divers don't find your package right away, we'll dredge the river until we do. It's over."

"Like hell." Joe lunged, slamming into Jonathan just below his sternum. As if he were a linebacker cutting down on a wide receiver, he tackled Jonathan to the deck. The collision jolted the phone out of Jonathan's hand.

"Throw it overboard," Joe ordered Molly as he and Jonathan struggled.

They rolled together in an indistinguishable jumble of arms and legs, then broke apart. Jonathan and Joe stood up slowly, both gasping for air. Jonathan, enraged, became the aggressor. He squared his shoulders, lowered his head, and charged Joe. His right shoulder collided with Joe's sternum and ribs, driving Joe backward into the bulkhead. Joe grunted but hung onto Jonathan, dragging him to the deck for another wrestling match. He flipped Jonathan onto his back and straddled his torso. Joe raised his right arm, clinched his hand into a fist, and thrust it downward. Jonathan twisted his head just enough to avoid Joe's fist, which crashed into the steel deck plate.

"Goddamn it," Joe said, his knuckles bleeding, his face wrinkled in pain.

With Joe distracted, Jonathan twisted Joe onto his back, stood up, and pulled out his handgun. Off to Jonathan's right, Mitch Broussard clamped handcuffs on Molly. Jonathan's phone rested where it had landed.

"It's really over, Joe," Jonathan said. "Thanks for acting like the guilty son-of-a-bitch you are."

Chapter Seventy: In the Rearview Mirror

Monday, January 5, 2015

Accompanied only by his thoughts, Jonathan guided his car along I-10 for the ninety-minute trip from New Orleans to Baton Rouge. After his encounter with Joe Haldeman, he was thankful for the solitude and calm—and, earlier, for the quick shower and change of clothes. Engulfed by the ubiquitous swampland, cane fields, and refineries that appeared on either side of the highway in metronome-like measure—cane field, refinery, cane field, refinery—each disappearing in his rearview mirror at the same rhythm. What a great opportunity to reflect on the ebb and flow of events since Robby's death.

Joe Haldeman and Molly Westcott were in jail. What a relief. Joe Haldeman had almost gotten off scot-free. Initially, factors like the nearly million-dollar payout from Bill and Maggie Haldeman's estates and tontine pointed to Joe. Then the real estate information led to Judge Haldeman. And, for a time, the evidence, from Betsy's perspective, painted Hunter into the picture as an accomplice or perhaps the killer himself.

In fact, it had been Joe Haldeman all along. What a genius at locating surveillance cameras. And lying. Having a criminal for a girlfriend, someone who would provide a false alibi, didn't hurt. Molly Westcott, the woman with the two-headed snake tattoo—the reason for her Dragon Lady nickname—who, conveniently, hadn't been at the Haldemans' holiday party. Molly, the pottery maker who traveled to Central and South America in search of antiquities, apparently returning with young, impressionable women whom she took under her wing and then sold to the human-trafficking syndicate. Everything had fallen into place. But it had taken time and going down many rabbit holes and dead ends to piece the puzzle together.

And what of the victims, the casualties of Joe and Molly's greed and corruption? That Jonathan hadn't been associated with Bill and Maggie Haldeman or Hunter Dejarnette or Esperanza Morales in life didn't matter. As Coroner, he was the ultimate arbiter of what caused their deaths. He would always feel linked to them. And to the Diaz family.

So many people's lives had changed forever, all in the span of a few days. Judge Haldeman, seemingly the prime suspect in his parents' murder, had been let down by the system, driven to some sort of psychotic break, and then suicide, before his innocence could be proven. Hunter might still be alive if Kathleen Haldeman hadn't pulled strings to get Hunter released from protective custody early just because she thought he was better off at home—and if the system hadn't allowed her to do so. The system.

Contemplating past events only strengthened his resolve. It was up to him, now, to advocate for reforming the system to better serve and protect people. He shook his head and sighed. Tomorrow would bring the Twelfth Night, the traditional beginning of the Carnival season. With each passing day, as people became distracted by Mardi Gras parades and parties, their memories of Hunter and the others would fade. His upcoming testimony took on a greater significance.

Chapter Seventy-One: Promises Fulfilled

Monday, January 5, 2015

The Louisiana State Capitol. Hard to miss. Located just north of where the interstate spanned the Mississippi, the edifice dominated the skyline. At four hundred and fifty feet tall, the thirty-four-story art deco structure looked more like an office building than a center of government. As directed by Senator Nichols's chief of staff, Jonathan pulled into the "Senators Only" parking lot, stopped at the guardhouse, and identified himself.

He entered the ground floor, which housed both chambers of the legislature. Energy and excitement—a glorious, democratic cacophony—echoed throughout the vast lobby. State workers scurried about. Several groups of school-aged children listened as docents lectured them on various topics. Individual tourists took photos of the area where Senator Huey Long was shot, and where his alleged attacker was killed in a hail of bullets, in the 1930s.

Jonathan gave the guard at the security desk his name and waited as the guard called Senator Nichols's office. Soon, an attractive woman with raven-black hair who was dressed in dark blue business attire emerged from an elevator and hastened toward him.

"Good afternoon, Dr. Gray. I'm Elaine Devereaux, chief of staff. I'm pleased to meet you face-to-face. Senator Nichols is in another committee hearing, or he would have been here to greet you personally. So much has happened. We were afraid you might not make it."

"Please call me Jonathan. And this legislation is very important. I *had* to come."

"Thank you, Jonathan. Is this your first visit to our Capitol building?"

"No, it isn't. I'm embarrassed to say it's been quite a while since I've been here, though. And one of the few things I remember is that the assassination of Huey Long happened right here, out in the open. Some say his assailant, a physician, was angry because Long was leading an effort to gerrymander his father-in-law out of his elected judicial office."

"All true, Jonathan. Huey Long, the Kingfish—what a political force *he* was. This building is a monument to his ability to get things done when he was governor, before his election to the U.S. Senate. But he also knew how to create enemies."

As their discussion continued, Ms. Devereaux escorted Jonathan on a brief orientation tour of the two legislative chambers and the hearing room where he would testify.

"You know," she said, "Huey Long isn't the only politician to think he's invincible. I worked for Max Jamerson when he was a state senator. Just like the Kingfish, he got caught up in his own self-image."

"Well put, Elaine. For what it's worth, my medical opinion is that some politicians act like they've undergone a lobotomy, with their common sense and humility sucked out and flushed down the drain. Present company excluded, of course."

Smiling, Elaine looked at her watch. "We still have nearly an hour left before your testimony. What's your preference for lunch?"

"It's been a whirlwind of a day. Can I go somewhere for a quick bite and to collect my thoughts?"

"Certainly. The Capitol dining room's just down that corridor. Be in the hearing room by a quarter of two. We can introduce you to the panel and go through any last-minute arrangements."

* * *

At the appointed time, Jonathan walked into the hearing room, which was already abuzz with activity. Senator Nichols called to him.

"Jonathan, welcome. Please come and meet the committee members."

Surprising, and refreshing, the relative informality. Along with Nichols, there were six other senators on Judiciary Committee "A." After introductions, Jonathan took a seat at a table in front of the panel. The senators sat in a mahogany structure that looked like a jury box. Senator Nichols called them to order.

"Good afternoon. We're here today to receive testimony from Dr. Jonathan Gray, Coroner of Orleans Parish, regarding Senate Bill 842. We've asked for Dr. Gray's views to assist this committee in determining whether to refer this piece of legislation to the full Senate for consideration during our legislative session convening in March. All committee members are present. So there is a quorum, and we may proceed. Dr. Gray was earlier sworn in by me as committee chair, and we will now accept his formal testimony into the public record. Dr. Gray, the floor is yours."

Hoping the last of his butterflies would leave, Jonathan cleared his throat and looked at his prepared remarks. Today was about fixing limitations in the legal framework and structure of the Louisiana coroner system. It was about Beatrice and being able to show her he'd made sure no more little ones would die the way she did—that no election campaigns would get in his way. *This* was the time. No more excuses.

"Mr. Chairman, members of Louisiana Senate Judiciary Committee 'A,' honored guests, and attendees, thank you for this opportunity to speak in favor of Senate Bill 842, the Louisiana Coroner System Improvement and Support Act.

"As Coroner of Orleans Parish, this legislation has my fullest professional endorsement and support. It represents a positive step forward for the historic system of locally elected coroners pioneered by the great State of Louisiana and rightly enshrined in our state constitution."

Jonathan paused and took a deep breath. Mental images of Beatrice running and playing with Mae's granddaughter, Sophie Louise, caused him to smile, at least internally. He nodded, almost as if to convince himself to go forward with his next step. He peered at the panel members, then deviated from his prepared text.

"And as a father who lost his child in a senseless shooting…" Jonathan gritted his teeth to keep his jaw from shaking at memories of Beatrice arriving at the morgue a dozen years ago. "…a senseless shooting perpetrated by a disturbed individual who slipped through the cracks of a flawed mental health system…" He exhaled and again looked at the panel, calmer now, more determined to rectify past wrongs. "…a mental health system in a parish where the duly elected coroner lacked basic medical and psychiatric knowledge…" Another pause and a deep breath. "…as a *father*, this bill has my *personal* support as well, and I urge its passage."

Jonathan reached for a glass of water, partly for dramatic effect, but mostly because his mouth was dry. He returned his half-filled glass to its silver tray, cleared his throat, and again made eye contact with each senator.

The words lightened the burden he'd been carrying—the heavy, emotional weight holding him down. Jonathan had fought through the challenges and regained control. He was Coroner of Orleans Parish. He had survived. Justice, in its immutable way, had triumphed. Robby would be proud. And Beatrice. Jonathan closed his eyes. Now, perhaps, the nightmares would end.

Jonathan opened his eyes and inhaled the first breath of his new reality. Reading from his prepared testimony, he spoke with confidence and conviction.

"I believe we are servants of the people. We must be good shepherds of their trust. Senate Bill 842 fulfills that responsibility. This important legislation benefits the State of Louisiana and its citizens for the following reasons…"

Acknowledgments

Mentioning everyone who helped *Voices of the Elysian Fields* along its path to publication would take several pages, or perhaps an entire chapter. For, as the trite—but true—saying reminds us, it takes a village. Success, indeed, has many parents.

Becoming a fiction writer presented challenges—especially for someone focused on a legal career emphasizing "just the facts." So, thanks to individuals and organizations shepherding me through the transition, an ongoing process. With me at the very beginning, a special thanks goes to Hampton Roads Writers and its founder, Lauran Strait. My colleagues in Mystery By the Sea—the Virginia Beach chapter of Sisters in Crime—provided support and guidance, and published one of my short stories in the *Coastal Crimes: Mysteries by the Sea* anthology, a key milestone in a new author's career. The Muse Writers Center in Norfolk, Virginia, under the dedicated stewardship of Executive Director Michael Khandelwal, served as a great source of instruction and enlightenment.

I can't overstate the importance of author Heather Graham and her conference, Writers for New Orleans. The conference gave me an extra reason to visit the city, allowed me to meet many interesting fellow writers—and fans—and provided an environment where I could develop my identity—my voice—as a writer. Thank you, Heather.

New Orleans. Iconic. Unique. Mysterious. Pick your favorite description. Likely, each would fit. That's why I refer to New Orleans as the "Chameleon City." Depending on your outlook, the city can be almost anything you want—or need—it to be. Because I don't live in New Orleans, I read a lot about the city and traveled there often, "for research," including participation in several Mardi Gras krewes. I listened and learned from my many new friends in the Krewes of Cork, King Arthur, Freret, and ALLA. I hope I captured the rich essence of life in The City that Care Forgot.

Dealing with the Medico-Legal issues facing a coroner required many hours of research, and advice from individuals much more knowledgeable that I am. The experience I gained while attending the Writers' Police Academy over the past few years proved invaluable. Thanks to Lee and Denene Lofland for their dedication in developing and fostering the academy. The many books by D. P. Lyle, M. D. on forensics and related topics were important as well. And to Howard M. Rigg III, M.D., thanks for helping me navigate the interesting world of autopsies and coroner topics specific to Louisiana. You're my favorite brother.

I'd be remiss if I didn't give a special shout out to Katrina Diaz Arnold, owner and chief editor of Refine Editing, for her thoughtful guidance and comprehensive edits. Thanks to you and your team—especially the excellent Jaime Brockway—for firmly but diplomatically encouraging me to "kill my darlings" on the way to a better manuscript. Beta Readers Doug Lutz and Stephanie Brannick provided insightful comments that helped me "keep it real."

To the team at Level Best Books—Shawn Reilly Simmons, Deb Well, and in particular my editor, Verena Rose—thank you for your confidence, encouragement, and support. I hope I don't let you down.

That brings me to the most important acknowledgment. First, last, and always, thanks to my family—especially Martha, my spouse and life-partner—for putting up with me since the day I declared "Hey, I can write a novel. How hard can it be?"

Laissez le bon temps rouler.

Michael Rigg

Virginia Beach

About the Author

Michael Rigg, an attorney for more than four decades, writes mysteries and thrillers set in two very different locations: Virginia Beach (where he lives) and New Orleans (which he visits as often as possible "for research," including participation in three Mardi Gras Krewes). He is a retired Navy Judge Advocate and a retired civilian government attorney, formerly working for the Department of the Navy Office of the General Counsel. He is a member of International Thriller Writers, Mystery Writers of America, and both the Sisters in Crime national organization and its Southeastern Virginia Chapter—Mystery by the Sea.

AUTHOR WEBSITE:
www.michaelrigg.com

SOCIAL MEDIA HANDLES:
Facebook: **www.facebook.com/michael.rigg.author**
Twitter/X: Michael Rigg@MDR102030
LinkedIn: www.linkedin.com/in/michael-rigg-4567b591

Also by Michael Rigg

Ghosts of the French Market – A Novelette (Witchduck Press)

Short Stories in the Following Anthologies:

"In a Faubourg Far, Far Away" – *Mardi Gras Mysteries* (Mystery and Horror, LLC)

"The Courier" – *Coastal Crimes: Mysteries by the Sea* (Wildside Press)

"Ghosts of Sandbridge" – *Virginia is for Mysteries, Volume III* (Koehler Books)

"Grandma Connie's Strawberry Pie" – *Coastal Crimes 2: Death Takes a Vacation* (Wildside Press)